M000215067

The Black Lions of Flanders.

#blacklionsofflanders

www.kingsgermans.com

A dedication.

To my family, for the love and laughter that has been ever present in my life, even in troubled times.

To Ned, my son, for all that we have done and for all that is ahead of us.

To Cathy, for holding the maps and for happy memories.

To my friends at the Shed, where Thursday night is a highlight of everyone's week; a true band of brothers.

To Sarah, my editor, for turning a bloated draft into a real book (two real books in fact) and those hours in which she generously shared her knowledge of all matters publishing.

To Neil Braddon and Neil Bosher for their constancy in proof-reading and feedback.

To Jen, for her beautiful cover and creative brilliance

To Adrian, for his patience with the maps.

To Jacquie, for her P.R. genius.

And to you, for reading this story.

We cannot enter into alliance with neighbouring princes until we are acquainted with their designs. We are not fit to lead an army on the march unless we are familiar with the face of the country—its mountains and forests, its pitfalls and precipices, its marshes and swamps. We shall be unable to turn natural advantages to account unless we make use of local guides.

Sun Tzu - Art of War.

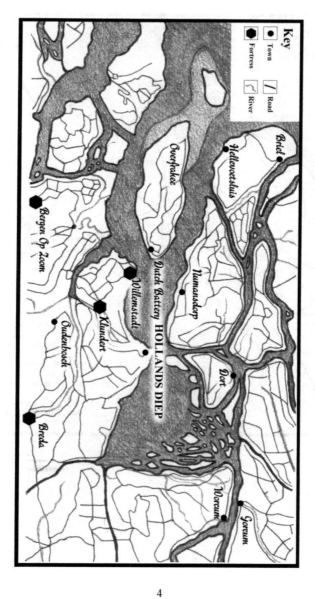

Key locations across the Low Countries, Flanders and Northern French border, west of the Sambre River.

Road
Town River
Fortress French Border

Scale in British Miles
0-5 10-15 20-35 30-35 40-45

CHAPTER ONE

The Rosanna and the Perseus.

The English Channel: 29th January 1793

The pin-prick of light on the horizon was the ship's only salvation.

The *Rosanna* had always been considered a lucky ship, but ten days held in Bristol dock by storms that roared in from the Atlantic had burned away what little money the crew had saved. The prospect of delays in profits for the vessel's London owners had brought a steady stream of messages of rising urgency, demanding immediate action of the ship's captain. Finally, Captain Uriah Johnson made the fateful decision. He could ill afford to listen to the protestations of the first mate's Celtic superstitions. O'Malley claimed that life as a Galway urchin on Ireland's rugged west coast gave him near mystical powers on reading the weather. He could sense the slightest change in the air and was rarely wrong on such matters. Passengers had been summoned from nearby lodgings, supplies renewed, and cargo and human freight were secured below decks.

Johnson took the merchantman out into the Bristol Channel considering the storm to have passed. O'Malley crossed himself, kissed the weathered silver pendants of St. Christopher and St. Patrick that hung on a thin leather strap around his neck and said a silent prayer at the ship's wheel. Seventy souls had placed themselves into the captain's hands. O'Malley feared that the lull was the great eye of a giant storm, the likes of which came once every score of years. Whatever had been in the days before, much worse lay on the other side.

The *Rosanna's* steady passage to Ilfracombe on a favourable tide improved by strong winds that had veered round, westerly to easterly. Accordingly, Johnson set a course wide of the Devon coast and aiming to slingshot wide of the tide around the treacherous Cornish coast ahead, round Land's End and strike south into the Atlantic. In the distance, winter skies that shone an azure blue overhead were filling in. The captain consulted his charts but he had sailed the stretch of water more times than he cared to remember. Beyond this point there was nowhere for his merchantman to hide. He had room and time to bring the vessel about, return to Bristol and face more delays or strike for Land's End and hide in Falmouth if the storm came. He considered summoning O'Malley to smooth over their differences, but a captain could afford no sign of weakness; least said, soonest mended.

When the *Rosanna* had found the warmer waters off the West African coast the events of today would be a distant memory. The ship would press ahead.

The merchantman made the passage around Land's End, a graveyard for vessels as long as man had sailed, and the place the *Rosanna's* luck finally ran out. The easterly winds died, overwhelmed by strengthening westerlies which brought ominous banks of cloud to fill in the sky and smother the remaining daylight.

The storm was upon the ship in a matter of minutes.

Initially, Johnson had hoped to run on the power of the fierce westerly wind and make Falmouth but within minutes such ideas were abandoned. In the ferocity of the encroaching night, the sea clawed at the *Rosanna* and sails were ordered to be reefed, to protect the vessel.

Then the first of the crewmen started to die.

Two hands were swept away from their precarious perches aloft, within minutes of each other, as they fought to gather in the sails. Others refused to take to the ropes above as the ship rocked violently; for what seemed an age the top sails remained only partially secured. Eventually all was made secure but by then another sailor had been plucked by the sea, no more than a yard from where O'Malley fought to control the giant ship's wheel.

Any hands that could be spared were sent below. Those few that remained above lashed themselves to

the nearest secure structure as the timbers of the
Rosanna groaned. The vessel rose out of the water to be
pitched a hundred foot down as the storm surged
through the Channel. Captain Johnson crawled and
then slid along the stern towards the wheel, one of the
few remaining deckhands darting out to seize him by
the scruff of the neck and then lash tight the loose trail
of rope from around the captain's midriff before the
next breaker could batter the ship.

"What do you think O'Malley?" Johnson bellowed.
He was no more than two paces from the first mate but
the wind tore the words away into the night.

O'Malley shook his head and gestured above, "We
can't make Falmouth now. Let her run, sir. She's a
sound old girl, so she is. Let her run. We can do nothin'
more."

For the rest of the night and all of the following day
the Rosanna did just that. Above decks, the world was
towering grey breakers; below decks, scenes of sickness
and desperation from novice passengers to the most
hardened sailor greeted Johnson whenever he went
below. Rest was impossible and even the simple task of
unrolling the navigational charts was a struggle. Any
sort of accurate calculation on the Rosanna's position
had long since passed; they were likely to be nearer
France than Britain. While the two countries were not at
war such were the tales of deprivation that it was likely
that cargo would be seized or payment demanded

before the ship could return on her way. Such a levy was the least of the *Rosanna's* problems.

In the early hours of the second night of the storm, Johnson posted a volunteer to a perch on the crow's nest; no more than a flat rectangle of platform high in the night sky. He watched the man disappear into the darkness, half expecting to see a body dashed to the deck such were the exaggerated pitches of the vessel, tossed about by the sea. By the best of guesses the French coast was very near but finding a port or shelter would be a miracle.

No more than an hour later the deckhand reappeared.

Prayers had been answered.

A light on the horizon.

O'Malley slipped his rope and made the perilous passage above to verify the sighting and reckon a course by eye. For what seemed like an age Johnson was alone, with only the storm as his companion. When the Irishman returned, it was with the look of a man who had seen salvation.

A light.

More than a light, a beacon on the coast.

The first mate fought the giant tiller and felt the ship respond. The beacon could just as easily signal rocks as the path to a port but in the hours of daylight ahead perhaps the *Rosanna* could find salvation. The news of the light was carried below deck as weary hands from the skeleton crew that remained above deck sought respite from the elements above. Sixty-seven souls pinned their hopes on that distant star and the skill of the captain and first mate to deliver them from the jaws of the sea.

Soon the beam of light became obvious to the men huddled around the ship's wheel. Still some distance away and lost each time the ship dropped into the giant swell of water behind waves that drove the merchantman along. Then O'Malley thought he heard a dreaded sound, carried above the howling wind. Instinctively he fought the wheel to bring the ship hard to port. In the next instant the *Rosanna* was lifted on a giant wave and his worst fears were confirmed.

"Breakers, Cap'n, breakers!"

The ship was pitched forward and then swung hard to port, little to do with the actions of the first mate. The *Rosanna* found herself broadside on to the sea. One moment upright, the next pinned by a sandbank and battered onto her starboard side. Spars were torn away from the sails, screams filled the night air from below decks and men around the wheel were plunged into a black, freezing foam. Another wave broke over the ship pushing it further ashore. Timbers cried in agony as the sea tore at the keel and the *Rosanna* began to break apart.

The exhaustion of the last thirty-six hours was momentarily shed from the Irishman's limbs. There were no orders, this was self-preservation.

The *Rosanna* was dead.

O'Malley slipped the knot of rope and slid into the water, briefly touching the pendants of the Saints before the dark consumed him. The sea carried the first mate to the shore yet his mind remained still, calm in the moment, knowing that his fate lay in the hands of his God and the force of nature. Yet as he struck his first weak strokes towards shore, one question came to his mind: the light, the beacon had been in the wrong place.

A false light.

It was then that the first mate of the merchant ship that had once been the *Rosanna* knew where he was. His arms pushed forward in his best imitation of breast stroke, on the return the right hand felt the reassuring shape on the dagger still at his hip. If he survived the sea, he would need the help of St. Patrick and St. Christopher to leave the beach alive.

Hanover: 31st January 1793

The sentry box at the southern perimeter gate was a lonely post. Sebastian Krombach cheered himself with the thought that he resembled something like the rather melancholy bird that had occasionally nosed its way out of an ornate clock in his grandmother's kitchen that had fascinated him as a child. At one time mounted cavalry troopers had stood sentinel here but now the barracks were the home of the 2nd battalion of the 10th Regiment.

The wooden box, which had long since lost any vestige of being water-tight, shook from the drumming of rain driven along by fierce westerly winds. The skies had threatened as Krombach and another redcoat were marched past a solitary line of tents where the aroma of breakfast taunted the reluctant and hungry sentries. There were perhaps one hundred privates in 2nd Company and they were rostered to maintain a watch at the southern gate for one week.

Krombach rested his musket to the floor momentarily, aware that such an action was an offence and pushed back strands of thick brown hair which had become plastered across his brow, stuffing them untidily under his bicorne hat and gingerly trying to touch his swollen right eye. Taller than most of the soldiers around him, he was three inches short of six foot tall. Bright green eyes burned with fierce determination. His youthful frame was lean, muscles honed by years of working with the men on his father's fishing fleet before enlisting with the battalion. At nineteen he was one of the younger recruits, yet his travels with his uncle across Hanover, Holland and France had shown him more of the world than many around him.

He could also count. Two redcoat privates and one corporal or sergeant for every two-hour watch; twenty-four rankers a day. A private should perform a watch once every three to four days. This was Krombach's fifth day straight. It was Corporal Gauner's bidding and when Krombach had tried to discuss the matter with the corporal, the blackened eye had been the response.

2nd Company was in chaos.

The young redcoat had barely seen Captain Hoyt before the officer resigned his commission. Ensign Schafer, the senior lieutenant and no more than a boy himself, had become dependent on senior soldiers, Gauner in particular. The corporal was cruel; a thug who ruled the unhappy barrack block. Bully, dominate, divide and conquer seemed to be the man's mantra. Acts of violence and humiliation were all too frequent. In the three months of Krombach's service, it had been a painful lesson learnt but not accepted by the young redcoat. Thankfully the worst excesses of Gauner were held in check by Sergeant Winckler but it was an uneasy truce. There was little point in complaining to a senior officer. The battalion barely had enough of those to function.

He shouldered the musket and not a moment too soon. Corporal Krogh paced to the open sentry box, carried out the most cursory of inspections, then turned to march back to his own place of shelter. Krogh, a tough-fighting Dane was one of Gauner's men. For all of that, there was something about Krogh that suggested the Dane was not always at ease with Gauner's methods. One fact was certain, one of Gauner's lackeys would bring Krogh some breakfast, it would be another hour or more until Krombach ate and then only if one of the Pinsk brothers, his only true friends in the company, had managed to save food for him.

There was a pointlessness to sentry duty that Krombach's father had warned him of in their many heated discussions about his choice to leave the family business on the banks of the Elbe and enlist. In fact, the only sight in the five days of duty, other than the snap inspections of the duty corporal, were the two officers and the regimental surgeon who had ridden out at seven that morning.

The 10th had not been the local regiment for Krombach but a family friend had known the colonel and it had been hoped that the redcoat's time in the ranks might serve as an apprenticeship to a commission, at least that was his mother's expectation. Father and son both knew that the world moved in very different ways. Money and position brought commissions; the son of a fisherman would never be the toast of Hanoverian society.

Worse still, Colonel Dohman had died before Krombach had ever set eyes on the man. Sebastian Krombach, dutiful son, tried to keep a cheery tone in the letters home and answer his father's worried questions with reassurances. It was for good reason that the name of Corporal Gauner had never featured in those letters.

Dunkirk: 31st January 1793

"It's been lit. I thought as much."

Jean-Baptiste Mahieu closed the wooden shutter but not before observing that the windows of half a dozen houses opposite held small votive candles. Rain fell in heavy downpours like a giant wave which had breached the harbour wall and broken over small houses packed into the old port town.

A voice called from the other room, "What are you mumbling about?"

Mahieu returned to a chair by the fire in time for his wife of eighteen years to bring a charred pot of coffee and two fragile porcelain cups. Having poured the coffee and offered his wife a cup, he placed the remains of the blackened pot near the fire and settled back for the inevitable question.

"I'm sorry, light of my life and master of this house, what did you say?" Donatienne's voice was tired and tinged with the anger that came with days of meagre meals.

"The tower, I said, they have lit the tower."

"And?"

"And what?"

"Jean-Baptiste Mahieu, you know very well what. My mother always said that I was a fool for marrying the honest Mahieu brother, God rest her soul."

Whenever his wife used his full name, the dutiful husband knew the depths of the trouble he was in.

"Perhaps she was right. Marrying a fisherman and a smuggler is a wiser choice than a soldier. At least you would never know hunger."

"Of course she wasn't right, Jean," Donatienne retorted, "but you cannot let your pride stand in the way. Think of Michelle and…"

"Don't say another word, woman. I need a moment to…"

Jean-Baptiste stared into the black of his cup, lost in thought at the reflection of the firelight on its surface, a reminder of the beacon that now shone across the town. The Leughenaer, 'the Liar's Tower' was a false light that steered merchant ships to their doom while the good citizens of Dunkirk slept and those with questionable morals joined the scavengers on the shore line for a share of any salvaged bounty. He felt her hand on his and a voice as soft as the touch of her fingers.

"Light the candle, please Jean."

"You know the risks, if I do?"

The question needed no answer. The candle was confirmation a householder was prepared for the call in the night, should it come. But also, it was an acceptance that if a child was pulled from the sea, the householder would take it in and raise it as their own.

The candle in the window meant a share of the spoils and the guilt from earning them but also the potential burden of another mouth to feed until the first crops could be harvested.

There were rarely any other survivors.

The 'Code of the Sea' ruled the beaches of Dunkirk. The lives of the shipwrecked who made it ashore were extinguished for the common good of the citizens of the town. No survivors meant no witness. Only in exceptional circumstances would a life be spared. Her hand pressed his again, seeking a decision.

"Very well," he whispered.

Mahieu scooped up a small candle, which had long ceased to be used for prayer as the Church of St-Éloi had been closed the previous summer. A shiver passed through him as he remembered the violence of that night and the power of the mob. With this simple offering at the window, he would become part of that mob. He slumped back into his chair and drained the last of his coffee, praying quietly to a God who had turned his back on France that the moment would not come.

Four hours later, with the storm still in full force, the pounding on the door shook the household and woke him from the chair in which he dozed.

"Mahieu, come quickly."

He knew the voice. Jean-Francois Grison; Mayor of Dunkirk; smuggler and part owner of the *Perseus.*

A man not to be crossed or trusted.

And a man on whom the lives of the citizens of Dunkirk depended.

Mahieu had given little thought about what to bring. His Charleville musket and bayonet seemed the logical choice but now using these weapons felt like a betrayal of his military principles. He had served more years than he cared to remember and had hoped that this year might be his last. While he had been born and raised in Dunkirk, he had spent only five winters in the last twenty there. Every year, Arnaud, his brother, had offered him work as a hand on the *Perseus* but Jean steadfastly remained in the army. The *Perseus* would be the first to leave the port and raid any wreck that had floundered; it had never paid to ask too many questions about what his brother actually did; these days, it paid to ask no questions at all.

Turning up the collar of his old greatcoat, he felt the spray and rain as waves boomed along the shoreline and threatened to drench the dozens of torches that fought vainly for light and life in the darkness. The cold forced him to withdraw further into the warmth of the woollen jacket while his eyes searched the shoreline and ferocious sea beyond for the sight of the vessel. Somewhere further along the chain of vultures that patrolled the shoreline the cry of the sighting had gone up and been passed along. Mahieu found himself running along thick sand, wet with the dregs of a tide that had begun to turn. Shapes began to appear. Boxes, trunks and packages; the flotsam of a dying ship.

Then the first of the killings began.

A body more dead than alive stumbled from the surf before being clubbed mercilessly. Mahieu moved on. He had experienced the ferocity of war. Five years fighting alongside the rebel armies of American colonists had exposed him to more horrible methods of killings than one man need experience in a lifetime. Yet the savagery of his townsfolk appalled him as it had the summer before. There was no honour in this, just murder and piracy.

He pulled at a box and another man came to help him, together they stumbled back through the surf to deposit the salvaged booty above the high tide mark where Grison and others would assess the merchandise. The mayor was nowhere to be found so Mahieu grunted an instruction to drop the box and the pair returned to the surf to harvest more of the night's bounty.

Had it not been for the warning of the other citizen he would never have seen the body that lurched out of the darkness of the night. The silver of a blade ripped past Mahieu's shoulder and he fell back to avoid another blow. But the attack was a tired lunge and another pass was checked by the cudgel of the man who had carried the boxes with Mahieu. The pair were now locked in a deadly dance of thrust and counter-thrust. For a moment Jean-Baptiste watched in a stupor before struggling to his feet in the now sodden coat and unslinging the musket. Even if the Charleville had been loaded, the water-soaked pan would never ignite, so he satisfied himself with the command to stop and the levelling of the musket at both combatants. At first neither man took any notice and Mahieu racked his brain for the language he had not used in ten years.

"Stop, surrender, now!"

He hoped the English made sense or that the seaman was even English at all but the words did the trick: both men parted. It was not in Mahieu's nature or training to kill a foe who had fought valiantly and surrendered his weapon when called upon.

"I claim this man for the crew of the *Perseus*," Mahieu shouted to his compatriot across the roar of the sea and the rain.

It was an old custom; a custom rarely used; it was a custom of the sea though. Mahieu marched the rescued seaman up through the sand, past stranded lifeless bodies, to stake his claim.

Ahead, torches clustered around the growing collection of treasures. Mahieu prodded his prisoner in that direction but was intercepted by Grison before he had made it to the thick line of debris that marked the high-water mark of the storm surge.

"What the hell is that?"

"I claim this man for crew of the *Perseus*."

Grison blew out his cheeks and sighed, shaking his head. Mahieu saw the mayor's hand reach inside the nankeen jacket and the flash of silver was followed by the brilliant white flash of a pistol shot. The bullet lodged somewhere in the right side of the sailor's brain and the lifeless body collapsed to his knees and toppled forward into the sand.

"I refute your claim."

Mahieu looked with horror and hatred at Grison.

"You are not of the *Perseus*, Mahieu. This…," Grison wavered the pistol in the direction of the corpse, "was not your claim to make. All you bring me is another mouth to feed. We have two months grain left, at best. Your Generals are demanding half of what I have. What I do, I do for the good of the Dunkirk."

The mayor walked away, stepping over the dead man without a second look and paced towards the torches to bay out instructions.

The soldier stood there for a moment and then watched a torchlight move nearer to him. A small child no more than ten years old offered the torch to Mahieu, who dumbly held out a hand. The boy proceeded to loot the body, making gurgled sounds of pleasure at the knotted pouch of coins that had survived the ordeal.

Small hands tugged nimbly at a leather string and in the torchlight and spitting rain of the dying storm, bloodstained silver pendants of two saints, St. Christopher and St. Patrick, became the booty and property of the scavengers of Dunkirk.

CHAPTER TWO

Private Duels.

Hanover: 31st January 1793

"Perhaps they won't come?" Erich von Bomm's voice, usually carefree, betrayed the tension of the moment.

"Perhaps not," Brandt attempted reassurance but was sure that his own effort sounded thoroughly unconvincing.

He smiled at his junior officer and received the weakest of responses. With his rugged, youthful complexion and blonde hair swept rakishly forward the young bachelor's easy manner made von Bomm the focus of much female attention.

"Pah!" a voice grunted indignation behind them. "If that had been my daughter's window I'd caught 'e backing out of, I'd have bloody shot 'e on the spot. And bugger me medical oath, I'd have let thee bleed out on the lawn. Good for the roses, a bit of blood."

Behind the pair, stood a stout man with a plump, ruddy face and receding russet hair who replied in a thick Derbyshire accent that both men had learnt to follow.

"Regimental Surgeon Harris, it really wasn't like that, I..." Von Bomm's voice trailed off as the lone rider came into view. The three men, two of whom wore their regimental red jackets, stood out in the drab green and winter brown of the open heathland, south of Hanover.

A duel, though a matter of honour, was frowned upon, expressly forbidden under the command of the previous incumbent, Lieutenant Colonel Marcus Dohman. With a funeral ceremony due in the next few days, a new man would take over and not a moment too soon; though just who was unclear.

Dohman had been ill for some time and the battalion's discipline had drifted badly. Major Johann Volgraf had become the senior officer, not that Brandt had seen much of him in the previous year. The major had preferred the task of running his family estate and was rarely present unless there was a social function. The four infantry companies and Brandt's Grenadier company had become like strangers to one another, despite sharing the same barracks.

Captain Brandt had taken it upon himself to do something to rectify this and had spent a great deal of time with the hapless Ensign Schafer, trying to sort the administrative mess of Second Company. Though the companies were officially numbered, each assumed the name of its captain; Hoyt's Company, had been an unhappy place, the fines and punishments detailed in the daily books attested to this.

"Oh not him. God above Werner, could you not find anyone else?"

For the first time that morning, there was a note of genuine alarm in von Bomm's voice.

Brandt smiled, "Erich, he was the easiest one to bribe, besides the regimental surgeon will do the real work, won't you, sir?"

"Aye, aye. Unless it's a pistol shot to the privates. In which case, I will let the good Doctor Wexler thrash around for a bit. Might save us all another scene like this once spring comes along."

The colour had drained from von Bomm's face as the horseman slowed and dismounted a few paces from them.

"Good morning, gentleman. Apologies for my tardiness but I see I haven't missed the main event. I had a private patient to attend to on the way here."

August Wexler strode unsteadily towards the three men. The doctor from Hoyt's Company was symptomatic of the malaise of the current days. Rarely sober and hen-pecked by a wife who controlled every aspect of his life apart from his spiralling gambling debts of which she knew precious little, Wexler's life revolved between earning money to satisfy both wife and creditors and keeping enough aside until his fortunes at the card table changed.

"You have my fee, Captain?" Wexler asked, somewhat sheepishly.

Brandt nodded and tapped a breast pocket.

"Aren't you forgetting something, Doctor?" Harris spoke from behind the pair of redcoated officers.

"No, I don't think so, sir."

"Your bag, man! What are you going to bind this poor man's wounds with? Kind words and a receipt for your services?" The contempt in Harris' voice was ill-concealed and it was a bashful Wexler who re-joined the group, clutching a medical bag and reeking of brandy fumes, despite the early hour of day. A silence descended upon the four men. It was still ten minutes before the allotted meeting time of that morning, eight o'clock.

"So, here we are. Any sign of the opposition?" Wexler asked, sounding more nervous than von Bomm.

The lull in conversation had accentuated the sound of the wind that whipped across the open heathland and the heavy rainclouds that were building in the west.

"Yes, they are over there hiding between that group of trees!" Harris answered gruffly.

Brandt stifled a laugh, "No Doctor, no sign as yet."

"Perhaps they won't come?" Wexler offered.

"No, they'll come."

Brandt swept back a fringe of fine dark-copper hair that threatened his brow. Despite being two years past his thirtieth birthday, he bore the countenance of a man much younger. Around amber-brown eyes there were dark shadows, testament to the worries which Brandt carried. While the comfort of married life had bulked out his frame, the infantry officer still retained the youthful vigour that had allowed him to win his wife amongst a throng of suitors.

"What makes you so sure?" Wexler asked.

"Because young Erich was caught with his arse dangling out of some young lady's bedroom window," Harris growled, as if such news had been common place for those sober enough to have heard it.

"It really wasn't like that, Regimental Surgeon Harris. Honest it wasn't," von Bomm interjected, a little of the humour and assuredness which Brandt found so endearing was alive in his voice again.

"Well that is a relief," offered Wexler, "perhaps the matter can be explained, the gentlemen shake hands, the physicians be reimbursed for their time and the whole incident never referred to again.

Wexler paused, "The matter can be explained, can't it?"

Brandt chuckled. "It's Erich von Bomm, of course it can be explained. The last two duels that I know of were both unfortunate acts of fate, as was this."

"Sometimes Captain, I find your faith in my moral fibre somewhat lacking," a broad smile broke over von Bomm's face which pleased Brandt. A man must be at his most ebullient if he was to survive a duel: personal experience had taught him that.

"Yes Doctor, the matter can be explained. The young lady, who for modesty's sake shall remain nameless was at a ball. We had danced together once but as she is engaged, I made no advance other than good-natured small talk. The weather that evening was particularly foul. On the way home, my buggy passed another on the road that was broken down. It was the carriage of the same young lady, alone on the road with just her servants."

"No chaperone?" Wexler interrupted.

"Yes of course. I offered my buggy but it only seats two and neither of the women felt able to drive it in dark of night. So, giving my word as an officer and a gentleman…"

Harris cleared his throat and raised his eyes skyward; von Bomm paused and turned to stare in mock admonishment at the surgeon.

"As I was saying, I gave my word. The road led into the face of the rain and by the time we reached her father's home we were quite soaked. Her dress was almost gossamer under the weight of the rain and even as the servants who opened the doors summoned her father, a stern and patrician type, I found it hard to avert my eyes. Well, I'm only human."

Doctor Wexler giggled as Brandt took his turn to shake his head in mild disbelief, "This is your best defence, Erich?"

Von Bomm shrugged and continued, "I explained the situation as best I could, he thanked me and instructed another carriage to be sent to rescue the first. There was an unspoken look which suggested that my services, honourable as they had been, were no longer needed and that any future contact with his betrothed daughter would not be welcomed."

"Sound's a good judge of character to me," Harris offered.

Von Bomm feigned a look of indignation.

"As I said, to those who have ears to hear, I was the perfect gentleman. However, Sophia and I had talked on the journey home."

"This is the lady who shall remain nameless?" Brandt offered, in case there was the slightest degree of doubt.

"The very same," von Bomm replied. "It turns out Sophia's heart is set on another."

"I knew it!" grunted Harris.

"Not I, sir but another gentleman at the ball, who's name appeared more than once on her dance card and had been a suitor deemed unsuitable by her father. The infatuation is known to the chaperone but this is the boldest that the pair had been in public. When I returned to the buggy, the bag containing her dancing shoes had fallen to the side of the seat. One of the small oil lamps on the front of my buggy was still lit and something made me look inside the bag."

"Your impeccable sense of honour, no doubt?" Harris interjected.

"If I hadn't spotted that letter none of this would have happened. I turned the buggy's light toward my seat and sat reading every word. They were the most daring plans of an elopement. The letter was unsigned, but it was obvious that it was the beau from the dance. What was I to do? To return to the front door was the obvious conclusion, but what if the father should pry into the purse. The course of true love demanded action."

"So, you clambered up the lattice like some knight errant to save the young lady's honour and play at cupid?" Brandt spoke, his voice distracted by movement on the road ahead.

"And when caught, the father of the house assumed the letter came from you? If I hadn't of had to get up so early this morning the matter would be comical, quite comical." It seemed that Regimental Surgeon Harris was rather enjoying the implausibility of the tale.

An austere black carriage pulled by a team of six chestnut horses rapidly closed on the ground where the four men stood.

"Well at least it's not the first time that intrigue at a ball has caused a duel, is it sir?" von Bomm nudged at Brandt's elbow and then shielded his eyes from the weak morning sunlight as the strong winds whipped across the open heathland. The only wind-break above

31

the low fern scrub was a solitary oak whose thick trunk glistened in the dawn's light. "Try and have me positioned with my face to the sun, Werner but with my back to that tree. Delay proceedings as much as possible. The strength of the wind will be an issue. Stall as long as you can. The advantage of the sunlight in my eyes will be lost but that tree will still glare."

Brandt nodded, understanding at once.

"There's a few thalers worth there and no mistake," Wexler let out an involuntary whistle as footmen worked to secure the carriage and then help each of the six occupants from the body of the vehicle. "Whose society feathers have we manage to ruffle, I wonder?"

"Wexler, man, do you live on the bloody moon? If you spent less time playing cards and more time listening to battalion gossip you would know that the young lady Sophia is the daughter of one of Hanover's strictest judges and her betrothed is a Guards officer, some blood relative of Field Marshal Freytag. Baumann is the family name. Our Erich is in a bit of a pickle!" Harris sounded almost cheery.

All three men turned away from the carriage to look at Harris who had returned to rummage into his medical bag, stopping only when he he found the long-handled bullet probe. Harris met the gaze of the three.

"What's the matter now?" the surgeon asked.

Brandt motioned his eyes towards von Bomm, "Perhaps you might like to find a few words of encouragement, in our current situation."

"Hmmm," Harris considered the matter before puffing out his cheeks. "He's a Guardsman, Erich, so pistols are a wise choice. He probably spends half his day at a fencing school but won't be able to shoot straight to save his life. Try not to kill him. I know that's what the rules of honour say, blood has to be spilt or a party must yield. It doesn't say how much blood, so as little as possible, please; and none of it yours."

Harris having dispensed wisdom, returned to the contents of his medical bag after placing the bullet probe into a jacket pocket. Brandt paced away from the group and headed towards the carriage. Of the six men, three gentlemen in morning dress stood apart from a physician who remained a respectful distance to the rear. Around them, servants who had ridden as outriders on the carriage, assembled a small card table, arranging drinks and refreshments. Striding towards Captain Brandt, the opponent's 'second' wore an elegant velvet jacket. Behind marched an officer who wore the same redcoat as Brandt, although the tailored uniforms spoke of a deeper red hue, deep blue cuffs to the dark green of the captain's.

Both regiments shared a strong bond. Should the drums of war call, the Grenadier companies from the Guards battalions and the two battalions of the 10th

Regiment would combine to form the 1st Grenadier battalion, an elite formation. With just the faintest hope that such a link could be exploited to ease matters away from the potential disaster of a duel; Brandt discussed matters with the two men.

There was no middle ground to be made though.

Only if von Bomm was prepared to sign a statement that the matter had been impropriety on his part, admit to plans of elopement and resign his commission would the matter be considered closed; Erich's standing in society would be ruined. Brandt knew that for all von Bomm's faults, the young lieutenant was telling the truth. In the matter of a duel, rank held little sway. The second was at the bidding of the man he had come to serve.

Pistols had been agreed in a stream of terse communications the day before. The two brothers, Ludwig and Leopold Baumann, shook hands before Ludwig, the younger of the pair, marched away and removed his red jacket, throwing it in the direction of a servant and took a glass of wine from a tray proffered by another. Brandt was left alone with the older brother, a wealthy man of Hanoverian society.

"Thirty paces?" Brandt suggested.

Baumann nodded his head. It was Brandt's right to dictate the terms, disagreement would be settled by negotiation and the toss of a coin, if needed.

"We will take our position over there," Brandt pointed towards a tree bathed in warm sunlight, despite the heavy grey clouds.

Again Baumann nodded, perhaps already calculating the trouble that von Bomm would experience in the glare of the morning light but Brandt knew his task.

"One more matter, Herr Baumann," Brandt said, weighing his words, "I respect that you second for your brother. The man I second for is like a brother to me. Loyalty to his wishes forbids me to discuss the matter with you but whatever the outcome, the moment that honour is served, this matter dies here. And let us hope that the memory of this misunderstanding is all that dies here today."

Brandt offered a hand, Baumann accepted, took a pace back and marched in martial manner towards his brother and the solitary wine glass that remained on the tray.

It had been a blessing to find an inn open at that hour and just yards from the barracks. Wexler went through an elaborate performance of patting his pockets down, like a man appalled at his own stupidity for having forgotten to bring his purse, despite having pouched the envelope containing payment for his troubles from von Bomm. Fortunately, those troubles had amounted to little other than the best part of an hour of the morning. The doctors and infantrymen were glad to be out of the chill. Heavy raindrops began to pelt the inn's windows and within minutes swollen streams of water were collecting in the road outside.

Steaks and medicinal red wine were the instructions from the regimental surgeon and von Bomm was badgered to recount the passage of events. Despite protestations of modesty, even Brandt found himself urging on the reluctant hero; von Bomm raised his hands in mock surrender and told the tale from the moment he took his mark.

"The ground had been paced out as you know, and the captain had positioned me as close to the tree as he dared, without our opponents guessing the ruse. The sunlight would have been in my eyes had there been a punctual start but with every moment that passed the matter moved to my favour. The bark of that tree glowed a bright orange when I stood against it. I could see very little of Baumann, but I didn't need to. I had no intention of firing first."

"Damned brave, if you ask me?" Wexler interrupted.

"We didn't. Let the boy speak," Harris growled.

"By the time the moment came, Baumann had been standing into the wind for a minute or more. I could see his eyes streaming from the buffeting of that westerly.

The glare off that tree would have made focusing almost impossible. All I had to do was stand stock still and hope."

"And then he fired..." Wexler interjected.

"Yes. I felt the ball whistle past my shoulder on the left and thud into the tree. I had to hold my nerve a moment longer. If I chose to fire and had missed then the pistols would have been reloaded and Baumann would surely have asked for new ground, as was his right. But until that moment, the initiative lay with me."

"Well I am with the doctor, Erich. Such a strategy takes bravery. How did you know he would drop the pistol and submit?"

"Human nature," chortled von Bomm, "I had already got a good glimpse of the body of the bride to be in that wet dress. Women do love a man who is prepared to die for them, but I was betting on him wanting to be a groom rather than an honourable corpse. I'm sure they will kiss and make good."

Despite the officer's tradition never to discuss politics, religion or the business of the battalion at the meal table, when the food arrived the matter of the successor to Dohman came to the fore. All that was known was that, against tradition, the post was to be made outside of the family of officers from the 10th Regiment. Brandt had kept his council while the other three discussed the current ills of the battalion until von

Bomm, buoyed by the release of the morning, pressed him for an opinion.

"Erich, I had been meaning to say something for a while but before Christmas I promised Katerina that…Well, you know that Aleksander is a sickly child and Eliza is headstrong, just as her mother. They are in Celle and I am here. I don't need the army for an income and…"

"You're leaving? Werner, no! When?" von Bomm sounded as if he had just been winded by a punch to the ribs.

"Two months. Three at the most. I have told Katerina that I will help the new man find a successor for Hoyt's company."

"But who will lead the Grenadiers?" von Bomm whispered in near disbelief at the words.

"A man brave enough to face down an opponent intent on killing him and wise enough to let the matter die on the field," Brandt placed a hand on von Bomm's shoulder.

"Bravo," Wexler said, "a glass to celebrate? You know that Baumann had wet his breeches."

"Aye, and worse no doubt. Thank God you positioned us up wind of him, Werner. But as Brandt says the matter died on the field and is never to be referred to again," surgeon Harris replied.

Brandt wanted to believe those words but the cold eyes of the second, Leopold Baumann, at end of the duel suggested the result merely heaped defeat upon dishonour.

CHAPTER THREE

The Army of the North.

Sint Niklaas: 31st January 1793

Ancient timbers groaned under the fury of the storm that ravaged the winter landscape of eastern Flanders. Antwerp was another day's ride away, two if this weather held. Captain Julien Beauvais drove any thoughts from his mind of the pleasures his return could yield and concentrated on tightly wedging a length of wood between the wooden arms of the barn doors and its gnarled door frame. There had been accommodation available in the town. The credentials from General Dumouriez would have ensured a warm room and a hot meal but a knife across his throat in the pitch of night was a near certainty.

No French soldier could trust the citizens of Flanders any more. And the citizens of Flanders no longer trusted the French.

After Jemappes, the Army of the North had been heroes to a man. A professional Austrian army had been defeated in open battle, Flanders had welcomed the sons of France, sensing that their moment of liberty from Imperial rule had come. The revolution had been brought to the cities and towns of Flanders.

But then winter came.

The National Assembly in Paris, unable to feed her northern army, made it lawful for soldiers to take what they needed from a people who had nothing to give. In the space of a week, looting, rape and murder had become common place. Discipline evaporated; battalions had become gangs of brigands. General Dumouriez ordered summary executions of those who stole while supply wagons were summoned from Dunkirk, Lille and Valenciennes but these towns had barely any food to spare for themselves. Politicians in Paris frightened by the power of the army had set about trying to shackle it when the whole of the Low Countries were ripe for deliverance from Austria. The miracle of Jemappes had been utterly undone.

Not that either Dumouriez or Beauvais should still be alive, a joke that the General shared with his envoy in the darkest of moments.

In the hours before the battle, Dumouriez and some of his staff had blundered into the path of Austrian infantrymen, no doubt scouting for food or shelter. A squadron of the 3rd Dragoons, Beauvais' regiment had been stationed close by. Whatever sixth sense had alerted him, the cavalryman had ordered a troop of his dragoons to follow him before the first shots had been fired; the order to 'Charge!' was a full-throated cry on Beauvais' lips a second later.

The village was a press of bodies.

Soldiers in grubby white uniforms and heavy grey greatcoats pulled at the reins of a dozen horses, some were already unseated. Then Beauvais was among them, slashing like a demon at the wicked silver of bayonets that rose to meet him. He never saw the bayonet that jabbed up under his sword arm and towards his exposed chin. A fraction lower and the tip would have torn through his throat. His assailant and a dozen other white jacketed Austrian infantrymen had died under the weight of Beauvais' cavalry sword before the loss of blood had overwhelmed him.

Dumouriez' personal doctor had tended to the dragoon once the killing was done; a fact that may have saved his life. The pain of that wound had long since passed. The reflex action of running thick fingers over the ridge of vermilion skin that ran to a dead right eye and the revulsion of his own reflection had not. Heavily stitched skin ran taut, pulling together what the infantry bayonet had torn apart. But General Dumouriez had lived, Jemappes won and Austria vanquished.

A broken smile fleeted on his lips.

Behind him, his horse whinnied, unsettled by another gust whistling through the unsteady rafters. Somewhere in the dark of the loft space above,

window-shutters thudded against exterior walls.
Beauvais made a mental note to secure it before settling
to rest but there was still work to do. Calming his white
mare, he removed the saddle and halter and set to work
drying the animal, before placing a warm blanket on
her back.

"Unrideable, eh? Good work, Gypsy," he hissed
softly, the sound of his own voice distorted. Those had
been the very words of the riding master after trying to
make the horse fit for service life, along with the
warning to Beauvais that the mare was headstrong and
troublesome. He had chosen her nonetheless with the
casual reply, "Headstrong and troublesome are just
how I like my women."

Not that there had been many of those in Beauvais'
life. Such dalliances were the realm of the hussar, fit for
little other than parading for the ladies of every town
that the army passed through. His wife, had she lived,
would not have recognised him now, certainly not the
youthful dragoon officer that she had married. But she
had given her life, giving birth to their only son, three
winters ago. Somewhere south of Paris, a child would
be sleeping, left to the care of the wives of the regiment.
And when the army had done with him, Beauvais
would return to claim little Armand and find a part of
France to settle where he might again know peace.

Outside the wind bullied the building, sprays of
misted rain driven through the thinnest of spaces

between the timbered walls and dragged Beauvais' mind to the tasks to be done. His waxed riding cape, which had shielded Beauvais from the worst of the weather rippled on a rope line that had once passed for tether line in the stable. Any other horses were long since gone, stolen or sold. That was another reason for not letting the mare from his sight. With the aid of a small lantern the powerfully built dragoon clambered up a ladder and squeezed into the loft space, crawling on hands and knees towards the shutters that had been blown open. For a while neither wooden fixing would move, the force of the wind pinning them to the outside wall. Across the landscape, lightning ricocheted and thunder peeled almost continually.

A momentary lull allowed Beauvais to free one side and then the other and work to secure the window space but now his torso was soaked. Returning to the empty bay next to his mare, he scooped together handfuls of straw to make both blanket and bed. Peeling off his jacket, he considered using the wax cape as a cover against the damp chill but thought better of it.

Instead, he lay his worldly goods beside him, at least those that might keep him alive. A pair of duelling pistols, a smaller hand-held pistol and his straight-bladed sword. If the knives in the dark came for him, then they had better come prepared to die.

The candle had long since burned through when sleep took Beauvais. He had hoped that sleep would bring him Juliette, instead it brought him the farm. One like his present surroundings but Beauvais knew the dark path the dream would take.

Winter daylight.

The open doorway to a ram-shackled building. A pair of feet, protruding lifeless from an open door. A small boy stood helpless, looking at the body and then at the scene in the farm for help.

None would come.

Three soldiers crowded around two bodies coupling in the dirt. A dragoon, riding breeches around his ankles thrust wildly into a woman who screamed in vain. One soldier stood with his boot pinning her outstretched arm into the mud of the farmyard.

Two other troopers had found a pig. While one held the animal down, the other slit the animal's throat with a sabre's stroke. Red jets of blood streaked over the limbs of the rutting cavalryman. There was wine, laughter and screams that had turned to a deep sobbing.

In Beauvais' darker dreams, the woman's face had become his wife, the child Armand. Tonight, his mind had spared him that torment.

What never changed was the rage that Beauvais felt inside as he slipped noiselessly from his white mare.

He killed the dragoon who stood over the woman with the first pistol shot, the bullet tearing the man's skull and showering the soldiers around with blood and brain matter. The second pistol erupted and another onlooker fell. Beauvais strode forward, dropping both pistols and drawing the sabre, slowly, deliberately. The solitary watcher was dazed, dropping the bottle, clearly trying to decide whether to stand at attention in an effort to placate the heavily scarred officer or defend himself.

It mattered little.

Beauvais barely broke stride but rammed the full length of his sword through the drunkard's pelvis. For a second the man remained upright as the blade was withdrawn, then collapsed in a heap. The bucking dragoon had remained blissfully unaware until Beauvais' fist yanked him from his victim before a knee was driven into the base of his spine shortly followed by the full thrust of Beauvais' bloodied sword.

The remaining pair panicked.

The dragoon who had slit the sow's throat let the animal in the last contortions of life, slip from his grasp, pinning his fellow conspirator to the floor. He knew that his existence was forfeit. Killing the demon of an officer was the only hope of escape. He rushed Beauvais with the intent of doing just that but the wild blow was mistimed. Even to a man blinded on his right, it had been a poorly concealed attack; a fatal mistake.

In the dream the woman and boy vanished.

Only the bodies of the dragoons remained at his feet.

He felt the anger subside as he walked towards the trooper who fought to free himself from the weight of a sow's corpse. Beauvais' hand tightened around the hilt of the sabre which had come to rest on the struggling dragoon's throat. He woke to find his arm outstretched into the darkness of the barn. Dawn was still some way off but that sixth sense honed by war had told him it was time to leave.

The killing of the troopers had not bothered Beauvais. The men would have hung from the nearest tree. Had they been from his own squadron, the matter would have never proceeded further. But they were under the command of another officer, a man whom Beauvais had little time for. The matter caused enmity which was a luxury of peacetime. Colonel Courtois, a fair man and friend to Beauvais had been left with little choice. The savagery of Beauvais' actions was blamed on the results of the wounds received in battle and some time away from the regiment would help these heal.

War had demanded his loyalty over family but the laurels of victory had been the stitch and needle of a surgeon.

The regiment had demanded loyalty but in upholding its honour he had been dishonoured.

Dumouriez had demanded loyalty and in Beauvais' hour of need had offered him succour. The General's envoy prepared his mount. He would reach Antwerp today. Dumouriez depended on him.

Before daylight had yet to trouble the horizon, a dozen torches closed in along the waterlogged track that lead to the barn where a Frenchman had taken shelter for the night. It was an error that would cost the Frenchman his life. The good citizens of St. Niklaas were determined to see to that.

Antwerp: 31st January 1793

A small pot of fresh coffee arrived but the scribe at the desk barely acknowledged the fact. A servant, wearing the livery of the deposed royal household gently placed the tray, bowed and left the room. Leaves of parchment, precisely ordered, written in Serge Genet's ornate hand waited for scrutiny and signature. Each page bore no blemish or correction. Twenty years as a legal clerk in Dunkirk had honed Genet's nature towards that of a perfectionist. In a world of uniforms, Genet had retained the simple black clothing of a clerk but wielded the power of an army from his pen. Only a tricolour sash denoted his rank and power; reputation did the rest.

Dumouriez, then Minister of War, had spotted the talent at once. Genet's work had shone amongst a myriad of reports that had arrived from across France.

His legal background coupled with an exceptional memory, were now thrown fully into the service of the Revolution. From the relative obscurity of a posting in Dunkirk, Genet was found a post at the Ministry of War, in Paris, where his intellect and methods earned him the nickname of 'the Spider'. Transfer from Dunkirk to Paris and on to the Army of the North had simply served to broaden his network; he had become a rising star in the ferment of chaos that was revolutionary France.

General Dumouriez never tired of saying that in a country that had forgotten God, Genet was a godsend; Serge Genet, the Chief of Intelligence to the Army of the North, never tired of such fulsome praise reaching his ears.

Between them, the two had set about to conceive victory at the battle of Jemappes: a miracle some had said. Poorly trained and ill-equipped, the French army had beaten and driven the professional troops of the Austrian Emperor out of Flanders, leaving Austria and Prussia paralysed in disagreement over how to deal with France and the mercurial Dumouriez. What Dumouriez and his soldiers had gained, the Convention in Paris had set about trying to lose almost at once, with laws that permitted starving soldiers to take any goods necessary from Flanders citizens, without retribution.

The result had been anarchy and hatred from a population that the Army of the North had come to liberate. When Dumouriez' orders for his soldiers to respect the property of the citizens of Flanders had failed, summary executions began in every battalion and regiment to try and regain discipline. Many soldiers, facing starvation, considered their part in the war over; starvation or the noose were a poor lot to choose between. There had been direct clashes between Paris and Dumouriez which made Genet nervous. In these days no man was immune from the reach of the guillotine. But Dumouriez had rebuffed such advice and had set about crossing the countryside and visiting various winter quarters to restore order. Slowly the situation had eased but by then the army had almost halved in strength.

Pouring himself a small cup of the newly arrived brew, he paused to examine a letter, new demands from the Convention in Paris. Somewhere across the hallway from the suite of rooms in the Grand Palace, which had become the headquarters of the Army of the North, a clock struck midnight. Outside a storm raged, rain driving hard into ornate wooden shutters which screened windows that rattled ferociously every few seconds.

The General was late, no doubt the severity of the storm the cause of the delay. Had it been anything else, surely Paris would have written.

Genet considered Dumouriez a most complicated man, compromised by his links to the deposed royal household. When the decree had been passed declaring that Louis XVI would face the guillotine, the 'National Razor', Dumouriez had returned to Paris. He had simply told Genet that he was going to wish an old friend farewell and that the army could not be in safer hands. The Chief of Intelligence had warned his superior that such a meeting would give politicians who feared the might of Dumouriez, ammunition to smear gossip and lies. It could even be a trap.

The Spider knew how Paris operated; the plea had been in vain.

Beauvais was overdue too but Genet cared little about him.

As long he reached Lille, the 'Queen of the Citadels' along France's northern border, then the orders would be dispersed east and west. Men, supplies and money; all must be found if the Army of the North was to campaign again. Besides, Beauvais could ride through Hell and come out the other side. There was something about the manner of the man that infuriated but fascinated the scribe. Somewhere in a compartment of Genet's consciousness was a list of those who had slighted him across the years. If greater power ever came to his hands then the pleasure of revenge could be enacted. He weighed the matter, turning the porcelain cup so that black liquid came perilously close the edge. An old memory surfaced, the black of the sea at Dunkirk on a night like this, perfect for the scavengers who lured ships onto the rocks, as vessels caught on the open sea, raced for port.

Beauvais was added to the retribution list for two reasons, neither of which Genet would have been prepared to vocalise. The first was that the dragoon reminded him of the lawless Dunkirk thugs who had made years of his life miserable. The second was that somehow Juliette favoured the dragoon. That thought utterly disgusted him.

Across the hall from the room that Genet worked in, the Countess de Marboré pulled bedsheets around her to keep out the winter chill in a room where the fire died away to smouldering embers. The title was one that she no longer cared for, the relic of a life before the revolution: now she simply used the name Juliette even though Dumouriez only referred to her as 'the Countess'. The revolution, which had taken husband, property and all the old assurances away from her, had also offered a strange path to a new life.

It seemed churlish to call the days that had come before tedious or even unhappy. Life in the village of Garvarnie in the shadow of a wall of mountains, of which Marboré was the highest peak, had been an idyll.

She had tried to give Michel, her husband and senior by some twenty years, a son but fate had not permitted children. Their relationship had softened and become paternal, as the world around them changed forever. The department of Bigorre, under whose laws the Counts of Marboré had lived for some five hundred years was absorbed into the new region of the Hautes-Pyrénées.

Such an act, seemingly insignificant, had changed the course of Juliette's life. Michel had been killed while leading a band of villagers who had repulsed an attack from marauding Spanish forces on a mountain pass near the view. New property legislation had been passed and the arrangements that Michel had made in the event of his death no longer held any legal sway. Juliette became invisible in the new republic. Property that should have been hers was instead now the right of any living male relative.

It was 'Liberty, Equality and Fraternity'. Revolution had not brought about the rights of woman.

As none could be found the new government seized the estate and its wealth for the 'people'. The countess could stay in her home for no more than a month, after which time she must make her life elsewhere.

In the panic of the days that followed, Juliette had read every one of her husband's papers and consulted with a local magistrate, a family friend of many years standing. He had spotted the name of Dumouriez in a series of correspondences from Michel's brief sojourn to the court of Louis XVI which had continued for some years after. If anyone could fight against this inequality, it was the then Minister of War. Rumour had it that Dumouriez had a lawyer of excellent repute working for him. Juliette had travelled to Paris but before the matter had been settled, Dumouriez had seized the chance to take up the vacant post as the commander of the Army of the North. The matter had never been fully resolved but his offer of protection had drawn her north.

Juliette slid gently from the bed, crossed the room and threw two logs on the fire, pausing to enjoy the heat and listen to the crackle as red embers singed thick bark before bright new flames burst into life. She made her way back to the bed, passing buff leather riding breeches and a dragoon's jacket that had been tailored to accentuate the curves of her body. It had been a gift from the officers on Dumouriez' staff. The General had of course approved and Genet had cast sideways glances. But somehow an odd freedom had evolved. Juliette had become a jewel in the pantomime crown that was Dumouriez' inner circle. Besides none of the officers, try as they may, held her fancy.

The moment that thought had crossed her mind, she caught sight of the small muff pistol tucked under the pillow and knew that it was a lie. There was a man who made her feel alive again. It was perhaps because they made such an improbable pair. The dragoon had once been handsome until the bayonet had torn a jagged scar into his face and taken the sight in his eye.

While other officers had complimented at every turn, Beauvais had remained disinterested; only speaking to her when she sat next to him and only when Juliette had forced conversation from the man. He had given her the small muff pistol, usually secreted on a lady's person for close protection. The dragoon had arranged a series of targets to represent the head, heart and groin and Juliette had demonstrated a natural prowess.

She peered at the locked door, tried it once more to satisfy her peace of mind and slid back into bed. She was alone in the building with Genet and some of the staff. If the lawyer, who found the slightest pretext to raise the matter of resolving her estate, developed the courage to make good on any repressed urges, he would certainly leave the room without a vital piece of his anatomy. Juliette never missed the targets that Beauvais had selected, even when he positioned a thimble which she had christened as Genet's manhood.

Beauvais was out somewhere in the storm and Juliette had the feeling that the dragoon was in trouble, the same dark doubts that had come to her hours before she had learnt of Michel's death.

CHAPTER FOUR

Engineers and Architects.

Nienburg: 31st January 1793

The house was full of industry, furniture being moved, luggage being packed. Half a dozen soldiers of the 6th Regiment in their white fatigue jackets, rather than their formal redcoats, worked alongside the domestic staff of the house. Frau Neuberg cast an eye over proceedings, nodded her assent as she moved through the rooms of the upper floor before proceeding down an elegant staircase of polished teak to the drawing room. She was not an overly sentimental woman; the wife of an army officer could ill afford such tendencies. However, she paused for the briefest of moments at the bottom of the stairwell to remember the occasions that each of her three daughters, radiant in their bridal gowns, had passed along the passageway and out of the main door. Jacob had stood in his parade uniform, ready to escort each of his girls between an honour guard of redcoats. The most wonderful times in a house that had been the happiest of homes for nine years, even while the army had thwarted her husband's ambitions for a rank beyond that of major.

Until now.

Perhaps the letter had come five years too late. Jacob certainly had said as much to her but she could still see the youthful energy that was now cloaked in the body of an older man. She entered the drawing room, where her husband sat in a chair near the fire, the letter folded gently on his lap. On the chair opposite two tunics rested on either stile, one a major's of the 6th, the other a lieutenant colonel's of the 10th. There were moments of occasional hesitancy in his abilities and Frau Neuberg would not allow one to take hold now.

"May I join you? You do look as though you are sat talking to those jackets."

She perched gently on the chair opposite her husband, careful not to crease either garment. For a moment she allowed herself to study a face careworn and creased by the middle years of life and the indifference of his peers to his methods. Thick dark grey hair and long-whiskered side-burns needed a trim but other than moments such as these it was hard to get Jacob to remain in one place for long enough. When he finally spoke, a voice gentle and warm sounded distant, his focus remaining on the flames which danced in the heart of the fire.

"The new house will not be like this, Hanne."

"I know Liebling, but it will be a new start. A new home for you and I."

"I know but..."

His fingers drummed anxiously on the letter.

"And the letter of introduction from Colonel von Hammerstein is a glowing recommendation of your abilities, Jacob. You should be proud of your time here and the work that you have done."

His faced turned to hers.

"Now who is being naive, Liebling. The Colonel is a rare man. He understood my methods but…remember my posting to Prussia?"

"You were away for eighteen months, of course I remember it. We postponed a wedding until your return."

"I was told it was to improve the staff work between our two nations, should we stand together in a time of war again."

"And wasn't it that?"

"No. Von Hammerstein felt he owed it to me to tell me that the posting was the idea of our glorious Field Marshal Freytag."

"Oh…"

"Yes, 'Oh', indeed. Freytag was hopeful that a spell of Prussian discipline would knock 'fanciful ideas' out of me."

"It didn't though, did it?"

"On the contrary, it showed that what I observed from the defeat in America was right. This promotion is going to be the testing of that theory, Hanne. War is coming."

"Are you certain?"

"It will take a miracle to avoid it. Von Hammerstein recommended me to von Diepenbroick before he had ever written this letter. They share the same view and 'Amen' for that. But the new house will never be the same as this one. This felt like a home and I fear that I will barely have time to live in the new one before the drum calls."

"Then I shall make it into a home for the day you return. You were born to lead men, Jacob. You understand them."

"I'm being posted to a battalion over the head of a senior major who expected the promotion for himself."

"Then clearly your Colonel von Diepenbroick thought he was not the man for the job and that you are. I look forward to meeting him, he sounds an excellent judge of character," Frau Neuberg's voice barely suppressed laughter. "Anyway, you have told me often enough that command is not a contest in popularity."

"Dearest Hanne, I'd hate to have you as an opponent."

"Then it's just as well that you have me for a wife, Jacob Neuberg. Now what shall we do with this tired looking major's jacket? Talking of which, I ordered a new dress to befit my station as a Colonel's wife. Come, we both have work to do. You, a battalion to prepare and me a household to organise."

Frau Neuberg looked through the window beyond, distracted by flashes of brilliant white against the drab grey of garden walls laid bare by winter. Thunder followed and rain hammered down with an unexpected violence that made her jump.

"I hope this weather passes for tomorrow. The road to Hanover will be nightmarish."

She felt his hand on hers.

"Liebling, if you command the sun to shine tomorrow, then I am sure it will," his voice spoke with love but with something more. It spoke with the confidence and authority which she found so reassuring.

Her husband, Lieutenant Colonel Jacob Neuberg, would succeed whatever the odds. War had carried him away before. If it did again, she would wait and have such a home ready for his return. He deserved nothing less than that.

London: 31st January 1793

The desk, a neat oblong of military precision, was spartan save for the pair of candlesticks, wooden trays filled with urgent correspondence or dictated replies that required an authoritative signature and a bronze ink pot, smeared with dried streaks of black ink from the efforts of the day. It had been a trying morning for Colonel James Murray. His ankle ached, a war wound from the battle of Brandywine fifteen years or so earlier. It had never fully healed and rain made the pain even worse.

The rain had been driven in on Atlantic storms from the Americas into France and over southern England, struck at the heart of the city. The plague of revolution had travelled in much the same way but at least Murray contented himself that such contagion could never take hold here. Especially now that a course of action had been decided upon.

An army was to be sent to the Continent and the Colonel had the honour of a prime post in it. There was much to do and he could ill afford the cold that was surely coming after his drenching from the short walk from Horse Guards, the home of His Majesty's Army, to Whitehall, the home of the enemy, the War Ministry and Henry Dundas, in particular. It was hard to find a man so vilified by soldiers, sailors and politicians. Yet Dundas held the confidence of the Prime Minister and that was all that mattered. With his years of Scottish trial law behind him, the Minister for War could make a 'hello' sound like an accusation of guilt.

At this moment there were no shortages of accusations to go around, only shortages in general.

Not enough manpower, uniforms, trained staff officers, engineers, siege weapons or money. Dundas levelled the responsibility for such matters firmly back at the doors of Horse Guards, while saving some invective for the colonies and their hopeless governors, those soldiers who malingered on the sick list at the nation's expense and the Irish. Murray had escaped from the meeting with his ears ringing, his uniform sodden and his ankle in agony.

Worse still he knew that today's meeting was not just about the very real prospect of war. Nothing formal had been declared by either nation but intelligence from Paris suggested that since the execution of Louis, war with Britain had been discussed in the National Assembly daily. Today's meeting was merely the opening skirmish between Murray and Whitehall. When an army was sent overseas, most likely the destination would be Holland, the Austrian Netherlands. The Duke of York had been appointed as the commander, Murray his chief of staff. Future battles with Dundas would be fought by pen and paper. Today's encounter felt like a resounding defeat. Murray had come away with the detailed rebuttal of deficiencies that Horse Guards had laid at the Ministry's door with a tome of such volume that there clearly hadn't been a shortage of pen and ink.

There were still half a dozen interviews and appointments before he could turn his attention to Dundas' missive. The Colonel's role at Horse Guards also found him dealing with dozens of different technical and official details, the termination of commissions by skilled officers, artillerymen and

engineers was part of his remit. Horse Guards, in a bid
to make the loss of such vital men in a modern army
particularly difficult, had insisted that all matters
needed to be dealt with in London, rather than at a
regional level. This final interview was a chance to
persuade those, often attracted by lucrative offers from
private ventures, that staying to serve His Majesty was
the correct and proper course. The next appointment
was such a case. Murray called to a guardsman who
stood sentry on the other side of the door, to bid the
gentleman enter.

A burly, broad shouldered man with a congenial
smile entered and sat in the chair that Murray directed
him towards. Auburn sideburns enclosed a thick mop
of black hair, streaked steel-grey at the temples; a face
tanned by winter sun suggested a man more suited to
life beyond the confines of a desk.

"Major?"

"Trevethan, sir."

"Ah yes, Trevethan. Wishing to leave his Majesty's
gainful employ?"

Murray knew the details but he prided himself on
wanting to know the measure of the man in front of
him. Was the officer worth retaining? More often than
not, the answer was 'no' but old habits die hard.
Besides there was an outside chance of something more.
Many engineers might baulk at the order to campaign.
If Trevethan had already made his peace with the local

battalion in the south-west, then he was fair game for Murray. One shortage to strike through on the list.

"So, what are you planning to do with your life once your chains of bondage are slipped?"

The man opposite scratched his head and looked a little bemused.

Murray repeated the question from a different tack, "What are your plans beyond the army, Major?"

"Oh, road building, sir. I'm sorry I thought 'e was speakin' another language for a moment," Trevethan's reply had a friendly Cornish lilt and Murray quickly surmised that it suited the Cornishman to play the fool, which intrigued the colonel all the greater.

"Roads, eh. Good solid work and heaven knows we need them improved. You travelled by land to get here?"

"Yes sir, three days, played 'avoc with me back. And these storms, fierce wind and rains. Rain's the killer you know, for roads. Good foundation and good drainage. Cambers and culverts, sir. Mark me words, cambers and culverts."

"Quite!" Now it was Murray's turn to look bemused by the technical language. "You have employment arranged then?"

Trevethan made a face that suggested the matter was a good as sealed but not quite.

"Well, Colonel, yes and no. There is a contract to improve the road from Falmouth to Plymouth. I have put in with a local group of businessmen for a share of the work for the turnpike. I'm to seek some extra finance while I'm 'ere in London, but I will be buggered if I have the first clue about how to go about it. Don't suppose you would be kind enough to suggest anywhere I might…err…um…"

Murray sat back, looked at Trevethan and then turned to face a window that looked out onto the main parade ground. It was all that he could do to stop himself from smiling. Campaigning would be a burden. A professional voice with a sunny disposition would be a welcome addition.

"Actually, Major, I do have a few friends who might look to invest. I will gladly write a letter of introduction but before I do that and, of course, sign the paperwork that honourably discharges your commission, well it crosses my mind that there is another way."

Trevethan sat forward, "Another way, sir?"

"Yes. Now it strikes me, forgive me but I didn't quite grasp the technical terms but water is the enemy of the road builder."

"Spoken like a true engineer y'rself, sir!"

"And which European people have mastered the art of dealing with water in their daily lives?"

"The Irish, sir?" Trevethan sounded completely confused as to the direction of Murray's thrust which suited the Colonel: intrigue would win.

"No, Major, the Dutch. Now imagine this," Murray paused to spread his hands wide in a dramatic fashion, "an engineer who has spent a year, two at most in that fine country, learning the techniques that working in that environment might bring. Why such a man could return to this country and not be the hand-maiden to some hard-pressed local businessmen but be the kind of capital fellow that capitol would follow. Why the very banks here in London would be falling over themselves to offer lines of credit to such a man. Mark my words, Trevethan, a man like that could achieve all he wanted in life and," Murray raised his finger to the heavens to accentuate the point, "be paid the rate of a king's officer on campaign while such skills were being learnt. What I wouldn't give for such an opportunity."

Murray paused and waited for the words to register, assured that the mind of the man opposite was already calculating the possibilities. The Colonel made a show of reaching for the quill that idled near the pot.

"I will just sign this form and you can be on your way. I will forward a letter to you regarding the contacts you need…"

"'Old on there, me beauty! Begging your pardon, Colonel, but just what were you drivin' at. Holland? Campaign? Are you tryin' to bamboozle me?"

"Not at all, not at all, Major. It's just that…Well you must have heard the rumours. An army is going to the Continent. The Duke of York will command and I have been given the honour of being the made the chief of staff. The potential for the man appointed as the Duke's engineer, once the campaign is done is, frankly, limitless. Reputations can be made with such a posting."

Again Murray paused, letting the matter ferment in the engineer's mind.

"Interested, Trevethan?"

The major ran thick fingers across his chin.

"Remind me never to play cards with 'e. I take it there will be more than just thee, me and his 'ighness on this jaunt?"

"All in good time, Trevethan. Horse Guards can only work so many miracles in one day. Shall I deal with this?" Murray looked at the paperwork that would have ended the Major's obligation to the King.

"Room's a bit chilly, if you don't mind me saying sir. The fire might be the best place for that bit of scrap."

Murray rose and offered his hand.

A small victory in the day and someone who had washed the gall of Dundas clean from his mind; Major Stephen Trevethan would be a boon in the days and months ahead.

CHAPTER FIVE

The Colours.

Hanover: 7th February 1793

It was an unhappy morning for the battalion as the massed ranks prepared to bury their former commander, a man that many of the newer recruits had never met. Sebastian Krombach's gaze fixed upon the coffin draped in the battalion's ancient flags, a rallying point in battle. The redcoats of previous generations had fought and died to save the Colours of the 10th. Losing them meant more than shame and dishonour in that moment, but a stain on the battalion's reputation for that lasted down the years. Krombach fought the urge to turn his head and follow the passage of the funeral cortege of Lieutenant Colonel Marcus Dohman as it rolled slowly past. The faded flags that shrouded the coffin like religious icons won out and Krombach's head twisted to stare; a wave of relief passed through him with the realisation that every other red coated Hanoverian infantryman had done the same.

2nd Battalion of the 10th lived on; even in death, there were the signs of renewal.

Behind the coffin rode the new commander, Lieutenant Colonel Jacob Neuberg. One of Neuberg's first actions had been to commission a new set of Colours made in rich silk. In all likelihood war was coming. The old flags were forty years old. They would not see out the rigours of even a short-lived campaign. Alongside the incumbent commander rode a small figure shrouded in a heavy blue cape. Colonel von Diepenbroick, the colonel-in-chief of the 10th, had appointed Neuberg, his reasons for doing so were his own but the decision had not met with universal approval. Von Diepenbroick's horse, a magnificent 'Hanoverian Cream', nodded solemnly into the face of a fresh northerly gust that heralded the return of a cold, clinging drizzle. Perhaps even the heavens disapproved of the appointment?

From the corner of his vision, they came into view. Two new battle standards, rich dark-green material chosen to match the collar facings of the four hundred redcoats on parade, were escorted by the battalion's senior officer, Major Volgraf. Knowing from bitter experience that sudden movement would cause the black, leather neck-stock to score into his chin, his head kept perfectly still as the new flags passed. On one, emblazoned under a relief of the head of King George, was a dais bedecked with captured flags and trophies with a motto that proudly read 'The Reward for Bravery'.

Krombach tensed and prepared for the orders to move. The swollen eye had recovered but his body ached, not from the morning march or the daily drills, but from a beating that had been more expertly concealed this time that soldiers endured. Bravery might have been the reward for the battalion in battle, but it was a necessity for a recruit in the barracks. Even now he knew that Corporal Gauner was scrutinising his and every other man's performance. Recriminations for the slightest imagined misdemeanour were bound to follow. Again, he considered whether he might mention these woes to an officer when the chance arose. But there seemed little point, the popular rumour was that the officers had troubles enough of their own; the arrival of Colonel Neuberg had caused that.

The last time that the 10th's headquarters had been so crowded with guests was to celebrate the end of the Seven Years war; paintings that lined oak-panelled walls detailed the scenes of victory for the proud redcoats. Then, the mood would had been one of feasting and celebration. Now the regiment had come together as a family again. Officers and their wives mingling with dignitaries from Hanover and relatives of the Dohman family while orderlies weaved in between clusters of people, refreshing glasses when required. The room resounded with the gentle murmurs of sombre conversations broken by occasional polite laughter, shared anecdotes of the man who had commanded for twenty years.

A great table had been placed against the far wall opposite the main fireplace where a sumptuous luncheon arrangement catered for the guests. Many had taken to warming themselves after braving the foul February conditions before moving toward the table of food. 2nd Company's doctor had approached the matter from a different perspective and already seemed intent on indulging in both food and wine before seeking a warm spot to sleep off the effects of the day.

Captain Brandt had considered whether he should remind the doctor to consider the other guests but was beaten to the task by Frau Neuberg. The new Colonel's wife had already sensed the danger and moved to gently steer the hapless Doctor Wexler towards a trio of young officers with subtle instructions to prevent any further wanderings by the physician. Relieved to be spared the task, Werner Brandt shuffled near to the warmth of the fire, nodding courteously to a sea of faces but seeking solace in his own thoughts. He wanted these proceedings over in order that he could move to deal with any outstanding matters regarding both the Grenadiers and 2nd Company, before returning to

Celle. Such were the current shortages that he had twice the workload as would normally be expected.

Katerina, his wife, had remained in Celle to look after their youngest child, Aleksander, who had been suffering from a fever. Had it not been for the funeral and the letter from Neuberg, Brandt would have stayed too. The last few weeks he had been plagued by the decision to resign his commission. As much as he was sure Katerina wanted just that, she had agreed that he must do his duty until the new colonel was settled in. Three months grace had been agreed.

The captain felt ill at ease without Katerina's presence. At social gatherings his wife's beauty and warmth shone through. In a crowded room she was always the most magnetic force in it, or at least so it seemed to him. Her confidence in these moments the perfect foil to Brandt's awkward manner. Giving orders to one hundred and sixty men was so much easier than small talk with a dozen politicians.

The touch of a gloved hand on his arm broke his chain of thought. Hanne Neuberg, grey-haired and matriarchal in an elegant, silk mourning-dress, had been performing the duties of the commanding officer's wife, circulating from group to group and rescuing slightly inebriated doctors. Even though Brandt had only met her once, she already appeared to possess a knowledge of everyone in the room, the perfect hostess. She pressed Brandt on the details of his wife, the progress of the three-year old boy and of his daughter Eliza. Brandt felt almost embarrassed to be sharing the private thoughts of his world with a relative stranger but the warmth in Frau Neuberg's eyes was evident, and Werner was glad of her company.

From another part of the room, raucous laughter broke the general murmur. Frau Neuberg stood with her back to the rest of the room, the warmth seemingly drawn from her complexion.

"Ah our exalted Major, no doubt," her voice carried a note of irritation.

Before she could continue Sergeant Roner, the Grenadier Company's sergeant, appeared at her elbow, coughed politely and bowed to both her and his captain.

"For you, Frau Neuberg, from the colonel," Roner handed a folded note and then retired a few paces, turned and then handed a further note to Major Volgraf. Frau Neuberg glanced at her message and neatly refolded it before handing it to Brandt.

"Would you place that in the fire for me please?" she spoke softly and as he held out an open hand, she leant forward to keep the conversation between them.

"People speak highly of you," Frau Neuberg paused, weighing her words, "My husband..."

Frau Neuberg let the note slip into Brandt's hand, "He has never commanded a battalion you know. When he came back from America, few wanted to listen or learn from his experiences." She seemed uncertain as to whether to continue.

"I have heard that your husband taught at an infantry officer training school at Nienburg. I hope that one day they will become compulsory. The 10th doesn't have one, we still rely on the gifted genius of aristocrats and gentleman professionals," Brandt proffered.

"Indeed, and regimental succession where command is concerned too," Frau Neuberg spoke quickly, another peel of laughter from where the Major held court. "He will need friends here. He wants to trust you, please do not let him down."

The moment caught Brandt completely off guard, a hint of fear on the face of the woman already dubbed the 'redoubtable' Frau Neuberg by fellow officers. Just as quickly, it passed and she turned and spoke to Sergeant Roner.

"Would you kindly announce me to the room, Sergeant?"

Neuberg's note had told his wife that a private meeting was running late. He had planned to speak to his officers by two o'clock, knowing that many would be keen to leave before dark to make the return trip to Hanover. Frau Neuberg withdrew the ladies and other mourners to another room, many using the moment to make good their exit. Devoid of guests, the lack of officers within the battalion became evident.

The room should have contained around twenty-five officers and five doctors. Brandt made a swift head count: eighteen men.

To his left sat the usurped Major Johann Volgraf, the longest serving officer in the battalion, his nephew Ernest Volgraf, commander of 1st company, in close attendance. Around them, new junior officers that Brandt knew by sight but not name. Cold disdain from the Major's hawkish brown eyes, a familial trait shared by both men, met Brandt's gaze for a moment. A forced smile of acknowledgement briefly registered before, somewhat dismissively, the Major returned to his conversation.

Across the room, August Wexler, Hoyt's Company's unwilling doctor had shaken off his young guardians, returning to help himself to a large medicinal brandy before moving unsteadily to talk shop with Regimental Surgeon Harris. Near the main door stood Erich von Bomm, the first lieutenant of the Grenadiers and a man that Brandt considered a great friend. Their paths had crossed little in the days since the duel but Werner knew von Bomm could take care of the day-to-day aspects of the Grenadiers. Hanging on every word of a story being told with gusto by von Bomm, was Lieutenant Schafer, incapable of the simplest of tasks within Hoyt's old company.

Brandt had tried to catch Erich's attention before the arrival of Frau Neuberg, but von Bomm had been deep in conversation with the very pretty grand-niece of the late Colonel Dohman and Brandt had wondered just what sort of consoling Erich was planning on offering? The previous week wasn't the first duel that had resulted from von Bomm's dalliances, but Erich had survived without a scratch and avoided marriage so far with a similar dexterity. Around von Bomm and Schafer, other junior officers craned necks to follow the tale of another conquest.

Brandt stood alone warming an aching back in the glow of the fire, the result of yesterday's journey and his own poor horsemanship. He considered himself too tall to ride: Being a shade less than six foot, he considered it an experience that neither horse nor rider enjoyed. Those thirty miles to Celle were a journey he would gladly endure again if he could be at his wife's side that evening.

Another wave of laughter erupted from the small group huddled around Major Volgraf. Brandt and the others in the room looked in his direction. Volgraf closed the case of an expensive pocket watch. His nephew, Ernst, looked at his uncle, who gently nodded. Ernst, taller than every man in the room, spoke assuredly:

"The Major was just saying that we have replaced a beloved late Colonel for a late Colonel."

The officers around him laughed with a false gusto at the repeated quip, while Major Volgraf drew assuredly on a long-stemmed pipe. Rapier like, his eyes scanned the room, observing reaction to the remark. Most of the men shied away, not daring to meet the Major's gaze. When Volgraf's eyes met Brandt, no ground was given; only the entrance of Colonel Neuberg broke the awkward silence that had suddenly descended on the room.

A slender man of medium height swept in, ruddy-faced complexion framed by a riot of dark grey hair and long-whiskered side-burns. Propelled forward at an impressive gait, Neuberg was a man more used to a life outdoors than wrestling with the fastidiousness of running a battalion from behind a desk. His uniform, an immaculate new red jacket adorned with wide Swedish style cuffs in the dark green of the battalion's flags, was adorned with heavy silver epaulettes and precise silver lacing signifying his rank. Brandt wondered how these symbols of office might sit on his shoulders in the days ahead; the battalion needed a strong leader but would Neuberg be ready for the task?

The colonel encouraged the attendant room to bring chairs and quickly a broad double-ranked semi-circle formed while he waited to the side of the fire-place.

"Gentleman, apologies for my late arrival," Neuberg checked his own pocket watch, frowning heavily at it as if it were the cause of the delay.

"I have just come from a meeting with Colonel von Diepenbroick. I wish to bring you up to date with that and formally, or perhaps informally, introduce myself. I know that many of you have carriages waiting and wish to be back to Hanover so I will be brief."

Neuberg paused, aware that he had rehearsed the phrasing of what was coming next for a while, a thorny matter that needed clarifying.

"I know that to some, perhaps most of you, I am a surprise appointment."

The merest twitch of agony passed over the face of Major Volgraf; his nephew wore an ill-concealed scowl.

"I am sure that my successor will come from this room, but for now the Colonel has asked me to command the 2nd Battalion. Why, you may ask? Well, I had spent time on the staff of the British Army in the American War. I may be one of the few officers in Hanoverian service who have seen action in the field. Part of my task is to pass some of that experience on to you." he paused, letting the words register with his audience.

"After the end of the American war I held a posting instructing new officers to the 6th Regiment in Nienburg. I also served briefly on the staff of the Prussian army. So I am here to put observation and some new theory into practice."

Again Neuberg paused, reading the faces around the room.

"Colonel von Diepenbroick thinks that war is coming: I agree. In the next three months we may be called to campaign somewhere." The room was now hushed, men leaning heads forward keen for every word.

Neuberg continued, "We have a number of challenges before that time. In truth, we may not even have that much time. I have agreed to transfer men to 1st Battalion, to bring them up to strength. We will be short of some three hundred in the ranks and ten officers. If we fail to bring ourselves up to full strength in time, Headquarters will no doubt select another battalion in our place."

The comment was met by a shaking of heads and general disquiet. The officers of 2nd Battalion did not want to miss out; the war may be over before they ever got the chance to see action. Neuberg considered this the moment to offer an olive branch to Volgraf.

"Major Volgraf, you have been good enough to stand aside from your promotion for now, but I need your help."

Neuberg waited. Both men knew that Volgraf had been overlooked rather than making some gesture of utilitarian motive, but Neuberg was offering him a way out, in front of his fellow officers. Volgraf would have been a fool to refuse.

"Of course, sir, whatever you ask," Volgraf replied in as carefree a manner as he could muster.

"Thank you. We are short of officers. I have made a note of what is required here. You are a man of influence within the community and the wider area. We need ex-officers to re-join us. If a gentleman can raise men to follow him, they will be preferred when the allocation of commands is considered. Once we have the number we need, you and I will discuss the organisation of the battalion."

Volgraf nodded as if such an arrangement was to be expected.

Neuberg continued "As for the rest of you, after the 24th of this month, all leave for officers is cancelled, until further notice. Settle your affairs at home. Then I need every one of you here. We will have new men to train and they will expect you to lead them, as do I."

A stir of whispers was exchanged as the gravity of the last statement registered with its listeners.

"Thank you, gentlemen, I have matters that I need to attend to elsewhere. I will post company orders tomorrow. In two weeks assume that we might be called upon at any moment."

The scraping of chairs and excited chatter died away as men exited from the room, keen to leave and spread the news of possible action for the battalion. Above the din, Neuberg called out.

"Before you depart, Captain Brandt, can you come with me to discuss a matter?"

Brandt groaned inwardly. Any chance of making it home to Celle that evening was fading fast.

London: 7th February 1793

The small waiting room was an island of tranquillity from the busy corridors of the War Office at Whitehall. A lean, weather-beaten man in a pale-blue, silk coat sat waiting for the oak door to his immediate left to open. He had arrived ten minutes early for his appointment. Brooks Jackson started to reach for his pocket-watch then chided himself; Dundas would keep him waiting, no doubt.

In an effort to exude calm to any of the clerks who frequently rushed by the open door and paid him not the least attention, Jackson drummed a cheery sea shanty that he had known from a world before politics. A teak walking stick with an ornate scrimshawed ivory shark added a rhythm, joined occasionally by the stamp of elegantly stockinged left leg and thump of a wooden right, the wood of which matched the cane and carried ornate carvings of a giant shark.

Jackson had filled half a century of living with more careers, scrapes and adventures than most men would struggle to fit into two lifetimes. He craved to be at the epicentre of events, but the past two years had been difficult. At the heights of his powers as a Member of Parliament and a successful banker, the American war had returned to haunt him.

The Colonies that had offered him a way to escape destitution as an orphaned child in the port of

Plymouth, helped him rise to become the Commissary General for the British army under General Carleton in the last year of the war, in the end became a weapon used by his many business and political enemies. Allegations of spying and profiteering were made though little evidence ever advanced. Eventually, Pitt, the Prime Minister, had turned his back on Jackson and the political life that he had made since returning from America withered.

Politics shunned Jackson; society did not. Jackson and the Minister of War, Henry Dundas shared mutual friends and through such channels it was made known that a man with Jackson's abilities would not be out of the picture for long.

Yesterday, the note had arrived.

The oak door opened and a clerk clutching a thick folder of documents appeared, nodded politely and bid Jackson to enter before scuttling out of the waiting room and disappearing from view.

Jackson rose, knocked once and heard a grunt of consent. Sitting patiently at a small desk in the corner of a large but frugally appointed room, a dreary clerk stared blankly at bundles of documents which never seemed to lessen, despite the long hours of work. Quill poised, he waited for the next blast of ministerial invective. A feeble glow emanated from a fireplace which radiated light more than warmth, seemingly afraid to burn in a manner which might be considered extravagant. The clerk rose, bowed his head politely and quickly resumed his station.

Henry Dundas waved Jackson in and pointed to an empty chair.

The men were of equal age but Dundas carried considerably more girth and little of the elegance of Jackson, whose trimmed grey beard and gold studded right ear gave him more the look of some well-to-do pirate who had just brazenly sailed up the Thames and popped in to Whitehall for morning tea.

Dundas looked every inch the politician wrestling with the burden of office. He was clearly deep in thought. Despite the chill of the room, perspiration had soaked into his powdered wig causing rivulets of sweat and starch to gather in the creases of his forehead before being dabbed away.

"We will send," he paused, consulting a register and ran his finger down a column "three third-rates and two hundred Marines and that's his bloody lot. If he can't keep order with that, I will have him flogged and bloody well replaced by some half-wit who can."

Another fierce dab of the brow was matched only by the sound of quill scratching on paper. Dickson, the clerk, through years of experience, knew which sections of ministerial dialogue could be left out. In the case of Henry Dundas, the final letter and the original oratory often had a degree of variance.

Dundas sat and looked over at Jackson and nodded in the general direction of Dickson.

"Bloody Governor of St Kitts; wants me to ship half the army out there so that he can sleep safely in his bed. The man is a complete fool. Tells me the entire Indies is unsafe since the French declared all men 'free and equal'. The whole bloody world is tipped on its head. Still this is what happens when you kill a King and free slaves."

Another knock on the door saw an elegant blue porcelain service of tea-pot, two cups and some pastries arrive at the hand of a junior clerk. Refreshments poured, Dundas shooed both Dickson and the younger man from the room, stepped around the table and offered a hand which Jackson rose to receive.

"Pleased to meet you, Brooks. Thank you for coming at such short notice. I have a job for which the Prime-Minister recommended you personally, you know."

"Thank you Minister."

Electric blue eyes beamed from the bronzed face, a warm smile stretched a well-groomed moustache which held the brown shade of earlier years while thick sideburns, flecked heavy with rebellious grey, reflected Jackson's age more acutely.

"Call me Henry please. You have been out of the picture for a while. Too long in my opinion and for no good reason; are you ready to step back in?"

Dundas fixed Jackson with a firm stare, akin to the ones he had used as a trial lawyer in Edinburgh and honed at Westminster. Still, Jackson felt genuine warmth in the Minister's voice.

"It's been a while but I will survive. I've encountered worse", Jackson's eyes flicked down to the wooden right leg.

"Indeed! Shall we?" Dundas motioned to their chairs and returned to his side of the desk. He was a man focused on business and Jackson found that refreshing from his previous remembrances of political life.

Dundas sat and paused as if lost in a train of thought.

"We're sending an army to Holland, perhaps France. Who knows? I'm just the Minister for War after all and Horse Guards tries to keep me in the dark. There will be Hanoverians coming; Hessians too, no doubt. I want you to go to Holland and arrange the supplies for the campaigning season. No-one has the financial sense and experience that you have, at least no-one that I can trust. Horse Guards rather kindly provided me with a list of names too. Most of them, complete bloody fools, but you were on their list. If you accept, that fool Murray will already think he has a little victory over me."

Dundas raised his eyes to the heavens; War Office battles with both Horse Guards and the Admiralty were both news and gossip in equal measure.

Brooks Jackson stroked his moustache in momentary contemplation before the infectious smile returned, "Go on. I'm listenin'," excitement registered by the hint of a Plymothian accent.

"Hopefully it will be easier than New York," Dundas smiled.

"The army is to be nobly led by the Duke of York. The Austrians and all of their Princes have a penchant for spending money that isn't theirs. The Hanoverians will want to pay for nothing. As for the Hessians…"

"Do we have to use them? How many men are we talking about? What about supplies from the Navy?" Jackson had already started to make some mental notes, his mind alive with the possibilities that the venture could bring to him.

"Yes, we do have to use them. We are rather at a stretch for men. Revolution could break out in the Indies, not that I would give the Governor of St. Kitts the satisfaction of agreeing with him."

Dundas sipped thoughtfully at his tea.

"Perhaps five thousand British infantry; a similar number of Hessian infantry and fifteen thousand Hanoverians; we can spare twenty squadrons of cavalry. As for the navy, I will offer you all the help I can but…"

"But you can't have war so expensive it bleeds the nation dry or an army so large that it starves to death."

"Exactly!" Dundas smiled. "I knew you would understand. Interested?"

"Yes, 'enry, of course I'm bloody interested," Jackson answered assuredly, flashing a broad smile which again made him seem more pirate than politician.

Dundas smiled. He had heard a lot about Jackson, not all flattering, but he found his warmth a refreshing change from the bile of the political world.

"The Guards are going first as soon as they can be made ready. Holland is falling apart at the seams and if the Frogs open the Scheldt, the Home Fleet will be tied down protecting our shipping. Added to that, the Prince of bloody Orange is so bloody incapable. The situation in Holland is going to be a challenge."

Jackson shrugged as if it was a matter that could be managed. "No worse than New York, I doubt."

The minister gave a self-satisfied smile and returned to examine the pastry tray. "My quack tells me I should eat less and walk more. He's another bloody fool. The world is full of them."

Another pastry disappeared. Dundas spoke as the bolted pastry cleared his throat, "Don't be thinking this will be some easy victory. Those Frogs and their 'Revolutionary Army' beat the Austrians and the Prussians a few months back. And Dumouriez is as slippery as they come. Keep your wits about you."

"Anything else?"

"Not for now. I have ordered that the Duke operates on the northern bank of Hollands Diep. That's causing a stink at Horse Guards, as if I cared: they don't want their man's hands tied. Colonel Murray can handle the supply issues until you take over. When you do, we might need to rein the Duke in from his Horse Guards orders. I'm sure there will be more later and little of it good news, I fear."

"Don't ever give up politics for a life in selling 'enry, you'd starve to death", Jackson smiled and chose himself a pastry from the dwindling selection.

CHAPTER SIX

The Devil's Emissaries.

Antwerp: 16th February 1793

Rain, driven by bitter north-easterly winds, ushered the 'Army of the North' away from Antwerp's Grande Place and on towards the Dutch border. Buildings wore sagging and weary tricolours and under these a handful of inhabitants had gathered, as glad to see the French leave as they had been to welcome them, weeks before. In the previous November, the southern provinces of the Austrian Netherlands had waited keenly to receive the victorious French army, a sentiment long since passed.

Serge Genet had watched the exodus from a partially frosted window for a few minutes before returning to a fastidiously tidy desk in one of the rooms of the Grand Palace, which formed part of the main square.

A gently steaming coffee pot awaited an imminent arrival. Parallel tables contained an undisturbed breakfast array of pastries and cold meats on one side and a series of maps and plans on the other. Genet surveyed the scene with a degree of satisfaction, before removing delicate silver framed glasses and cleaning them on the silken tricolour sash tied about his waistcoat.

"I'm not sure that's the prescribed use for a sash of office, Serge?" said an assured voice.

The double doors to the room had burst open amidst the task of spectacle cleaning. A slender, sodden figure unchained a blue cloak and hurled it in the vague direction of a cloak stand, followed by an equally saturated bicorne which cart-wheeled ribbons of spray over the varnished mahogany floor.

General Dumouriez strode across the room, made for the silver coffee pot and poured himself a cup while a servant, wearing the livery of the household of King Louis, tidied the abandoned garments before retiring from the scene. The General drew back a chair and settled back with his feet on Genet's desk, rivulets of water running down the leather and threatening the neatly arranged correspondence.

The servant returned with the intent of removing the heavy riding boots but Dumouriez shooed him away, wagging a playful finger.

"No, no, leave that. I'm leaving soon and you should be packing."

The servant bowed and left the two men. Dumouriez ran his hand through thinning silver hair; he had long since lost the pretention and taste for formal wigs. Having just turned fifty-four he retained a lean physique. Piercing dark brown eyes shone from a face that retained the vestiges of youthful charm that had made him a favourite at the Royal Court for thirty years. Allied to this was an air of command which drew unconditional loyalty. Men followed Dumouriez, but both he and Genet knew a test of loyalty for every soldier setting out towards the Dutch border might come sooner than either man might wish.

The man in clerk's clothes moved sharply to rescue documents from a puddle forming on the green leather covering of the desk. Even though he found this intrusion into his world of order deeply disturbing, he was too respectful of the General to voice a rebuke.

Refreshed by the hot coffee, Dumouriez contemplated the choice of overdue breakfast but instead seized a quill from the desk and motioned Genet to pass the documents to him. In truth only the last two were of interest but he took his time to read each before scrawling his signature.

"You will have our best people on these?" Dumouriez asked, already knowing the answer but betraying just a hint of the gravity that each message contained.

"Yes, sir," replied Genet.

"You will use the Countess for this?" Dumouriez asked, almost rhetorically, a relaxed smile returning to his face.

"Yes, sir. And Beauvais will carry the message to Dunkirk and then on to Paris with the dispatches. It will give us the time we need, I think."

Genet's words trailed away and Dumouriez looked at him but knew that pursuing the matter was of little value. Instead, he spoke with a reassuringly warm tone, "Don't worry my friend, all will be well."

Craning his neck, the General called out, "Julien, get your sorry backside in here!"

The door was flung open with a force that rattled ancient hinges, the void almost filled with the frame with of a man whose muscular torso was squeezed into a tightly fitted short green dragoon's jacket. As the figure advanced Genet could see the grey, dead right eye and vivid vermilion scar that ran from chin to temple. Captain Julien Beauvais stood to attention.

Genet never failed to find the sight of Beauvais both imposing and galling. The clerk had winced whenever Dumouriez recounted the tale that lead to an Austrian bayonet tearing the right-hand side of the dragoon's face apart. There was little doubt that Beauvais had saved Dumouriez' life and become a favoured pet in the process.

"Prepare yourself and two men. You leave for Dunkirk as soon as these communications are ready."

Beauvais nodded at Dumouriez' order.

"But before you go, help yourself to some of that food Julien, you are starting to look like a bloody scarecrow;

then Dunkirk. No stopping to ravage half the women in Northern France. And try not to kill any more villagers. The mayor of whatever shit-hole you slept in last week had the temerity to write and say that some demonic creature cut down half of the townsfolk before riding off into the morning."

"It was two men, sir and they did seem intent on killing me first," the dragoon hissed.

"Funnily enough the mayor forgot to mention that. These people already consider me the devil incarnate for the actions of the army. You are my emissary. Try and keep it to a maiming or two next time and you will make Genet's task of drafting a suitably pliant reply a little easier."

Beauvais' faced twitched into an awkward, broken smile and Genet marvelled at the General's skill. With a few well-chosen plaudits and a thoughtful act, men like Beauvais would follow their General time and again, whatever the personal cost. While both soldiers breakfasted, Genet sealed several documents handing Beauvais all of the communications bar one.

"You might find this useful in dealing with the Mayor of Dunkirk," Genet paused. "Should his co-operation be less then complete, find the town's garrison commander and have everyone on this list arrested."

Genet knew Grison, Dunkirk's new mayor, would not buckle. Only by a display of naked power could Grison be brought to heel. Without proper leverage Grison would protect the man he and Dumouriez needed.

"His family and friends that I know of. Choose some and have them…" Genet waved his hand, the words dried in his mouth. Spying was Genet's business, killing was Beauvais'.

The dragoon pouched the note in a waistcoat pocket, nodded and turned away, returning for a final sortie at the breakfast table. The chief of intelligence had found a skill in setting challenges that one might previously think were beneath the compass of a cavalry officer. But in the month since his posting to Dumouriez' staff, Julien Beauvais was clearly enjoying the freedom and opportunities that life at headquarters provided.

Dumouriez had moved to examine a series of maps, gently drumming his fingers before looking at Genet, "How are you getting on with those diamonds? Paying the bills?"

Since the arrival of the French, what little trade there had been in the port appeared to have ceased. Most of Antwerp's diamond trade had relocated to Amsterdam. Genet had struck a deal with those who remained, a protection tax, but it did not yield anywhere near the money that the army needed to make good a deliberate shortfall from Paris.

"Diamonds have been difficult, sir; to trade with I mean. We end up selling them back to the traders we had collected them from, who tell us the market is depressed because we have driven the buyers away. Gold would be more useful in that regard," Genet offered.

"Diamonds, difficult? You have clearly never had a wife and a mistress, Serge!" Dumouriez chuckled and then coughed almost apologetically at seeing the face of his Chief of Intelligence, a hapless bachelor.

"You are right of course but in three weeks' time none of that will matter. Amsterdam: that is all that matters." Dumouriez returned to study the maps for a few moments.

"We are going to capture Amsterdam, collect half the gold of Europe sat in its banks and win the war! That should bring a smile to even your worried face, my friend."

The General turned and swooped on an unmolested croissant on the breakfast table, polished it off and flashed a self-satisfied smile to his spy-master.

Valkenburg: 23rd February 1793

The message to Prince Josias of Coburg, commander of the Austrian Forces, crossed the front-line of the river Meuse at Maastricht. There, the garrison commander permitted entry through the town, on the proviso that a formal escort of a dozen Austrian Hussars chaperoned the trio of French horsemen. Their destination, the main winter encampment at Valkenburg, lay a few miles east of Maastricht. Instead the riders were turned south, passing through the camp of the Esterhàzy Hussars. When the commanding officer of the Esterhàzy saw the carrier of the French message, the compliment of twelve hussars became a squadron, the Hussar's regimental standard carried proudly ahead of the main body of troopers.

Juliette, Countess de Marboré, was received into the Austrian camp at Valkenburg in the style of warring tribal queen come to make peace with Caesar himself. Even with the rigours of the four-day journey, she was clearly very beautiful. On dismounting and removing her riding cape, heads of soldiers strained to view a dark-green dragoon's jacket tailored to accentuate a slim waist and skin-tight buff riding breeches which bordered on the immodest. No man could ever remember seeing a woman dressed in such a way, excepting in Vienna's most exclusive brothels. When the Countess removed the plumed dragoon helmet, long dark blonde hair tumbled out.

Had Dumouriez wanted to negotiate the cessation of Austrian hostilities, he might have simply offered the Countess as a prize and most would have considered the matter settled. News of her arrival spread. By nightfall, numerous Counts and Generals who had found a reason to absent themselves from the camp during the harsh winter and lodge in the relative comfort of Maastricht had returned. But the Countess was more than a vision for soldiers who had been campaigning for the last few months; Dumouriez had chosen her because he trusted her to negotiate peace on his behalf.

London: 22nd February 1793

The British army had been delivered into a crisis and Horse Guards had offered up a rare moment of clarity.

In St. James Park the seven battalions of Foot Guards formed an open rectangle, ready for inspection. Behind the Foot Guards, two ranks of squadrons of the Household Cavalry were formed. Beyond this, thousands of Londoners pressed around to gain some vantage point; in the atmosphere of a carnival, the bands of the Foot Guards led the crowd in a rendition of 'God save the King'.

With crisp precision a young officer, scarlet tunic bearing the dark blue Foot Guards facings edged in thick gold braid, walked his horse forward aware of the full gaze of the soldiers. Seven pairs of battalion standards dipped in salute. The officer, with sword drawn, returned the gesture.

At twenty-nine years of age, Prince Frederick, Duke of York and Albany had taken the parade of the Foot Guards more times than he cared to remember. But what he was about to do, he had never done before. Consciously he loosened the grip on the reins of his mount and reached forward to pat the animal's neck, in an effort to calm himself as much soothe his mount, well versed to these occasions.

When the Duke looked back up, he felt the weight of some five thousand redcoats looking back at him. There had been rumours of course. Every barracks, every town hall, every home had been alive with them since the death of Louis.

The moment had come.

Prince Frederick cleared his throat, hoping his voice would carry the necessary gravitas instead of the high-toned excitement that critics cruelly jibbed from the safety of the House of Commons.

"Soldiers of the Foot Guards, Our King has entrusted me with three battalions, the 1st battalions of each regiment, to form an expeditionary force to journey to Holland and save that country from the scourge of the French Republic."

He paused, as much to catch his own breath as to allow the words to sink in.

"I ask only for volunteers. Vacancies in each 1st battalion will be filled by volunteers from the 2nd and 3rd battalions."

Major-general Lake, who stood fifteen paces away in front of the Duke of York, offered a salute with his ornate sabre and then wheeled about in a precise manoeuvre and issued an order that had never before been uttered.

A strong voice of unquestioned authority rang out across the park.

"Parade, Volunteers of the Foot Guards, one pace forward."

In the weak, late February sunshine, five thousand men stepped forward as one.

CHAPTER SEVEN

The Black Lions.

Mont Cassel: 25th February 1793

Mont Cassel, atop an escarpment that steeply rose to over a thousand feet above the countryside around it, was shrouded in thick skeins of cloud which, having deposited heavy rain before dawn, were now starting to part. On clearer days, the English coast could be seen and the sea never seemed to be empty of British ships. It had long become the occupation of many a citizen to sit and watch the sea from the gardens by the windmill atop the hill which rose above the main town square. To the north lay the road that led to Wormhoudt, the Fort at Bergues and the canal towards Dunkirk; east, the road to Flanders and south-west, the road to Paris.

The squall of the early morning gradually gave way to sporadic sunshine and the cobbled stones of the Grande Place soon rang to the sounds of market traders, draught horses pulling heavily laden carts and the residents of Mont Cassel swarming between stalls and coffee houses. Men in the white of the old royal army or the blue of the new republic made their way through the town to re-join the Colours.

One of those, a heavily moustached man in his late forties, sat alone on a small bench on the north side of the square, basking in weak February sunlight. It was February not Ventôse, or whatever the term for the month was, under the new revolutionary calendar.

Jean-Baptiste Mahieu set out his immediate worldly goods on the table before him and then repacked them carefully into his calfskin backpack. Spare boots; fresh linen; cleaning equipment; socks and a bonnet de police for barrack duty. These were the bulk of his belongs.

As his black coffee cooled, he divided a large cheese, fresh bread and smoked sausage into three sections, wrapping each into waxed papered parcels. Food for the next three days in case the army failed to deliver; whatever else he needed would be acquired.

Tied under his backpack in loops of old string, were sticks for kindling, depositing flakes of bark onto the table as he pressed the food parcels back inside the pack. Finally, at the top and easy to reach were the necessaries; an old tin cup and small, rectangular tray with a two-pronged fork attached with old knotted string. His cutlery had travelled the globe with him, surviving war with the British in America, the revolution and war along the borders of France and finally, Jemappes.

In the November rain of the previous year, a rag-tailed French army had kicked the Austrians out of Flanders. Afterwards thousands of conscripts had deserted thinking that their part in the war was over. Murder, looting and the guillotine had become the cycle of events during that fateful winter. Finally, Mahieu and his battalion had received two weeks leave but now he faced recall and the new season of campaigning. A revolution, born of the hope of freedom from hunger and taxation, had instead brought constant war and the fear of execution for those who failed in their revolutionary zeal. The guillotine, assembled just a few yards away from his seat, stood testimony to that.

The Grande Place held as many men in uniform as it did townsfolk, though Mahieu was unsure as to what his battalion's uniform was meant to be. He wore the white of the old *Ancien Regime* army, but only because no new issue of clothing had been forthcoming. His old battalion had been disbanded and he and several others from it found themselves posted to this new national battalion. Many of the new recruits levied from across France had come to the camp at Cassel, on the plain to the south of Mont Cassel, where new battalions had been formed and drilled as best as possible. Experienced soldiers bolstered the ranks of the raw revolutionaries, but that didn't stop the new recruits deserting and selling their muskets and just about anything else they could, in an effort to get home.

All Mahieu had to show for his transfer of status, from a soldier of the King to one of the Republic, were three concentric circles of cloth: red, white and blue sown into his bicorne. The National Assembly in Paris needed an army just strong enough to hold its borders, but not strong enough to threaten the fledgling government.

Last year, before Jemappes, such a scenario had nearly happened.

Lafayette, the hero of the American Revolution, had tried to lead the Army of the North over to the Austrians. Once, Mahieu thought, he would have followed Lafayette anywhere, but that was another war, another lifetime. Lafayette had been lucky to escape the aborted coup with his own life. Now General Dumouriez was in charge, a soldier who had delivered victories at Jemappes and before that at Valmy, over the Prussians. A General who brought victory with this army was worth following. What had happened in Flanders in the winter was not of Dumouriez' making. That blame lay with Paris; every soldier knew it.

The clamour of market-day died away as drums were heard. The Colour Party, led by a blue-coated officer on a chestnut charger, made its way through the centre of the Grande Place, the horse walking to the beat of the drum as regularly as the men behind it. Soldiers kissed wives, children, anyone they knew, in those last few moments of freedom.

A thousand men, a fraction of the 300,000 men who had been drafted to arms in the previous year, formed into a series of marching columns.

Jean-Baptiste Mahieu hurried across the cobbled square, musket, backpack and worldly possessions stowed away; the only evidence of his passing were the flakes of bark, a drained cup of coffee and two coins.

The Colours were slowly paraded past for soldiers and the citizens of the new republic to see while sergeants and corporals cajoled men into their correct formations. The French tricolour had symbolised the new union between monarch and people, red and blue the medieval colours of Paris, white the *Ancien Regime*. Except, of course, the monarch, Louis XVI had been a poor revolutionary. His execution a month ago had changed France and the world. Now the cries were *'Vive la Republique'* as the officers took station.

Behind the new national flag came another banner, sewn by the ladies of Mont Cassel. A giant, black, heraldic lion on a yellow background, a standard from a bygone age, had been patched and repaired. Ribbons of red, white and blue adorned the new flag-staff.

The townspeople of Mont-Cassel knew of the uncertainties in the year ahead. The revolution could end in the next few days or months and occupation by armies from Austria, Prussia or any of the German states which chose to send 'mercenaries', would more than likely be brutal. The death of a king would see reprisals on the inhabitants of Mont-Cassel, so soldiers and citizens sang *'La Marseillaise'*, the battle anthem of the Army of the North, with all of their hearts. Their men, the 14th National Battalion, was heading to fight the Austrians, Prussians and the English too, if they came.

'Grab your weapons citizens!

Form your battalions!

Let us march! Let us march!

May impure blood water our fields'

The battalion left the Grande Place and not a single man felt the biting weight of his pack or musket; the 'Black Lions of Flanders' were going to hunt and kill their enemy.

The table recently vacated by Jean-Baptiste was soon occupied by two men deep in conversation. One, who wore a long indigo cloak, fastened by a simple leather knot, brushed away the flakes of bark with a faded red Phrygian cap, the *bonnet rouge,* symbol of solidarity with the revolution. As the cloak fell open, a tricolour sash was revealed. Jean-Francois Grison, Mayor of Dunkirk, a man of slender frame, somewhat at odds with a plump, bronzed face, straightened a shock of tousled black hair and exhaled an involuntary sigh. Both of his sons had marched away with the 14th Nationals. Before he faced the return journey alone, he had arranged to meet his counterpart, friend and accomplice, Gilles Tabary.

Tabary sat on the bench opposite. He watched Grison with a degree of mirth. Tabary was a bulk of muscle and while he shared some of Grison's more colourful past, he shared none of his pretention of grandeur. However, he did have mayoral airs of his own to uphold, so he swept a rather large scarred hand over closely cropped hair, pushing ridges of perspiration back across his head and down towards the nape of his neck. Almost unconsciously he flicked his right ear-lobe, where a thick gold earring nestled.

One of the daughters of the owner observed her mayor and smiled approvingly. She bustled over to them, whistling snatches of 'the Marseilles' and generally lightening the mood of the overcast day. Tabary sat back and rearranged his sash, straightened a white cravat which retained traces of pale green imprint, then preened and plumped at a striped nankeen jacket which matched the pattern of the cravat.

Wine and a very thin rabbit stew were delivered while Tabary and Grison fenced with an easy small talk. The tables near them were now occupied and Grison made a point of acknowledging the passers-by. Somewhere during the conversation Grison whispered the names of Genet and *Perseus*.

Tabary signalled silence, concealed in the motion of wiping away remains of the stew from his lips with a

napkin. Even Tabary, fearless Tabary, was afraid to
have part of a conversation overheard that might be
reported to Paris or Genet.

The Church of our Lady of the Crypt had survived
eight centuries of love, worship, death, plague and
desecration. Currently, it served as stables for a
squadron of dragoons. Having finished their meal,
Tabary and Grison followed a path through piles of
soiled straw awaiting removal and scattered pages of
manuscripts that had escaped the ransacking mob of
the previous September. In conversation designed to be
overheard by the troopers acting as stable hands, both
made small talk about wanting to see the progress of
the battalion on the road to Wormhoudt; the pair
climbed the stone steps to the square tower for a view
over the town and the certainty that their conversation
would not be overheard.

Grison recounted how he had been visited by the
disfigured Captain Beauvais five days ago, the events of
that evening tumbled in a series of muted sentences.
The messenger from Genet had wanted to find a mutual
friend of both men. Beauvais held a list of names,
counter-revolutionaries hiding in Dunkirk, he had
called it. Grison's wife; his sons in the Black Lions;
family friends were listed; Tabary too. Genet's
knowledge of Dunkirk had been put to good use.
Grison prayed that he and Genet might meet in the

future so that Genet could feel a slow, lingering death at the point of his blade.

Beauvais gave his own assurance that no harm would come to Arnaud Mahieu, the man he sought, and Grison's complete co-operation would be reported to Dumouriez. The dragoon had been well informed. He knew of the unlawful use of 'the Leughenaer', the Liar's Tower; how Grison, Tabary and the crew of the *Perseus* had killed any hapless sailors who scrambled ashore and scavenged the broken wrecks for booty. Somehow, he even knew that both Mayors still took a share in the profits from smuggling.

Jean-Francois Grison, mayor of Dunkirk, wine-seller, smuggler, father and husband chose to risk the life to protect those around him.

Within the hour, Arnold Mahieu, captain of the pinnace *Perseus* and brother to Jean-Baptiste had been found on board his ship by Beauvais. Grison had led the way around the dock and identified the ship, nestled in the fleet of fishing vessels moored around the harbour. The vessel had been boarded, fresh provisions loaded and as soon as the tides permitted, the *Perseus* had sailed.

That had been five days ago and there had been no sign of her since.

Hanover: 25th February 1793

A series of dirty white canvas tents had been established around the interior of the main camp. Some communal structures had awnings open to the elements from the front where camp fires fizzled against the damp mist which hung on the morning air. The scene was akin to a travelling town having moved in to the barracks of the 2nd Battalion. Women were chatting, mending uniforms, washing, cleaning or cooking over the open fires. Children played at soldiers, chasing one another around the tents and engaging in mock sword fights.

The heavy single beat of a drum made most look up. Soldiers and new recruits who were spared the morning drill, emerged from the tents or the series of small barracks which formed the perimeter buildings to watch the spectacle. The tented city ceased at the edges of the red gravelled parade ground. Four roads bisected the tented camp, the southerly road led from the camp and toward Hanover. The sound of the drum came from this direction and soon a column of redcoats, marching three abreast, came into view. Behind them twenty more men in civilian clothes, carrying knapsacks slung over their shoulders, did their best to ape the motion of the soldiers. At the head of the column, mounted on a rather tired looking horse, Lieutenant Schafer sat uneasily in the saddle, wishing that he had opted to march with his men, rather than to ride out.

At the edge of the western road Brandt and von Bomm watched the progress of the column. Neither spoke; behind them three paces back, stood Sergeant Roner. Both officers could quite plainly hear anguished mutterings. The progress of the new arrivals was clearly an affront to all that Grenadier Sergeant Roner held dear.

"Very nice, Captain Brandt; and to think you gave up the Grenadiers for this," von Bomm was in radiant mood despite the grey morning and the rather shambolic column that had now come to a halt before them.

Brandt bore a pained expression. He had braced himself for the fact that his new company would need some polishing up, but this was worse than any of his imaginings.

Von Bomm chirped, "You won't actually be planning to stand next to us at any time in the firing line, will you? That lot looks as if they will wet themselves the first time they fire a shot, let alone see the enemy."

"There are times, Erich, when your comments are about as welcome as a dose of the pox."

"Oh, you are all charm this morning."

Brandt pulled his tunic straight and marched onto the parade ground. Schafer had dismounted in a graceless fashion and was now unsure what to do. He held the reins of his horse in one hand but noticed Brandt moving towards him. The young officer fumbled to draw his sword to salute his new captain, while calling the men to attention. Fortunately, a corporal from Volgraf's Company, who had been watching with the crowd, stepped forward smartly to take the horse. The beleaguered Schafer cast a look of deep gratitude to the man before turning and facing Brandt.

Brandt acknowledged the salute as he approached. The lieutenant, a flaxen haired boy of twenty years, cut a jaded figure. Even his thin straw-coloured moustache seemed to droop from his mouth in unspoken resignation. Brandt knew that he had struggled to cope with the unwanted task of company commander. At least, now that Brandt had arrived, the chore was relinquished and Schafer would have someone to follow, rather than have to lead.

"The company is ready for your inspection, sir."

Schafer spoke with a perceptible air of relief and then sheathed his sword as if the act absolved him of the burden of command.

"Thank you, Lieutenant. And thank you for commanding them. You have done a fine job."

"Thank you, sir," Schafer stammered.

The compliment brought a flush of pride to the junior officer, manifesting itself in an embarrassed grin. The accounts and ledgers that Brandt had seen were a mess, but that wasn't Schafer's fault, not directly anyway. He was one of two junior officers who had been left to do the work of more senior men. 2nd Company, such as it was, looked poorly clothed, poorly drilled and disinterested. But for all that, Brandt wanted the men to hear that he was grateful to the young man who had been out of his depth since the departure of Captain Hoyt, just before Christmas.

Brandt moved to position himself in front of his new command.

"Men, my name is Captain Brandt. I am your new commanding officer."

Brandt looked up and down the three lines of men that now faced him. Several heads in the rear ranks weaved and bobbed to get a clear view.

"I am sure that many of you have heard that we might be heading to war. Well I can tell you that it is true; we may get orders to march at any moment. We and the battalion must be ready. I look forward to serving with you, wherever that might be. For now, we must make the most of this time to train and improve. Assemble here in one hour for musket drill."

Then Brandt returned to Schafer. "I have commandeered some tents over on the far side of the barracks," Brandt pointed as Schafer seemed slightly lost at the mention of directions.

"The officers are to move out from their lodgings and into these. I want everyone used to the rigours of campaign. We will run the company administration now as if we are in the field. Is that understood? And send the sergeants and corporals to me there, as soon as the men have returned to barracks. I want a discussion with them out of ear shot of the men. That is all, Christian."

Brandt made a conscious effort to use Schafer's first name. The young officer nodded and turned with far more assurance than he had dismounted earlier, passed on a series of instructions to the men, then dismissed the redcoats. Brandt returned to the watching Von Bomm and Roner.

"Nicely done, sir; you almost have me believing you," von Bomm smiled as his friend drew level.

"Erich, can we agree that the Grenadiers are fine in your capable hands?"

Brandt glanced sideways and Von Bomm gestured as if that matter went without saying.

"And that you won't manage to destroy them over the course of the next few months or let them fall apart at the seams?"

Von Bomm knew Brandt well enough. "What is it that you want?"

Brandt smiled "The services of Sergeant Roner for one month to help me whip this lot into shape."

"And if I were to refuse?"

"Well actually you can't. I became commander of 2nd Company this morning, so I approved the transfer of Sergeant Roner with the Colonel yesterday. Think of it as a parting gift. Don't worry, he will probably be back to hold your hand before the war breaks out. Now let's see if we can scrounge refreshments before the Sergeant and I have to spend the rest of the morning sorting out this disaster."

Brandt clapped his hand on the back of von Bomm's shoulder and the trio headed off across the parade ground in the direction of his company's command tent.

The column of redcoats broke ranks and headed towards the main barracks, Krombach racing to catch two beanpole frames. The Pinsk brothers loped one behind the other. Tomas, the elder by a few minutes, led; Henry dutifully following. At six feet four inches tall with dark blonde, tightly cropped hair, their ranging strides threatened to carry them off the parade ground before Krombach could reach them so the young redcoat sprinted and overhauled them just before the barracks entrance.

"Well, what do you think of all that?" Krombach panted.

"Alright; fine words but let's see if he actually sticks around though."

Tomas could find fault in the perfect sunset, but despite his almost constant gloomy outlook, Krombach found a great deal of pleasure in the company of both men.

"God, you're a miserable turd," Krombach's voice rang with laughter, in between drawing deep breaths from the run to reach two men.

"He is a distinct improvement on Hoyt the invisible, and at least has to shave every day unlike the Little Brother. Satisfied?" Tomas, under a seemingly great effort, broke into a half smile.

'Little Brother' had become the company nickname for Schafer, as he had sought to ingratiate himself with the N.C.O.s and the men of 2nd Company. Whatever effect the young officer had been hoping for, the outcome had been rather different. Sergeant Tobias Winckler and Corporal Conrad Gauner had filled the void left by the disappearance of Hoyt. Schafer had found himself swayed by both men, the company likewise; 2nd Company had two masters and the young officer found himself subservient to both. Where Gauner ruled by fear and strict discipline, Winckler cajoled and encouraged, earning a cut from the public houses at which his men drank. Krombach and the Pinsk brothers had long since decided that Winckler's geniality was better than paying homage to Gauner. This meant that Gauner took every opportunity to punish Winckler's men.

"Sebastian is right, Tom, you are a miserable turd!"

Henry joined in, sharing none of his brother's melancholic view of the world. Both men towered a heads-length over every man in the company save Thilo Hartmann, 'the Ox', who had lumbered across the parade ground and pushed past the three men, swatted a half a dozen queueing redcoats aside and ducked into the doorway of the barracks. There were few grumbles from the men waiting to enter the barracks.

Along with Krogh, Hartmann was Corporal Gauner's enforcer. The three men peered around to see where Gauner might emerge from. Both Pinsk brothers wore thick-lens glasses, which only served to make their eyes seem like round marbles. At long distance, without the glasses they were almost blind, squinting heavily whenever their glasses were removed.

Some men chose to hide their previous lives when they enlisted. The brothers made no secret that had worked on their family's farm before a succession of poor harvests had forced their enlistment; two less mouths to feed. Krombach had hidden the fact that his father was a moderately wealthy fish-seller until Fuchs, a weasel of a man, had overheard the three men talking and reported the news to Gauner. The voice of the aggressive corporal was heard bawling out instructions and Krombach nodded with his head in the general

direction of the doorway. The three broke from
conversation to jostle their way into the barracks.

CHAPTER EIGHT

Departure.

Greenwich: 25th February 1793

The children stood, peering out of open windows, staring into weak midday sunlight. They could hear the heavy rhythm of drums: the soldiers were close. Stronger now came the wail of pipes, caught on occasional gusts which tumbled across the quadrant of the Royal Naval Hospital at Greenwich, whipping white-capped breakers on the muddy-brown water of the Thames. Everywhere, there were people; every vantage point had been seized. Either side of the grey Portland stone columns of the hospital, thousands had gathered, some clambering onto exposed window ledges.

From the windows the offspring of King George III and Queen Charlotte waved across to the crowd and a huge cheer erupted. A sea of waving hands and smiling faces returned the gesture. More than a hundred small boats were anchored around the three large transport ships and handful of frigates moored at the steps which led up from the Thames into the open quadrant of the hospital. Others, not able to find a spot to anchor, beat a crazed motion against the incoming tide. The day was momentous. The British army was going to war against France, against Tyranny.

The march from Whitehall, some six miles to the waiting ships at Greenwich, should have taken around two hours but even with those guardsmen not selected for deployment and ten battalions of red coated Fencibles called in from surrounding counties, keeping the mob at bay was an impossible task. The massed band, drawn from the three regiments, led the procession, followed by an escort of cavalry and behind that, the 1st battalion of the Guards.

Today every guardsman was a hero. Once the cavalry had pushed through a gap, the red coated infantrymen were swallowed up in a mass of hysterical Londoners. No soldier escaped the kisses from amorous and intoxicated civilians. Bottles of wine and gin were thrust into the hands of redcoats, pint pots shared. The scene resembled that of any army returned home from an impossible victory rather than that of one heading out to war.

By the time the third Battalion arrived, the parade consisted of as many drunken or comatose redcoats, propped up in fruit carts or bundled onto wagons. When the last battalion passed the gates of the hospital towards the main steps, it bore more the look of a village outing, rather than the smart body of men which had left the northern part of the city.

Even the Prince Regent, who had complained about being forced to attend, stood and waved at his younger brother who had forced his way through the ranks of the mob into a open area where three ranks of sober and very serious looking Coldstream Guards pushed back the great throng, to create some space for the parade to move into. Everywhere the chorus of cheers rang out, heightened further when an inebriated corporal was wheeled past in small hand-cart through the mass of bodies. The soldier had retained a redcoat to cover his modesty with the balance of his uniform and worldly goods put to use as bedding against the rigours of the journey. Once level with the Royal party he found the co-ordination to raise himself to his knees and salute his monarch.

"Never fear, King George, we'll kick the Jacobins in the arse for you, Sire, never fear."

With that the corporal toppled back into the cart, as helpless and bare as a new-born baby. From the balcony the crowd witnessed their king, German King George, roar with laughter. Another round of 'God save the King' echoed from the walls and columns of the great building.

But the Duke of York saw none of this. Amidst the tumult he had slipped away, his yacht taking advantage of the turning tide and freshening winds. The British Ambassador at The Hague, the royal palace of the House of Orange, had sent word. As yet no preparations had been made by the Dutch for the arrival of the British forces and William, Prince of Orange, was in no mood to be rushed into a decision. The Duke's yacht slipped out of the Thames to meet her protection, a Royal Navy sloop to try and resolve matters before the arrival of the main army.

Lieutenant Simon Henson-Jefferies, a junior ensign with the 1st Battalion of the 3rd Guards regiment, was tasked with shepherding the remnants of the drunken soldiers through the throng of the rejoicing mob and into lines, where soldiers made the precarious journey up thin, whitened gang-planks onto the last of the transports. Six hundred men were being crammed into a ship designed to carry four hundred. The decision had been made due to the short distance of the journey and the lack of immediate transports at hand. One or two nights of discomfort could be borne by the men.

The Englishmen and lowland Scots from which the 3rd Regiment were drawn, clambered up the gang-plank, straining under the weight of packs burgeoning with gifted wines and spirits. Hands clutched at support ropes on either side the plank, while holding heavy Brown Bess muskets. Suddenly a figure slipped, toppled through the rope and crashed onto the cobbled quay side. A small patch of red bloomed in size below the knee of the white linen trousers, closely followed by a scream of pain so loud that the din from the press of people around the cordon of soldiers died away to nothing. Several heads appeared over the side of the ship curious to see the source of the sound.

The Queen sent the young Princes and Princesses in from the balcony. They could see the full horror of the guardsmen writhing in agony, his right leg shattered below the knee. Doctors of the battalion were called for but, apart from alcohol to ease the pain, none of the medical baggage could be found on board the transport for the 3rd Regiment. Word was sent to the other two transports but it soon became apparent that no medical baggage was present on any of the ships. Whatever turmoil might be on the other side of the Channel, the lack of preparations within the Brigade of Guards was now laid bare.

After half an hour of agony, eventually a stretcher from the hospital made it through the crowd and the distressed soldier was carefully carried back through the silent mass which parted respectfully. Previously intoxicated guardsmen resumed the boarding of the transport in a gloomier disposition. There were whispers of bad omens and a sense of foreboding in the ranks.

Valkenburg: 25th February 1793

Colonel Karl Mack von Leiberich's head ached. His gaunt face contorted in concentration knowing that each word of the communiqué to the Emperor's trusted adviser Baron Thugut would be scrutinised for meaning, any hint of criticism accentuated by Thugut to the Emperor.

Thugut hated Mack. Most of the princes, counts and generals in the army hated Mack. Prince Josias trusted him and to the Colonel, that was all that mattered. He held the post as the Chief of Staff to the Prince. For a Protestant serving in the Catholic army of the Emperor, never having held a front-line command and benefiting only from the patronage of his superiors and a society marriage, his standing was remarkable.

Mack had long since made a rule of only sipping wine during toasts, on all other occasions he drank hot apple tea finding that the drink soothed the strongest of his headaches. He rubbed a ridge of scar tissue as he re-read the letter. Like the tea, that too was a reminder of the Turkish War. In the dying moments of the battle for Belgrade, Mack had ridden to rally an infantry battalion from a last desperate attack by the Sultan's elite Janissary troops, when his horse collapsed. Pinned helplessly under the animal, Mack could do little as a Turk aimed a fatal blow with his yatagan blade. At the very moment of impact, the man had been killed in a storm of musketry from the Austrian battalion. The dying man's blade had slipped and sunk into the right side of Mack's face, stopping just short of the eye socket.

Colonel Mack mulled over the events of the past few days to ensure that he had missed nothing.

On the morning of arrival of the Countess, he had been briefing the Prince and his three most senior corps commanders. The preparations for a Spring campaign against the French, each with a myriad of pinned flags, representing regiments and supply routes had been presented. Mack was sure that Count Ferraris, one of the Generals presented, had taken a great deal of pleasure in permitting the entry of the Countess, even though sensitive military information was set out on the table. Mack had found himself the only person bothered by such a threat and his attempts to roll up his strategic maps served only to dislodge various unit markers and brought barely suppressed titters from the three bored Generals.

The colonel stepped back to watch the Countess, escorted into the room with regal ceremony, led by Major Brennen of the Esterhàzy Hussars, who had seen fit to personally lead the escort. Juliette, Countess de Marboré, realising that the act of a curtsey would have looked faintly ridiculous in her cavalry uniform gave a somewhat stiff bow and then bore the note from General Dumouriez directly into the hands of Josias, Prince of Saxe-Coburg-Saalfeld, commander of the Army of Emperor Francis II.

Brennan bowed his head then raised it and spoke, "My Prince, I have the honour to present Juliette, the

Countess de Marboré," throwing his right arm back toward the Countess in the most theatrical style.

The Prince for his part took the note and then reached forward to kiss the hand of the Countess. Clearly delighted with himself, Brennan stepped away and stood next to Mack. The two officers could not have been more of a contrast. Both were in their early forties, Mack wore a long white jacket edged with a thin gold band, his only act of ostentation to show his rank. Brennan bore the full-dress uniform of the Esterhàzy," with consummate style. Both his sky blue jacket and blue pelisse, set rakishly over his left shoulder, were both covered in thick horizontal gold braid and buttons, the pelisse further adorned with white ermine fur. Below this Brennan wore cherry red riding breeches and supple calf-skin boots trimmed halfway up his shin, with more gold braid. As he took up a position to admire the movement of Juliette toward the Prince, the cavalry officer's hand instinctively checked for any signs of imperfection on a rigidly waxed moustache.

"Madame, France honours us with your company," the Prince spoke warmly in perfect French; Josias was a man who enjoyed perfection. He rose early each morning in order that his valet could dress him in a crisp fresh shirt, his wig could be powdered and arranged and he could present himself to his officers for a formal breakfast served punctually at a quarter to seven. The appreciation of perfection was the reason that Josias persisted in retaining the services of Colonel Mack, even when his senior officers conspired against the man. For all of Mack's visible physical and religious flaws, he could make an army function better than any man that Josias had met. It was to Mack that the Prince handed the note as he led the Countess to a red velvet chaise longue.

The Countess, aware that the days of travel had taken their toll on her appearance, spoke in a gentle tone, despite the discomfort that the eyes of the room were upon her, "I must apologise for my appearance, it is not the most flattering of looks."

"On the contrary, I have never seen a French dragoon, look so becoming. Just as well come to think of it," the Prince said, causing a warm ripple of laughter from his Generals and the half a dozen Esterhàzy troopers who had accompanied the Countess into the main room.

"But we must get you out of those clothes into something more becoming a lady of your status, Countess." The Prince spoke with a concern more paternal than amorous.

"I would settle on just getting her out of those clothes," whispered Brennan under his breath, once again tweaking his moustache and licking his lips like a fox spotting a particularly delicious chicken.

Mack sipped his tea meditatively; the meeting revealed that Dumouriez would be as dangerous an opponent in any future peace as he was proving to be in war. He had sent a Siren into the heart of the Austrian camp and it seemed that few men were immune. On Josias' instructions, the Emperor had been apprised of the offer of a peace accord with Dumouriez and the Army of the North. If agreed, the Prince and Dumouriez would join forces, march on Paris and restore the Bourbon Monarchy.

In Mack's view, life rarely ran that smoothly, so he returned to his strategic maps, convinced they would yet be needed. At least he had convinced Prince Josias to include the details of a campaign for the year which did not rely on the cooperation of Dumouriez, a small victory. Savouring the flavour of the apple tea, Mack felt the tension of his headache begin to recede.

CHAPTER NINE

Toy Soldiers.

Hanover: 26th February 1793

Sergeant Roner drilled the company under Brandt's watchful eye as Colonel Neuberg rode back into the barracks; the afternoon performance had followed a similar pattern to that of the morning, ragged at the best of times. However, when Brandt stood his redcoats to attention Neuberg doffed his bicorne to acknowledge the salute and paused to praise the men for their progress; a simple act but one that brought smiles to even the glummest of faces. Rumours circulated that the battalion was to move, Brandt knew that Neuberg was returning from meeting General Wallmoden at the army headquarters, so the speculation would grow unless Neuberg brought definitive news.

The men of Brandt's Company tumbled exhausted from the parade ground and went in search of something to eat. Krombach, the Pinsk brothers and others from the company fiercely debated the latest gossip as they journeyed to the tavern. By eight o'clock Sergeant Winckler had rounded up his men and marched them back from the Harvest tavern which the foot-sloggers had long ago christened the Three Nuts due to its rather dubious drawing of three full bags of barley grain.

The 10th had taken over their current home from a regiment of light dragoons about twelve years earlier. In that time, many of the stables had been converted into six large oblong barracks buildings, three on each of the eastern and western flanks of the compound. These easily housed the private soldiers and junior corporals when the battalion had been below strength but with the influx of new recruits, the barrack buildings had been deemed inadequate.

The northern perimeter contained a series of small terraced cottages comprised of the lodgings of officers and senior non-commissioned officers; wedged centrally between the dozen cottages were the battalion headquarters. Only the southern perimeter currently remained undeveloped, its low walls a border to the world beyond the camp. Foundations for two new barracks had recently been dug either side of the main southern gate but the buildings would not be ready for some weeks. The battalion had already outgrown its current accommodation. Neuberg's solution had been to order the erecting of a double row of tents around the borders of the parade ground; as Krombach returned to the barracks it was the yellow light from lines of camp fires that guided him.

The large oblong room had recently been repainted. One of the Colonel's first orders had been to overhaul each barracks block. The men had been glad of the work: broken cots had been mended; rotten mattresses filled with fresh straw; two fireplaces which dominated the centre aisle had been cleaned; dirty mirrors which hung above each had been washed. Similar attention had been spent on the large hearth at the far end of the room, an area reserved for the corporals of the company. Gauner and Winckler had clashed over the matter.

At full strength, each company required five corporals but Brandt's only had three, Gauner, Krogh and Möller. As the instruction was to fill every cot, Winckler had planned to put senior soldiers there, people who might owe him a favour for that privilege. However, Gauner had filled the spaces with his men. Fuchs, weasel-like and odious, sat picking his toes with a knife and flinging the debris of his activities towards the fire. Next to him was Krogh, the Dane, the only man ever to fight Hartmann, the Ox, to a standstill. The two had become friends since. Across the aisle were the beds of Gauner and Hartmann.

Winckler had relented. Most of the rest of the company were secretly glad to be shot of them from various cots around the barracks. Only Corporal Möller found the situation distasteful. Möller seemed a thoughtful, dependable man and Krombach had overheard him telling Winckler that he felt betrayed by the sergeant; Gauner was gaining control of the barracks in Möller's eyes.

However, the refurbishment of the room had done much to lift the men's spirits. Two elongated rectangular tables set in either half of the walkway were a hive of activity as most of the company sat cleaning their woollen redcoats, whitening belts or polishing kit. Water that boiled in giant pots on the fires was regularly scooped into mugs and then carried outside to pour down the barrels of muskets, before drying and checking every piece of metal work.

Most of the recruits who had arrived the previous day had received trousers and a dull white undress jacket which bore the regiments green facing, which experienced soldiers called 'fatigues'; few had yet to receive their redcoat; none a musket. Fuchs worked alone, cleaning the kit of Gauner, Hartmann and Krogh.

Chores completed, the tables were cleared and games of cards broke out. Krombach considered replying to his parents' letter. He had turned nineteen four days ago. The event had passed unmarked in his new life. The arrival of a letter from home had brought a joy which he had shared only with the Pinsk brothers. Fetching paper and pencil from his backpack he returned to a place at the table, catching sight of his shadowy reflection in the yellow light of the room, in one of the mirrors over the central fireplace. Dark brown hair, thick and parted above the left eye, looked unkempt. He pushed back a mass of hair with his right hand. Long wispy sideburns needed cutting too. His face was more drawn than he had remembered. When had he last paused to look in a mirror? Tired eyes looked back from under bushy eye brows. Four months in the army was turning the handsome fisherman's son into a man. All he had to do was survive the process.

The letter started well but six lines in Krombach was joined by Henry, who religiously unravelled a cloth about a yard square, brushing it so that the creases were removed. In doing so a map of Europe and the other continents was revealed. Henry had traced, named and painted detail into it with loving care. Most the map had stayed faithful to the world some forty years previous.

The brown of the Ottoman Empire controlled the areas of large parts of Greece and Turkey and along the North African coast. The Austro-Hungarian Empire shaded as rich ochre, sat as its uneasy neighbour, the brooding house of Hapsburg controlling some of the finest troops in Europe. Across the German mountains and plains was a patchwork of colours, a deep red representing a patch of land belonging to Hanover. It shared the same colour as Great Britain and it was more comforting to some to view Great Britain as an extension of the House of Hanover. To the East lay the dark blue of Prussia, beyond this a green expanse of

Russia, dynasty of the Tsars. To the west the light blue of France, more ochre for the Austrian Netherlands and down toward a faded brown and green for Spain and Portugal and another patchwork of colours for the boot shaped land which comprised Rome and the Italian states.

Krombach had fallen in love with the map as soon as he saw it. He had watched as Tomas brought a beautiful rosewood box to the table. More religious relics would be unpacked, the eyes of several men were now watching from the outer edge of the candle's glow. The box lid softly slid open and revealed more than a hundred figurines. Infantrymen, cavalry and cannons, painted in accordance with the colours on the map. In a central well of the box was a hollow horn tumbler, with a pair of ivory dice. The two men began to position figures on the map.

More light was brought, the crowd around the table swelled. Chairs were drawn up, vantage points sought. Soldiers offered favours of kit cleaning to join the game. Winckler and Möller enjoyed the spectacle as much as everyone; bets were being laid on the next move, the next roll of the dice, each throw and the respective moves on the board bringing a reaction from the men. After a testing day the game brought laughter and comradeship.

Krombach had not noticed Gauner, Hartmann and Krogh return, fuelled by several jars of ale. At first the late-comers were content to watch. Then, bored with being on the periphery, Gauner beckoned and Hartmann pushed several bodies aside. Complaints from the disgruntled died in the throat when they looked up at the mountain of muscle towering about them. The sound of a swift blow to an obstinate man's ribs and deep exhaling of air were followed by a chair being offered to Gauner: unease replaced the laughter.

Flanked by his henchmen, Gauner demanded to take a role in the game to which the elder Pinsk brother finally assented, sensing it might be the best course of action. Krombach, sat directly ahead of the three interlopers, was lost in concentration on his next move, little realising that Tomas had quit his position, apologising to Gauner as he handed him the horn tumbler.

"Not much life left in the game Corporal,"

"I can see that Pinsk. Remind me not to make you a General eh?" Gauner mocked. Nervous laughter emanated from the outer circle. "Well, well. Let's see if we can rescue the disaster, boys."

The game was reaching a finale. Krombach had been drawn into an alliance with Henry and was having more than his share of luck. Players dropped out. More dice, more betting, and the return of laughter in the room as the game concluded. Henry had won aided by his alliance with Krombach: Gauner had little influence on the turn of events.

"Well, well what a pair of little arse merchants we have here," Gauner snarled contemptuously. "Next time count me in from the beginning, otherwise you will have the lads thinking we can follow a farm hand and the idiot fish boy into battle and all live happily ever after."

He paused, his eyes sweeping across the room, waiting to see if anyone would dare challenge him. The Ox lent forward and picked up one of the tiny crafted cannons with a delicacy that belied his strength. Tomas's eyes moved from the cannon piece down towards his brother, seeing the tension and hatred etched into Henry's face and his left hand curled into a fist. Tomas signalled 'No' with just the merest shake of the head, but Gauner missed nothing.

"What's this, afraid that your little brother might lose his head? Good, it's about time someone showed some sense in this company. What do you ass-wipes think is waiting for you when we fight the French, little cannons and toy soldiers? Real men, with big long bayonets to ram in your guts; some of you might not like me, not that I give a shit, but when the time comes you will be glad you are all on my side. Real men like Hartmann and Krogh here: they will keep you alive." he sneered waiting to see who reacted.

Hartmann and Krogh shared a grin of triumph; no one dared move except Winckler, who shifted uneasily in his seat.

Gauner waited, "But don't worry lads. We are all a happy family now. We'll be alright. Me, the lads, even good old Sergeant Winckler, we'll protect you from those nasty Frenchies," he waved his hands as if it was an act of kindness that needed no thanks.

"Careful now Corporal..." Winckler spoke softly, knowing that if things slid out of control he would be forced to act.

"Apologies, if I startled anyone Sergeant. No offence meant." Gauner rose as gracelessly as possible, snapping heels together in mock salute.

But Gauner was not finished. His would be the authority over the company. Winckler's time had been and gone. He swayed forward and grabbed the box of figures that Tomas was hurriedly trying to clear, "Gather round men. Let me show you how we are going to beat the French and end up knee deep in tasty French tarts. Is that OK with you boys?"

Again, Henry bristled with ill-concealed rage. Tomas knew that unless he acted there would be a very short but bloody squabble, which would not be a contest. As well as a beating, he and his brother would be singled out for punishments, far beyond tonight. Reluctantly he collected the other figures and pushed them in the direction of Gauner. The scraping of several pairs of chair legs against the stone floor rang out as various soldiers gave way to allow passage around the table for Gauner's muscular frame. Tomas stood up and

Gauner sat in the chair at the centre of the table. He took the opportunity to press considerable bodyweight on Krombach's shoulders as he moved past and exerted a pincer like grip that made the boy wince.

Tomas deployed the armies of the great powers as the belligerent corporal directed. Opposing these, he placed forces to represent the French. Henry gathered back the box at an opportune moment, swiftly salvaging any unused pieces from the reach of Gauner or the Ox. What began as a demonstration of the grasp of world affairs from Gauner soon broadened into a lively discussion, the edge of tension subsiding now that Gauner was firmly at the centre of events. He even generously acted as judge allowing voices from the edge of the circle of faces in the half-light to share an opinion. Some were even given credence. Troops were moved around the map, armies deployed. No dice was rolled. Gauner decided the outcome.

By the end of the evening the musket men of Brandt's Company had decided that Austria and Prussia couldn't be trusted. Austria might kick the French but would hold troops back in case the Turks decided to raid from the southern flanks of their empire. Russia needed Prussian permission to send an army across their sovereign soil which wouldn't be forthcoming. Both would squabble over the remains of Poland. This would stop the Prussians having a dart at Hanover while the army was away. Prussia also needed to maintain an army against the French, to make sure that the Austrians didn't snatch all the glory. Troops were paired against troops. When all was said and done, there were no French forces left. Some were placed to fight the Austrians in the south and over the Alps; others against the border with Spain. France was undefended.

All that the Hanoverians and the British, who would land in Holland, had to do was march into France, drinking and whoring their way to Paris. Catcalls and choruses of approval rang out. Gauner sat back, soaking up the adulation, raising his hands to encourage the mob of redcoats. Even Winckler broke into a smile. Krombach pulled the box of figures from Henry's grasp, placing rank after rank of infantry and cavalry in France. Gauner noticed the new arrivals. His hand conducted the crowd for silence.

"What's this? The idiot fish boy is awake. Play time is over, young lad." The contempt was back and the air of joviality punctured. Krombach continued building ranks of troops.

Winckler leaned forward "What is this Sebastian?" He was as puzzled as the rest of the company, who were now transfixed on the map again.

"Alright then, let's see what we have?" Gauner spoke with magnanimity, secure in his position, encouraging Krombach and sensing the chance to belittle him, a perfect end to the evening.

"This is the French army" muttered Krombach. Muffled, nervous laughter drifted out of the gloom.

"Pardon me, young sir," Gauner cupped an ear. "The elderly ladies at the back can't hear you." Again, more stifled laughs. "And where, pray does this army come from? No army in Europe is this big."

Krombach and Gauner fixed one another in ill-concealed repulsion. It was Krombach's turn to pause, feel the room watch him. He found strength in that moment and felt a surety in his voice. "It is the army of France. Rather it is the people of France. They will fight and die for the revolution," he said slowly.

"Boy, you are talking complete cock!" Gauner waived a hand dismissively, nodding to the faces around, repeating the phrase to a wave of general relief.

Krombach stood slowly.

Gauner matched him, closely cropped hair revealing a muscular neck and broad shoulders barely restrained by his corporal's redcoat.

Hartmann shifted his position. If Krombach dared to throw a first punch, the Ox would ensure that Krombach would never throw a second. Not that Gauner would need his help. The corporal fought the urge to snap Krombach's neck, too many eyes were watching and the idiot fish-boy was not worth risking the noose for.

"You may think what you like, Corporal," Krombach spoke.

The room fell silent. He began again as Gauner was still attempting to lap up adulation for his skilled rebuttal.

"You may think what you like Corporal, about the French and my opinion. But they will fight and die for the revolution, and we had better be ready."

Gauner stared at Krombach, eyes full of cold hatred. Krombach did not flinch but continued, fear overcome by a pulsing rage.

"I have been there. Two years ago. I shall never forget it. I have witnessed the guillotine and fury of the mob. It was a hatred that I have never seen before. From that mob last year, the French built an army of the people, ready to die for their Revolution and their country. They defeated Austria. They defeated Prussia. So, if you are going to prepare us for anything, I suggest you prepare us for a war where the enemy is going to stand and fight, because we will be on his land."

Krombach turned and pushed his way through the crowd of men and into dimness of the barracks to find his cot.

London: 26th February 1793

Brooks Jackson cleared a small section of a clouded window with his cuff and peered down and across Whitehall, looking for the returning carriage of the

Minister for War. Dickson, Dundas's moribund clerk, had tried to jab some life into a miserable fire before Jackson dismissed him. Meetings between the two men had taken an increasingly confidential nature now that Jackson's appointment had been confirmed.

A black carriage slowed to a halt. Sir Henry Dundas pulled himself out through the door, cold fury etched on his face. The trip to St. James Palace had not gone as the Minister would have scripted it. Jackson braced himself for stormy waters and a minute later the heavy door swung open and slammed shut and a gale of Scottish invective raced across the office.

"That money grabbing bastard; what in God's name is he thinking? I've a bloody mind to send the Hanoverian army south and kick his royal arse."

The Minister of War mopped his brow, thick with sweat despite the chill of the day. He marched towards Jackson, stood in the large bay window, sending papers spiralling from his desk as he did. Another curse then he turned his gaze onto the busy Whitehall street below and took deep heavy breaths, trying to regain some control. Instead, fresh insults tumbled out.

"That German piss-pot, Louis the insignificant of Hesse-bloody-Darmstadt; if we didn't need his men…He's nearly unhinged the King before a shot has been fired!"

Jackson edged his way around Dundas and made his way to a silver tray where a selection of bottles stood in a neat row, waiting for moments such as these.

"Drink?" Jackson asked in a Plymothian burr.

Dundas nodded. "King Louis has only gone and sold his bloody troops to the Prussians last month. Of course, we are paying him more so he is happy to oblige us. But there is a problem." Dundas accepted the glass, took a gulp and felt the scotch burn into the back of his throat.

"Financial or...?" Jackson asked, sipping at his glass.

"Very financial; all of the money that the Prussians have coughed up has disappeared. How much royal whoring can one man do?" Dundas could feel the rage returning. "So not only are we bearing the cost of the Hessian troops on our campaign, we must pay the Prussians off too."

"The trials of public office, 'enry"

Dundas shot Jackson a sideways glance suggesting that the moment was still too raw to find any humour in it.

"And then the question was asked by his Majesty as to why we don't have enough troops of our own? Why must we use the Hessians? Who must we blame for this? Need you ask?" Dundas turned sharply to see Jackson trying his best to suppress a rather broad grin.

"Yes, good question, Sir 'enry. Why do we need the Hessians again?" Jackson grinned.

"Bugger off, you dozy Cornish pirate"

"Plymouth's in Devon, 'enry."

"Same bloody difference."

The Minister found it hard to maintain anger. "Anyway, you may well sit there and grin, but all of this comes out of the budget that you have to work with."

Jackson did his best to look suitably crestfallen but he knew that military budgets could be skillfully extended by men of means.

"Sorry 'enry of course. So are we still going?"

"Going? Of course we are still going. The King still takes the credit for it being his idea; he'd just rather not have to pay twice for the Hessian troops. And I have to find the savings. Fox and his scum in Parliament will be all over me like the 'pox for this, unless we are very clever." Dundas took another heavy gulp.

"I thought you were meant to sip it?" Jackson asked.

"Not in emergencies. Now we need to get to work. By tomorrow, we need to have a plan drafted. I want you in Holland by the middle of March at the latest."

"Why not earlier?" Jackson said, staring at the last of the whiskey, letting it run around the sides of the glass.

"Without a Commissary General, he can't go disappearing into the sunset. I don't trust the Dutch, I don't trust the Austrians and I'm not entirely certain that York's head won't be turned. Before you know it, he will be trying to march on Paris. And we aren't carrying the cost of provisioning the bloody Austrians."

Dundas drew deep breathes to try and calm himself.

"York knows his orders. No troops south of the Diep. And you will have to make sure that is adhered to. Understand?" Dundas continued, Jackson listening, knowing that the best course was to let the Minister vent some steam.

"This operation is controlled from here and everyone needs to realise that sooner rather than later: York; Fawcett at Horse Guards; most of all you, don't go native on me the moment you get out there."

Jackson grinned and nodded. "Is there anyone you do trust 'enry?"

Dundas turned to stare down across Whitehall. "God perhaps? And sometimes I think that he is a secret Catholic. Get me another drink before I attend Parliament. I need to find a way to make the finances of this Hessian mess work."

CHAPTER TEN

The Conspirators.

Hollands Diep: 26th February 1793

Before dawn, the *Perseus* had drifted on the incoming tide into a tributary which cut into the southern coastline of Hollands Diep. Beauvais had ordered that the ship stay to the west of Willemstadt, the Dutch fortification that linked a chain of defensive positions that covered the road network threading across the waterways at Klundert and Breda. There had been no specific detail in his orders about a precise location to rendezvous after Dumouriez' message had been successfully passed to a British vessel. He and Mahieu would use their cunning to find the army; the smuggler had no choice in that matter.

Beauvais had reasoned the situation as best he could. Protracted sieges made little sense to the cavalry-man, but this flank of the Diep would need to be masked if Dumouriez intended to sweep around it and reach Amsterdam. The French army should be close at hand. The *Perseus'* crew began dropping pots and netting, taking on the appearance of a vessel searching for crab or shrimp on the waters of the inlet. At the sign of any close inspection by Dutch troops, she was to slip her moorings and leave. If either man was not back within forty-eight hours, the *Perseus* was to leave. The crew would return to Dunkirk and report to Grison, the mayor. Mahieu had bargained this much with Beauvais in the hours before.

Beauvais grunted, "I shall be glad to be on dry land. Your ship smells of fish."

Mahieu shrugged and pulled on a long grey fur coat. "It's a fishing vessel, what do you expect it to smell of? The art of smuggling is to look like the chicken and be the fox!"

The morning air was chill, thin skeins of mist rose from the still water of the Diep. Neither man bore the countenance of a local. The dragoon, clad in a dark green cape and the sailor, wearing a long whale-skin coat, which reached down to his knees, and oilskin boots, set off south to find a French patrol. It was still dark when they skirted the village of Oudenbosch and followed a raised road. To their right, a watercourse which fed into the tributary that the *Perseus* was now berthed in; to the left, a series of open fields were just visible through the spaces in the trees and bushes which grew on the bank of the dyke road.

Mahieu's feet hurt. The oilskin boots were not a great choice for walking the cobbled road but he drew some consolation from the fact that Beauvais cut a faintly ridiculous figure, trudging beside him in knee-length riding boots. Arnaud Mahieu, a man who had braved storm- tossed seas and towering waves, decided it was a thought best kept to himself.

At just after eight, with an hour of walking behind them and the late winter sun beginning to warm their faces, the pair ran into a patrol.

"Ours?" Mahieu asked.

The horsemen were about five hundred yards away, appearing from an opening in the tree line which edged the road. Both riders wore black, conical Mirleton helmets, vivid blue ribbons of material streaming from behind. Sombre black dolman jackets, buttoned up against the chill of the morning, served to accentuate the same vivid blue facing on the jacket cuffs.

"No!" Beauvais hissed, after a moment, "Dutch hussars."

The dragoon spat heavily. "You have your pistol?"

"Yes."

"Good. Draw it and point it to my back. It's loaded?" Beauvais spoke without turning around.

"Yes."

Two Dutch hussars had become six. One horseman turned left trotting away from the group, while the rest turned right and approached in single file towards the two men.

"I am now your prisoner, understand? Know the Dutch for prisoner?" Beauvais whispered hoarsely.

He made an adjustment under his cloak then raised his arms slowly.

"No, of course I don't know the bloody Dutch for prisoner," Mahieu muttered.

"German?"

"No! Unless you want to order beers or whores, we are talking in French."

The hussars were less than two hundred paces; the front pair riding with carbines slung across their saddles. It was likely that they had been out hunting, rather than this being an official patrol. Trees either side of the road were thinly spread, beyond these the fields were open. Running was likely to end in death. Mahieu could see a young officer motion instruction to the first pair of troopers.

"Then just wave and point. And don't shoot until I do. Remember I'm blind on the right. Deal with anyone on that side," Beauvais whispered. "And leave the officer to me."

"Anything else?" Mahieu asked.

"Yes. Try not to blow my head off, however tempting."

"Are you some sort of mind-reader?"

The leading troopers, who had drawn their carbines, skirted around the pair of men and positioned themselves behind Mahieu. Both heard heavy clicks as weapons were cocked but there was a casual air about the horsemen. The officer, a youth who Mahieu guessed could not be more than twenty from the thin dark moustache which had grown in uneven patches on his upper-lip, gave instructions to which the four troopers chuckled. Then the young subaltern spoke to Mahieu but the Frenchman understood none of the words.

There was an awkward silence. Mahieu gestured with his free hand at his prisoner. He did not want to move the pistol in case one of the troopers behind him took the movement as a threat.

English. He would speak in English, he knew enough words of that; it was just at that precise moment he couldn't remember any.

"He...bad man. Very bad," Mahieu spluttered.

The Dutch officer repeated the phrase slowly and nodded his head, his moustache turned into a long broad smile as he repeated the words to his troopers. He replied to Mahieu in fluent English, of which Mahieu understood the word 'French' and little else.

"Oh for God's sake, you are going to get us both killed!" Beauvais spoke up.

"What? What are you talking about?" Mahieu's voice full of horror at the dragoon's outburst.

Beauvais turned sharply on Mahieu, repeatedly pushing a thick finger into the bemused smuggler's chest. The trooper closest to Beauvais raised his carbine, the weapon less than a foot away from Beauvais' temple.

149

"What sort of smuggler can't talk his way out of a situation? I have hated every minute on board your ship! It smells of fish! You smell of fish! You're nothing but a useless Dunkirk fisherman! Why Genet made all this fuss about finding you, I don't know. I'm going to knock his head off when we get back!"

"When we get back? Are you quite mad? And I am a smuggler, a bloody good one! I don't normally have to do a lot of talking as my pistol tends to do it for me!" Mahieu replied fiercely.

"Good. First sensible thing you said!"

Beauvais raised a left hand that had secreted its way to his hip during the outburst at Mahieu. A small flash of flame erupted from it. The hussar to Beauvais' left was thrown back, the dying embers of a smile extinguished by a fine jet of blood that sprayed into the air. Beauvais dropped the small duelling pistol, grabbed at the carbine to his right and slammed his body weight into horse and rider. Another explosion, inches from his ear, then a second. He tumbled to the ground and rolled in a tangle of cape and boots.

When he unravelled himself and regained his footing, Mahieu stood among three dead bodies. The officer was slumped over the saddle of his horse, heavy globules of blood cascading onto his horse's fetlock and hoof. Behind him, a second dead trooper, whose horse had bolted, lay spread-eagled; a dark claret sea of blood creating small islands of stone in the cobbled road.

The trooper whose horse Beauvais had shoulder-charged, had managed to control the frightened animal and was picking his way down the bank sixty yards to their rear, nervously glancing back at the two men. The other hussar trooper had galloped along the road and was making toward the compatriot who had separated from the group as they had emerged from the tree line.

Beauvais looked at the carbine on the floor.

"Seems wrong to shoot a man with his own weapon."

Swiftly crouching, he picked up the carbine, gave it a cursory inspection, stood and aimed instead at the trooper on the road. The rider was shouting and gesturing wildly to his returning colleague. Beauvais pulled the trigger; there was a momentary pause before the flash and bark of the carbine. The weapon kicked into his shoulder but his frame absorbed the impact. When the small cloud of smoke had cleared, both hussars had raced into the tree line and were now beginning to work their way through the heavily muddied field.

"Think you had better stick to targets about a yard away. Leave the real work to us fishermen," Mahieu muttered.

"I hit him," Beauvais growled, offended at the sleight on his marksmanship.

At the far edge of the field, the two troopers were joined by the third who Beauvais had shoulder charged. The leading hussar gestured defiance in the direction of the two Frenchmen, then disappeared into the thin wood-line which separated the fields. As the last horse followed, it slowed momentarily. The trooper, who had fallen behind the others, slumped from his horse into brown, fertile earth.

Beauvais pushed past Mahieu, a smug lop-sided grin on the dragoon's face, and seized the bridle of the officer's horse which had taken to grazing thick strands of grass, near to where the young hussar officer had fallen. With surprising grace, he mounted the animal and trotted off to collect the horse of the trooper killed by the first pistol shot. In no more than a minute, the animal soothed, he returned to Mahieu.

"Can you ride in those ridiculous boots?" Beauvais asked.

For twenty minutes they headed south and then east, across a flat landscape intersected by raised roads. Mahieu's poor horsemanship mean that his mount struggled to keep pace with Beauvais'. He was glad when the dragoon slowed to a halt, pulling his mount into the shelter of the tree-line. Mahieu followed him, nudging his horse into cover.

"What is it?" Mahieu asked.

"Soldiers. Three, I think."

"Where?" Mahieu peered along the empty road.

"Which of us has one eye again? There!" Beauvais hissed.

Around three hundred yards distant Mahieu could make out the shape of a horse and then saw a dismounted soldier, carbine pointed at the two Frenchmen.

"Ours or theirs?" Mahieu muttered. "Damn, I haven't reloaded my pistol."

Beauvais mounted his horse. "Come on. They're ours. In fact, I think they are mine."

He trotted down the road, leaving Mahieu struggling to re-mount and by the time that he had caught up, Beauvais had transformed into a gregarious character, full of laughter, sharing an embrace with another dragoon, a younger man, a foot shorter than Beauvais but who's jacket bore the same worn scarlet facings.

"We were told to look out for you. We have been up and down this road for the past two days," the young officer gently chided.

"Ah, I'm sorry Demont, truly I am. My new line of work isn't an exact science," Beauvais beamed.

Two dragoon troopers touched the peaks of their bronzed head-dresses in salute and returned to a dutiful lookout. Mahieu, feeling like a forgotten party guest, slid awkwardly down from his horse and crunched heavy paces through the wooded undergrowth to where Beauvais and Demont now crouched. Both men had tied the horses and Demont was busy sketching a map. He stopped and sniffed the air.

"My God Beauvais, you smell like the harbour sewers at low tide."

"Ah, yes. Demont meet Arnold Mahieu. Don't ask any questions, it's better for everyone. As for the smell, apparently, it's what a smuggler's vessel smells of," Beauvais shot a glance at Mahieu but for once there was the hint of mirth and a smile drawn from enjoyment of the moment.

Demont nodded at Mahieu then returned to sketching a map from one that Mahieu assumed the dragoon must have made over the last two day's patrols.

"The army is here, at Breda. It's rumoured that the Dutch have a huge arsenal there. The General is desperate to seize it. You should only find our patrols on the road now. Every time we see the Dutch, they retreat. Quite tedious really."

Demont continued sketching, Beauvais nodding at the marks on the map, clearly understanding the annotations his fellow officer was making.

"Not every time," Beauvais smiled. "You can add two against my name when you return to camp."

"Really? That explains the horses."

"Even pocketed one of them with this," Beauvais reached to the side of his cape and withdrew the small mahogany muff pistol and grinned, the bright vermilion scar more vivid than ever.

"Wait until I tell the Colonel that. No wait, better still, come back and tell him yourself. Give up whatever it is you are doing now and come back. There's bound to be real action soon."

"Perhaps. I promise to put in an appearance. But for now, we must find Dumouriez. He asked for this fisherman. God alone knows why, Genet's practical joke, I think." Behind the hissed reply, there was the slightest trace of respect for Mahieu.

Following Dumont's directions, the men made good progress. They heard the bombardment of Breda before they saw the trails of smoke that threaded into the low cloud base of the late winter morning.

The riders slowed to look at the scene.

"At least we know where the army is," Mahieu said. "Something has puzzled me. Well more than one matter, actually."

"What?" Beauvais asked, reaching under his cape and uncorking a small wooden water bottle, drawing heavily from it.

"Why did you ask him, that officer, to list the men you have killed? And what was that pistol about? Looks like something a woman would carry!" Mahieu asked, nodding with thanks as Beauvais passed the water bottle to him.

"The pistol was a humorous gift, after Jemappes, after…" his hand waved in the general direction of the wound on his face, "I went to work for the General. The officers of the regiment sent me a matching pair. I don't think I was ever meant to use them. I supposed some might have thought what I'm doing now isn't the job of a soldier. Not a real man's work, certainly not honest work for an officer of the 3rd Dragoons."

Beauvais broke off and looked away from Mahieu. His frame heaved a heavy involuntary sigh.

"As for the dead count, it might seem a bit morbid to an outsider but it's a tradition. The officer with the most enemy slain on each campaign wins a trophy. It is highly honoured. I really don't expect you to understand."

Mahieu asked mockingly, "Because I'm a smuggler?"

"No, not that. Well, perhaps a little." Beauvais seemed almost embarrassed to admit his opinion of Mahieu but the man from Dunkirk merely shrugged.

"So, what is the prize?"

"Even though I missed the battle, I won the trophy for the last season. It was…Really you wouldn't understand."

"Tell me."

"It was a teaspoon with a bronze elephant mounted on the handle. It bears my initials and is used at regimental dinners now."

Mahieu coughed on the water bottle he was drinking from as Beauvais talked.

"You suffered all of that," he gestured at Beauvais' face, "for the reward of an elephant on a spoon? Thank God my nephews are in the infantry."

Breda: 26th February 1793

Sparks leapt from the heart of the fire as Arnaud Mahieu prodded a damp log into it. He sat back and ran thick fingers through a mane of greying hair. A shave and hot bath would have been most welcome but neither seemed a likely prospect. Smuggling was a younger man's occupation. Perhaps it was time to sell his stake in the vessel? He watched the flames greedily lick the damp wood, boiling sap spitting out. Mahieu knew that such plans were a mere fantasy. The sea was his mistress and she would forever have him at her mercy.

"Here, put these on."

A pair of black leather knee length boots descended from a height and landed with a thump at his feet.

"What are those for?"

"You ride like a cripple. The boots will help your feet in the stirrups. A couple of hours riding with me and we might even make a dragoon out of you," Beauvais had the same ragged warm smile as when he had spoken to Demont. "And thank you for this morning."

Mahieu shrugged.

"Other men would have panicked. I won't forget it," Beauvais offered a bottle of wine, a third of the contents already missing.

"It's nothing. It was self-preservation as much as anything," Mahieu smiled took the wine, sat back on an upturned crate that had previously contained howitzer shells before the morning's bombardment, and drank.

"You are in a good mood," Mahieu smiled; the red wine was delicious. "Is this the cause?"

He held the bottle toward the sun to study the liquid, tilting it gently, however other movement caught his attention. A dragoon was approaching, too small and slender to be a soldier, long blonde hair nestling into a wax riding cape. She nodded at the two men.

"Or that?"

He twisted back towards Beauvais but the dragoon had already turned on his heels and followed the woman into a large, white tent. The guards at the tent flap closed the entrance as soon as Beauvais had ducked inside. General Dumouriez was holding a council of war: Breda must fall tonight.

The message that Juliette had brought back from the Austrian camp at Valkenburg was positive. Coalition between the two armies was accepted in principle by Prince Josias. There was no response yet from Great Britain. But soon London would know Josias' position and it would force the British hand. King George wanted the Count of Province, uncle of the rightful heir,

Dauphin Louis-Charles, to act as Regent until the young prince came of age. But the boy of nine was held in Paris, his fate uncertain and Province an unpopular figure. That outcome could still be made to work in Dumouriez' favour. If the masses decided that they did not want the return of the Bourbons, the General who controlled Paris would have the power. Dumouriez was King-maker and held a powerful hand of cards. He could choose to play the faithful revolutionary or restore a Bourbon to the throne.

The great unknown was General Miranda.

"Look at the gifts that Ares and Aphrodite have brought me."

Juliette smiled at Dumouriez' comment, "Are you playing Zeus then, General?"

"Why not? In this tent we are immortals with the power to reshape France and countries around it. This is our moment."

"Well Zeus, any chance that you could order the God of War here to take a bath? He smells as if he has spent a week living in Poseidon's midden," Juliette could barely finish the sentence before laughing. Beauvais turned a shade of crimson and apologised again for the stench that came from his uniform.

"Now, now, children, I will not have squabbling. Beauvais has done a great service. Genet tells me that this Mahieu is the best and bravest of the Dunkirk smugglers and we shall test his nerve," Dumouriez paused, looking up from the documents signed by Prince Josias. "You are covered in blood, Beauvais!"

"We ran into a spot of bother on the road, a Dutch patrol."

"And?"

"There are four less Dutchmen that you have to fight, sir. This time at least you won't be troubled by a letter of complaint from the town's mayor."

"I don't know about the Devil's emissary, seems to me you are an agent of the Grim Reaper himself."

"Shouldn't that be Hades, if you are keeping true to your Greek analogy, sir?" Genet spoke, his voice sounding piqued.

Juliette guessed that he felt excluded from the conversation and the plaudits being offered. She took an obvious step nearer to Beauvais knowing it would annoy Genet further, and surreptitiously looped a finger around one of his, feeling it gently squeezed in return.

"Either way, did this Mahieu prove his mettle to you in the fight, Julien?"

"Yes, sir."

"Good. Paris tells us that the British will land across the water soon. I need to know every last detail. Get as close to Helleveotsluis as you dare. There is an island too…"

"Overfrakkee, sir," Genet offered.

"Yes, thank you, Serge. Overfrakkee. I want to know the garrison strength and landing places."

"Countess, when can you be ready to ride again?"

"Tomorrow, why?"

"Find General Miranda's army. I want to know his intentions. This is going to take a degree of care and you are of course at liberty to refuse."

"Continue. You just sent me into the camp of the enemy. How much worse can this be?" Her mind was already intrigued. The nights of sleeping in the wild had been strangely appealing to a woman who had lived a life of modest luxury in the days before the revolution.

"Worse. The Army of the Ardennes has representatives from the National Assembly at every meeting. You will do well to get a private audience with Miranda. But then he is just a man so I am sure you might find a way. Before we set out, Paris transferred 16,000 men from my command to his. So far, the Assembly has left us to our own devices. I doubt that will last and when the time comes it will force our hand. I want those men back and Miranda to hold his ground. Paris has sent orders too this morning, telling us to co-operate with the Army of the Ardennes while it chases shadows all over Eastern Flanders. Serge have you drafted the reply to Paris yet?"

"Yes, sir. Are you certain that you wish to remind the Assembly that the Army of the North controls the movements of the Army of the Ardennes and not the elected representatives?"

"Serge, Serge, Serge, you must learn to worry less. Yes, I mean to spell it out to those fools in Paris. The tail cannot wag the dog. We must be free. They have done what they thought was best for France. If we can force our way to Amsterdam, then we can make France powerful again. If we can force one more battle from Josias and win, we negotiate the peace from a position of strength. And if these plans fail, then we have an assurance from Austria. Boldness will win. I will sign the dispatch today and have it on its way."

Juliette watched Dumouriez as he gazed at the roof of the tent, clearly calculating other matters. The silence lasted for a few seconds and then was broken as the General jumped to his feet and loudly clapped his hands twice. On cue, the tent flap peeled open and royal liveried staff deposited two trays containing cold cuts of various meat, warm bread and wine.

"Refreshments and then the thorny issue of Breda."

After devouring slices of chicken and beef and delicious bread, Juliette lay back in a small folding campaign chair, her feet perched on a second, listening to Dumouriez outline the problems of the campaign. She drew occasional sips from a small glass of wine clutched in her right hand which returned to rest on the flat of her stomach, rising and falling to the rhythm of her breathing.

Genet dragged himself away from the sight of her, before his mind wandered or Beauvais caught him staring. The dragoon loomed over Dumouriez' shoulder; he examined the map and listened intently to the General as he outlined his ideas for the next few days. The scribe didn't need his famed spiders-web of informers to know that Beauvais and the Countess were lovers. He had wondered how a woman could give herself willingly to such a disfigured man. His stream of thought was interrupted as he realised that Dumouriez had asked him a question.

"How many, Serge? And how soon can we get them here?"

Genet scrambled through the paperwork on his desk to give his mind time to think. Dumouriez was still discussing the bombardment; he searched for the facts in his mind.

"Three more batteries will arrive tomorrow, sire. It leaves one in the Corps that you have sent to seize the crossing at Gorcum," Genet looked up from the pile of notes to see Dumouriez staring at him.

"Everything alright, Serge?"

Genet nodded, his blushes saved by Juliette, a soft voice cutting through the momentary silence.

"Why don't you just send him?" the Countess had raised her head, lifted an outstretched leg and aimed a playful kick in the direction of Beauvais buttocks which presented a tempting target as he stretched over the table to reach for his own glass of wine.

"What do you mean?" Dumouriez asked.

"Well forgive my poor feminine insight but you don't have enough men to blockade the town; guns to reduce it or the time to starve them out. Without a miracle the army will run short of food, gunpowder and ammunition within the next fortnight," Juliette returned to stare up at the ceiling of the tent as she spoke.

"That would be the size of the matter, yes." Dumouriez admitted turning to look at Juliette, "So what are you suggesting?"

"Send Julien. He will frighten the life out of the commander, I'm sure. Especially if you send him as he is now," she giggled, raised an apologetic hand in the general direction of Beauvais and continued, "tell him you have the garrison surrounded, offer him clemency but only if he surrenders tonight. Move some troops around the town after dark. Light more camp fires. I don't know. Be creative."

Dumouriez smiled and looked at Beauvais and then to Genet, who shrugged and smiled back. It was an utterly ridiculous plan but could it be made to work?

Twenty minutes after Beauvais had entered the tent, the flap was flung open and a voice Mahieu recognised yelled for a messenger. A young cavalry trooper of the 1st Hussars, who had been stood at the side of the tent, seized a handful of messages and some whispered instruction. Within moments he was gone, galloping towards the position of the massed batteries that were carrying out an unhurried bombardment of the fortified town.

The man looked at Mahieu but showed no recognition. Mahieu stood, knowing the short, thin figure. Dark-brown receding hair closely cropped; small eyes, enlarged by the silver framed glasses. A man who Grison, the mayor of Dunkirk would find and kill if Mahieu failed to return home. Serge Genet held the gaze of Mahieu for a moment, before turning and fighting with the flap of the tent, ducking back into safety.

The bombardment concluded at 6pm; the meeting between Beauvais and the garrison commander, Count de Bylandt, lasted twenty minutes. The Count faced a difficult choice, not knowing the size of the French army. Dumouriez' messenger, a towering hulk of a dragoon with a ravaged face and dead right eye, smelled worse than a rotting corpse. His uniform was stained with the blood of other men.

Julien Beauvais had lied. He told the garrison commander that the army numbered some forty thousand. Last night the camp fires had suggested a tenth of that number. Tonight, they had been spotted north and east of the town, not just in the south as they had the night before. The Frenchman offered the commander passage from the fortress with the full honours of war, retaining all equipment but their artillery. Furthermore, all officers could take their personal baggage, in exchange for swearing an undertaking not to fight again on the south bank of the Diep. One company of Dutch infantry and one squadron of cavalry would be held as prisoners until the garrison had retired to Willemstadt and begun to cross Hollands Diep. At that point, the last prisoners would be released. The civilians of Breda could leave; if they chose to stay, their lives and goods would be protected by the word of General Dumouriez.

When Beauvais had finished reading the terms, he looked at Bylandt.

"Sir, I am a cavalry-man. I don't understand sieges. If I should die in battle, I would hope it would be for something more significant than this place. No soldier could think less of an officer who saves the lives of his men from needless slaughter. That is what will surely happen here."

Beauvais stated the matters plainly, as facts that needed no counter.

"My General will expect an answer within an hour."

At 6.45pm, the Colours of the House of Orange were lowered from battlements of Breda. The following day, Genet undertook an inspection of the stores left behind by the Dutch which took him nearly three hours. One hundred and sixty cannons had been left in perfect working order. Food, gunpowder and artillery reserves had been captured that would supply the Army of the North for the next two months. The Dutch, in their haste to leave, had not destroyed a single article.

CHAPTER ELEVEN

Allies.

Hollands Diep: 26th February 1793

Hellevoetsluis sat under a blanket of cloud causing the waters of the Hollands Diep to reflect a chill slate-grey. The southern bank, two miles across the Diep, was no more than a dark green smear to the naked eye. Major Stephen Trevethan, wrapped in a thick blue jacket to keep away the worst of the day's chill, tracked slowly across the landscape by way of a powerful naval telescope mounted on a brass tripod. Satisfied, he returned to a cheery whistle and compared his observations to a map of the Diep, running a finger along the coastline. In the distance a thunderous rumble could be heard.

Willemstadt. That was the key. The Duke of York had said as much on the journey over. If the Dutch held Willemstadt, it would leave the British free to manoeuvre. If the British were drawn into that fight, matters would become trickier.

Major Stephen Trevethan studied the map again, tracing the shoreline beyond Willemstadt, knowing he needed to visit the stronghold. The expanse of the Diep was better than a castle wall against the French, the tract of water fragmented into a myriad of tidal waterways running across Holland. While the Dutch controlled the Diep, the French would need to take a much wider passage to The Hague, the Dutch palace and symbolic seat of power, leaving their supply lines exposed.

Earlier that day, the Duke's yacht had made good progress and reached Hellevoetsluis on the early hours of the morning, having left Greenwich on the afternoon before. All the talk had been of the campaign. Trevethan had shared a berth with Captain Charles Craufurd, the Duke's Aide-de-Camp. However, the Duke had accepted just about every spare bit of baggage from staff officers who were following with the Guards Brigade. Every space below decks was filled with trunks and the paraphernalia of campaign that such gentry had deemed a necessity. Even an ornate, gold-leafed table and several dining chairs had been stored for the expected social parties that lay ahead. Trevethan would have gladly tipped the lot overboard. He had considered a wager with Craufurd that most of the baggage would be discarded if the campaign lasted a year but thought better of it. Both men, along with the Duke and Sir James Murray, the Duke's Chief of Staff had been glad to see land. The same winds which had propelled the yacht briskly to Holland had brought discomfort to all but the Duke, a keen sailor.

Arrival dampened that enthusiasm; Hellevoetsluis was totally unprepared. The yacht moored in the Diep until a berth in the harbour could be found. When the vessel finally slipped anchor and entered the narrow canal leading into Hellevoetsluis, the reason for the delay became apparent. Seven third rate Dutch seventy-fours were tied up alongside dock, in a haphazard manner, leaving ships to operate in narrow lanes barely wide enough for two ships to pass. Stores for these Dutch 'men-o-war' stood piled on the dockside but there were few signs of crew working to service the ships. A handful of men lazed, watching the commotion around them with disinterest. Where the skeleton staff of a ship's crew was working, tasks were being performed at a dilatory rate. A threatening musical score accompanied the scene; French guns could be heard bombarding Willemstadt, the main fortress on the southern shore of the Diep. If Willemstadt fell, Hellevoetsluis' fate would be in the balance. When the Duke's party finally made it ashore they had been greeted by a further dark comedy, a General and the town's mayor holding an animated and very public argument. On the whole, the spectacle reminded Trevethan of a marionette show that he had witnessed as a boy at a fair in Falmouth.

Pieter de Haan, mayor of Hellevoetsluis, a tall thin man who craved quiet, order and for the tumult of the times to pass him by, was being roundly harangued by a figure in a Dutch General's uniform. The conversation had changed from Dutch into English as soon as General Bentinck spied the Duke of York and his party of officers approaching. Bentinck's lavish blue jacket, bedecked with gold trim and rich orange sash, strained at the seams as he jabbed a short fat finger in the direction of the slighter man. His opponent wore a black hat, plain and broad-brimmed with equally austere black clothes. The mayor clutched nervously at his own orange sash of office, the only item that the two men had in common.

Bentinck had arrived from the Royal Palace to ascertain the progress of preparations in the matter of the housing of British troops, a matter that De Haan was claiming to have no prior knowledge of. It had taken the Duke's good nature, allied with Murray's calm words to resolve the matter and agree a plan in which all parties could save face. Bentinck would immediately escort the Duke and Craufurd to the Hague; there would be no time to unpack. The Dutch General groaned, knowing that the journey would take a dozen hours on horseback, a prospect which neither he nor his mount would enjoy. Murray would arrange the temporary deployment for the arriving troops on the northern banks of the Diep. Trevethan was to reconnoitre the area and gather some intelligence on the designs of the French.

Trevethan had the better end of the deal; whistling a Cornish sailor's shanty, he returned to the map. The sound of footsteps was followed by a polite cough.

"Yes, what is it?" Trevethan spoke without turning.

"Major, forgive me but your Colonel sent me. Perhaps I can be of assistance to you?" de Haan spoke timidly.

Trevethan turned and looked at the tall figure of de Haan, who peered back nervously through pebbled spectacles, giving him the air of a startled owl.

"Yes, actually you can. Take a pew," Trevethan shifted his position so that de Haan could perch next to him on a large boulder mounted at the edge of the premonitory which formed the canal walls into the port.

"When will your men arrive?" de Haan asked staring at the map which Trevethan cradled in his lap.

"Soon, tomorrow perhaps, two days is more likely. What about the French, de Haan? Any news on where they might be?" Trevethan shared the map he had been studying.

"No, nothing. Yesterday they attacked Willemstadt but were beaten back. Today, perhaps Klundert." De Haan pointed south-east across the water, and then identified the town on the map.

"Their cannon sound further away today. If they can't cross here then, they will need to come around the Diep and cross the Island of Dordrecht." De Haan was now pointing east, parallel to the Diep. "Once they cross there, we only have the ramparts for protection."

Trevethan had already walked the perimeter of the port's defences as a means of stretching his legs after the voyage. The design was a very basic star shape and imitated the style of the great fortress builder Vauban, but with none of his deadly killing grounds to strengthen the defender's hand. The walls looked suitably sturdy though and with two thousand British Foot Guards manning them, they would be impregnable.

"Those ramparts look enough, don't fret. Anyway, the French won't get that far." Trevethan spoke with more assurance than he felt.

"I hope not." De Haan was still hesitant, weighing his words carefully. "Not every Dutch citizen is for the Prince of Orange. If the town falls it will go badly for me and my family." De Haan looked over Trevethan's shoulder as if he was expecting the French to appear at any moment.

"It will be alright. Really it will," Trevethan smiled again his voice full of warmth made friendlier by his Cornish burr.

"Now, what about the island here?" Trevethan pointed at the mass of land around two miles from the entrance to Hellevoetslius harbour. "Are there Dutch troops there?"

"Overfrakkee? Yes, an entire battalion has been posted there by General Boetslaar. He commands the forces at Willemstadt." De Haan pointed south east across the Diep. "Would you like to meet him?"

"That I would." Trevethan smiled at de Haan again, slapping him on the back with a muscular paw of a hand "Please, as soon as you can, Mister Mayor."

The Dutchman smiled weakly. "Pieter de Haan," the mayor proffered a hand expecting a crushing hand-shake and relieved that the muscular hand extending from Trevethan's stocky frame possessed a firm but not overbearing grip.

"Stephen Trevethan. Don't let the uniform fool you, I'm an engineer rather than a soldier. Would rather be building roads than blowing up perfectly sound architecture, but Colonel Murray is a silver-tongued devil. Still it is beautiful country an' no mistake."

De Haan felt himself cheered. He hadn't followed every syllable of the Cornish-man's words but there was friendship to be found in the sentiment of them. A degree of order was being restored to a day which up to that point had been uncomfortably turbulent.

Liege: 27th February 1793

At first, there was nothing but white snow set against the black of pine trees in the dark of a sky that had yet to feel the morning sun. Jean-Baptiste

Mahieu rose, small patches of solidified snow falling from the creases in his great coat. He unravelled a large discoloured rag from his head and face, which had done its best to keep out the chill night air, then searched inside his tunic pocket pulling out a cloth bag full of dried moss and grass. Inside his backpack, he found a flint and some small lengths of kindling. The weather had deteriorated over the last week and so as a precaution Mahieu had taken to storing fuel for the next morning's fire at the top of his pack which also served as his pillow. Each morning, despite the hail and snowstorms that the Army of the Ardennes had endured, Jean-Baptiste had provided a warming fire for the men around him. Slowly the dawn landscape was alive with black shapes moving among the grey white background; the Black Lions stirred.

Jean-Baptiste pulled a small green fern branch from the pile he had torn down to use as bedding the night before and fanned the remains of the previous night's fire, hoping that there was still some life in it. Blackened charcoal embers floated away on the breeze but then there was the unmistakable orange glow. He set about reviving the fire and under his expert attention within a few minutes a healthy blaze had developed as kindling and larger sticks were broken up and added to the flames. Somewhere in the undergrowth of fern and bodies a voice enquired, "Is it morning already Sergeant?"

Mahieu grunted. He was just getting used to the title. The colonel of the 14th had promoted an assortment of men. Within the spirit of blending two armies together, old Royalist and new Republican, half of the promotions had been new recruits and half old campaigners. Within the hour breakfast had been scrounged and dawn light began to pierce the woodland in which the Black Lions had camped.

Mahieu recalled the wild horses that roamed the Great Moor around Dunkirk. In the dead of winter, the animals had stood together for warmth, great clouds of steam billowing from them at every breath. Mahieu could see the same scene around him now. An army had emerged from under the snow and palls of warm breath and smoke intertwined. He saw his company commander pace heavily towards him, feet sinking into the freshly compacted snow. Captain Davide a heavy-set man with dark hair, in his late twenties wore the new blue uniform of the French Republic. He had been a soldier for a year but Mahieu found him to be a good officer, a decent man. Brave too by all accounts.

"Mahieu, morning," Davide's voice gruff in the early dawn air "Slept well I hope? Tonight, we might sleep under cover."

"How do you reason that, sir?" Mahieu asked cautiously.

"Because we have found a bridge over the Meuse that the Austrians have left unguarded. Rather careless of them really. It's about five miles from here. We have some hussars there now but they can't hold it should the enemy appear, so whoever gets across the bridge first grabs the best place to defend on the other side and sits in the dry while the rest of the army crosses."

"And who has that dubious honour, sir?" Mahieu asked, already sensing the answer.

"Thirty minutes, Jean. And check every man's weapon. Just in case we must fight our way across," Davide nodded and strode off to pass on the news.

Having been transferred by Paris from the Army of the North, the Black Lions were crossing the Meuse. General Miranda's command was struggling to serve two masters, advancing as slowly as he dared, but his soldiers could no longer be a force that just observed. The National Assembly needed a victory.

CHAPTER TWELVE

The Island.

Hollands Diep: 28th February 1793

"Please stop that."

"What?"

"That! Tuneless humming, I preferred it when you were miserable."

Arnold Mahieu put down the telescope and stared hard at Julian Beauvais. The hum broke into a whistle, punctured by a slight hiss due to Beauvais' broken smile, interrupted by a long yawn. Satisfied that he had irritated the smuggler sufficiently, the huge dragoon returned to following the tree-line through the view of his own telescope until he found the gun battery. He glanced down and traced the outline of the map drawn by Demont. The position and distance of the drawing seemed to agree. The Dutch had positioned a half battery, three six-pound guns and a howitzer, to cover the passage of the Diep and protect their own life line to Willemstadt. Both men were couched on a low bank near the water's edge having crawled through a belt of tall, straw coloured grass, to observe the island of Overfrakkee in the early morning light.

"I don't suppose you would care to share the reason for your cheerful disposition today? In fact, I didn't even know you could smile until we ran into your cavalry patrol."

Beauvais paused his whistling, cocked his head as if giving the matter consideration and merely said "No," before yawning again and returning to observe the island.

The less people that knew, the safer she might be. In truth, Julien Beauvais wanted to shout his good fortune from every steeple.

"No sleep and you smell like some Arabian brothel. On second thoughts don't tell me, I will only hate you more," Mahieu scanned the shoreline of the island. "Pass me that map."

Beauvais freed a hand from the telescope and slid the map over to Mahieu.

"Well, since you have clearly made the effort to perfume yourself, let's assume the role of smelly fishermen and take a closer look at the island."

Mahieu slithered back through the long grass, leaving Beauvais alone with his thoughts; memories of Juliette.

The previous night, the Governor's room in Breda Castle had been a gift from Dumouriez, for the man who had delivered a bloodless victory. Besides it seemed that the General took a degree of satisfaction that his two most useful assets had found solace in one another, his Ares and Aphrodite. It was the first night that the pair had slept together with any form of privacy. Sharing the same horse blanket under the open skies in the balmy summer days ahead had an appeal but the last time Beauvais and Juliette had huddled together to share bodily warmth as rain and hail stones peppered them throughout a long night.

Beauvais had not found his way to the room much before seven in the evening. He had taken time to visit the colonel of the 3rd Dragoons. Hours earlier, Beauvais had arranged that his regiment would be the leading formation to enter Breda and take possession of the Dutch prisoners. Normally this would have been an odious task, tying up men and officers in mundane work. Apart from the opportunity of petty pilfering for the rank and file, the task added an additional layer of administration before the regiment could set about the task of housing itself and three hundred and seventy horses which badly needed care, attention and some shelter from the Dutch winter.

Horses were another challenge facing every cavalry regiment in the army; the 3rd Dragoons were currently short of one hundred and thirty. Beauvais' old squadron had given up their mounts so that the other three squadrons could deploy fully; his men had become little more than skirmishers. A dragoon was prepared to fight and skirmish on foot but it was poor-man's work compared to that of a horse-soldier. Beauvais had suggested to Dumouriez that the Dutch be made to keep a squadron of cavalry as part of the prisoner bond that had been arranged; he was determined that his regiment would profit from it.

When he finally found the colonel, the baggage of the Fourth Squadron had arrived in Breda and Dutch horse wear was being pulled from horses by gleeful troopers. Behind them were two large wagons packed with the squadron's saddles and equipment, ready to be unpacked. More than the gift of horses Beauvais had come to ask a favour of Colonel Courtois, a friend of a dozen years. Only when their conversation was concluded did he allow himself to think of Juliette.

Breda castle was alive with warmth, music, light and laughter. As many as two thousand officers and soldiers had found lodgings under its roof. The building, four wings with towers at each corner, arranged as a square with an open interior, had been a barracks and military hospital over the last three hundred years. Now every room and corridor on the three floors was packed with soldiers relieved to experience a night away from the open winter skies. The rest of the force that Dumouriez had besieged Breda with were lodged around the town.

The dragoon had bounded into a torch-lit hallway, turned left and taken the staircase built into a corner tower, threading his way to the third level. Once here he raced along the stone corridor; straddling prone bodies; soldiers sat sharing a meal or game of cards, until he arrived at the next corner turn. Two infantry-men in the blue jackets of the Republican army guarded the entrance to the next wing. For a moment they might have considered stopping the dragoon in full flight, but on recognising the scarred face, perhaps somewhat relieved, both men snapped to attention.

Dumouriez had taken the top floor of the wing of the castle which overlooked the main canal. He had housed himself, Genet and officers on whose loyalty he needed to be certain of. Some of these doors stood ajar, laughter or snatches of conversation briefly registered with Beauvais; he spotted the door, pale blue paint with ornate gilt patterning setting it apart from the varnished brown timber of the others. From underneath the doorway soft yellow light stretched out into the darkness.

Beauvais slammed his heels into the stone floor, skidded and came to an ungainly halt. His chest thudded and he paused to catch his breath, suddenly feeling acutely dishevelled. He yanked a calf-skin glove off with his teeth and ran a hand over four days of growth. He felt more like a vagabond than an officer of the French army. It was more than just that, he felt nervous, almost unworthy. Straightening himself, he removed the brass dragoon helmet, ran his hand through the long black hair that had been encased by the armoured head-wear. He knocked once, listened and was about to knock again when he heard her voice.

"Enter."

He had seen the room earlier that day. Then it had looked much like Beauvais felt now, a bedraggled mess. He could not believe the transformation. To his right, the four-poster bed, previously a broken skeleton covered by a grubby mattress, had been transformed into a sea of satin sheets and plush pillows. Rich purple curtains were tied back at each post. In the warm orange glow of the roaring fire in the central hearth the bed looked as if it had been transported from a children's fairy tale.

Beyond the bed, by a large window, stood a small table with five small closed silver cloches; a sixth stood uncovered, a large side of pork rested, thin skeins of steam rising from it, next to an uncorked wine bottle with a single glass beside it. To the left of the fire, a large copper pot stood in front of a four-piece folding screen, each panel showing a relief of Greek nymphs engaged in some rather curious activities. Between a pair of the panels a thin Turkish towel rested; from behind the screen, occasional clouds of steam gently rose entwined with the sounds of gentle singing.

"Is that you, Casimir?" Juliette broke from the song at the sound of the door closing.

"No, it isn't. It's me." Beauvais paused. "Who in God's name is Casimir?"

"Oh, you! At last my hero has arrived!" From behind the screen came the sound of splashing followed by the slight impact of feet on the wooden floor and the disappearance of the towel. A hand emerged wagging an empty glass.

"I'm so sorry my darling but I started without you. Would you fill me up?" There was delicious intent behind the question

Beauvais took the glass. "Who is Casimir?"

"Well you have a choice. He is either an admirer from my army of lovers, or…" There was another knock on the door. From behind the screen Juliette bade the person enter. An old man wearing the gold and green livery of the House of Bourbon, opened the door and nodded to Beauvais. Behind him, two boys struggled with a large copper pot, similar to the one now empty by the screen. Juliette's head shot out from the side of the screen, wet blonde hair looking much darker in the amber light of the room.

"Thank you, Casimir, thank you boys. That will be all for now. I have clothes that will need a good scrub."

She disappeared and a dragoon's uniform, white blouse and riding breeches dropped over the top of the screen. Dumouriez' servant finished overseeing the boys' efforts to set the new pot of water over the fire, collected the clothing and withdrew from the room, nodding respectfully at Beauvais first, before saying "Thank you, Countess," in the general direction of the woman behind the screen.

Juliette stepped out from behind the panels as Beauvais stood looking thoroughly dumbfounded, empty wine glass still in hand. She wore nothing more than a plain short-sleeved white petticoat but Beauvais could not move or take his eyes from her. She walked up to him, casually wound her fingers into the hand that held the wine glass and pulled it away, with a gentle but wicked smile. She looked up to kiss him and Julian leaned forward but as he did Juliette placed a solitary finger to his lips.

"After you have bathed and shaved."

Juliette turned, placed the glass on the dinner table and then led him to the waiting water.

From somewhere across Breda, Beauvais heard a clock chime a solitary sound. Moonlight cast a milky light into the room adding to the red of dying embers in the hearth. He could feel Juliette's breath hard against his face, her warm body coiled against his right arm. She had let him sleep for a while but the delicate touch of her finger on his face had stirred him. In the dark, he felt her trace the scar line, a delicate dance from temple to chin.

"Does it hurt still?"

"No, not now; some days, but not now; would you rather it wasn't there?"

"No, darling, no, not at all; I think this is how you were meant to be, Julien. It's perfect." Her fingers worked their way down through chest hair and rested on his muscular torso. "You are perfect."

Beauvais felt her kiss his chin, just to the side of the scar, the kiss ended with a delicate bite. Her hand started moving lower again until it found its target.

"Don't you ever tire?" Julien coughed in mock surprise and turned to look at the Countess.

She feigned an innocent air and smiled. "We will both have time enough to sleep but not this night." In a languid motion, she slithered downward and mounted the dragoon.

"Whatever happened to the art of conversation, woman?" Beauvais laughed, embarrassed at how easily Juliette had manipulated life back into his tired frame.

"A soldier and conversationalist; usually I can barely get two words from you and now you want to talk?"

He reached up to caress her body but she batted his hands away.

"No sir. I don't think so; pray, delight me in conversation while I enjoy a gentle trot on my charger."

"What, now?"

"Why, yes sir; now, sir. Conversation appears to be your pleasure. My pleasure is …"

The rhythm of her body slowed and only when she was ready, she spoke again.

"What do you think of our chances of living through these next few days?"

Julian began to protest but Juliette expertly used a heel and drove it into thigh muscle, a faint smile caught in the corners of her mouth as she did so.

"Answer the question."

Julian tried to concentrate. "I don't know. If Dumouriez succeeds then we might have more nights like this. God help me!" He laughed until his left thigh stung with another well directed heel and a smirk of delight from Juliette.

"And if he doesn't? We die?" She asked.

"If he doesn't you have two choices. Go with him. Wait out the war."

"Or?"

"Or stay; stay with me. I spoke to Courtois about it. I would return to the regiment..." Beauvais was finding concentration on the conversation increasingly difficult. Another heel stung him.

"Until the worst is past... I have a plan." Beauvais could barely form the words. He felt her heel shift and braced himself for another blow, but Juliette merely increased the trot to a canter.

"As long as there is a plan; I have no intention of leaving. I have seen what mounts Austria has to offer and it doesn't match this."

In the dark they lay together.

"Are you asleep?"

Beauvais was tempted to feign sleep but a hand stretched over his chest, entwined hair around delicate fingers and yanked firmly.

"Ouch...No, no, I'm not asleep, not now anyway."

"Good. I need to know something." Juliette's head lay across Beauvais chest, rising and falling with his breathing. "What do you want me to do?"

"Let me sleep?"

Another sharp tug of chest hair followed.

"No. If Dumouriez fails; if we fail; what do want me to do?"

Beauvais ran a hand through her soft hair.

"Live. I want you to live. I'm not sure that I will be able to offer you that." There was silence between them.

Juliette spoke in a whisper, "You want me to follow Dumouriez?" She felt Beauvais' chest shudder with a deep drawing of breath.

"You could choose from the eligible men of Europe. Why would you want to spend a life on a captain of dragoon's pay, even if I survive the witch-hunt that will follow?" Again, the darkness was filled with silence.

"My life before this was filled with people making decisions for me. As much as I loved my husband, I was never allowed to make a choice. I don't want counts, princes or kings. I want what I have now."

"I can't allow myself to think of a new life, of peace, not yet. Too much is uncertain. I have a son and to have the prospect of a life with you, a family again and then lose it all would be too…" Beauvais stopped. In the dark he pulled Juliette to him and kissed her. "If you stay, we are vulnerable. You can see that? I will be implicated. Dumouriez will look out for himself and as for that weasel Genet."

"Genet?"

"Yes, every army has representatives from the Assembly but not this one. The most powerful of all France's armies. Dumouriez thinks it's because the Assembly wouldn't dare send men here. I am not so sure. Besides, Mahieu told me a few home truths about our friend, Citizen Genet. I will need to silence him. In the meantime, I will return to my regiment. Courtois will not follow Dumouriez, if he allies himself with Austria."

"But what about that other captain, the one who wanted to court martial you? La…"

"Lavigne is now a major. I don't know. He could be a problem. How do you know about that?"

"Genet told me. He tried to warn me that you were a tainted man; a man without honour. It would have been a little sincerer if he hadn't been staring at my breasts while talking to me."

"I can't blame him. He is only human, at least I think he is."

The couple giggled and kissed again.

"So why did he want to court-martial you? Do you have problems making friends, Captain Beauvais?"

"Well I'm not as adept as you, clearly." Beauvais winced as Juliette kissed him and found a soft patch of chest hair to pull. "Anyway, did your friend, Monsieur Genet, not tell you?"

"Yes, he did. He told me that you killed five men; five of your own men. Part of me has wanted to know, another part feels that our lives beforehand no longer matter. Everything has been torn up. Only the future counts."

"Now you sound just like a revolutionary. A Phrygian cap would really suit you." Beauvais kissed her head tenderly.

"So, is it true?"

"Yes, it is true. They were men from Lavigne's squadron. One day I will tell you about it, but not now. I need to sleep."

"Did they deserve to die?"

"For what they had done, yes, yes they did."

Juliette kissed Beauvais and turned in to cuddle up to his warmth. In a matter of hours Juliette would be miles away, riding to find the army of General Miranda and he would return to the fishing vessel. He allowed himself the luxury of dreamless sleep as the clock tower struck three chimes, across the silent town of Breda.

The Hague: 1st March 1793

Servants of the royal household of William the Fifth, Prince of Orange and Stadtholder of the United Provinces greeted the weary travellers just after one in the morning. The Duke and Captain Craufurd had been found rooms and fresh linen delivered. The journey from Hellevoetsluis had been remarkably smooth; the bluster of Bentinck had transformed three changes of horse into remarkably efficient affairs.

By the time of their arrival though, Bentinck had spent twenty-four of the last twenty-seven hours in the saddle. Exhaustion and four servants had carried him to his bed. Of the Prince's staff, only a man shrouded in an admiral's jacket to ward off the night's chill, was on hand. Admiral Jan Hendrik van Kinsbergen, a man of heavily creased features and thick greying hair, greeted the Duke and told him a meeting would be convened just after breakfast. The sloop that had followed the Royal Yacht to the mouth of the Diep had travelled further along the coast and brought word to The Hague of the British arrival. At least the morning meeting would allow a meeting of minds between the royal princes and a joint plan of action to be struck.

At the appointed hour, both men were received into a grand dining hall; the Prince with a thick comb of auburn red hair flanked by wire grey sides was of a surprisingly slim build considering the food already piled onto his plate. Admiral van Kinsbergen took the other breakfast berth. After introductions, breakfast was resumed. Craufurd sat next to an empty table setting.

"Seems you have worn my finest General out," the Stadtholder said dryly.

"Forgive me, but I thought it best that we agree on where you might like my troops deployed, your Majesty, as a matter of some expedience," York spoke carefully.

"Yes, a plan, of course, what to do?" Orange scoured the table, "butter, where is it?"

A servant stepped forward, found the butter dish and placed it next to the Prince. Without the slightest hint of acknowledgement, the Prince sliced open a pastry before smearing it with butter and devouring it.

"Yes," Orange finally spoke after considerable chewing. "Well, discuss the matter with Bentinck and my admiral," a brief nod in the direction of Kinsbergen, "I'm sure whatever you decide will be acceptable. Admiral, will you annotate the decision for my approval?"

Kinsbergen nodded.

"Now tell me, what news from London?" With that the Prince of Orange changed the subject and no further military matters were discussed until the meeting after breakfast.

Admiral van Kinsbergen unfolded a map showing the territories of the Provinces. Bentinck had still not appeared and he sat alone with the Duke and Craufurd.

"I fear the General has been detained on another matter this morning." Kinsbergen seemed pained to continue, "It seems…" He traced the line of the Diep on the map, "That yesterday, the Governor of the fortress of Breda abandoned his position to the French. Under the terms of the agreement he has marched his men to Willemstadt. Count de Bylandt, commander of Breda, arrived here in the last two hours to explain his actions to his Majesty."

York and Craufurd looked at the map.

The Duke spoke "What do you think, Admiral?"

Kinsbergen stroked greying stubble. "I don't know. If the French intend to take Willemstadt, why send our men in that direction? Dumouriez is shrewd but this makes no sense."

"And so, this is a feint, sir?" Craufurd leaned forward.

"Maybe; I'm not the soldier. That is your department. What would you do?" Kinsbergen asked.

York looked at Craufurd. "What would you advise me, if the roles were reversed?"

The young captain studied the map. "Well, we don't know the size of the French army, so we are all guessing. But, if he sent the Dutch west on this road…"

Craufurd pointed at the track from Breda, he clearly doesn't want them in the way for his crossing…here."

"Gorcum," Kinsbergen nodded, "from there, he can turn left towards Numansdorp. If he can bounce the Diep and cross the Island of Dordrecht, then we have problems."

"Can he cross? What about the Dutch navy. You are the admiral," York offered a smile, in case there should be any doubt in the matter.

Kinsbergen smiled, "Yes, the navy. Well we have one or two challenges it seems" he uttered in a resigned manner. "You know in my time, I have fought in the service of the Russian Navy and a couple of years ago, briefly, in a joint operation with your Royal Navy. In all of my years at sea and in the service of the Stadtholder, I have never known such fear as exists now."

Craufurd looked anxiously at the Dutchman, "Because of the Revolution in France?"

"That and more; six years ago, there was nearly a revolution here. I was implicated. Oddly enough, the late King Louis may have funded it. There is irony for you! Now, for every ship that I can man, three more lay idle. Sailors have been called in to shore up the gaps in the army's ranks. Others have left to seek a better paymaster. And some actively crave a revolution here. Crossing the Diep might be easier for the French than we think. His Majesty knows this. He has kept me close because he doesn't trust anyone, least of all me."

"Surely sir, you cannot mean that?" There was ill-concealed horror in the young captain's voice.

"Whatever you decide on the deployment of your forces, decisions here will be delayed, obfuscated over. The letter that Bentinck sent to the Mayor of Hellevoetsluis still sits unsigned on the Prince's desk. In his mind he is still considering whether he needs your help. He will still be considering the matter when the French arrive here."

"But it won't come to that," York offered a calming voice. "Dumouriez will be defeated. Still, we mustn't let him cross the Diep."

"Or capture Willemstadt," Kinsbergen muttered.

"I thought you said he was going for Gorcum" Craufurd said, checking the map again.

"He is, I'm certain but he is wily, perhaps a gambler too? Perhaps he sent Bylandt's men by way of Willemstadt to weaken the resolve of the soldiers there?" Kinsbergen stroked his chin again.

"Would that work, sir?" Craufurd asked glancing worriedly in the direction of the Duke.

"Not if I know General Boetslaar. Dumouriez has his match in that man!"

"So, can you keep Willemstadt supplied? And support my men if we move to…" York studied the map, "Numansdorp and Dort on the Isle of Dordrecht."

"Yes, I will find a vessel. Crew her myself if I have too. Of course, the orders may not be authorised from the Prince in time. And I may need to find a new employer afterwards," Kinsbergen smiled.

The Duke of York smiled, rose and shook Kinsbergen's hand, "My father has one or two connections in the Admiralty."

"I might hold you to that. I will meet you in Hellevoetsluis by tomorrow morning. The port is a bit congested from what I understand. I must seek His Majesty's approval before I leave. If he thinks I am keeping a weather eye on you, then assent will be granted all the easier for it."

York half-smiled, somewhat surprised by Kinsbergen's statement, "This isn't how I thought allies were meant to be?"

"In my experience of the world, sir, it is how allies are; now, more than ever." Kinsbergen bowed deeply.

CHAPTER THIRTEEN

Reifener.

Hanover: 1st March 1793

Both battalions of the 10th Regiment were on the move, heading northwest from Hanover to Celle to drill with another battalion of infantry. At last rumours transformed into certainty, the 10th would be deployed and excitement had spread across the barracks.

Thankfully for Krombach, since his clash with Corporal Gauner their paths had not crossed. The company's fortune seemed to be improving under Brandt; at least that was the consensus between Krombach and the two Pinsk boys. Roner had been transferred as the Company Sergeant-Major; the corporals had moved out of the barracks; more cots could be crammed into the main building and recruits had arrived with more still waiting in Celle.

The musketeers of the 10th had drawn ahead of wagons which carried tents, baggage and supplies for the seven days which the battalion was expected to be away; the warm spring morning making the march pleasurable. With the ache of his pack and the dead weight of musket rubbing against his shoulder gone from his mind, Krombach remembered what he had planned to share with the Pinsk brothers before the news of the battle training had broken. After an hour on the march, he had a chance to do just that.

The road ahead stretched through the unbroken landscape of small farms set in clearings. Conifers, ash and elm flanked the boundaries of the farmland and bordered the road ahead, at least as much as Krombach could see. When the order finally came from Captain Brandt, the men fell out and scrambled for any decent spot to sit. Krombach looked for the brothers and soon found Tomas and Henry chatting to one of the new recruits.

"Hallo, you two." He smiled at Tomas and Henry and nodded to the new man.

Tomas busily filled two brown-headed clay pipes with tobacco while Henry fished a small bag from the side of his pack, expertly unpacking a cloth; a bundle of fine dried grass; a steel striker which fitted over his large knuckles and a large sharpened piece of flint. Within a couple of swift blows of the striker across the flint, he had transferred the spark to the dried grass; a dozen soldiers appeared to light up from the healthy orange glow of the brothers' pipes. The boys smiled at their proficiency and passed the pipes for Krombach and the recruit, Andreas Reifener, to try. Krombach declined but Reifener drew heavily before turning a very grey colour and coughing violently.

"Krombach this fine specimen of Hanoverian youth is Andreas Reifener. No less than Sergeant Winckler himself told us to look after him for some reason. He can't march straight and is dangerous with a musket, to friend and foe. However apparently, he can cook, so who knows, he might yet come in handy." Tomas spoke, his voice full of teasing warmth.

Krombach offered his hand which Reifener shook rather limply. "I'm Krombach; don't worry about these two. When they first joined up, nobody let them near a musket for two months and they still can't shoot straight now."

Reifener cut a rather sorry picture in his uniform, looking like a boy of no more than fifteen when he was, in fact, some ten years older.

"You do look a bit thin for a cook, though." Tomas added, rather unhelpfully, but Reifener shrugged it off with a smile, which had barely left his face since Krombach had seen him.

"Actually, I'm a baker, or was, until my uncle made me enlist last week," Reifener spoke with a gurgle of laughter at the end of his sentence, as if joining the army was a matter which hadn't concerned him at all.

"Why is Old Boots being so charitable?" Krombach asked. 'Old Boots' was the company's nickname for Sergeant Winckler, when he was out of earshot. "There is something in this for him, no doubt."

"He seemed friendly to me. Spoke to my uncle for a while and then said that I might come to be of great service to him and the nation," Reifener chuckled.

"Are you planning to bake for the French?" Tomas said quickly, Reifener threw a friendly punch towards Tomas' shoulder.

"Apparently, Andreas already left a bun in some girl's oven in Hanover, that's the reason he has joined our merry band."

Henry perched with his back against an elm tree; spoke between heavy draws on his pipe, his bicorne drawn down to shield his eyes from the glare of the bright morning sunlight.

Reifener blushed and gurgled laughter.

"Anyway, look at his bloody uniform Krombach. Couldn't you have sorted out something better than this?" Tomas pulled at the sleeves of the jacket and Reifener's hands disappeared inside.

It was as if he had shrunk by a third on the morning march. "What's the point of having someone on headquarters duties that can read and write and then this sort of nonsense occurs?"

"Honestly boys, you wouldn't believe what goes on at headquarters," Krombach smiled and tapped his nose as if there were secrets he dare not tell. "But as for uniforms, we did have a tailor present, but he was only there to measure up the officers. For the rest there were a few uniforms to fit the likes of Hartmann, for everyone else there was one size and that was it. Why didn't you take him to the tents?"

In the tented city that had grown up in the barracks, a number of wives offered services to alter jackets and trousers, but since the news of the battalion's impending exit, the queues had grown daily.

"We tried but Gauner was drilling us like a maniac. We were always the last to finish, last to find a meal. You really have missed some fun," Tomas quipped.

"Old Boots did you a favour I think. Gauner gave us a bit of a rough time but had you been there, you would have had it ten times worse," Henry added, rather unhelpfully.

"Thanks you two. Well, I suppose there's some advantage to being able to spell after all," Krombach retorted, but the three knew that Krombach had not been sent to headquarters duties because he was literate, but to keep out of the grasp of Corporal Gauner.

Krombach could in fact read and write in German and some English and spoke enough Dutch and French to sell a variety of fish. Had he gone on many more selling trips with his uncle, his vocabulary may have improved enough to aid him in other areas. His uncle rarely went to bed alone, having made some conquest which Sebastian had always pretended not to notice, if only so that he would not report those encounters to his mother, who always wanted to know the details of every trip the pair had been on.

"Get up and get ready to move," Gauner's voice broke across the conversation, "very nice of you to join us, Mister Krombach," Gauner passed by the four soldiers, his eyes full of hate and his stare locked on Krombach.

"Corporal," Krombach nodded. When the corporal had moved on down the length of the column, Krombach quickly whispered. "Listen, there is something not right about Gauner."

"You mean beside the fact that he has fists bigger than your feet and he wants to knock your head off?" Tomas whispered, slinging his pack back on.

"Remind me, why I like you again Pinsk?" Krombach said, struggling with his own pack. "No, not that. Well, not just that. Before we left he delivered a message to headquarters. Neuberg was away and Major Volgraf was commanding in his place."

The boys listened as they tightened up equipment and checked one another's packs and strapping, wary of leaving anything that Gauner might seize on.

"And?" Henry said, his eyes flicking around for any patrolling N.C.O.s.

"Most messengers were in and out of that room in under a minute. Gauner delivers a message and he is in there for ten. And when he comes out he and the Major are both smiling, sharing a private joke. Just then

Captain Brandt arrived to see if there was any post for him and saw the faces on the Major and Gauner. The captain didn't seem too happy about it, but didn't say anything. Don't you think that's odd? "

"What do you think it means; other than Brandt might just have been unhappy at seeing you?" Tomas asked, his humour failing to conceal his own nervous tension as the young soldiers waited for the call of the company sergeant to form up into a marching column again.

"I'm not sure yet. Old Boots might know. Either way, it probably won't be great for us." Krombach smiled weakly at the three men and headed back to his place in the column of red coats forming up on the road.

London: 1st March 1793

Dundas studied the brief dispatch from the Duke of York, noting the date and time of the letter. The Brigade of Guards would be landing imminently, if they hadn't already. Still the words 'chaotic' and 'disorganised' sprang off the page, making Dundas shudder. Holland was in a worse situation than either man had imagined.

If that matter were not challenging enough, the preceding letter from Lieutenant General Fawcett directly impugned Dundas' control of the Ministry. Fawcett, the most senior soldier in the King's service, ruled Horse Guards and the pair clashed regularly as demands of government were borne by an under resourced field army. At least that was how Fawcett saw the matter. Dundas had read the report from Fawcett three times and each time brought contorted howls of rage. Indeed, he had only read the Duke's dispatch as means of escape from the accusations of Fawcett but now he wished he had not bothered.

The door swung open without knocking and Brooks Jackson entered.

"Thought you might need...?" Jackson unveiled a bottle of whiskey from inside his jacket. Dundas motioned him to sit which Dickson, Dundas's chief clerk, took as his queue to leave and slipped noiselessly out of the room.

"Are you sure you care to drink with a man who's..." Dundas searched for the phrase in Fawcett's letter. "Treatment of the army is endangering the nation," Dundas peered over the top of the letter at Jackson.

"I've drunk with worse 'enry. Much worse," Jackson grinned bearing more of a resemblance to a pirate from the age of Drake than a respectable Commissary General.

"So, what are you supposed to have done now?"

"General Fawcett has seen it fit and proper to set the world straight about the next infantry brigade that is being prepared for Holland. Not only to me but to His Majesty, the Duke of York, Sir James Murray, the Duke's Chief of Staff and Major-general Abercrombie, the man appointed as the Brigade commander." Dundas spoke with ire in his voice.

"His words: 'The Brigade is wholly unfit for overseas service and there are no others that can be sent'…and… 'I was not consulted upon the subject until it was too late to remedy the evil,' " a scowling Dundas peered over the document at Jackson before continuing.

"And whose fault is this? Why mine, of course; lack of manpower; the Fencibles draining Fawcett of men. Shall I continue?"

Jackson had retrieved two tumblers from the silver drinks tray, "Depends. Is it making you feel better?" Jackson smiled. "Broad shoulders 'enry old mate. That's what you need for this job and that's what you got. Will all be forgotten the moment we sweep the Frenchies from the field."

"And if we don't?"

"Then a toast to the man with the foresight to raise the Fencibles. Cheers 'enry."

Brooks Jackson had already drained the single malt and was searching for a refill before Dundas had put the glass to his lips.

CHAPTER FOURTEEN

Bridgehead.

Herstal: 3rd March 1793

Herstal was uninviting on the eye. Squat cottages, wreathed in smoke, gave way to open caste mining on the periphery, thawing snow stained black by the unceasing labour of mineworkers. Its one redeeming feature to General Miranda was the old roman bridge whose solid stone arches spanned the Meuse and offered roads leading north and east.

Miranda had occupied one of the few two-tiered buildings at the heart of Herstal, the Stadhuis, a tired and decidedly functional looking building in a town of craftsmen and mine workers. To here, a stream of reports had filtered throughout the day on the position and strength of the Austrians. A bridgehead had been seized on the eastern side of the Meuse the previous morning but caution had dogged Miranda's every decision. If the army of the Ardennes crossed the Meuse so too would any supply column; if the army was forced to retreat, it would be caught hard against the banks of a deep river. Disaster would surely follow.

Just three miles to the south stood Liege, garrisoned by the Austrians, strength unknown. The enemy could advance overnight and cut Miranda's line of supply or retreat. Ten miles to the north stood Maastricht and beyond that, the main Austrian winter quarters. The conservative estimate was fifty-thousand of the enemy camped within three days striking distance. The National Assembly had ordered Miranda to strike first. His force of thirty thousand would catch Prince Josias off-guard and drive him back across the Rhine.

Sebastián Francisco de Miranda y Rodríguez de Espinoza had powerful friends at the National Assembly. He could imagine speeches given exalting the success of such far-sighted orders. For a moment, even he had been caught up in the bold direction of such a strike, but now the reality was somewhat different. At forty-three, Miranda, a Venezuelan born professional soldier, had fought on three continents and travelled to more countries than he cared to remember.

He was popular amongst the ranks too; his soldiers had christened him 'Le Toréador'. Rugged good looks, still bearing the testament of a handsome youth, blended with gentle middle-age. The first flecks of greying temples nestled in the rebellious wave of jet-black hair, which Miranda casually pushed back, when deep in thought. Warm brown eyes and a face that rarely delivered a scowl made Miranda a man who had conquered hearts during time spent in the royal courts of Russia, Spain and Great Britain where the soldier and adventurer debated and discussed the politics of rebellion and revolution in the New World.

He counted few men as enemies and had struck an easy friendship with Dumouriez and now he wished he had heeded his friend's advice. Orders and a private message had been delivered an hour earlier by an angel masquerading in the dark green of a dragoon's uniform. Even three days of living in the roughest of conditions had somehow added to her earthy beauty. Were there time she would be another conquest he would aim to make but the general sensed that such sport would be denied him. Juliette was somewhere in one of the dingy rooms above enjoying the luxury of a hot bath and then clean sheets to rest her head on.

Reluctantly he dragged his mind back to matters at hand.

In all of Miranda's military experience, from North Africa to America, he could not remember dealing with so shambolic an army. Dumouriez had been right; the army of the Ardennes was at best an army of defence, a 'Corps of Observation'. The army lacked cavalry to find the enemy and artillery to match the Austrians in battle.

Miranda had studied his formations at length. There were perhaps half a dozen of the battalions in whose abilities he had absolute trust and two of those were posted on the far side of the Meuse at this moment. A sharp rattle on the door disturbed the General from his thoughts.

A young hussar officer stepped into the dim light of the small library room that Miranda had taken for his own use, leaving the door ajar. The General, a tall, slender man, deep-olive tan set against a crisp white silk shirt and clean white breeches, frowned at a map of the Meuse. Casually draped on the leather chair behind him was his jacket, a rich blue encrusted with gold ribbon around the cuffs and neck. His posture suggested that he was untroubled, his voice suggested otherwise.

Miranda spoke, barely looking up, "Report?"

The pallid hussar gulped for air, drawing deep breaths. "Yes sir, just returned. My Captain said you would want to hear from me; The Austrians, sir …North."

"Show me; where?"

The hussar walked over, studied the map and placed a gloved finger.

"How many and when did you see this?"

"Two thousand infantry with guns. And cavalry. Dragoons, three squadrons." The hussar checked his pocket watch. "Around two hours ago."

"Two hours ago?" Miranda fixed the hussar with a look of disbelief.

"Yes, sir; I lost two men in my patrol. Two other patrols are missing, long overdue. We hid from the

Austrian cavalry, to see what was coming behind. As we tried to work our way back around, one of their patrols caught us."

Miranda looked at the young cavalry soldier. He was exhausted, shocked. Of his three-man patrol, he was the only one to escape with his life. Even in such a small command, guilt of survival would play on a man's conscience, for months, perhaps years. Miranda was considering a few words of comfort when he noticed movement outside the door way; another hussar.

"Come in." He spoke quickly and smiled as reassuringly as he could to the young Hussar ensign.

A corporal from the same regiment, the 6th Hussars, marched in, snapped swiftly to attention.

"Report, sir," the corporal spoke assuredly, Miranda nodded.

"Hussars, two squadrons with horse guns; north on our side of the river."

Miranda looked at the map. "Show me."

The corporal pointed and both the General and ensign leaned forward.

"Corporal, take a message to the troops at the bridgehead. They are to withdraw at once, 3rd Legere, then the 4th Legere. The ..." Miranda paused and looked at his orders, "the Fourteenth Nationals to hold the perimeter until the Legere are across then begin their withdrawal."

The men of the Legere battalions were a precious asset, they had proved their worth in the American war. The Fourteenth, the Black Lions, were one of the National Battalions. It pained the General to think it, but such troops, in this circumstance, were expendable.

Across the river, the bridgehead resembled something of a wide horseshoe in shape, both ends resting on the banks of the Meuse. The 4th Legere held the right flank and Black Lions, the centre. The left-hand side was covered by the 3rd Legere which guarded the single road to Maastricht. The bulk of this battalion was posted behind a thick wall of pine trees, far too dense for most troops to stand up in, let alone operate in. Two companies had been deployed in thin skirmish lines, operating in obscurity on the far side of the pines. The road plunged straight through the woods for three hundred yards and the opening beyond was no more than a thin sliver of light. However, the colonel had rotated his companies through skirmish duty in hourly shifts and all had experienced at least one bout beyond the safety of the pine wall. Save for the passing of friendly cavalry patrols, there had been little action.

Now, however, there was the sporadic rattle of musketry. For the first time today, something was happening in the rolling terrain beyond the forest. The men of the two companies waiting to move up to relieve those now in action, began to check their weapons and equipment in earnest as a lone figure burst from the road between the pines. The runner found the Colonel of the 3rd Legere just as a messenger from General Miranda arrived.

The 14th Nationals, the Black Lions, had spent the day toiling along their section of the perimeter with an array of tools 'liberated' from the miners on the outskirts of Herstal. Half a dozen pioneers from one of the line battalions had also been ordered forward to aid the battalion's effort in building a defensive position. The pioneers bore the distinguishing features of their profession. Each wore thick leather aprons and matching calf-skin gloves, functional and a symbol of their elite status and retained the white uniforms of the ancient regime. Pioneers were the only men in the army permitted to wear a full beard, another symbol of their prestige and each strutted with bold arrogance, carrying wickedly-honed axes.

Their arrival was an imposing sight.

Even though their battalion colleagues were nestled in the relative safety of the western river bank, the bearded warriors seemed to take a perverse pleasure in being called upon for such arduous work.

Until the arrival of the various digging tools and the pioneers, the men of the 14th had taken to clawing at a stretch of open farmland with bayonets, musket butts or stones. The left of their position rested on pine woodland currently held by the 3rd Legere. To their front lay a small tracked road arrowed across bare fields to another farm settlement, some three-quarters of a mile distance. The ground was flat, featureless apart from the field boundaries of bushes, no more than knee-high. To the south of the Fourteenth's position lay another large, thick pine wood, held by the 4th Legere.

If the enemy were to attack the bridgehead, the ground ahead of the Black Lions was the safest to manoeuvre in. It could also have become a deadly killing ground, if the French had positioned a battery of artillery to support the infantry. The artillery had been expected earlier in the day, but by three o'clock none had arrived.

Jean-Baptiste drew heavily on a clay pipe and watched four large redoubts in various stages of construction, each a mixture of pine trees, mud and snow. His hands ached, two hours of work had just finished and now the company was being rested. Nearby muskets stood in triangulated clusters, should the call to arms occur. Jean-Baptiste, enjoying the sensation of the tobacco in his lungs, sipped steaming black coffee from his battered tin cup then noticed most of the men in his company had turned and were looking past him.

The messenger had raced from the position of the 3rd Legere and was now bearing down rapidly on the Black Lions. The hussar slowed to speak to Captain Davide, before tearing off again towards one of the two central redoubts, either side of the small road.

Davide resumed his course towards Mahieu and the blackened coffee pot which sat wedged on three large stones and a small flickering fire. The captain carried a small charred mug which one of the soldiers stood near the fire took and filled; Davide nodded his thanks before turning to Mahieu.

"I shouldn't let the men get too comfortable Sergeant."

"What did the messenger say?"

"Nothing to me; wanted to know where Colonel De La Faye was. We will find out soon enough." Davide sipped the black tar brew.

"This coffee is awful, Jean." Davide smiled.

"Thank you, sir" Mahieu smiled weakly and reached inside his jacket pocket for a small polished silver flask.

"This might help." A small tot of brandy was added to Davide's cup.

The message delivered, the hussar raced towards the position of the 4th Legere. The crackle of musketry had increased from the north, beyond the woods and behind the positions occupied by the 14th. Both men watched movement in the ranks of the light infantrymen: men were packing equipment and extinguishing fires while non-commissioned officers barked orders. Soon three of the four companies had hastily formed into a column of march, turned about and begun to retire towards the bridge and the safety of the west bank of the Meuse.

The remaining company had spread into pairs of men, a thin skirmish line poised for orders. As it did so, figures began to emerge from wood-lined road. As these soldiers passed through the waiting skirmish line and headed for the bridge, Mahieu could see that three men bore musket wounds, another, who looked deathly pale, was being carried on the back of a compatriot, both men's dirty white uniforms smeared with crimson.

As the men of Mahieu's company watched the majority of the 3rd Legere leave, the other battalion started to make similar preparations. Murmurs of unease passed between the men of Captain Davide's company, worried glances from one to another. Mahieu turned to face his fellow Black Lions, did his best to look unconcerned and poured himself some more coffee just as a runner arrived, looking for the captain who was watching the exodus of the troops from either flank with more than a touch of concern.

"Captain Davide?" The officer turned to see a boy of no more than sixteen.

"Yes."

"Colonel's compliments sir. You are to take your company and relieve the 3rd Legere. The battalion is to withdraw as soon as the Legere battalions have gone. You have the honour of forming the rear-guard."

"Fine, just fine." Davide drained his cup and turned to his men, most of whom had heard the order.

"Well gentleman, it seems as if the some of the best battalions in the army need our help. Let's show them that the Black Lions aren't afraid. *'Formez le Peleton'*, quick as you can."

There was a momentary pause where no one seemed to move.

"That means now. Move it!" Mahieu's voice snarled disapproval at the delay in the men's reaction to form into their platoons, ready to march.

Between them, Davide, Mahieu and the other sergeants of 6th Company jostled the men into position and by a quick march, more of a jog than a walk, covered the five hundred yards to their new position. The company halted, turned and straightened up to deploy into a close order line, fifty yards behind the skirmish line of the 3rd Legere and around four hundred yards from the prospects of safety. Not that much was moving on the bridge. The three companies of the 3rd Legere had arrived after the 4th and were now waiting while that battalion filed across the bridge.

The sounds of musket fire were now more audible, the crackles of fire answered by more distant replies but in a far greater number.

From the northern road between the trees one of the two companies posted on the far side of the woods jogged back towards the position of Davide's men. Mahieu watched a young Light Battalion officer blow three short blasts on a whistle and point in the direction of the close order company of the 'Black Lions'. Within a couple of minutes, sixty of France's best soldiers were sheltering behind the men of the 14th National Battalion. Mahieu watched Davide walk over and talk to the young infantry captain while most of the returning light infantrymen dropped to their haunches to recover their breath. Only then did Mahieu realise that the increased popping of musketry wasn't just coming from the north, but east too.

In the open ground beyond the four redoubts, fine traces of smoke could be seen, personal skirmish duels that were now being fought in the killing grounds ahead of the redoubts. The rattle of drums carried on the chill afternoon wind. Either side of the road, two long lines of Austrian infantry, in grubby brown greatcoats, had emerged from dead ground in the distance and begun a slow advance on the redoubt. A pair of battle standards raised in the centre of each battalion, dancing in the afternoon light on poles of yellow, red and black.

Davide had returned to examine his infantry line. The men's ages reflected the broad spectrum from which the previous year's draft had been drawn.

Youths of sixteen, who could barely grow enough stubble to shave, stood shoulder to shoulder with men in their late forties. A few had seen war in America. In the battles of the previous year the battalion had been held in reserve. The boredom of inaction and hard labour which dogged a soldier's life, as it had for most of that day, was now replaced by tension and fear in the ranks of Davide's command. Across the three lines, men had fallen out, desperate to relieve bodily functions. Many of Davide's men had never fired the Charleville pattern IX musket in anger. Good quality gun-powder had been in short supply in the previous year. The captain knew he needed to focus the men's attention on him.

More movement to the north, the men of the last company posted on the far side of the pine wood line began to make the trek back towards the security of the ranks of the 14th. As they did so, the light company who had only paused moments before to recover breath and composure, moved off back towards the bridge. More heads in the company turned, men were clearly wondering whether their best option was to run and join the queue at the bridge.

"Men of 6th Company," Davide's voice cut across the sound of distant battle and the scenes of confusion at the bridge. "Black Lions, *'Garde à vous!'*."

Mahieu cajoled a few stragglers back into the ranks, the rest of the company stood to attention at the instruction. Davide paced slowly down the line. He spoke now in a lower tone, forcing the men to listen.

"The army is watching us today. The General himself is watching us." He raised his right arm and pointed across to the west bank. "Why do you think he chose our battalion to fight alongside the Legere? He has heard of the Black Lions. Now he wants to see if we are as fierce as our battle standard."

As Davide spoke the first of two columns of the battalion left the redoubt, the tricolour danced in the breeze alongside the standard of a black lion on a yellow background.

"So listen," Davide continued, "listen to the orders when they come. In a few moments you will load your muskets. Take your time. The sergeants will check each man's musket. Stand together and the Austrians cannot beat us."

Davide smiled and nodded at Mahieu and then hoarsely growled the orders to load. Mahieu and the other two sergeants watched along the files, ready to move to any of the soldiers who were struggling with the drill. Davide strode past Mahieu and spoke quietly to him.

"I'm going to speak to the Colonel, find out what his plans are and then speak to that Legere captain. I have a horrible feeling that we are going to be left with our arses hanging out."

In the moments while 6th Company loaded, the men from 3rd Legere who had left the woods streamed past. All bore powder stained faces and hollow looks of exhaustion. At last, the marching columns of the 3rd started across the bridge. The company that had sought shelter behind the men of the 14th now waited their turn.

On the northern road there was movement, flashes of light and the sounds of musketry as a line of Austrian skirmishers sprang from the cover of the wood line. They were now four hundred yards from 6th Company. Skirmishers flooded the open field to the left and right of the road, behind them further movement. A third battalion of infantry, in brilliant white tunics, began to deploy, this time from the north. Mahieu turned to check the redoubts. The final two companies had left the field defences, which now looked wholly inadequate against the mass of the enemy. Thirty soldiers had remained to act as a skirmish screen to harass the approaching foe. Mahieu did not fancy the odds of survival of those left behind in the thin screen of defending skirmishers.

The two greatcoated battalions that closed from the east were now at four hundred paces. At one hundred or less they would fire and then charge. The redoubts would fall, the bridge was three hundred yards further. The Black Lions had six or seven minutes at most before they were caught up in a deadly crossfire, pinned to the bank of the Meuse and destroyed.

Davide returned, short of breath, having walked as fast as he dared, without breaking into an unseemly trot. He did not stop but hurried on to speak to the Legere commander, whose men were now exchanging long range fire with the advancing white jacketed Austrians. Mahieu could see that the Legere officer bore a look of mild insouciance to the whole situation. The conversation concluded, the officers shook hands and Davide walked as calmly as he dared back to the battalion. He allowed himself a moment then spoke.

"Black Lions, listen to me. In a few minutes, we will be across the river," Davide spoke assuredly, aware that every pair of eyes was on him. "But before we can cross, we must allow the rest of our battalion the time to cross. And then cover the retreat of the brave comrades who man the redoubt. Their lives depend on you!" As Davide finished speaking a spent musket ball disappeared into a patch of snow a few feet to his right. "14th, *'Garde à vous!'*" Davide barked orders and the muskets of the company moved in ragged unison.

To the north a line of Austrian infantry formed up. A thousand bayonets danced in the sunlight. To the east, a roar of musket fire; one battalion had stopped and opened fire on the redoubts to the left of the road. Mahieu could see two bodies slumped in the snow, others wounded. The men of the Black Lions left to man the redoubts were running. On the road between the two Austrian battalions was more movement; enemy cavalry. Three blasts of a whistle and the Legere were running too.

6th Company was the front line. Davide turned and walked to the left corner of the first rank, "*Appretez vos armes!*"

The Austrian skirmishers advanced, crouching low. They were still at one hundred paces when the first men around Mahieu were felled.

"*Armer! Joue!*"

Davide knew the volley would have little effect but if the men did not return fire, they would not stand.

"*Feu!*"

The muskets of the first two ranks crashed out. Davide barked out the orders to reload, another three of his men fell. A second volley rang out, more disorganised than the first.

"*Demi-tour a droite! Par le flanc droite!*"

The line turned about and wheeled quickly to the right, all pretence of parade-ground drill lost. Mahieu growled at men who attempted to move faster than the command warranted.

"*Halte!*"

The company had wheeled through ninety degrees and its flank was now exposed to the advancing ranks of white coated infantry, three hundred yards away. To Davide's front, the battalion in heavy brown greatcoats that had held fire was now no more than two hundred and fifty paces away. The line stood with its back to the bridge, still one hundred yards from the hope of safety. The last marching column of the 14th had begun to make the passage across and only the piquets remained forward of the company now.

At that moment, the thin screen of Black Lions who had held the redoubt broke cover for the safety of Davide's men. They were fifty yards away from the line when the cavalry caught them. Sixty Austrian hussars in sky blue jackets and blood red breeches had given chase. Mahieu watched as every man was mercilessly hacked down, those attempting to surrender given no quarter. The hussars peeled away in shouts of triumph, having little intention of attacking a line of close order troops, at least not until the right moment presented itself. Another troop of hussars moved in a column to the right of the company's position.

"*Demi-tour a droite! Pas accéleré! Marche!*" Davide intended to half the distance to the bridge by marching in quick time. At fifty paces the line halted. David could see the men of one of 3rd Legere companies; true to their officer's word, they had taken up positions on the bridge to offer some form of protection.

"Sergeant Mahieu, take the third rank. An oblique line to our right, keep that cavalry off our flank."

Mahieu nodded and while the other two ranks reloaded, he positioned the line to cover the movement of the hussars, who had now broken from a column and formed a double line. The cavalry were no fools; they remained two hundred yards distant. Out of musket range but close enough to cut off the Black Lions before they had made the fifty yards in the heavy ground. Even if the Black Lions made it, the bridge would become a killing ground. The cavalry would hack their way through fleeing men and the hussars had shown little evidence of wanting to take prisoners.

6th Company waited.

To their left flank enemy skirmishers circled.

Behind them now just one hundred and fifty paces, the wall of white coats advanced. The 3rd Legere provided supporting fire but still more men in files on the left of Davide's command fell. Two of the wounded attempted to crawl back towards the bridge but were cruelly targeted by the sniping of the enemy.

To the centre, the enemy infantry that had halted to let the cavalry, fresh from their easy victory over the Black Lion's forlorn hope of skirmishers, pass through their ranks, began to advance again.

To the right, hussars poised for the killing blow.

Mahieu heard a deep rumble, followed by another, then a third. He watched a large patch of earth shudder, brown mud deposited violently onto thawing snow. A cannonball skipped sixty yards, a second tear in the

ground and then it murderously smashed into the
Austrian cavalry. Four horses, on the left of the hussar
line facing him, collapsed into a smear of blood and
stricken flesh. The second round had missed but the
third also registered a hit. To the left of the line, the
cannonade roared with even more intensity.

The line of white coats which had advanced from the
northern wood had also received fire from the French
twelve-pounders firing from the protection of the west
bank. The enfilading fire had plunged into the long
lines of the two companies nearest the river bank,
causing death and confusion. Davide looked at his men.
The was no drill book instruction follow the next order.

"6th Company…*Courir!*"

The guns crashed out again in support and the Black
Lions ran for their lives.

CHAPTER FIFTEEN

The keys to the Diep.

Hollands Diep: 3rd March 1793

The plan to capture Overfrakkee had been bold.

The *Perseus* had scouted the island at dawn and dusk for four days. Half a dozen jolly boats and a cutter had been moored on a pontoon on the northern shore of Overfrakkee and in all that time the collection of vessels had not moved. Dumouriez decided that under cover of darkness the *Perseus* would seize the boats, bring them back to the southern banks of the Diep and then ferry a landing party of soldiers to a small beach that Mahieu had already reconnoitred. More men would follow.

Seize the battery, seize the island and with it wrestle control of Hollands Diep from the new British arrivals.

The weather had been with them, a new moon and heavy sea mist; perfect for a surprise attack. The *Perseus* had set out to find the boats at around an hour before midnight. Two hours later, the ship had drifted silently back.

The boats were gone.

In the darkness there had been disagreement. Beauvais had suggested landing men in the *Perseus* and trying to ferry enough men over before the force was discovered. The infantry colonel, Cassin, whose men had been selected for the assault, was not persuaded. The Dutch had at least seven hundred men on the island, perhaps more. The attack was over before it had ever begun.

Beauvais pulled his cape around his frame, drawing nearer to the warmth of the fire. The same sea mist and chill of the morning offered no hiding place for him. Juliette had avoided him, punishing him for being kept away from her bed by Dumouriez' scheming. Four nights before, Beauvais had promised he would leave the world of spying and return to the regiment. But now was not that time, especially after the fiasco of the previous few hours. When Beauvais and Cassin had returned to camp and broke the news to Dumouriez, the General exploded in a fit of rage at the incompetence and cowardice around him. Beauvais had never seen Dumouriez act like this.

Mahieu had stayed to scout the Diep, in search of answers to the failure of the previous hours, until a phantom wreathed in mist appeared. Mahieu cursed and whispered quick instructions. The *Perseus* lowered her sail and slowed noiselessly and then began to drift in the pull of the Diep. Mahieu drew in a deep lung-full of air. It was a little after eight in the morning. A faint breeze and the watery outline of a morning sun were testament that the mist would not last.

But sound carried. Noises of a vessel preparing to make the sharp turn into the narrow harbour passage. The ghostly silhouette of a British ship of the line began to form on the wall of mist, her sails reefed. Behind that, translucent light hinted at the bulk of a second. A moment of clarity and the British Seventy-four was revealed in all her glory, her deck full of redcoats.

"We need to leave, now!" Mahieu hissed.

In moments the *Perseus* had hauled her single sail, turned with the breeze and felt the pull of the current draw them towards the safety of the southern bank.

It was just before midday that Arnaud Mahieu completed the journey from the Perseus' berth to the camp, securing a horse from a reluctant hussar, who had been left as part of a screen of troops now observing Overfrakkee and the fort at Willemstadt.

By the way the animal tossed its head on arrival at the camp, both horse and rider were glad to be parted from one another's company. He found Beauvais sat on an upturned empty crate, using another turned on its side as a table and in the act of cleaning a pair of pistols, a cavalry carbine and the small muff pistol that he had killed the hussar with a few days ago. Mahieu looked at the weapon and tried to remember when that was exactly but the days had tumbled into one another. He wasn't even sure which day it was anymore.

"You took your time. Thought you might have sailed away from our happy adventure; can't say I would blame you if you did." Beauvais had not looked up but was busy running a dry rag over the pan of one of the pistols before carefully re-examining it in the now bright sunlight of the spring day.

"And miss your smiling face? Besides you would only ride back to Dunkirk and drag me back here or somewhere worse." Mahieu spoke only partly in jest.

"Not me, Arnaud, not me. I'm quite done with that line of work."

Mahieu cast the dragoon a sideways look. "You going soft, Beauvais? The last person who called me Arnaud was my mother, and then only when I was in trouble."

"Perhaps you are now. Dumouriez wants to see you. Wants to know where his boats went. Of course, he has already blamed Cassin and me for the whole thing."

"And what did you say to that?"

"I blamed you," Beauvais looked up, his crooked face forced a weak smile, "you are still riding like a cripple, despite the boots."

"Thanks. I feel like one after that ride. Where is Dumouriez by the way?"

"In his lair with Cassin and Genet plotting, no doubt." Beauvais had changed weapons and was now checking the mechanism of the '77 pattern weapon, testing to see if the flint, wrapped in a leather flint pad, held firmly in the jaws of the hammer and met the frizzen squarely.

"It's a pity you can't arrange for Genet to come with us on one of our little excursions. It would do him good to see the outside of that tent."

"He's probably afraid that you might not bring him back."

"I might not. He was a slippery bastard before he left Dunkirk for Paris, by all accounts. Now he is playing at being Caesar's clerk in there. Would Dumouriez miss him if he were to disappear one morning?"

"Dumouriez might. But no one else would. Make sure you make a good job of it, unless I beat you to it."

"You, a captain of dragoons, a man of impeachable honour?" Mahieu grinned broadly.

Beauvais rose, leaving the weapons on the upturned crate. "Come on, let's go and fill that tent with the perfume of rotten fish!"

The two men found Dumouriez and Cassin studying a map, deep in conversation. Genet sat at his desk, poised to take fresh instruction. Dumouriez looked up then returned to the map, tracing his fingers along a road and muttering to the infantry colonel.

"So, my wandering sea captain has returned. Did you find the missing boats? Last night's escapade was rather ...unfortunate."

Earlier that morning, as his ship had withdrawn from the stretch of water near Hellevoetsluis, where Mahieu had watched the British manoeuvre into the narrow channel that led to the port, he had indeed spotted the missing vessels and more besides. The craft were ferrying Dutch troops from Willemstadt; the Dutch troops that Dumouriez had forced to retreat in that direction. Had the Dutch been sent elsewhere, the boats would not have been called from the island. It was an unforeseen consequence of the easy victory at Breda.

Beauvais watched as an interested neutral as Dumouriez turned and faced Mahieu. The implication, however slight, that Dumouriez' own plans had been at the root of the problem, threatened to re-ignite the anger of the early morning. But instead the General offered a look an air of calm indifference.

"Mahieu, my friend, it does not matter. An unfortunate set of circumstances, yes? Anyway, it was never in the plan, a side wager, nothing more." Dumouriez stood, palms raised in tacit acceptance of guilt. "Is your ship ready for action tonight?"

Dumouriez continued, not waiting for the answer.

"Colonel, I want a dozen of your best men here in one hour. They answer to Captain Beauvais. Understood?"

Cassin nodded.

"Good," Dumouriez turned to Beauvais and continued. "I want you to return to Overfrakkee. One trip; take gunpowder, find that artillery battery and destroy it. No excuses this time, Julian. Get the job done and by a quarter to eight."

Dumouriez turned and examined the map one last time. "Tonight, timing is everything."

He looked up, turned to face Beauvais and Mahieu and grinned broadly. "While you cause mayhem in Overfrakkee, we are going to capture Willemstadt and the British will scuttle away as quickly as they arrived."

Numansdorp: Sunday 3rd March 1793

Rain spat against the dark of the small windows in the Minister's cottage, nestled in the quiet narrow avenue that led to the church. On any other Sunday, the priest would have been returning from his evening service, a hot meal waiting for him. This was not a normal Sunday. Numansdorp, battered by the squall of a late afternoon storm that arrived to viciously drive away the sea-mist, soaked Dutch soldiers desperate to find cover.

Trevethan could see shapes moving in the dark of the street outside. The weather would put an end to the ferry of small boats that had run throughout the day from Numansdorp to Willemstadt, bringing the remnants of Count de Bylandt's men back to the northern shores of Hollands Diep. The soldiers had marched out of Breda with the full honour of war according to their commander but rather ignominiously in the eyes of everyone who heard the account. Now the church had been thrown open as a temporary shelter. Troops had arrived over the past three days but no decision had been made as to their destination. Many were still camped in Willemstadt. Some had set out for Hellevoetsluis, before being sent back. Accommodation there was already overstretched, now that the British Guards had arrived.

Major Stephen Trevethan chased the last morsels of his stew around the plate and then mopped up the balance with a chunk of fresh bread. For the moment he was alone in the priest's house but no doubt space would be found for some of the officers in their lodgings. Trevethan borrowed an extra candle from the small table opposite his, careful not to disturb a dress that the Priest's wife was in the process of repairing, pushed his plate away to make space and opened a large leather journal. A stabbing pain in the small of his back combined with sore buttocks and calves reminded him that in five days he had managed more riding than he had in the last five months. The engineer considered himself a reasonable horseman but approaching his forty-eighth year in a few months, the elasticity of youth had long since left him. Too much of his sister's cooking had left a layer of insulation and every day this week the riding had been more painful than the day before. Even the boat journey across the choppy Diep had been a blessed relief. Another rattle of rain drove against the window. Thank goodness he would not have to make the journey across the Diep tonight.

Trevethan opened the book and studied his notes, the map that Murray had given to him pressed inside the cover. He unfolded it and began the process of comparing his scribbled observations against the geography of the Diep. Three days ago, he had finished his report and delivered it to the Duke and Sir James. There was a question that had nagged him then and he had yet to find a satisfactory answer. Why had Dumouriez let the Dutch troops return to their lines? Why through Willemstadt?

He studied the map again. Breda had cast fresh doubts amongst the Duke and his staff on the stomach of the Dutch for a fight. There were three key places, all defended by Dutch troops, as the situation currently stood. The fort on the southern bank that the French had been besieging for a week was the most secure of the trouble spots in the British opinion. Trevethan had visited twice, met the abrasive General Boetslaar and liked the man almost immediately. He was all that De Haan, the Mayor of Hellevoetsluis had intimated. The fort was well supplied, the soldiers looked well drilled and their morale good, despite the occasional shelling from French howitzers. Even the influx of the soldiers from Breda had not ruffled Boetslaar. The General had set about finding shelter and accommodation for the new arrivals. Willemstadt was in good hands, despite being the last Dutch stronghold on the southern shore. It was the crossings on the northern side of the Diep that worried Trevethan.

The island of Dordrecht was the next concern; if it fell, then Hellevoetsluis would be besieged. However, earlier that afternoon, Trevethan had witnessed two old barges ferrying soldiers from the 1st Guards battalion towards Dort, the main village on Dordrecht. By now, guardsmen would be safely posted on the island. Besides, Dordrecht was only in danger if Gorcum fell and tomorrow, the plan was to ferry the full battalion of the Coldstreams there. A bit of British steel to stiffen the Dutch resolve, Murray had called it. But that depended on the British battalions being able to find the dock space to unload.

So far, the campaign had been dogged by poor cooperation with the Dutch. Only providence had prevented a full-scale disaster.

Trevethan had come from Hellevoetsluis that afternoon when a Dutch frigate had limped into the port having been battered by huge seas. Had the flotilla been delayed by a few short hours the Seventy-fours, dangerously over-crowded, would have been in serious peril. The army could have been lost before a shot was fired.

They were here now and that was all that mattered.

Despite Admiral Kinsbergen's best efforts, six dirty coal barges were the fruits of his labour. The Duke has graciously accepted them and Trevethan pitied those guardsmen who would have got off one transport, only to be dumped onto another which was stained with coal and lord knows what else. The redcoats were needed further along the Diep to hold vital crossing points.

Trevethan looked again at the map. Twenty-four hours and all would be well. Dordrecht was secure now, Gorcum would be secure. But still it didn't make sense. Where were the French?

Bylandt had reported that the French had surrounded him with an army of forty thousand men. The Duke and Murray doubted the figure. General Boetslaar had even more uncharitable thoughts. His furious Dutch oaths needing little translation. Scouting reports had put the French force at no more than fifteen thousand. The French weren't forcing the issue at Willemstadt with any vigour because they didn't have the numbers. Only three field batteries had been deployed against the fort, none of the guns a heavy siege calibre. The whole attack felt like a ruse, nuisance value and nothing more. Boetslaar almost seemed slighted by the lack of effort by Dumouriez.

Furthermore, travellers who had passed through the French lines just south of Worcum, the village on the southern bank of the Oude Maas river facing Gorcum, had seen no more than a battalion of infantry, a handful of cavalry and no artillery at all.

Whatever the French were planning, it wasn't obvious to the Duke or to Trevethan. But then he was just a humble engineer since becoming the chief of staff's personal choice as the staff engineer for the army in Holland.

Road building in Falmouth and beyond could wait. Rebecca would understand, eventually. He had lived with his sister and her family the four years since his wife had died. Rebecca had pleaded with him not to go. In the night after she heard that Trevethan had taken the post she had experienced one of her visions that presaged disaster.

The Cornishman looked once more at the map, folded it and closed the book, rubbing fingertips over the worn cover. The rain had eased and he patted down his pockets feeling for his pouch of tobacco. He needed to smoke and knew that the priest and his wife had both wrinkled their noses at the fumes from his pipe. A stroll first to walk off the stew and maybe something would come to him about the French plan, to his engineer's mind; it was a puzzle that needed solving. He could call in on the officers from the 3rd Regiment and be sociable.

Trevethan heard the Guards officers before he saw them.

The avenue contained a row of white-washed terraced houses, each clean and tended. Whatever else the Dutch short-comings were, from what Trevethan had seen, they were a house-proud nation. From one of these, an oblong shaft of yellow light illuminated the narrow track between the houses and threw shadows onto the wall of the house opposite, riotous puppet shows of movement being projected out, broken by an occasional head which popped out to exhale a lung-full of smoke and be refreshed by the stiffening breeze. As Trevethan strode past he was greeted by a cheery 'Hallo' from a youthful face that had clearly been used to receiving a range of responses in Dutch to his salutations. A gruff, Cornish reply was not what the young officer had expected, still the engineer took the chance to cadge a light for his pipe before walking on. The tobacco was calling him more than the need for conversation with someone less than half his age, whose father had probably bought the promise of a Guards commission while the infant boy was still at his wet-nurse's teat. The system of commissions had been the same for two hundred years. It produced as many good officers as bad. No reason to harbour a grudge and the young man had been kind enough to offer a light for the engineer's pipe. He chided himself and resolved to make amends on the return journey.

Trevethan quickened his pace, climbed a steep bank which rose to the edge of the dyke road and then found steep stone steps that led down to the pontoon. The delight of the dyke system had still not left him. Now there was an engineering task! Numansdorp, like so many of the towns around the Diep, was below water level. De Haan had told him that the fields were fertile in the summer and yet homes rarely suffered from damp, even though they stood below the water table. The engineering of the project, completed two centuries before, fascinated the Cornishman and had made Murray's pitch all the easier.

Trevethan found a sheltered spot to crouch down and look across the waters of the deep. The rain had died away and the wind was lessening all the time. Across the water, a mile and three quarters away were the lights from the fort at Willemstadt. In front of him was a small harbour, where several small craft were moored, riding the slight swell of the Diep.

The ship; it was the other matter that Trevethan couldn't fathom.

Throughout the last five days he had noticed the vessel. Nothing unusual struck him about it at first. On Thursday afternoon he had sat enjoying a rare moment of relaxation at the end of the promenade at Hellevoetsluis. De Haan, ever the genial host, had brought a bottle of beer and the two men watched the fishing boats in the late afternoon light. The mayor had made the connection first. Few ships, if any, returned to the south banks of the Diep with their catch. Most came back to the north and to the safety of his port. He knew them by sight, even at a distance. But the silhouette and shape of the lone boat anchored near Overfrakkee looked…wrong. It wasn't the type favoured by the local fishermen at all, more like one of the deep-water vessels which sailed from Ostend or any of the ports where men fished the Channel. Also, most of the fishing vessels and crews shared camaraderie, yet this ship never anchored with the others, it just poked around the western tip of Overfrakkee at odd times of the day. At the best times for fishing, the dawn and dusk tidal runs in the Diep, the ship was rarely spotted at all.

The conclusion had been that the French were spying on Overfrakkee. But to what end?

Seizing the island without the fort at Willemstadt was just gaining a short-term victory. With only one boat sending a force there would be a painfully slow process. However, if Willemstadt fell, then possession of Overfrakkee became a different matter. Hellevoetsluis would cease to be a viable port for the British. Any ship trying to make the slow turn into the narrow harbour passage would be mauled by any gun batteries that the French could capture or ferry across. But that was a sequence of highly unlikely events, made irrelevant because Willemstadt stood.

Trevethan rose, pushed back a tangle of dark thick curly hair, drew on his pipe and watched the embers glow orange. The heavy night clouds had begun to drift apart and light from the thin crescent of the moon spilled across the waters of the Diep. The Cornishman decided to walk to the end of the pontoon, before turning back and exploring the card game that was evidently in progress at the Guards' billet. The planks of the pontoon wore a silver sheen, soaked by the earlier downpour. Trevethan reached the end of the wooden walkway, coughed heavily and ran a hand over his jacket and trouser pockets searching for a handkerchief. As another fit of coughing came on, the night sky to his right, turned from black to a momentary brilliant white, then a mixture of ambers and reds. A second later a series of booms crashed against him, causing the engineer to crouch for cover and sending his favourite pipe rattling onto the planks of the pontoon before slowly disappearing with a silent splash into the deep. For a moment, Trevethan followed its course and then returned to the scene of fire on the shore opposite. Another explosion and then another.

The western edge of Overfrakkee, where the Dutch had hidden an artillery battery was on fire.

In that moment Trevethan understood.

Willemstadt was about to fall.

By the time that Trevethan had scrambled back up to the road, it was already lined with people, staring across the water towards the flames and smoke that billowed into the night sky. Trevethan headed for the avenue and the Guards billet but ran into a gaggle of the junior officers who had been drinking and playing in the card school, as he picked his way down the bank.

"You!" Trevethan pointed at the young officer whom he had earlier borrowed a light from. "Where is your Major? Where are your men? Get them at once!"

The young ensign looked somewhat stupefied. Behind him a voice called out, "What's this Henners. Who's your uncle?"

Trevethan looked around as the officers piled passed him, but Trevethan caught the arm of the man he had first spoken to. Lieutenant Simon Henson-Jefferies inebriated and excited to join his friend in the dash to see the spectacle shook at the grip of Trevethan but couldn't break the Cornishman's grip.

"What the hell is going on?"

From the darkness and the crowd of figures surging along and up the bank came the figure of the man that Trevethan had spoken to earlier that day.

"Sir," Henson-Jefferies was doing his best to stand to attention, the cold night air working to dampen the effects of the alcohol. "Sir, I think this man is quite mad! He wants to see you. He wants…"

The Guards officer drew up to Trevethan.

"I'm Major Fletcher, 3rd Regiment. And you are?"

"Major Trevethan, an engineer with the Duke's staff. Look I don't have time to explain; when we are in the boats maybe. Yes then." Trevethan paused, composed himself. "Major. I need you to take your men from here and get them to Willemstadt, now."

Fletcher looked at Trevethan.

The engineer spoke again. "The fort is going to be attacked, maybe it is already. If it falls, it will be a long walk to another port and then home for all of us."

Major Fletcher scratched the back of his head, weighing up the preposterous nature of the supposition.

"Sir, it's against the standing orders," Henson-Jefferies spoke in the silence, while around them a press of bodies moved, more and more people coming to see the source of the orange glow in the night sky.

"Sir the standing order from Horse Guards; no deployment on this southern bank of the Diep without authorisation from…"

"Oh shut up, Henson!" Fletcher looked at Trevethan. "How certain are you?"

"As certain as I can be. It's the only explanation that makes sense. We don't have any time to waste."

Mercifully, the currents across the Diep were light, the tide having turned in the last half hour. The storm had blown itself out, the chop of the water buffeted by the occasional blast of cold air. By the time that the three boats had landed by the slipway which led to the fort, nearly thirty minutes had elapsed since the first explosion. Redcoats, unused to rowing, had pulled at the oars and eventually each boat settled into a spasmodic forward motion, occasional oaths exchanged as men and oars clashed, mid stroke.

From the direction of Overfrakkee, smaller flashes of light pricked the night; musket fire. Thankfully, the fires that had been caused in the initial explosions had failed to take hold; the vegetation was too sodden to burn. While the lead boat made its way across Trevethan explained his theory to Fletcher.

It had taken fifteen minutes to assemble just thirty guardsmen. The soldiers had not been confined to their encampment and it seemed many had taken the advantage to go and explore the local hostelries in villages along the northern road that ran between Numansdorp and Hellevoetsluis. Others had perhaps taken advantage of the darkness and confusion to simply blend into the crowd. Trevethan only hoped that thirty men would be enough. It had to be.

The redcoats tumbled out of the boats and formed into a two-man wide column while Trevethan ran ahead and banged at the main door, exchanged words with the sentry and eventually called for the man to fetch General Boetslaar. Seconds ticked away, Trevethan had now been joined by Fletcher and the two exchanged anxious glances. While they waited, Fletcher ordered his men to load their muskets, trying to make use of the passing seconds. What seemed like an age was in fact just over four minutes.

Boetslaar appeared, followed by a series of loud Dutch oaths and orders. A bicorne tumbled out of the darkness and landed in amongst the waiting Foot Guards. Trevethan recognised his own name in the stream of Dutch instructions and Boetslaar had cuffed the hapless sentry around the head as he looked over the walls at the British below. Once inside, the new arrivals turned left and up a flight of stairs to the main allure, the walkway that ran inside the walls of the pentagonal fort.

Boetslaar stood at the top of the steps by a large torch which flickered and danced on the dying northerly winds.

"What are you doing here? Overfrakkee is being attacked. I've already sent fifty men over there." Boetslaar nodded at the salute from Major Fletcher as soon as the officer had crested the steps.

"Sir, the attack isn't there, it's here. The Dutch prisoners from Breda, you still have lots of them here, don't you?"

"Yes. Why?"

"I think Dumouriez has got his own men inside the walls now. Overfrakkee is a signal to them to seize the main gates to troops waiting outside."

Boetslaar considered the matter for the briefest of moments. The eastern walls of the fort were crammed with hundreds of soldiers jostling to watch the spectacle of lights on Overfrakkee. Perhaps the guards at the main South Gate had been drawn away.

"This way. Follow me!" Boetslaar grabbed the torch from the wall and moved swiftly along the allure, pushing men aside as he did.

Trevethan, Fletcher and the handful of redcoats followed on as best they could, dodging the obstacles of men and muskets thrown aside in the wake of Boetslaar's charge. In the moonlight the soldiers could see why the General had led them on this route. The interior of the fort was a cluster of small buildings around a large barracks and Church, the palest of moonlight catching the series of water-ways which cut between the houses. For men unfamiliar with the terrain, the fort's interior was a maze of waterways and blind corners. By taking the walkway along the main wall, all of that had been avoided; the main gate reached in less than three minutes.

Boetslaar stopped and waved the torch above his head. Two sentries stood in place. Boetslaar shouted and one of them raised an arm in reply. Boetslaar shouted the same challenge again and the same response occurred.

The Dutchman muttered something under his breath. Trevethan looked at the two men. They were positioned above the main gate. The gate was closed and Trevethan drew a heavy sigh of relief and sank to his haunches to catch his breath. As he did so he noticed movement in deep shadows under the gate-house.

"It's not right, it's not right." Boetslaar muttered. "They aren't my men."

In the pitch of night, the sounds of a column of horses could be heard. Then the heavy clank of bolts being drawn and timber being moved.

The South Gate was being opened.

Boetslaar roared like a wounded lion and threw the torch into the mouth of the gate. As it spiralled down a dozen soldiers were illuminated momentarily before the torch hit the cobbles and broke apart. Boetslaar drew his sword and threw himself down the steps into the street that led out onto the gateway, musket balls jagging after him from the two guards on the rampart at the main gate.

"Fix bayonets!" Fletcher screamed. "Kill those men. Close that damned gate!"

The Guards officer dived down the steps after Boetslaar. More musketry, this time from inside the gatehouse, whistled past his shoulder. From behind him, Fletcher heard a guardsman grunt and collapse from the stairs and fall into the darkness of the fort.

Trevethan had made for the two sentries who fired at Boetslaar, both now scrambling to reload. In the seconds before he reached the first, the Cornishman had the momentary realisation that he didn't have a weapon on him. His sword and pistol were both hanging up on the door in the Priest's cottage. A brief glance over his shoulder worsened the matter. All the redcoats were descending the steps to the main gate, following their officer. Trevethan made an instant decision. The soldier nearest him had spat out cartridge paper, loaded a ball and was frantically trying to prime the weapon as Trevethan slammed into him, wrapping his arms around the Frenchman and driving him hard back against the wall of the fort. He felt the man crumple as the air was forced out of his body. Before releasing him, Trevethan arched back his neck and drove his forehead into the sentry's nose, hearing the snap of bone and feeling the metallic taste of another man's blood in his mouth.

In the second that Trevethan let the Frenchman go, he felt a whipping sound cut through the air and rolled down and away as the second soldier lunged with a bayonet, now fixed to the end of his musket, having abandoned the task of loading. Trevethan had rolled away and knelt facing the sentry who stood over the body of his colleague. Around the Cornishman, the percussion of muskets and pistols rang with the scrape of metal on metal and the cries of men wounded or dying, but he was oblivious to it all.

For a moment, the Frenchman cast an anxious glance over the wall and then turned to face Trevethan, a look of triumph on his face. Below, three of his compatriots had manged to drag the timber beams used to secure

the door and tip them into the lake by the main gate.
French dragoons had crossed the bridge and were
dismounting to join the fight. The numbers were going
to tip heavily in the French favour very shortly. The
gate would be held and Willemstadt would fall.

Trevethan drew himself up. The musket of the first
sentry was wedged under the man's motionless body.
Trevethan patted down his coat quickly and thrust his
hand into a jacket pocket. A sturdy handkerchief was
released and as the Frenchman stepped forward,
Trevethan wound this around his left hand. He had
avoided fights in the ale houses of Falmouth but had
certainly seen more than a few in his time. He drew a
deep breath and gave more ground, aware that step by
step, he was being forced away from any help.

The Frenchman lunged once, a feint to the body.
Trevethan followed the move and arched to avoid it.
His attacker grinned, a second lunge, more purposeful
and to the right, Trevethan swayed left. The Frenchman
sensed victory, his target seemed off balance and the
sentry drove the musket will all his force towards the
chest of Trevethan.

Trevethan saw the blow coming and rolled slightly to
his right, wincing as the bayonet sliced the fleshy palm
of his left hand. It took all of Trevethan's might to grasp
the end of the musket barrel and then yank it sharply
back and down. The Frenchman, unbalanced by this
change to his own momentum, was pulled closer to the

249

engineer, who drove a right hook into the infantryman's ear, followed by a second and third into the face. Trevethan pulled again on the musket. This time there was no resistance. The Frenchman had collapsed at the Cornishman's feet.

Around the engineer were the sounds of hundreds of Dutchmen, troops loyal to Boetslaar. The sounds of musketry had drawn men to the South Gate. For a short while, a pushing match had broken out. There was no way to close the main gate, other than the press of bodies. The French soldiers inside the gate had been killed or captured. Fletcher had managed to withdraw a dozen guardsmen who now positioned themselves around the crenellations of the main gate, happily taking pot shots at the French dragoons stranded outside.

In the dark, French infantrymen having reached the bridge, now faced the prospect of rushing at the closed gate and trying to force it open again by weight of numbers. All the while, musketry from the main wall thickened, as the Dutch defenders added their muskets to the British fire.

For the second evening in a row, Colonel Cassin aborted his attack.

Breda: 5th March 1793

Genet saw to it that Colonel Cassin was replaced. Dumouriez had wanted him executed on the spot, threatening to do the job himself. Yesterday had not been one of Dumouriez' finer moments. Willemstadt stood and Dumouriez had lost men needlessly. To many Generals, the outcomes of such risks, once taken, had little consequence, but to Dumouriez, popularity and standing amongst his men was paramount. If he was going to ask them to follow him and rescue France, they had to believe in him. Armies believed in victorious Generals far more than they believed in defeated ones. At least in his experience, they did.

The failure of Willemstadt was further compounded by messages from Paris and General Miranda. The National Assembly were questioning the purpose of the campaign against the Dutch. Paris was determined that Dumouriez should move to combine his forces with General Miranda and defeat the Austrians. However, Miranda's message was that the Army of the Ardennes was facing a superior quantity of Austrian troops who had outmanoeuvred him.

The Army of the Ardennes was on the run.

Dumouriez had driven everyone from his tent, even Genet. For an hour he sat alone. Only when he was ready did he recall Genet. Again, the storm had broken;

Dumouriez was the relaxed soldier, a man in charge of his own destiny.

"Ah Serge, apologies for earlier," Dumouriez waved a hand casually as if the matter warranted no further discussion. "Three messages, if you please. The first to Paris, agreeing to the wishes of the Assembly; dress it up how you like. Next, to General Miranda; urge him to regroup his forces. They are falling back on the road to Brussels."

Dumouriez looked over at the map.

"Tell him to make no further attempt to engage the Austrians before our forces join. We can meet up with him within ten days. We must risk a great deal in this final moment. How we fight will determine how we can negotiate. Finally, to Prince Josias; inform him that we have been ordered to give battle and it may be that only after having done so, will we be free to seek the terms of an accord in a personal meeting."

Dumouriez reasoned that if he asked the army to follow him before another battle with the Austrians, the men might refuse. Win or draw, his stock would rise again. Lose badly and the outcome was far from certain. He poked his head out the tent and searched for Beauvais, who was deep in conversation with Mahieu.

"Julian, come in and bring that sea-dog with you," Dumouriez turned and strode towards the table of maps, where a large bottle and selection of glasses were arranged, poured himself a brandy and filled two other glasses, knowing that Genet would not drink. The two men had filed in, the brief glimpse of the outside world lost as the tent was secured.

"A toast, gentlemen?"

Both men took a glass.

"Mahieu, France thanks you for your services. Serge will arrange some payment for you. Return to Dunkirk, our adventure here is over, for the moment. But stand ready, in case you are called for again."

Arnold Mahieu nodded gratefully, he and the crew of the *Perseus* would be happy to leave the Diep at the earliest moment. Sheltering the ship would become increasingly difficult, especially if the rumours of a withdrawal were true. Dumouriez' words hinted as much.

"Julien, I know you want to join your regiment. A little bird has been petitioning on your behalf, but one last mission with me and I think all will be well. What do you say?"

Julien Beauvais intended to say no. It was what he had told Juliette he would say, but those were not the words that left his mouth.

"To France," the three men toasted and Genet respectfully stood.

Outside of the tent, Arnaud Mahieu offered his hand. "Next time you come to Dunkirk, don't come and see me; unless it's to drink yourself senseless or to join my crew."

"And smell of fish for the rest of my life?" Beauvais shook his hand.

"Julien, a man could disappear in a town like Dunkirk. Make a new life, especially when he has something to live for."

In the distance, the unmistakable figure of Juliette was bearing down on them, riding from the direction of Breda. She had ridden two days to return from Miranda's headquarters to bring the news of his reply and defeat. Dumouriez had sent her back to the luxury of her room to rest but he might as well have ordered the wind to stop blowing.

"It's a nice thought. But a man like me cannot hide. And if I did, she would not want me. Now go, before you see some real bloodshed."

Beauvais smiled a crooked smile, patted Mahieu hard across the back and turned to face the Countess, wondering just how he might break the news that he was leaving with Dumouriez early the next morning.

CHAPTER SIXTEEN

Promise.

Celle: 7th March 1793

Four days of training in the rolling plains and wooded copses to the north of Celle had been a tremendous adventure, each evening the men of Brandt's Company had returned to the lines of small canvas tents to chat excitedly about the events of the day. Gauner's mood appeared to have lightened, he even nodded a smile towards Tomas and Henry as he stalked past one of the blackened wide-bottomed pots which bubbled with a delicious smelling stew. Reifener may have been a baker, but he seemed to be at home organising the contents of the cooking pot, tasting it and adding salt, which he had managed to scrounge from Old Boots. The men made sure that there was enough for any passing N.C.O and the news of a well-cooked stew clearly travelled quickly. Most of the corporals and sergeants appeared and pulled rank to draw their share of the meal before the other men.

As the soldiers, some in redcoats and others in green barracks jackets, settled to find a dry spot to eat in the gathering gloom of the late afternoon. Krombach perched himself next to Henry Pinsk, who was busy tucking away his meal, a wooden spoon scraping against the sides of the tin mug the stew had been poured into.

"He might be a hopeless soldier, but he will make someone a lovely wife", Henry grinned.

"It looks delicious", Krombach agreed, only just having received his after being pushed back down the queue when the scramble of non-commissioned men had muscled in. "Where is Tomas?" Krombach noticed a mug of stew steaming gently by the side of Henry.

"Gone to see the captain; Roner came looking for him as soon as we got back. A couple of the other lads were tagging along too."

"Did Roner say what it's about? He's not in trouble, is he? He really looked the part today and yesterday, for that matter", Krombach mused, hoping that his friend wasn't in any bother.

Tomas Pinsk had indeed caught the eye of Captain Brandt and acting Captain von Bomm. In the two days of exercises, the three battalions had been joined by two squadrons of light dragoons and a half battery of guns. The battalions had practised facing attacks from the cavalry, manoeuvring from columns of march to lines of three-deep or into the protection of a four-rank deep square. They had stood under the fire of artillery as the four field pieces fired blank charges at around six hundred paces distance. The jets of orange flame and grey smoke and the thundering boom of those guns, small in calibre as they were, had unnerved some of the men.

The battalions had simulated attacking the guns while being wary of the cavalry prowling on the open flanks. Into these open spaces, detachments of grenadiers had been ordered by Major Volgraf. Von Bomm had led his men to find cover and skirmish positions to deter the cavalry as much as possible. At the first signs of the cavalry showing an interest in forming up, the skirmishers began to withdraw in pairs back to the safety of the nearest company. Depending on the flank being threatened, Volgraf or Neuberg wheeled part of the line to face the potential threat. If musket fire from a company was deemed not to be enough, or the light dragoon numbers too great, the battalion formed square and six hundred men knelt or stood in tightly packed ranks as the horsemen rode around the outside waving swords and shouting good natured insults.

It was obvious to Neuberg that ten of the compliment of Grenadiers were simply too old for active service with the battalion, let alone with the grenadiers who might spend large parts of their time in battle, moving from line to skirmish duty. To find suitable replacements, the colonel had sent out selected men from various companies to work with the grenadiers. Neuberg had witnessed countless skirmish battles in

America had spoken at length to his officers of the proper skirmish training for a war that now felt imminent.

Krombach had taken no more than two mouthfuls of stew before Old Boots found him.

"Krombach, get your backside over to Captain Brandt. You can thank me later." Winckler stood over him.

"Yes, Sergeant; I'll just have my food," Krombach wolfed another mouthful.

"Unless I missed the moment that you started giving the orders, now means now!" Winckler's voice was stern but not unfriendly. "Leave your stew. Pinsk will finish it; he's a growing boy, though if he grows any more his trouser legs will end around his knees.

Krombach passed his bowl to Henry, rose glumly to his feet, and trotted slowly off behind the brisk pace of the sergeant. A few minutes later he stood in front of the captain to receive a hastily written note which Brandt had sealed, folded and then handed to the boy.

"Be sure this gets there. Then take yourself to the Blue Angel. The battalion will march through Celle at 9.00am tomorrow. Report back to the battalion there." He pushed some coins across the table. "Tell the innkeeper that you are there on my business and this will cover the cost. Do not get drunk and do not try and bed Herr Westerberg's daughter."

Captain von Bomm, who was sat at the end of the same table, carving slices off a leg of pork, tutted reproachfully, waved his knife as if to chastise the young soldier, then smiled and winked.

"Don't encourage him, Erich." Brandt sighed "Company Sergeant-Major Roner has arranged a horse. You can ride I take it?" Brandt asked, suddenly feeling slightly foolish that he hadn't checked that before.

"Yes sir" Krombach snapped back, eager to be away, but feeling the gnawing sensation in his stomach as von Bomm demolished another chunk of pork.

"Have you eaten? Never mind, deliver the message and eat at the Angel", Brandt slid another coin to join the others, "well, off you go."

The evening had grown dark when Krombach had finally negotiated his way across the town of Celle, found the white-walled Schloss and taken the road south-east towards Eicklingen. Following the directions that Captain Brandt had written, Krombach had rather nervously presented himself to the servant who answered his hesitant knock, suddenly very conscious of having been in the field for the last four days. The house was on three floors as best as Krombach could make out. In the small reception area in which he stood, patterned tiles covered the floor and an ornate wooden staircase spiralled to the first floor and beyond. An elderly butler dressed in a simple black jacketed uniform descended the stairs, bowed respectfully, and bade the young soldier to follow him. Krombach was led to the first floor, through a pair of intricately decorated doors which had lost some of their original lustre and into a large reception room. Rustic paintings hung between large tapestries of rural scenes, the most wonderful gilt-edged furniture glowed in the rich amber of candle and firelight.

Katerina Brandt, who cast a rather melancholy gaze into the warmth of the fireplace, rose from her chair with such elegance that she seemed almost weightless. Her hair fell about her shoulders in loosely-wound ringlets, rich mahogany-brown, bleached by sunlight at the tips. Krombach guessed that she must have been a similar age to her husband. Care-worn with faint creases at the corners of her eyes, she cast an awkward smile towards Krombach.

"Frau Brandt, a note from the Captain."

"Thank you." Her voice cold, distracted.

Katerina received the envelope; opal green eyes met Krombach's momentarily before turning away to open it hurriedly. When she turned to face Krombach a few moments later he detected a glassy reflection in her gaze though her face beamed with obvious delight.

"Thank you. Private?"

"Krombach."

"Has my husband made preparations for your lodging tonight?"

Krombach nodded.

"Yes of course he has. Werner is so organised." Lightness and warmth radiated from her voice and smile.

"The Blue Angel, I take it? But we cannot send you out of this house dressed as you are." She glanced at a heavily lacquered long-case clock which stood between tapestries depicting workers bringing in a harvest and another showing fishermen with the bounty of a catch.

"Follow Martin; leave your uniform here tonight. Put on the fresh clothes that he will provide for you."

"But…"

She held a hand up to stop him and smiled.

"Private Krombach," her voice aped the military world of which she knew so much, her voice told Krombach there was no room for discussion. The contents of the note had transformed Katerina Brandt.

"My husband sent you to represent him. When you leave this house, therefore you represent my family and me. Gentlemen of this household, whatever their station, have standards to maintain. Isn't that so Martin?"

The man merely nodded solemnly.

"Tonight, you are a young gentleman who is off duty. Go and enjoy your freedom. Martin will deliver your

261

uniform at breakfast tomorrow. Before you leave, you will take some tea or coffee with me and tell me of your life and the battalion. Werner... Captain Brandt tries to shelter me from that life but I wish to know all that there is."

Tea arrived and Krombach, freshly washed and dressed sat nervously, perched on the edge of a chaise longue, dressed in what he assumed from the shape and fit were old clothes of Captain Brandt. He feared he might despoil the garments or the finery of the room as he sipped at a rapidly cooling cup of tea while Katerina pressed him for news of the battalion and her husband, then delighting in finding that they shared another common link. Katerina's father had owned a fleet of fishing boats from his days in Gdańsk before a new venture had sent him and the family to Prussia.

Fifteen minutes passed in pleasant conversation and Katerina Brandt had decided to ask what she most feared to know.

"Sebastian. One more question. Do you think we will go to war?"

Krombach stopped. He had thought the matter over for several days, everyone in the company had.

"Yes, yes I do ma'am."

A taut look of powerlessness returned to Katerina Brandt's face.

"Werner and the children are my life. I cannot think of one without the other. Our son has been ill and...", her voice trailed off and she turned from Krombach to gaze back towards the comforting light of the fire. "And I have no right to ask you…"

"Madame, please whatever it is, ask", Krombach was captivated by the woman's beauty.

"Bring my husband home to me." She turned to meet his gaze, her opal eyes again held a watery glaze.

"Promise me. Promise me you will." She stood and offered her hand.

Krombach stood, bowed deeply and kissed her hand. "Yes ma'am."

III

The fine weather had broken and the central square in Celle was shrouded by heavy grey clouds which threatened to douse its inhabitants. The small daily market had been restricted to the right-hand side of the town-square, each face flanked by decorative wooden beamed three-floored town houses. From the windows of these, people had perched to get a bird's eye vantage point of the parade, much as their forebears must have done in the previous three centuries, as many of the houses bore dates of construction to attest to their longevity.

Krombach pushed his way through the crowd, pulling an unwilling mount behind him. He had considered riding the very short distance from the Blue Angel tavern to the market square, but the density of the people moving in the small streets convinced him that walking the mare was the best option. The last thing he wanted was to arrive on parade as a mounted soldier, a privilege reserved for officers, or worse still, be mistaken for a cavalry trooper. He was a soldier of the 10th and his brief flirtation with horses was hopefully over.

As he settled in a spot at the front of the crowd, he relaxed briefly. He had been terrified of being late for the arrival of the battalion and he was exhausted from the events of the past few days. Freedom from the battalion and the life of the messenger had not been his only flirtation of the night before. His redcoat and breeches had arrived early that morning and he marvelled at the colour of the jacket, a crisper cleaner shade of scarlet than he had ever known it. Loose stitching repaired, and some adjustments made to the turn-back on the sleeve. It felt like it was made for him rather than the ill-fitting garment which it had been previously. The prodding and measuring of Martin and one of Frau Brandt's staff had transformed the jacket.

Inside the jacket, a simple patch of material had been sewn to make a deep pocket and there lay a note which read 'Messages from the heart should be carried next to the heart - good luck - K.B'.

There was something else too, a pair of pink and green flowers which had been tied together with lace. The note was from Katerina, but the flowers were from Herr Westerberg's daughter's dress. She had clearly read the note when she placed them there.

Krombach looked at the clock; the time was approaching nine o'clock. Was there time to return to the Blue Angel and explain?

As the thought raced in his head, the whistles of flutes and the heavy boom of drums began to sound in the square, following shortly by the ringing clatter of two hundred sets of hooves as the 7th Light Dragoons entered the market square on the road that led from the Celle Schloss.

Maren Westerberg had noticed Krombach before he had seen her that previous evening. Four years older than Krombach, she ran the Blue Angel in all but name. Her father had been taken ill some two years previously and now found working, even for short periods of time, too much effort. Instead he sat and drank for an hour or two with some of the regulars before retiring to bed to leave his only daughter and half a dozen staff to serve in the busy tavern. Herr Westerberg, unshaven and generally dishevelled, had found the energy to remove

Krombach's money from him after quizzing the young man about his reasons for staying. He pointed to a space on a table nearest the door, making some comment on the morals of soldiers; no guests or unsavoury business were permitted in the room. His energy spent, Westerberg had returned to drinking, which he managed with surprising skill for a man incapacitated by the strain of illness.

Krombach's food had arrived, Maren had intercepted the platter from another waitress, and weaved her way through the small groups of oblong tables, avoiding the majority of groping hands, enjoying the choice comments that came her way and retorting with practised ease. Blonde hair fell around her bare shoulders and the traditional dirndl dress, a green silk top and pink skirt held tightly around her waist with a pink bow, which only served to accentuate her figure. The white blouse, under which the green silk top was tied with thick lace, restrained cleavage that was the beer-soaked dream of many of the Blue Angel's customers.

Krombach, his thoughts full of the conversation with Katerina, was unaware of the woman who studied him. He had given a promise, but how on earth was he to keep it? He was a man of the ranks. If and when the time of battle came, he would be looking toward the decisions Brandt made. Such choices would preserve the lives of every man in the company but he could not tell Katerina that. She wanted to believe that Krombach could vouch for her husband's return.

He sat with his head in hands contemplating this when a plate of food slid under his nose and the rich aroma of freshly cooked pork reminded him of his gnawing hunger.

"Hope she is worth it?" A soft voice spoke close to his ear above the general din of the tavern.

"I'm sorry?" Krombach was lost as to the meaning and looked up to see a pretty, petite waitress setting down a small pot of beer and some fresh cutlery.

"The woman you are thinking about." Her eyes shone with mischief and her tone gently mocked.

"I like to know the business of all of our regulars. With most of these, it's obvious. Their minds follow their hands and other parts no doubt. But you, you are a challenge. It took a while longer, but I have worked it out, I think."

"I'm sorry" Krombach repeated "I don't understand. I'm a bit tired, I..."

"Well, let's see. You arrived on a horse, which my stable boy tells me has the stamp of the 10th Infantry. They aren't in Celle, but I know they are arriving here tomorrow. The saddle bears the initials W.J.B, which might just be Captain Brandt, who is in the 10th and has a house in Celle. How am I doing so far?"

Krombach, who had taken the cutlery and started slicing though the pork and wolfing mouthfuls down, could only nod as juice dribbled down his chin.

"They do feed you in the army?" the waitress laughed "Glad you are enjoying it."

Krombach looked up, wiped his mouth with the cuff of the jacket and then glanced in horror at the brown smear that had been left on the rich blue material.

"Oh, that's a bit clumsy. And then there are the clothes; very fancy but not a soldier's clothes and not yours; borrowed from that look on your face. I do like a man in a uniform too, so I'm quite disappointed. So I worked out that either you have deserted and stolen the captain's horse and clothes, or you have carried a message to his wife and somehow ended up wearing his clothes."

"I can explain," Krombach spoke through mouthfuls of pork and rich gravy.

"Later," the waitress teased. "I can always ask my father to investigate you. He is more direct than me!" She motioned in the direction of Herr Westerberg, firmly ensconced with drinking partners but casting a wary eye over in the direction of Krombach.

"I am Maren. Let's find some bread to mop that gravy up and a pudding for later."

She turned and cut a swathe back through the tables, cuffing some of the patrons who had attempted to grope her on the outward journey, when she had been fully laden. Krombach had not noticed her arrival, but certainly noticed her departure.

For the second time that evening, Krombach found himself sharing the story of his life with a stranger. As the tavern had cleared, Maren brought a candle to the table and sat, exchanging stories. Hers, of a life around the tavern, all she had ever known. Krombach shared stories of journeys to Holland and towns around the Rhine, life in the army in search of an adventure and the disappointing reality. And of his meeting with Frau Brandt and an impossible promise, which already felt like a heavy burden.

Somewhere around one in the morning, Maren led Krombach up to a room on the first floor. She passed him the candle. "Your room is there. My father sleeps in here," she pointed to a door ahead of them, slightly ajar. "My room is down this corridor and to the left." She smiled in the yellow light of the candle, leaned forward, kissed him on the cheek and then turned to make her way along the dark passage.

Krombach's room was small. A chair and table were set near an unlit fireplace. The bed was set inside an oblong cupboard, the double doors of which were open. He hung his clothes over the chair placed the candle on the table, blew it out and felt his way to the bed. It was cold and felt slightly damp but it was a soft mattress and pillow and Krombach was not fighting the urge to sleep. He pulled the doors closed and the bed was now encased in a set of wooden walls, which rose into the ceiling. Shafts of moonlight entered through ornate fluting at the top of the door panels.

None of that mattered to Krombach. Thick with a wave of exhaustion, he slept within moments of resting his head.

The market square had filled with soldiers. The cavalry and four small four-pounder cannons had formed the rear ranks while four infantry formations comprised the main body of troops. To the right was 1st Guards battalion, next came 1st battalion of the 10th then 2nd. On the extreme left was a smaller formation, which carried no standard but Krombach recognised the profile of Captain von Bomm and realised that this must be the Grenadier companies from the three battalions. He moved his way through the crowd, just as sleeting rain caused many of the onlookers to fall back under the canopies of shop doorways to find shelter. As he drew level with Brandt's company, the captain acknowledged him with a cursory nod in his direction but remained at attention.

As Colonel von Diepenbroick bellowed the order for the parade to be dismissed a small figure dressed in pink and green raced along the front of the crowd. She saw the redcoat holding a horse and staring intently at the parade and cut towards him.

Krombach was jolted by the sudden appearance of an indignant Maren Westerberg.

"Sebastian Krombach, you have much to learn about women. When a lady tells you where her room is, it's a clear sign that she might require some company." She managed to sound slighted.

Krombach, sheepish and confused at the outburst, could feel the eyes of the redcoats nearby, along with a few stifled chortles. Maren could not hold the air of feigned rage any longer.

"I read the note, when I placed the flowers inside your pocket."

Maren had delivered the cleaned uniform to Krombach's room while he had breakfasted, read the note and the words had filled her with envy, which she had regretted the moment she had thought clearly and reasoned the matter out. By then Krombach had left.

"I'm sorry I shouldn't have. I spent all of this morning feeling jealous, but those words aren't for you, are they? Frau Brandt is only thinking of him."

She pointed in the direction of Captain Brandt, who was striding towards Krombach, undecided whether to rescue the soldier first or his own horse. Krombach's delight at seeing Maren was tempered by the deep embarrassment. Used to shouting to make herself heard in the tavern, her voice carried across the square with ease. Krombach stood to attention and thrust the reigns towards Captain Brandt. The captain took them, smiled politely at Maren and shot a look at Krombach suggesting that there might be a conversation later about his evening at the Blue Angel. Only thirty yards away, his wife watched the unfolding drama with some amusement and perhaps a little envy of her own.

"That's Katerina Brandt, isn't it? She is beautiful."

"Yes. whispered Krombach. "Maren, quietly please, everyone is watching." Brandt had remounted and trotted back to his position with the battalion.

Maren looked around and then smiled, unabashed.

"So? Let them."

"She is beautiful, in her own way, I suppose." Krombach looked at Katerina who gave the hint of a smile.

"But I will prefer to spend my days and evenings ahead, thinking of you," his fingers wound tight curls in the blonde hair which lapped her shoulder and he bent forward to gently kiss her.

"Come back to me Sebastian, promise you will come back. When this war is over, come and take me to all the places you have been."

Maren had spoken softly, between a cascade of kisses and tears. Catcalls and applause rang out from the men of 2nd battalion, who had just fallen out from the parade.

"I will. I promise Maren."

Brandt had informed Lieutenant Schafer and Company Sergeant Roner that they would be responsible for the Company for the next day or so. Frau Neuberg had seen to it that Brandt was given an additional day to spend with his family. Colonel Neuberg had persuaded him to command the company for the year and lead the men on campaign. He would need to convince Katerina and then catch the battalion up at some point before they reached Hanover. He glanced left and saw a truly marvellous sight. Katerina mounted on her chestnut mare had drawn the attention of Colonel's von Diepenbroick and Neuberg. After both had reached across their mounts to kiss her gloved hand, she trotted to the side of her husband.

"Hello," he smiled, aware that the eyes of many of the milling soldiers in the square were upon his wife.

She held out a gloved hand, which he kissed before leaning over to kiss her lips.

"My, such public displays of affection are quite unbecoming" Katerina laughed. "We should be doing what those two are doing."

She glanced over at Krombach deep in conversation between kisses with Maren. "An interesting young man; you should try and make something of him."

273

"Is he? I really don't know him. I asked for a messenger and Sergeant Winckler brought him along."

"Honestly Werner, what have you been doing these last few weeks?" she teased, "besides deciding to stay in the army?"

Werner Brandt felt the colour drain from his face, "How could you possibly know?"

"While you have been camping with your men and practising war, we had a house guest."

Brandt was still none the wiser.

"Frau Neuberg," Katerina eventually put him out of her misery.

"Ahh..." Brandt felt as though the matter had already been decided.

"There is a greater good that you are doing. The lives of all those men. And it is only a year."

Brandt shook his head in disbelief. He had spent the last few days wondering how he might find the words to tell Katerina. Colonel Neuberg was the commander of the battalion but the redoubtable Frau Neuberg was a tactician of the highest calibre.

Krombach could have happily spent the rest of day just kissing but was aware that the minutes were slipping away and then of movement out of the corner of his eye. Krombach looked to see the Pinsk brothers nudging each other and grizzling. Behind them was Reifener, who looked embarrassed to be in the presence of a woman.

"You might need these, if you are actually planning on doing any fighting that is?" Tomas had produced Krombach's pack and musket, which he had placed with the mule train and had set about retrieving when he saw that Krombach was otherwise engaged.

Conversation and laughter filled the square around them as the redcoats spent the last minutes of precious freedom before forming for the march ahead. Maren and Krombach kissed for one more time and reluctantly he dragged himself after the other three men. Tomas dropped back to speak to him.

"Sebastian, listen, I have something I want you to do." Krombach was still grinning and giving sideways glances at Maren, who was courting admiring glances from a number of other redcoats.

"'Bastion, this is important, "Tomas shook him roughly and with a degree of impatience that he had not known from his friend. "I've been transferred to the Grenadiers, Henry is staying with you."

Krombach looked at Tomas blankly, "When?" he mouthed.

"Yesterday, last night, look it doesn't matter when, it's happened. Please look after Tomas. Despite being a giant, he is my little brother. I swore to our mother that

I would look out for him. Now I'm asking you to do what I can't. And watch out for Gauner. He hates you and Henry. Now I'm gone, I'm afraid Henry will get drawn into something, one way or another. Please promise me."

Krombach looked up at his friend who towered a full head height above him. For the first time he realised that Tomas was sporting a black eye and cut nose. "What happened to you?"

"You have startling powers of observation. Henry and I disagreed over my transfer. I don't want to leave him but he told me that he can take care of himself. Perhaps he can? I never knew he could punch that hard," Tomas smiled, wincing with pain. "Just keep him alive. Who knows what we are heading into."

"I will Tomas. I'm going to miss you. Henry and I will stay out of danger and out of Gauner's way."

Krombach embraced his friend, before turning to wave to Maren for the final time. The two were fifty yards apart. Another heavy shower of rain crashed onto the cobbles of the market place but they held their gaze until Krombach heard the voices of Roner and Winckler calling for Brandt's Company to fall in. With a last look, he turned to find his place in the column.

CHAPTER SEVENTEEN
Old Boots.

Hanover: 12th March 1793

Rumours of the 10th Regiment's orders had circulated throughout the ranks during the church service, well in advance of their official announcement two days later. Krombach listened as Neuberg spoke of the workload in the days ahead and how each soldier would be expected to uphold the honour of the battalion. Beyond that, he could offer no clue as to the destination of the army, although Krombach had pieced together enough information from various whispers in his continued duties at headquarters for Captain Brandt to know that the army would march to Bentheim. There each Hanoverian battalion would be taken into British service.

Such small information had been invaluable to Winckler, who had pressed Krombach to keep his eyes open and report to him. The Sergeant seemed to have a scheme brewing but he was not keen to share his plans. Old Boots had taken Reifener under his wing and the ex-baker's boy had told Krombach that the sergeant planned to pay a visit to his uncle. It had become painfully clear that Reifener was utterly clueless as to the mechanics of conception, a scapegoat to carry both the blame and cost of the child. It was not until the following day, a week before the battalion was due to leave that Krombach had a chance to discuss the matter with Winckler.

Twelve wagons had arrived at the barracks and Krombach had found himself and a small handful of other soldiers selected for the task of escorting these into Hanover and returning with supplies and victuals. Lieutenant Schafer had been allotted as the officer in charge but Winckler had already established the true seniority for the journey and the task ahead. Schafer had been pleased to acquiesce, with obvious relief at Winckler's expertise in the matters ahead, tempered by the knowledge that a blind eye might need to be shown to the sergeant's activities on occasion.

The narrow roads into town were busy with traffic as carriages and caissons from the battalion joined a swollen stream of other travellers heading toward the centre of Hanover. Several times the journey was halted to allow the supply-wagons, heavily laden with stores, to pass by. Another time, the wagons were driven onto the grass verges to clear the road for the magnificent sight of a cavalry regiment and battery of horse artillery, heading south from Hanover.

Neuberg had worked some minor miracle in acquiring the transport, but experienced wagon-masters were even harder to find. Various districts which fell into the regiment's area were scoured, very reasonable purses offered for wagons and drivers. Winckler was experienced in handling a cart and half a dozen of the wagons were driven by men from the battalion but nevertheless a journey that should have taken some forty minutes took the best part of two hours. As the morning had lengthened toward lunchtime, Krombach sensed that the cheerful mood of the Sergeant was ebbing, the lost time encroaching on his plans.

The yard itself, a requisitioned cattle market, was set on three sides of a large cobbled open courtyard. The surrounding buildings, each with a terracotta tiled roof, had freshly painted signs denoting the stores that could be drawn from that area. There was a small wait to enter the courtyard and the soldiers had taken this as a reasonable excuse to light pipes or eat rations that had been issued for the journey.

Krombach joined a small group of soldiers sat at the verge of the road, enjoying the lull before the work of hauling the stores began, and watching a steady thick stream of blood gushing from a pipe and staining the damp mud road. The nearest warehouse to the left of the entrance had a slaughterhouse attached to the rear of the premises and the overpowering stench made Krombach draw heavily on a borrowed pipe and decide that lunch could wait. Hartmann, Gauner's henchman, had no such inhibitions. He sat and watched the blood spurt across the road weaving a path into the verge opposite where it drained into a water-course, all the while gnawing on a piece of dried beef and swigging from his canteen.

As the wagons had arrived at the victualling yard, Winckler had passed his own instructions to the men, and disappeared, returning around an hour later to oversee the balance of the work. Hartmann lifted twice the load of most of the other men allowing the wagons to be packed inside two hours. By the time Krombach took his place next to Winckler, on the eleventh wagon in the train returning to barracks, there were long queues of other vehicles waiting to access the yard. Trailing in the wake and ordered to maintain a distance, was a lone civilian wagon-driver, the rear of the procession. The battalion's supply of gunpowder had no passenger; the soldier who had sat in the wagon on the outward journey had squeezed onto a seat of one of the lead wagons for the return. Winckler's good humour had returned and Krombach felt the moment safe to raise the matter of Reifener.

"Did you manage to see Reifener's family while you were away?"

Winckler broke off from humming some melody "Yes, I did, as it happens. His uncle is a sly old fox and no mistake. The army will have young Andreas for the next twenty years, if he lives that long. Still it's not a bad life, eh, on a day like today?"

The Sergeant smiled and returned to his tune, while gently encouraging the pair of heavy horses pulling the cart to keep an even pace as the road gently inclined.

"But what happened? The child was never his, was it?"

"No, I very much doubt it. You know what the family business is, don't you?" Winckler asked and Krombach nodded.

"Well it turns out they aren't just bakers here in Hanover. They follow market-days and feasts all over Northern Germany, even into Holland. They have this mobile bakery. Seems they can feed the Five Thousand. Perhaps they should team up with your old man and do a loaves and fishes special." Old Boots chuckled deeply to himself.

Krombach flapped away at a fly that had been circling one of the horse's rumps and had now moved to bother him.

"Thanks Sergeant, I will suggest it next time I'm on leave," he said, with as much disinterest as he dared muster.

"Anyhow turns out they had been in Osnabrück last April and returned there in November for some Saints feast. On arriving in the town, the old man's son is seized by the town's burghers on behalf of the bishop. It seems a local farmer's daughter, a young virgin, is carrying a child, but this is no immaculate conception.

The Lutherans in Osnabrück feel the Catholics had already cornered the market on that front."

The observation drew another chuckle from the Sergeant.

"Where was I, oh yes? So, the uncle goes to see the Bishop and meet with the farmer. And behold a 'miracle', suddenly the girl isn't sure it was the uncle's son but suggests it might be our very own Private Reifener. How much money changed hands for that decision to be made? Your guess is as good as mine. Never the less, it now presents the bishop with a bit of a dilemma. The farmer wants a regular payment for the upkeep of the child, the bishop doesn't want a foundling on the doorstep or the girl thrown out of her home, as that will come out of his stipend and old Uncle Reifener doesn't want to be paying out any more money to anyone than he must. Turns out when the mobile bakery returns to Osnabrück in February, near the time of the birth, the bishop has had an idea, perhaps even a 'vision from on high'."

Winckler spat heavily, coughing out a lapsed Lutheran disgust at all things connected with the church in general. Krombach waited patiently for the Sergeant to continue.

"It seems the bishop has a relative who is an officer in our cavalry. He has told him that the army is short of men, war is coming, usual story. So, our hard done to farmer draws up some legal letter which the bishop submits to the good burghers of Hanover, saying that unless reparation is made, the bishop will raise the matter with the honourable Duke of York no less, who happens to be Archbishop of Osnabrück, in his spare time."

Another chuckle from Winckler turned into a cough and a salvo of phlegm.

"Hanover wants no fuss, Osnabrück wants no fuss, so young Andreas presents himself to the nearest infantry battalion that he can find, the army withholds part of his pay for the next twenty years and the farmer, the baker and the bishop all congratulate one another for not being out of pocket."

"Bloody hell," Krombach said softly.

"Could be worse, he could have had to marry her too. Bit of a sour maiden by all accounts. Seems the farmer still thinks he can pass her off as undamaged goods as his wife is bringing up the child. It's a strange world, Sebastian; mark my words, a very strange world."

"But it's not fair," Krombach suddenly felt very sorry for any time when he had mocked Reifener's rather frequent failures at basic tasks, even if it had been done with a large slice of good humour.

"It's not about fair. That's not for the likes of you and me to decide. We just have to get on with things as they are. When you are on campaign, things won't always be fair. You will have to keep your eyes open and share

your council and opinions with those you trust."
Winckler looked sideways at Krombach.

"Listen up boy. You have got enough about you. You
aren't daft. But you haven't got these." he said tapping
the three chevrons that indicated his rank.

"Don't go picking fights with those who have until
you've got stripes of your own. Standing up to Gauner
took guts but was stupid too. One of these days Roner
won't be there and Gauner will pick and pick and pick
at you until he gets a reaction."

Winckler had transferred the reigns into one hand
and with his free hand, firmly pinching Krombach's
shoulder with each 'pick'; Krombach's cast a stern look
sideways.

"There, that's what he will look for. That eye contact
will say 'insolence' to him. He will make chance after
chance to belittle you in front of the men but never in
sight of the captain. He's a tricky bastard is old Conrad.
And if he is sniffing around the arse of Major Volgraf,
then Captain Brandt might be hard pressed to
intervene."

Winckler returned both hands to the reigns and
proceeded to check the pace of the team. The wagon
had crested the small rise and he eased the pace on the
gentle descent. In the distance they could make out the
shape of the barracks, a mile away.

"I know Sergeant. Thank you for the words of
advice," Krombach rubbed his left shoulder hard, "And

thanks for sending me to headquarters as often as you have. It's kept me out of Gauner's way."

"Yes, well it won't last. And I'm not always going to be around, you know; for now, I will settle for getting shot of this lot and keeping us as far away from those fireworks, as possible."

The last cart filled with the battalion's gun powder allocation had just crested the ridge. Winckler clucked a sound to the horses and urged them to close on the cart in front and returned to his tune.

Captain Brandt had taken the manifest details from Schafer, who had appeared at the headquarters office on the northern face of the barracks. He had drawn the duty normally performed by Major Volgraf, who had been sent to Hanover to press officers to return to the Colours and meet a gentleman keen on a commission in the battalion, who had promised the requisite number of recruits. Neuberg had spent the day in his office and Brandt, completing a final list of equipment shortages for 2nd Company, had witnessed breakfast, lunch and a flurry of messages come and go from the room. Schafer's successful trip would resolve some matters but shortages would not be made good before departure. The current transport shortage would even mean men carried heavier packs than they were used to.

"Hold my post a minute Lieutenant, would you?" the captain asked as Schafer stood in front of the duty desk, rocking nervously from foot to foot, "I need to see the Colonel a moment."

Schafer nodded in relief, as much from being given a clear task to do. He sat down on the chair vacated by Brandt and then a panicked look spread across his face.

"If someone comes in Christian, you represent the Colonel. Any problems, ask one of the orderlies here to come and fetch me," Brandt pointed to two clerks who sat copying out a series of company orders.

Knocking and hearing Neuberg's muffled voice, Brandt stepped into the small room. A table, uncluttered on all the previous visits, was now covered with loose sheets of orders, lists and maps. The colonel was leafing through paperwork, a thick pencil clutched between his teeth, consulting documents and then scratching various notes in a ledger on the desk.

He raised his eyebrows in mock despair, before withdrawing the pencil "Who is minding the shop?"

"Ensign Schafer"

"Make sure he doesn't set fire to anything! Your birthday list?" Neuberg nodded toward the list in Brandt's hand.

"Hardly sir, more like a list of miracles for someone to perform."

Brandt smiled. He had found Neuberg a very easy man to get along with and much of an improvement upon Dohman, the previous incumbent. He may have been loved by the men, but these last few days would have overwhelmed him.

"Any news about the greatcoats, sir?"

"No, nothing yet; I have sent requests, so has Colonel von Diepenbroick, but we might have to improvise somewhat, I fear. In fact, I will be surprised if we don't get lost on the way to Holland or France, or wherever the hell it is we are headed."

Neuberg's ironic voice was couched in a smile.

"Why, sir?" Brandt asked, somewhat quizzically.

"Why? I must be working you too hard, Werner. Haven't you heard? Our glorious leader for this expedition is Field Marshal Freytag. He has somehow found the energy to rouse himself from his frequent septuagenarian afternoon naps and lead us to glorious victory," Neuberg returned to leafing through the sheets of paper on the desk.

"Is there going to be a problem?" Brandt was unsure of what to say.

"Well that depends…" Neuberg continued to search through a document until he found the detail he was looking for and then entered that in a column on the ledger.

"On?" Brandt asked.

"On Freytag's belief that this war will be like the battles of forty years ago; the Field Marshal and I once shared a rather enlightening, if somewhat brief, discussion on the future of campaigns when I ran the training academy at Nienburg." Neuberg stopped his search through the documentation and looked at Brandt.

"As I recall, he arrived just before lunch, which he tucked into with much energy and gusto, watched some of the musketeers training in skirmishing drills for about five minutes, and then pronounced that such practises were not the way that 'Armies of Honour' fought. Our glorious leader then retired to his carriage to return from whence he came, no doubt to sleep off his lunch. After that he arranged for a posting to Prussia for me, in order that I might disavow myself of such foolish notions. But those words stay within these walls."

"Oh!"

"Oh indeed, Captain Brandt, oh indeed. Let's hope that the French soldiers that spent half a dozen years fighting the British in America didn't learn a thing from that war, despite having just beaten the Austrians and the Prussians in the last few months. Let us also hope that General Dumouriez commands an 'Army of Honour'. From my knowledge of them you can be sure, Werner, that plenty in the Austrian and Prussian ranks held the view of the Field Marshall, right up to the moment that their arses got a good kicking."

London: 15th March 1793

"What about Austria?"

Jackson drained the last of the single blend malt whiskey from his glass and looked longingly at the empty bottle on the table of the Minister for War. If there was another bottle Dundas wasn't making a move to reveal it and Jackson with his resourceful scrounging skills hadn't discovered any other hidden cache of booze in the last five weeks. Still he already knew that this was his last evening in London, so he had arranged a meal at Bradshaw's, a gentleman's club just off Mayfair Street, through Dundas's membership. Jackson had resolved to pick up the tab for their evening, to spare any ministerial blushes.

"Why do you think we even went at all?"

"Oh I gave up trying to fathom government policy a long time ago, no offence like. I'm just a merchant at heart," Jackson again played the humble south-western sailor.

Dundas rolled his eyes, "My dear man, we went to Holland for two reasons. Firstly, if we hadn't, it would have fallen into the sea under the weight of an invading French army. Secondly, the King heard a splendid idea. Not had, as in an original thought, mark you, but heard!

One that he has since subsumed as his own, as is the way of majesty. That is why troops are needed. And in a few weeks, when York tries to slip his chains on some combined crusade with Austria, you will get to earn your corn, instead of drinking my whiskey! Is there any more of that?"

Jackson smiled and shook his head. "Not unless you are keeping secrets from me, on that front?"

Dundas made for the door that partitioned his office and the waiting room, grabbing a long black velvet coat as he did. "Come on then, let's make a move."

Outside of the Ministry a covered cab was waiting and both men clambered in and settled back as the buggy began the short journey to Bradshaw's.

"You didn't ask me the obvious question?" Dundas growled.

"Which was?"

"Where did the 'splendid idea' come from?" Dundas replied.

"Well 'enry, I knew you would tell me and to be honest, I thought I might need a drink to take it all in, so 'twas best not to delay."

Dundas smiled "I shall miss your warmth and charm... eventually."

In the half light of the buggy, Dundas saw the broad grin on Jackson's face.

"The idea for our co-operation came from our very own minister in Vienna. A man I sent to Austria precisely because he lacked any sense of wit to come up with such hare-brained schemes. He could offer the Austrians nothing of significance, because he knew nothing of significance."

"So whose plan is it?" Jackson asked.

Dundas snorted, "Thugut; this has reeked of him from the beginning."

It was an open secret that the two men loathed one another.

"Thugut is afraid. He wants to embroil us with his cause but we mustn't get wrapped up with the Austrians."

"Then why are we going to co-operate with them?"

"Honour of course; we cannot refuse the call. When those bastard upstarts in Paris have been defeated and France has a new King, Thugut is afraid the new man will look more to London than Vienna for guidance."

Jackson could see it too and the possibilities for trade and finance that it could bring. The balance of power across Europe was going to shift in Britain's favour. Dundas smiled at the dawning realisation of the man next to him.

"Thugut wants the British alongside him but very much as the junior partner. He is a wily bastard! He has some plan or other, mark my words. I don't know what it is yet, but in the fullness, it will be revealed. And until then, I need you to understand this. Your orders come from here, my office. Do you understand? If this whole campaign unravels the Prince can walk away. But men like you and me will be held to account."

Jackson nodded, "So what is the plan and what's in it for us?"

"Baron Thugut wants our help but has also suggested a fit and proper reparation as Austria sees it. But under no account are you to provide supplies for the Austrian army. I tell you this because I believe that if we advance into France, the Austrians will try and bleed us of men and money. When our reparation is claimed, there must be no doubt over who possesses it. Thugut will strike when we have the most to gain. Once he has us in the field, he will shift heaven and earth to deny us our prize, or change the price already agreed."

"And what is the prize 'enry?" Jackson asked.

"The prize, my friend, is Dunkirk. To put a Bourbon arse back on the throne, the Duke of York will take possession of Dunkirk and Great Britain shall have a piece of empire on the continent.

Liege: 15th March 1793

The Esterhàzy Hussars led the Austrian advanced guard, horsemen riding with the sun warming their backs along the road that led west towards Brussels. The army had rested on the western bank of the Meuse for ten days but the arrival of Thugut's message had finally galvanised Prince Josias into action. Colonel

Mack had tried to stir the Prince from the torpor that he had slumped into but Josias was not to be moved. Miranda's army had been routed by manoeuvre, Mack had submitted plan after plan to follow up the French but Josias was adamant. The peace plan with Dumouriez would be given time to develop. The campaign would be ended with the minimum of lives lost.

As much as Mack and Baron Thugut loathed one another, they both shared common-ground. The response from Emperor Francis, written by Thugut, left the Prince in no doubt. Defeat the French army in the field, swing south and take the road to Paris.

Thugut had also written to Mack, the letter full of false warmth, wanting to know the precise positions of the British, instructing Mack that their forces must be utilised fully in the coming campaign, and under Austrian leadership. The Duke of York must be woven into Mack's plan of campaign and then given time to capture Dunkirk, so that Austria could be seen to have asked for nothing in delivering a victory in which she had given and paid much more.

To Mack, the machinations of Thugut seemed rather transparent, but his survival stood on reading the politicking of the Baron. If Britain seized the bribe, surely Austria would be permitted reparations of her own. While the British took control of a French city, Thugut would fashion a suitable prize for the Emperor, denying any deals made, no doubt; all the while whispering in the royal Bourbon ear that London had seized Dunkirk when it had no right. Britain was the natural enemy of France and Austria her true ally.

All of this stank of politicking, to Mack. The British had not moved from their positions on the northern coastline of Hollands Diep. Captain Craufurd, the Duke of York's aide had delivered a message to Prince Josias three days before. The British would move south only when their cavalry arrived and that was not expected until the end of March at the earliest. The French attacks in the Netherlands had stalled, that was a small mercy at least, but the British forces barely constituted a small Corps in Austrian terms. How the redcoats would capture Dunkirk without vastly increasing their commitment of forces or without significant help from Austria, was beyond Mack.

Before the British had assembled such a force, Austria would settle the matter of the French revolt. Colonel Mack would see to it. If such an outcome dislocated Thugut's plans, that was an additional bonus. Mack scanned Thugut's letter again. Soon they would have a chance to clash over such matters, face to face. The court of Vienna was locating to the Austrian Netherlands for the summer months.

Emperor Francis II was coming to the front.

Tirlemont: 15th March 1793

Julian Beauvais pushed his riding boot into the heavy turf and watched with concern as bubbles of dirty water ran over his boot. Open farmland around Tirlemont, a landscape savaged by winter storms, had been broken by ploughing. The gentle gradient of the terrain sloped down towards the first of two parallel branches of the river Gete. Beyond one of these, the Petite Gete, stood the Austrian army. Their camp fires had been visible for the past two evenings. It was difficult to judge the full scale of the Austrian forces. Beyond the Gete, the ground rose with a series of ridges and what lay behind those was more supposition than fact. French cavalry patrols had failed to pierce the screen of Austrian skirmishers and light cavalry formations which patrolled its eastern banks.

Scanning the horizon, he saw the road to St. Tron that he had followed earlier that morning, to find his regiment, the 3rd Dragoons, transferred from the siege of Willemstadt to journey across the Brabant province with Dumouriez.

Tomorrow, the 3rd would be in the thick of the action. Dumouriez already knew that the Austrians would have a superior number of cavalry in the field. Trying to press home an attack when the enemy outnumbered you in the most mobile arm on the battlefield would be difficult. The ground at least would hinder the Austrians as much as the French, the fields on the far side of the 'Petite Gete' looked as saturated as the one that Beauvais stood in now. Control of the roads would be vital. Once thousands of infantrymen had churned up the ground, moving horses and artillery on anything but the cobbled roads, would be impossible.

Beauvais turned and headed back towards Dumouriez' tent. No longer the clean, white lustre of the first days of the campaign, it now resembled the faded yellow calico sails of the *Perseus*. Beauvais found himself wondering where Mahieu was before his thoughts returned to Juliette. Dumouriez had ordered her to Tirlemont too. Even though it had meant a few more shared nights, Beauvais had wanted her anywhere else but here. Events were moving much faster now than anyone could control, even Dumouriez; his moods had begun to mirror his fortune. Each setback triggered irascible behaviour, more violent than the outbreak before.

However, the morning had been fruitful enough for Beauvais. His visit to the 3rd had yielded the beginnings of a plan that would see Juliette protected if Dumouriez' plans failed.

Colonel Courtois handed Beauvais a pair of sealed letters; the colonel was one of the few men outside of Dumouriez' inner circle who knew of the possibility of a pact between the two armies.

"You look a wreck, Julian. Too much easy living at headquarters eh?" Courtois smiled warmly. "When are you coming back to do some actual soldiering rather than playing at being an overgrown errand-boy?"

"It's a pleasure to see you too, Colonel," Beauvais replied dryly, his face contorting into a broken smile. "Soon, I hope. Headquarters has mentioned how poor the scouting reports have been of late, so I don't imagine you will be without me for too much longer."

Courtois motioned the captain towards a set of four woodworm-ridden chairs in the barn that was currently making do as the regiment's headquarters. Overhead, beams thick with old cobwebs held three lanterns which provided much of the light. The only other source, a small rectangular window, was obscured with further layers of cobwebs and masked by a bush which, despite growing outside of the building, had thrust a branch in through a gap between window frame and wall. Freshly strewn straw had done something to mask the smell of the cattle that had inhabited the building only yesterday afternoon, but the cavalrymen seemed oblivious to the cloying smell. The only other occupant of the room, a junior officer who Beauvais did not recognise, was acting as officer of the day and in the act of scribbling out a report into a book wedged across his knees.

"Anton, can you find some coffee for Captain Beauvais and me? Then post yourself outside the door, I don't want to be disturbed." Courtois spoke with an easy authority.

Two steaming mugs of black coffee arrived in a few moments.

"You're a good lad, now outside and keep the well-wishers away." Courtois watched the young dragoon leave, a boy of perhaps seventeen years old.

"They will be sending us children next. He's a good lad, great horseman, but wet behind the ears." With the young dragoon safely out of earshot, Courtois continued.

"Let's keep this brief, you know how tongues wag. This note is for you. It is signed by every officer in the regiment with the rank of captain and above. It tells of your devotion to the Revolution and France and that the actions you have taken for Dumouriez were done without the knowledge of the General's treachery. Keep it safe, if Dumouriez manages to emerge victorious, destroy it."

Beauvais nodded. "Every officer; even Lavigne?"

"Juliette is most persuasive, Julien. When she visits the regiment, she commands far more attention than a mere colonel. It seems Lavigne has been moved to sign the document. Anyhow, he is the least of your current problems." Courtois waved the issue away as if swatting a fly.

"Juliette?" Beauvais spoke softly.

"Yes. It's bound to come out that she took the note to the Austrian camp. Paris will assume that she was complicit in the matter. And, let's face the fact, she is hardly inconspicuous, so this is for her." Courtois handed a second sealed note.

"At the first opportunity, she is to ride to Valenciennes. General Ferrand controls the garrison. He also happens to be a longstanding friend who owes me a favour or two and a few thousand livres. The man is an atrocious gambler but as tough as teak. If the Convention comes sniffing around, he will see them off. When the dust settles, the Countess can reinvent herself as someone new. But for now, and the duration of events, she has become my niece." Courtois whispered the instructions and smiled affectionately at the dragoon opposite him.

Beauvais chuckled, "You have not changed, Alain. Thank you."

Both men grinned like children who had stolen apples from a neighbour's tree and were now enjoying the booty.

"It is a danger to follow Dumouriez. One moment his plays the ardent revolutionary, the next he is courting Austria. You know that he requested to command the army, when he could have stayed safe in Paris. His ambition knows no limits. I don't think he intends to bring any Bourbon back to the throne. He knows that most of the country won't stand for it. He wants France for himself. I've been blind to that fact in more than one way," Beauvais whispered hurriedly. "Don't follow him over to the Austrians, Alain."

Courtois nodded in silent agreement and the pair drank in quiet contemplation before Courtois pointed at the door and then spoke loudly enough should the young officer on the far side of the door have been eavesdropping.

"Thank you, Captain, a pleasure to see you. I look forward to you returning to our happy fold."

The colonel called the young officer back into the room, the door swinging open with such speed that it suggested the young dragoon had indeed been straining to hear the conversation. Beauvais had returned to the lair of Dumouriez with a far happier outlook than when he had left.

The flap of the tent was still sealed shut but a congregation of Generals and staff officers had gathered outside. Within the canvas walls, Dumouriez was holding discussions with General Miranda, General Valence and Louis Philippe, Duc de Chartres, a member of the house of Orleans and distant cousin to Louis XVI. Genet was on the inside of course; Revolutionaries and Royalists, strange bedfellows in the tent of the General.

Beauvais guessed that the plan of battle had already
been agreed but now was the moment for private
discussion. Jean-Baptiste Valence was a firm friend of
Dumouriez and Beauvais had overheard enough letters
drafted between the two to know that Valence's
support could be relied on. The Duc de Chartres was
only two years older than the young dragoon who
stood as officer of the day for the 3rd, but already a
capable soldier. His family had supported the
revolution at some considerable personal cost. Failure
for Dumouriez would have repercussions for so many.
Beauvais scanned the faces of the assembled officers,
doing their best to pass the time before battle with small
talk. Whatever the rank, the habitual need for soldiers
to find moments of light relief to puncture the growing
tension always surfaced. A few moments later Genet
pushed the tent flap back and bid the group to enter.

CHAPTER EIGHTEEN

New Stripes.

Hanover: 18th March 1793

Brandt's Company had been at musket drill for half an hour when the runner arrived. The redcoats had marched to an area of farmland which the battalion had hastily requisitioned where three elongated white targets, twenty feet long by five feet tall, had been erected. Two thick parallel black bands, placed a foot from the top and bottom of the heavily pock-marked boards, marked the boundaries of a successful volley. Captain Brandt divided his company into three platoons and he and Company Sergeant Roner moved between them, observing the drills and instructing when needed.

The battalion was at full strength at last, a final draft of men arriving two days before. Corporal Möller had made a sergeant, along with a man called Richter who had returned to the Colours, having left only four months earlier. The older hands of the company knew Richter as 'Moustache Georg', a nickname earned from the black, broad, bushy moustache which sprouted from under his nose. When Moustache Georg drilled the men he stood ramrod straight, yet each movement involved an involuntary thrust of the head, rather like a flamboyant cockerel. Richter had fought in a British battalion in America, a musket ball having grazed his windpipe, leaving him with a deep scar but clearly no damage to his voice as it boomed out drill orders above the din of musketry. He made a good foil for Roner, another man who wore the honorific sergeant's moustache with a distinguished air, although with less volume and considerably more flecks of greying hair. With Roner, marginally the taller of the two men, large sideburns stooped and threatened to meet the moustache. Both presented a fearsome spectacle to the new draft of soldiers and Brandt was at last happy with his compliment of non-commissioned officers. Two soldiers had been promoted to the rank of corporal and for one of them, Krombach could not have been happier. Henry Pinsk had arrived at breakfast that morning, sporting two new stripes neatly sewn onto his scarlet uniform, grinning from ear to ear.

With each volley, Krombach felt increased satisfaction, the drill movements felt automatic. His platoon was commanded by Winckler whilst Gauner patrolled behind the double rank of redcoats. The section had fired at one hundred yards, reloaded and advanced to seventy-five yards of the target. Here, the effect of the fire at shorter distance was far more visible, patches of bare wood revealed where musket balls slammed home. A further reload and the ranks advanced to within fifty yards, halted and fired another successful volley. More fresh timber had been exposed, every musket had fired.

Winckler and Gauner moved along the ranks checking that the muskets had been made safe, particularly in the case of the newer recruits, none of which had experienced a volley of fifty muskets. Misfires were commonplace but the three volleys had provided none. Satisfied with the outcome, Winckler stood the platoon at ease just as the runner, who had reported at first to Brandt, sought out the Sergeant.

Brandt had decided that Winckler was best suited to fulfil Doctor Wexler's list of requirements and had permitted him to take one man from the platoon with him and carry out the matter with all haste. The message was a godsend to Winckler, who had been looking for a reason to return to Hanover and had planned to ask for permission from Brandt that evening. This order gave him the chance to return without questions being asked. Winckler left Gauner with instructions to train the platoon in misfire drill, ordered Reifener to fall out of the platoon and the two men were soon out of sight to the remaining redcoats.

Corporal Gauner followed the instructions of Winckler to his own ends. As the other platoons continued various stages of their drills and with Brandt and Roner deep in conversation with Sergeant Richter, whose platoon was furthest away on the range from Gauner's, the Corporal sensed an opportunity. He marched the platoon back to their starting point, one hundred yards from the target board. Krombach heard his name mentioned. He had drifted in concentration briefly during Gauner's instruction, following the passage of the two departing figures without trying to obviously turn his head. Now several heads turned in his direction and the squat, muscular Gauner, beckoning him out of the rear rank.

"Wake up, Krombach. Just because there isn't someone behind you to kick you up the arse, doesn't mean that you can have a snooze."

Gauner's acidic tone brought involuntary laughter from redcoats secretly relieved that Gauner had not selected them. Krombach stepped forward and presented himself to Gauner, smartly shouldering arms.

"Very good; thank you for finally joining us." Gauner walked around Krombach and faced the two ranks of men.

"Now, we have all done very well today, firing at a wooden wall that isn't planning to fire back anytime soon. Except that the French won't be so obliging.

Today we fired in two ranks, but in battle you will fight in three."

Gauner had heard the discussion about Neuberg's ideas of a battalion firing in two ranks but had dismissed it as the idea of a man who had little experience of commanding troops in battle. Besides, Neuberg's wings would soon be clipped of such fancy. The corporal was backing Major Volgraf and his connections to win in that cock fight.

"We fight in three ranks so that when the enemy fire back and the men around you start to die, as they will," Gauner paused and stared at the now frightened faces in front of him, "others will take their place and the battalion will keep firing until it is victorious."

Gauner returned to a central position, stood with his back to Krombach but facing the rest of the platoon.

"However boys, don't worry," his convivial tone had returned, "for we have private Krombach in our midst, who knows everything about everything and he is going to demonstrate how a soldier who has been with the battalion for…" Gauner paused, "How long have you been playing at being a soldier, Krombach?"

"Four months, Corporal," Krombach answered, trying not to sound intimidated.

"Four months, Corporal," Gauner repeated in a mocking tone which sounded mildly coquettish to the sound of muted laughter.

The sergeant put the redcoat to the test, rattling through the orders to simulate the action for a misfire. As Krombach concentrated on the procedure, Gauner turned about sharply and in feigned accidental movement, he cuffed the back of Krombach's head sending the young soldier's bicorne spinning to the ground. Gauner turned to the ranks and pulled a face to the audience of the platoon, as skilled as any jester. Proceeding to pace around Krombach with deliberate care, he crushed the defenceless black felt hat into the soft turf. With the misfire drill carried out to Gauner's satisfaction and Krombach failing to respond to the belittlement, the sergeant tried a new tack.

"Private know-all, who has not yet learnt to shave, recently enlightened us with his vast knowledge of the French people and their army? Is that right, Private?"

Gauner now faced Krombach, bringing his face in close to the young soldier so that each burst of invective covered him in spittle and fetid breath. Still Krombach did not reply but held Gauner's stare.

"Answer me boy. You said the French were stronger than us! Stronger than YOUR comrades! Stronger than the men in MY Company!"

Gauner had waited for this moment for weeks. The timing had never been quite right. But with Brandt and Roner still involved with Richter's platoon he could at last enjoy revenge, but still needed to be wary. At a distance, should anyone observe, this scene still needed to look like drill and instruction.

"Don't cry, Private."

"I'm not!"

"Pardon me. Did you speak? I'm not...?" Gauner bellowed.

"I'm not crying, Corporal."

"No, not yet, but don't ever question me again boy, do you understand? Bugger off to your fishing village and leave the fighting to the real men or start listening and learning when men better than you give an opinion."

Gauner's voice snarled, loud enough for the platoon to hear every word.

"Do you understand me?

"Yes, Corporal!" Krombach snapped back an automatic reply. There were no tears yet but he could feel the burning shame in his face and wondered just where this would end.

"Good," Gauner lowered his voice to a whisper, "because if you don't, it won't be a French bullet or bayonet that you will have to worry about."

Gauner stepped back and turned two paces to the right of Krombach.

"Right, now that the little matter is settled lads, Private Know-all, sorry, Private Krombach, will demonstrate just why we will beat the French, should they ever be brave enough to stand against us in the field, won't you Private?"

"Yes Corporal"

"Good. Private Krombach will fire five rounds at the target from one hundred yards, hitting between the two black lines with every shot." Gauner's voice had returned to his earlier easy tone with the men. Then he paused. "Oh, let's make this interesting. If he misses, he will clean thirty muskets after drill. Yes, that's what we will do. I will choose the best soldiers on parade today and Krombach will clean their muskets."

Some smiles broke out in the ranks, soldiers subconsciously straightened their posture, silently appealing to be relieved of musket cleaning, an onerous necessity. A chance to dodge the task and enjoy more of the penultimate night in camp was a promising prospect.

The first three shots had struck home, well within the centre of the board, puffs of dust and splinters of wood attesting to the point of impact. Each shot had been accompanied with a mixture of cheers and groans from the watching platoon. Krombach had tried to cut out the noise and listen only to the orders. He felt a wave of weariness pass through him as he stood braced to fire the fourth round. At the command of "Make ready," he had cocked the musket; at the command to "Present," brought it to his eye-line. Despite the mild mid-March temperature, his forehead was caked in sweat and he felt this run along his brow and drop onto his right hand as he squeezed the trigger waiting for the final command.

"Fire"

There was the delay of a second while the spark from the flint struck the frizzen, ignited the powder in the touch-hole and the Brown-Bess musket kicked savagely into Krombach's shoulder. A thick white puff of smoke obscured his vision.

"Miss," shouted Gauner in triumph.

But other voices disagreed.

"What, what?" Gauner cocked a hand behind his ear, conducting the platoon, like some puppeteer performing for a town crowd.

"Hit you say; high on the right; near the top but under the line?" Gauner laughed enjoying his own bonhomie.

"One more to go then; you lot shouldn't be encouraging him. Think of the extra time at the tavern you could all enjoy."

The orders followed again. Krombach took the opportunity as he loaded the barrel with ball and powder to mop his brow; again, as he replaced the ramrod he drew the back of his right hand across his brow, hoping that Gauner wouldn't notice. But the sergeant had designs of his own. While Krombach loaded, he told the captive audience of the success they would achieve in war by overcoming tiredness,

overcoming the enemy and overcoming their own fears.
As Krombach stood left foot facing towards the target,
right heel touching the left, he heard the commands
"Make Ready" and "Present" in quick succession; but
no command to fire.

Gauner continued his soliloquy on the limits of
exhaustion that a soldier might expect to endure. After
three minutes he stopped talking and turned to face
Krombach, who had been holding the musket, ready to
fire while Gauner had deliberately ignored him.
Krombach fought the strain of aching arms at holding
Brown-Bess, aware of the barrel's sway as his muscles
screamed. If Krombach had been on the deck of a ship
rolling in heavy seas the movement of the barrel would
not have been much worse.

"Fire!"

The ignition, delay and then explosion of smoke and
flame a relief, but the delighted sound of Gauner's voice
was not.

"Missed!"

This time there were no voices from the ranks to
appeal the decision.

Dort: 19th March 1793

The room echoed with small talk and the occasional
burst of laughter but it did little to conceal the
unspoken tension. Brooks Jackson was finding his first

full day on Dutch soil to be slightly strange, very much on the periphery of events. An informal introduction to the Duke's staff had taken place the previous evening and he had found himself drawn towards the company of Major Trevethan, at first because of the close locations of their places of birth but then quickly through a shared humour and world view. Now the pair sat together in the bay window seat of a large cottage, sharing the room with another dozen British and Dutch staff officers. The house had been requisitioned by General Lake, the Guards Brigade commander, and the building now assumed the mantle of the command post for the Duke in his reconnoitring of the eastern fringes of the coastline of the Diep.

The room was a clean, crisp white, save for a dark mahogany cupboard comprising of three sturdy drawers and shelving above in the same timber, filled with richly coloured plates. On the far wall from the two men, a highly polished table nestled between four chairs and a large fireplace. On the table a map of the Diep, edges held down by an assortment of cups and crockery, had become the focal point of various officers, as comments and assumptions circulated. Other plates, clearly Oriental in design were hung on small sturdy shelves, off-cuts of the blackened timber beams which protruded between the freshly white-washed ceiling plaster. Opposite the open doorway that led to the main hall, another door stood ajar and from this came the delicious aroma of freshly cooked beef. From the hallway, a long-case clock chimed.

It was two o'clock and the Duke of York was an hour late. He and his party, escorted with a compliment of Dutch Hussars, had set off to scout the French lines at dawn. A missing Duke would scupper what promised to be an excellent meal. Another fifteen minutes elapsed before a body of horsemen came into view from the large bay window. Within minutes the Duke of York breezed into the room, apologising for the delay in what was clearly smelling like an exquisite lunch but could barely conceal the look of delight on his face. Drinks and fresh water were hastily brought so that he, Murray, Boetslaar and Craufurd could be refreshed.

The mood lifted as the news circulated. The French had fallen back as far as Breda; the threat to Gorcum and from a left hook along the banks of the Diep was over. It was not until four in the afternoon that the matter could be discussed around the map, the table having been cleared to permit the sumptuous array of meat dishes and puddings. Only with the clearing of plates by a stream of efficient Coldstream stewards were the sightings and details conveyed to the whole room. Officers jostled to view the map. York spoke confidently, outlining the tactical significance of his findings.

"The situation for us has not changed significantly, not yet. The French are in Breda, but we don't know how many and we don't yet possess the means to dislodge them. Perhaps Dumouriez has gone elsewhere? Generals Boetslaar and Bentinck have agreed to conduct widespread scouting either side of Breda and see what more information might be found."

Dutch and British officers nodded in approval and both men concerned returned the acknowledgement with smiles.

"Also gentleman, a new face to our ranks; our new Commissary General, Mister Brooks Jackson."

Jackson hauled himself from the seat, wedged in next to Trevethan and stood, to a gentle round of applause and warm greetings.

"My apologies for barely having spoken to you but I see that you have found a fellow west countryman. I hope you can understand the Major more than I?"

Again, warm laughter in the room, slightly more exaggerated from Henson-Jefferies and his fellow ensigns. Both Trevethan and Jackson exchanged a look noting the fact.

"Now, what news from London on the other brigades?"

Jackson raised a hand to acknowledge the room.

"Thank you, your 'ighness for the warm welcome. As Commissary General, I promise to keep you and the men in the manner in which you are accustomed, though after today's meal, I may already need write to London for more money."

Trevethan coughed heavily, "Good luck on that, Mister Jackson."

The general mood of merriment continued at the interchange between the men.

"When I last spoke to the Minister for War, an infantry brigade was preparing to march to London, from where it will embark to join us. Within two weeks that force should be here and ready for deployment."

Jackson thought it not the opportune time to express the reservations of Horse Guards on the quality of the men. The Duke would probably already know the thoughts of General Fawcett on the matter.

"Twenty squadrons of cavalry are also due, within the next few weeks. Along with that will come Hanoverian and Hessian infantry, guns and cavalry; in six weeks, sir, you will have an army of twenty thousand men or more." Jackson finished speaking and the Duke nodded his thanks.

"That is all gentlemen. Return to your posts, thank you." Murray spoke at the signal from York.

The room was filled with footsteps and the scraping of chairs on polished wooden floor boards. Murray's voice cut across the din.

"Commissary General, a moment, if you please?"

The room cleared and the door closed, York, Murray and Watson remained.

"Do you think those timings are accurate?" York spoke, a hint of concern in his voice.

"Yes sir, I do. Why?"

"Boetslaar wants to fight the French tomorrow. The man is like an angry bulldog spoiling for a match." York shrugged. "That is not the concern, he can be handled."

The Duke smiled and nodded towards Murray, signalling that the task was one best continued by the Chief of Staff.

"Was there anything else from London? Were you given orders?"

When Murray spoke of London, Jackson knew he meant Dundas. Horse Guards would have no doubt briefed the Duke; Jackson saw no reason to pull his punches. Besides, telling a truth now might give him room for a few fictions later.

"Yes sir. To make sure that you don't get swept along with the Austrians and end up doin' their biddin'; I am only authorised to purchase victuals for the British, Hanoverians and the Hessians. Even supplying the Dutch would be heavily frowned upon, I expect."

The Duke and Murray exchanged glances and then York offered Jackson his hand.

"Thank you, Brooks. Thank you for your candour. We shall progress quite well, I think."

CHAPTER NINETEEN

A Position of Strength.

Neerwinden: 18th March 1793

The battle had raged for half of the day but it had passed Major Brennan and his squadron of Esterhàzy hussars by. They could not even have claimed to be spectators. The whole regiment had been positioned as a reserve to the left of the central ridge that formed Prince Josias' position. Apart from the occasional troop being sent on scouting duty towards Dormael to observe the ponderous left hook that the French had attempted to deliver there, there had been no call made for the services of the cavalrymen.

Instead the horsemen had spent most of the morning dismounted, their mounts stood patiently under heavy horse blankets while ominous skies threatened overhead and early spring greenery shone bronze from a midday sun that offered no warmth. Soon cooking fires had sprouted into life, Brennan had signalled for his troopers to follow suit. It was often the perverse luck of the soldier that rare moments of luxury were spoilt and the arrival of a mug of coffee to warm the officer's hands on, coincided with the appearance of riders along the ridge. Brennan watched the passage of the men with interest. Even at the higher elevation the ground looked heavy going. The sodden ground where the hussars had been posted was a poor location for his horses to spend any length of time.

A hundred yards behind the Esterhàzy, a tributary of the Gete ran swollen, the ground on either side a morass of standing water which had been churned brown by the passage of troopers making their way to and from the river. One of the riders had a distinctive red jacket and Brennan knew the British officer from his recent posting at Prince Josias' headquarters. Information had been relayed to the colonel of the regiment and the rider had been about to head further along the line when he spotted Brennan and pulled his horse towards his fellow Englishman, who fought in the bold sky blue jacket and cherry red riding breeches of the Esterhàzy Regiment.

"Craufurd, what news? Any work for us?"

"None yet sir, but there is bound to be action later today," Captain Craufurd touched his bicorne in recognition of Brennan's rank.

"So, what's happening on the other side of the hill?"

"The French are putting in a serious effort on our left, probably to draw the Prince away from the Liege road. Neerwinden is being heavily contested. They drive a battalion out, we feed another one back in. Infantry work, pure and simple and most of it at the point of a bayonet."

"Sounds grim."

"The French are having much the worst of it, sir. I would say their losses are three times ours. And the ground is stodgy, I don't think your chaps would want to be anywhere near the town right now."

"Don't let their eagerness to entertain a spot of lunch fool you. They are bored rigid. I am too, a bit. Someone else is taking of the glory," Brennan sounded rueful but winked at the mounted officer, in the confident expectation of the moment later in the day when the Esterhàzy would be unleashed.

"Any sign of the enemy cavalry, Craufurd?"

"It's not been deployed in great force, sir. Colonel Mack has estimated that we outnumber them two to one in sabres and many times more in quality. The colonel is advising His Highness to let the French punch themselves out against Neerwinden, meanwhile we have given ground on the right to stretch the communications between the enemy's attack columns and weaken their centre. We remain largely unscathed so I'd say that Prince Josias is holding all of the aces right now."

"Well we will certainly be glad to move from here. And the prospect of being left in the lurch as the rear-guard on ground like this was giving me the willies, I don't mind admitting. As long as we don't have a second Jemappes on our hands!"

"That's a name we have been banned from mentioning," Craufurd smiled. The action had been an ignominious defeat for an Austrian force at the hands of Dumouriez, late in the previous year.

"One last thought, sir. When you do move, you are not to use the main Liege road. Colonel Mack has reserved that privilege for the cuirassiers."

"I told you someone else would be taking all of the glory."

"By the time this day is out there will be plenty to go around, sir. I must continue; good luck and good hunting, Major," Craufurd again touched his bicorne and headed towards the Liege road.

The afternoon passed in splendid isolation. Messengers criss-crossed the ridge but none brought news for the Esterhàzy. When orders came at last, troopers busied themselves for action. As Brennan and two of his sergeants carried out a final inspection of the now mounted hussars, the Englishman witnessed the incredible sight of twelve hundred cuirassiers, the elite heavy horsemen of the Austrian cavalry, who considered themselves unrivalled in Europe. Black breast-plates stood out against crisp white uniforms. The column which passed along the Liege road seemed infinite and on the other side of the ridge Austrian artillery peeled out a massive cannonade, as much it seemed to announce their impending arrival rather than crush the enemy's exposed infantry.

The cuirassiers disappeared.

Fifteen minutes later the order to advance was issued. The Esterhàzy would cross the ridge, find a crossing over the Gete and pursue a broken enemy.

The Brabant countryside, made open by farmland, offered few hiding places. Even the mud would now work in Austria's favour. Every step the enemy took would sap their energy.

It would be fine sport for the Esterhàzy.

South of Neerwinden: 19th March 1793

The war-club had materialised out of the darkness. Had Mahieu not already been shifting his weight to load his musket, the blow would have killed him. Instead, the impact was oblique and the darkness of the American night disappeared into the darkness of dreams. He felt Mohawk warriors rush past him; felt the crush of pine needles as he collided with the forest floor; heard the ragged musket volley.

Images of his life swam through his mind, each overlapping another.

The tree where the boys had made a swing; Donatienne, giving birth to their daughter; a long August night in sleepy Dunkirk. Visions collided together in impossible combinations while the scent of fresh pine filled his lungs.

The silence of dreams was shattered with an explosion of sounds. He could hear voices that sounded familiar though he could not place a name to any of them. And the pain was back. The left side of his skull where the war-club had struck years before pulsated again with unbearable pressure. His fingers clawed into bare earth in torment. Pine needles dug into the skin, some sliding under finger-nails, piercing the soft nail-bed but even this new agony failed to draw the sting of anguish inside his head.

Jean-Batiste tried to open his eyes: only the right eye would respond. He looked up into the early morning sky. Clusters of lights, distant stars floating amongst the clouds, came slowly into focus. Tentatively he raised his left hand, along his chin and cheek towards his eye socket, finger tips feeling streaks of blood. The well of his eye socket had filled with a mixture of blood and pine needles. He tried to scoop the congealed mixture away when he heard a voice.

"Here, Sergeant, leave that to me."

He thought he recognised the voice; one of the Grison boys, the smuggler's sons. But those boys were striplings, ten years old at most.

He felt the jolt of ice-cold water against his face followed by the gentle motion of a cloth on his forehead, working downward into the orbits of his face.

More water.

Mahieu was awake. Alive but nothing made sense; just a searing pain in his head. Slowly, he blinked. Both eyes were open, functioning. He levered himself up and the man whose voice seemed familiar, helped the sergeant, propping him up by the base of a tree.

The woods were alive with movement. Small campfires crackled as resin-soaked wood burned, a rich golden light piercing the gloom. Another man that Mahieu recognised strode out of the darkness. The pressure in his head was back and concentration seemed impossible. The man knelt next to him put a water bottle to Mahieu's lips and he drank freely, slaking a sudden thirst which felt unquenchable.

"Glad you are back with us, Sergeant."

Captain Davide turned to the soldier who had been treating Mahieu. "Thank you, Fabian. Good work. We need this old war horse."

Mahieu saw the Captain smile; the present time began to make sense; the Black Lions, Fabian Grison was a soldier now, not a boy.

"Any sign of the patrol, sir? Is Guilbert back yet? Grison asked trying not to show anxiety about the fate of his younger brother.

"Yes, just back. That's what I came to tell you. We are leaving in the next half an hour. The camp fires will stay alight. Just carry essential equipment. If we move soon, we might just catch up with the army. Spread the word among the company while I talk to the sergeant for a moment."

Grison nodded and moved silently away.

"What happened to me?" Mahieu's eyes followed the movement of Grison. "I remember him as a boy." He looked at the Captain; more fragments of the previous day were resurfacing.

"The battery... did we protect it? My head... it's bursting..."

Mahieu spoke a stream of short phrases, overcome by the latest rush of pressure which felt as if it was squeezing his head between a vice.

"Rest, my friend, rest," Davide said. "We are alive and that is all that matters for now. Can you walk, do you think? The army has retreated. We are part of the rear-guard. The colonel has ordered our withdrawal now. It's going to be hard going, I'm afraid. Our cavalry and guns have buggered off sometime in the night. We are here on our own for the moment."

Davide was not surprised at his sergeant's confusion. Had Mahieu not stumbled as the cuirassier aimed the killing stroke, the Frenchman would not have lived to be carried from the field of Neerwinden. Instead, the cavalryman's sabre hilt had contacted with the left temple of Mahieu. The blow alone should have killed him but the sergeant had led a charmed life throughout the day and fate must have been protecting the veteran from Dunkirk.

In the confusion of the final moments of the battle, Dumouriez himself had ridden into the centre of the hollow square which the Black Lions had formed themselves into, as the Austrian cavalry stalked the battlefield in search of a beaten enemy to rout and kill. The skirmish line, of which Mahieu had been a part, was trying to protect the flank of a gun battery, in the act of limbering up and preparing to withdraw. Out of the smoke of battle, fresh cavalry charged the screen, severing the escape route back to the battalion and spearing the skirmishers back against the stricken guns. Dumouriez and the massed ranks of infantry could only watch on in horror. Mahieu had collapsed under one of the abandoned field guns. When the few survivors of the cavalry attack had returned to the safety of the square, the sergeant's unconscious body was dragged to safety by the Grison brothers.

The battle had achieved nothing, at least nothing that Davide could fathom. The Black Lions had lost over two hundred men, dead or missing.

The army was beaten.

Tirlemont: 26th March 1793

A week before, the town had been headquarters to the French on the eve of the battle from which Dumouriez hoped to be able to dictate peace on his terms.

The armies of the North and Ardennes had combined and caught the advancing force of the Austrian General Clerfayt by surprise, mauling his force and sending it limping to the safety of Prince Josias' army around the town of Neerwinden. Dumouriez and Miranda had followed close on their heels. The opposing forces were closely matched in number, 45,000 Frenchmen opposed 39,000 Austrians. The revolutionary fervour of the French set against the superior training of the Austrians soldiers in every arm.

The night before battle, a warning reached Dumouriez. It was only a matter of time until the Prussian Army under Prince Frederick of Brunswick forced a passage of the Meuse. Another ten thousand men, the professionally trained Prussians would arrive to turn parity to clear allied advantage and revenge for the embarrassment of Valmy. Prussia had no interest in negotiating for peace. Only by seizing Paris could the Prussian King, Frederick William the Second, gain meaningful leverage at the peace table and expand the Prussian state with the reparation of French territory.

Despite the better defensive ground, Dumouriez' only option had been to attack: defeat the Austrians; pin their army against the Meuse; negotiate as the victor. The gambit offered every prospect of success until the final hour when the Austrians unleashed their reserves of heavy cavalry, breaking the French centre, and the cup of victory had been cruelly dashed from his lips.

Two French riders and their Austrian cavalry escort headed past the working parties of French prisoners who were digging mass graves in the soft Brabant turf. A similar scene would be happening around the villages and ridge above the Petite Gete, no doubt. Some of the soldiers paused in their grizzly task of retrieving the pale and twisted corpses, robbed of the last vestiges of wealth and dignity to shout a weary "Vive La France," at the sight of the General and the giant French dragoon who rode behind him. But such moments were short lived. Many of the cries died on the wind or with a discouraging prod from the butt of an Austrian musket.

Dumouriez would negotiate as the vanquished and it had seared a malignity into his soul since the moment of defeat.

Mack waited for the arrival of the General being entrusted by Prince Josias to undertake the most insightful questioning of the Frenchman. If the colonel, a staunch sceptic of Dumouriez' offer, could be convinced, then others in the Austrian hierarchy could. Just as importantly, a Prince could not meet a vanquished inferior. Where was the honour in that?

When Dumouriez and Beauvais entered the tent, Mack, and the young Cuirassier ensign who stood at his side, bowed deeply. Dumouriez and Beauvais returned the gesture. A single gold-framed chair with an inviting soft red seat, had been placed in front of a white clothed table and the senior officers sat, leaving the cavalrymen to stand. Dumouriez spoke fluent German but French was not a language that Mack chose to speak, unless necessary.

While apologies from the Prince of his absence from the meeting were relayed in a formal letter read by the Cuirassier officer, Mack studied his erstwhile opponent.

To Mack, Dumouriez had always been a gambler, reckless with his affections; once, the servant of Louis; next, a redoubtable revolutionary; now, a friend to the Bourbon household again. The Austrian court would fall in love with Dumouriez no doubt, his elegant uniform, fresh and crisp, encasing a slender physique. While lines of worry had been lightly etched into his brow, the face suggested one more akin to laughter than despair. If Austria chose to accept Dumouriez, Mack would have to contend with the General for the duration of the campaign, in all likelihood. The thought that an émigré General would be more loved than a colonel who delivered victory after victory for the Emperor twitched at the edges of Mack's scarred face.

"General, we are both busy men. I shall be blunt. Why should Austria trust you?" Mack had decided that subtlety would not be needed; only firm questioning.

"Austria has nothing to fear from me, Colonel. She can only gain from this meeting and from this union. Our countries are not natural enemies. Did you know that I was the last person to speak in confidence with the King? It was the night before his execution." Dumouriez spoke assuredly, even in a foreign tongue.

"He ordered me to serve France as I must until the moment that his line could be re-established." Dumouriez edged closer and lent on the table, looking at the notes that Mack was scribbling. "He knew that the time was not right then but a time would come when the allies of France would come to her rescue, restoring the Monarchy and the Catholic Church. We prayed together that such a time might come."

Mack raised an eyebrow at the words but continued noting them.

"And will we be lucky enough to find that your men share these repressed feelings of love for a king sent to the guillotine in front of a baying mob?" Mack asked with near naked acerbity.

"A great deal will, I believe. But, with Prince Josias' permission, I would offer my men a free choice. Some of the men are from the old army. Of their support I'm certain. Some of the colonels, whom I have spoken to privately about the matter, would be prepared to speak out in support of this union. Those who don't, I would ask in all conscience, to be sent home."

Mack again scratched notes and at the mention of the word, looked up sharply.

"Home? We can't just send half of your army home." He shook his head in disbelief.

"Each officer would declare an oath on behalf of those men who wish to return, that they would not take up arms against our forces. If we keep the soldiers as prisoners, it would just create bad feeling amongst the other men. Besides it would cost you money and men to feed and guard them."

Mack shrugged at the comments. Such vows were not uncommon, but the colonel was still far from convinced.

"Pardon me, may I ask a question of your aide?"

"Yes of course. But may I first say the great wound he bears on his face was suffered in saving my life. He has given great service to France. Should Captain Beauvais wish to give no more and return home, I would still be in his debt."

"Then we have both given for our cause." The scar tissue on the right of Mack's face ran in a similar jagged fashion to that of Beauvais', but where Mack had retained the sight in his right eye, the wound of the Frenchman carried on toward his hairline. The vermilion had slowly begun drain from the scar tissue but it did not yet bear the pale flesh tone that Mack's had settled into.

"Captain, forgive me, but I must ask. Truthfully, will you follow the General? Could you, clearly a brave soldier of France, consider an act which some might see as treachery and to which you might find yourself away from home for another six months, perhaps even a year; truthfully now, on your word."

Beauvais fidgeted uneasily behind Dumouriez as the cuirassier ensign translated Mack's words into French. He had considered that he might be asked such a question. The response that Dumouriez wanted was clear but the cunning of the man had been to leave the dragoon an escape route should he want it.

"Sir, I am a soldier of France, it is true. And it is as a soldier of France that I will remain. The General knows my personal plan. I shall return to my regiment. If my colonel decides that he wishes to follow the General, then as a soldier, I would do duty to my regiment. If not, then I will take an oath and return home."

Mack listened and watched Beauvais as he spoke. Satisfied with the veracity of the answer, he etched the page with a few more notes.

"Thank you." Mack nodded at Beauvais.

"General Dumouriez, I will report to the Prince as soon as I am able. What are your plans now?"

"Move the army south, near the fortresses of Lille and Valenciennes."

Mack could not contain the mistrust he felt towards the French General.

"Why so far south? We will follow you, of course. If you try and run for the border."

"I understand your sentiments. But it is both a practical and tactical matter. My army is short of supplies now. We must feed ourselves or drain you of resources. A starving army is more likely to disintegrate rather than finish the job at hand. Also, as I'm sure you know, Valenciennes and Lille are the keys to Paris. Hold these fortresses and the road to Paris lies before you. If I am close enough, when the moment comes, I can ensure that the commanders of those fortresses are men loyal to me."

Mack had studied the maps. Grudgingly, he conceded that what Dumouriez stated was both logical and practical.

"General, Prince Josias has placed huge amount of faith in you."

Dumouriez stood and offered Mack his hand. "I will not let him down; you have my word, Colonel."

Mack shrugged acceptance, rose, and shook hands.

CHAPTER TWENTY

English Pay.

Valenciennes: 1st April 1793

Tired horses, sweating heavily, struggled to pull the carriage over the final incline of the scarp. Three-quarters of a mile further along the flat plateau, the walled city of Valenciennes revealed itself to the coach-team and passengers. The town's brickwork was bathed a dull bronze by afternoon sunlight. The walls were given the illusion of towering proportions, reflected in the gentle flow of the Scheldt River, tributaries of which ran either side of the fortress. The flow of the river left only three narrow avenues from which the town could be approached, marshland edged large swathes of the river bank. In the distant north-west, out of view on the plateau, roads disappeared on to Dunkirk and Cambrai. This town was one of the 'Keys to France' as many Generals had called them, Valenciennes and further north, Lille. Paris could not allow such prizes to be gained by her adversaries.

Behind the first carriage, a second struggled at the foot of the slope, both having travelled sixty miles or more already that day. Once Maurice Caillat would

have trembled at the thought of travelling in such
exalted company; ten years earlier, he had been a
stable-boy in a provincial town, in Bergerac. Since then,
France had changed, for the better in the opinion of
Caillat and he would offer everything to see that it did
not return to a world of rule by an absolute monarch.
The stable-boy would scarcely have dreamt of owning
the long velvet emerald-green coat and matching
breeches that Caillat now wore, or of the tricolour sash
of office wound tightly around a slim waist. But Caillat
had completed a metamorphosis, from stable-boy to
investigator and few in France were beyond his scope.

Of his travelling companions, he knew varying
amounts before the journey and had learnt much
during it.

Marquis de Beurnonville, Minister of War and the
man to whom Caillat reported directly, was seated next
to him. Even though Beurnonville was his senior, the
Marquis had insisted that his own personal conduct be
scrutinised due to his life-long friendship with
Dumouriez. There could be no hint of favouritism; the
General would be returned to Paris and answer the
grievous charge of treason.

Opposite Beurnonville sat Armand Camus, a man of
great renown in the National Assembly. His was the
second signature on the oath which had brought a
political challenge to the divine autocracy of Louis XVI
and one of the few who could survive without the need

for protection of either the *Jacobins* or *Girondins*. The opposing political factions had developed a deep hatred of one another, each wanting to control the course of the revolution. Even *'les Montagne'*, powerful voices from the court of the dead king, who still held sway and kept the political peace, heeded the council of wise Camus.

Across from Caillat was the man who interested him the most. Lazare Carnot was one of the brightest minds in the Republic. He considered every citizen a soldier and had been instrumental in raising hundreds of thousands of volunteers. An engineer by profession, his energy had driven the organisation of military training camps and the supply system for so many new recruits. Caillat admired Carnot's confident manner, born not from arrogance but from a disposition that all was possible. When Beurnonville and Camus had moved to praise Carnot for his efforts, in genuine modesty he stated that the credit was due to the many men and women around him who shared his vision. Yet there was a steely determination about the man which Maurice Caillat found inspiring. Carnot was nicknamed 'the Worker' by all sides of the National Assembly. Caillat had enquired of Carnot's current assignment and with a nod of assent from the minister, Beurnonville, the Worker spoke freely.

Beyond Valenciennes he was destined for the camps at Mont Cassel and Dunkirk. He travelled with an executive authority as powerful as Beurnonville's. His word was as good as if Paris had decreed the matter in that moment, yet he bore the responsibility with outward ease. His work was to make the defence of the Republic efficient in every matter, save that of sending people to the guillotine.

Despite having been informed of the seeds of Dumouriez' treachery for some weeks, Caillat only held the powers to investigate, interrogate and then report his findings; he wondered if he could trust himself to arrest people on the strength of his own suspicions. Beurnonville had yet to confer such powers on the men who worked for him. In the climate of fear that pervaded Paris, the necessity of proof was diminishing.

The carriage which trailed behind and had now crested the plateau contained three *Girondins*. Caillat had spent his brief political life fighting and investigating them. Two of the Girondins were to accompany Beurnonville and Camus. The third, also an investigator from the Ministry of War, was heading to Lille, no doubt charged with a similar task to Caillat. A fortnight before, Girondin spies had infiltrated the camp of General Dumouriez and made the potential treachery commonplace news on their return to Paris. The situation, previously monitored stealthily by Beurnonville's department, threatened a rift in the Assembly and pushed the Revolutionary Council towards its own civil war. The Girondins had crowed about the revelations to anyone who would listen. What

Beurnonville had done with the information he had
held for weeks was not for Caillat to know.

The coaches arrived into the western gates of
Valenciennes, slipped through leafy avenues and on
towards a hostelry. Tired passengers clambered out
and fresh horses were put on a single carriage. Only a
short stop was planned, the remaining passengers
would share the one coach and head toward the
headquarters of the Army of the North, near the
marshes at Raismes. Stable-boys and coach men
clambered over the carriage, transferring or unloading
baggage.

Caillat blinked in the sunlight and stretched a lean
frame before dusting down his jacket. Long straw
blonde hair was tied with a leather knot and fell in a
pony tail to the middle of his back. Youthful whiskers
grew around a thick golden-brown moustache, a similar
rectangular patch of growth on his lower lip. Ten years
ago, Caillat would have been one of the stable boy's
sweating to change the horses in quick time or bear the
consequences of a swift kick to the body. Caillat and
Carnot had chosen the backpack favoured by infantrymen to hold their worldly goods and both smiled as
they made sure that the cowhide packs were indeed the
correct ones, each backpack holding documents vital for
both men.

Inside the investigator's, a series of folded notes, each
written in a familiar scrawl. The man who had given

Caillat a chance to make something of himself, plucking him from the obscurity of a Paris market place on the whim of a chance conversation, had been Serge Genet. And it had been from the pen of Genet that Beurnonville had been receiving information for some weeks. Maurice Caillat was in the debt of his former mentor for his current position in the world.

The investigator, once of Bergerac, walked swiftly over to the passengers who remained, shook hands with Beurnonville and Camus, ignored the two Girondin ministers and turned on his heels to catch up with Carnot.

Bentheim: 2nd April 1793

Krombach sat alone in the empty canvas tent massaging the soles of his sore feet. The march from Hanover to Bentheim had taken eleven days and he was enjoying momentary solace in a camp now filled by the entire Hanoverian army. The flaps of the tent were tied back so that Krombach could witness the commotion of dozens of redcoats gathering around one of the kitchen tents, where a notice had been pinned by Company Sergeant-Major Roner. Before he had time to gingerly put socks and boots back, he spotted the figure of Henry Pinsk, loping over toward the tent like an excited schoolboy.

"We're off!" Pinsk had skidded to an ungainly halt before ducking into the tent.

"I know you're off Corporal, I have had to share a tent with you for the last twelve days," Krombach replied.

"Ha bloody ha. Very droll, private." Henry smiled. "My wind is the sign of an effective digestive system and if you don't like it you can always sleep in the west-wing of our little castle," gesturing outside of the tent.

"Don't tempt me," Krombach smiled back.

The tent which could comfortably house sixteen men was filled with the back-packs and laundry of twenty. Sleeping at the sides of the tent meant waking to a shower of damp and condensation each morning, sleeping in the middle meant that you were more likely to be trodden on as men came and went for watch duties.

"What's the news? I'm saving my energy rather than trying to fight my way through that lot."

The pair looked up again; Gauner had bulldozed his way to the front and was now reading the orders to most of the company who stood six or seven deep to hear.

"We leave tomorrow. We are now part of 3rd Brigade, us and the 5th Regiment. Nothing more than that, except that by tomorrow night, we will be in Holland," Pinsk spoke with the enthusiasm of a boy looking forward to the arrival of a travelling fair.

The army itself bore a resemblance to a travelling fair. In the space of a week, the population of the quiet border town of Bentheim had risen from some five thousand people to somewhere near twenty thousand as Hanoverian forces converged on the town. The battalion had arrived on the Saturday to camp at the walls of a medieval hill, which rose sharply above the predominately flat landscape. The following day the army paraded within its walls; every battle standard received a last blessing on German soil.

The two soldiers ambled over to join the back of the crowd and listen to the various excited chatter from the men about just where the orders might take them, Gauner's voice above all others, as usual. As the pair crossed the open space, they saw Captain Brandt with a British officer, a Major called Rifle, for whom the men of the 10th had paraded that morning. The men having been counted off, the battalion was officially taken into British service. The major had spoken briefly to the men in very fluent German; Hanoverian troops were subject to the same rules of discipline as a British soldier but also the same pay. King George wanted no favouritism between his loyal troops. That news had caused excited murmurs throughout the ranks and throughout the rest of the day. While no one knew what the rates of pay might be, it was rumoured that British soldiers were paid significantly more than the men from Hanover.

Captain Brandt had escorted Major Rifle through the entire ordnance list of 2nd battalion's equipment. Once the Major was satisfied that the numbers tallied with Neuberg's report which had been submitted two weeks earlier, he and Brandt had scrawled signatures into a ledger carried by the Major's orderly and Rifle considered his work of the last few days complete. The 10th had been the last regiment on his list and now he could report back to Commissary General Jackson as he returned to find the Duke's army, wherever that now was.

Brandt was rather hopeful of finding out what was happening across the front too, eager to be rid of Major Rifle. With the Englishman satisfied, Brandt made to Colonel Neuberg's tent to report. When he got there, he found both Volgrafs, major and captain, sat in close counsel around a portable table, with Neuberg at its head, which had become a fixture of the officer's tent. Across from them sat Bachmeier and Thalberg, the captains of the other two companies.

"I was just about to send out a search party for you" Neuberg said, gesturing to an empty seat. "I have come down from the mountain with the word."

Sheepishly, Brandt took a seat next to Bachmeier. Neuberg just returned from a meeting in the Great Hall of the castle under the gold and red heraldic banners of Bentheim Castle, had received a rather lethargic and lengthy briefing from Field Marshal Freytag, the army's commander. Colonel Neuberg proceeded to unfold a sketched map of the Belgium and the French frontier and the fortresses of Valenciennes and Lille.

"Right, this is what I know. The French are on the run from here, pointing to a mark on the map that represented Neerwinden. A battle was fought about two weeks ago and the French forces were beaten by the Austrians."

General cheering followed that news. "The Austrians have followed up sharply, pushing back the French to here." Neuberg drew a series of crosses around Lille and Valenciennes. "These two cities are the keys to Northern France. Hold them and Paris is less than two weeks march away. The French have pulled back against the British," he marked more crosses against Dunkirk and a thin line from the coast to Lille, "and the British have received orders to push up, for us to join them and then link up with Austria."

More cheers and applause from the faces around the table; even Major Volgraf bore the look of an excited man.

"And south from here, we have just received news that Prussia and Austria have forced crossings on the Rhine near Oppenheim and Spires."

More excited glances and smiles.

"Gentlemen, it seems the French are in full retreat. The bad news is that we are here," he pointed to a spot on the table, three inches off the map. Perhaps a month away, by which time Valenciennes or Lille may have fallen. This war may well be over before we get there."

The table fell silent.

Neuberg looked hard at the map. "But who knows. It could all change. Oh, before I forget," he looked at the Major, "Johann you and I, best dress. Field Marshal Freytag is hosting a dinner at eight."

"Yes sir." Volgraf showed no sign of the fact that he already knew that the invitation was coming.

The Volgraf and Freytag families had served the Hanoverian army for over a century and the Major had already shared a brief appointment the day before in which, amongst other matters, Freytag had promised him the command of the 2nd or another battalion, should one become available. He had also expressed his dismay at von Diepenbroick appointing an 'outsider' with no experience and from Freytag's memory, questionable methods on infantry drill. The Major could be reassured that the Field Marshal would not forget a family friend.

Raismes: 2nd April 1793

On a flea-bitten bed in the dark of a peasant cottage, near edge of the Raismes Forest, which Juliette had done her best to make clean, the couple fought and tussled in frantic love-making, the knowledge that the night could be their last together. She had relented to Beauvais' plan.

It had been a rare victory for the dragoon, but one made from their desire of a life together, after Dumouriez, after the Revolution. If Dumouriez failed to bring the army over to Prince Josias and Austria, Beauvais might gain protection from the regiment but the Countess would be made an example of, no doubt. Flee to Austria and a return to a world of servants and docility toward the protection of an Austrian admirer or stay and be hunted. If the Countess was caught, it would force Beauvais into a rash act of rescue and their fates would be sealed. Such stories of forlorn love played well with the mob, even as the guillotine fell.

With a grudging reluctance both left the bed and dressed. They kissed, perhaps for the last time; neither could be certain; then rode the short distance to Dumouriez' camp, on the edge of the marsh. The bulk of the army was posted further north near St. Amand, the General having already sent a division north-west towards Lille. He had neither the men nor ammunition to besiege either fortress. They would need to be won over by a combination of stealth, persuasion and veiled threat. Genet had drafted messages to both fortress commanders. Two hours later, the Countess de Marboré delivered that message to General Ferrand at Valenciennes.

There was a spartan simplicity to the quarters of Ferrand which sat at odds with his impeccable appearance. The walls were freshly white-washed and uncluttered with decoration; a solitary large painting hanging over an empty fireplace, a hunting party chasing a stag through a forest, the imposing fortress of Valenciennes in a distant valley. On three walls, pairs of narrow windows gave views out on the series of plateaus which surrounded and overlooked Valenciennes. Opposite a closed oak door stood a table, crammed with maps and papers and in front of this, two ancient wooden chairs sat unoccupied. Ferrand drew one of these back and gestured Juliette to be seated. Only when she had done so, did he sit himself and examine the communications that had been delivered to him, one from Dumouriez and the other from Colonel Courtois.

"Do you believe in this enterprise?" Ferrand had read the letter from Dumouriez and had folded it up neatly, before placing it on the desk.

Juliette spoke firmly "No. The revolution has robbed me of a husband and of my life before. I have come to love the life it has given me," she smiled at Ferrand, "and thank you."

345

Ferrand raised an eyebrow. "For what?"

"For asking my opinion. Dumouriez has used me for his own ends and I suppose that I have used him more than a little to gain some freedom. But of late I have allowed myself to become no more than a brightly coloured lure on the end of a fishing line. Even Julien…" Juliette stopped, fearing that in saying more she would somehow be unfaithful.

"Julien?"

"Julien Beauvais, captain in the 3rd Dragoons."

"Ah. Which brings us to this," Ferrand carefully opened the letter from Colonel Courtois, re-adjusting the frames of his spectacles and then read the note, his lips silently mouthing the words, breaking into an occasional smile in doing so. Ferrand folded the note carefully, then paused, stood and walked to the fireplace and began tearing the note into thin shreds.

"The colonel and I are old friends," Ferrand said, taking care to make sure that all of the pieces fell into the grate, "so I cannot risk that being seen. Even here, there are eyes doing the bidding of others now."

He returned to his seat and cleared some of the paperwork from the desk, searching the scrolled documents for a map of the fortress.

"The Assembly has posted an investigator here, a man called Caillat. He reports to the Minster of War. In theory, I am not supposed to have a door closed for a meeting, unless he is present. We haven't much time; he is currently inspecting some part of the town, probably noting the number of rats!" Ferrand smiled momentarily at the thought of the revolutionary fervour of the town's rodents being questioned before returning to the matter at hand.

"Anyway, take my reply to Dumouriez. Tell him that Valenciennes will only take orders from the National Assembly. The doors of Valenciennes are closed to him while he persists in this foolishness. Understood?"

Juliette nodded and studied the map, thick with heavy pencil markings, showing the positioning of redoubts to be constructed to aid the defence of the town. Ferrand slid a hand under his powdered wig and itched at his scalp.

"You need to change out of that dragoon's outfit. You are rather, umm, easily distinguished in it." He smiled as much to hide his own embarrassment at casting an eye over Juliette's physique. The itching finished, his hand returned to trace a path on the map, before turning over sheaves of paper to find some which was yet unused. Working quickly, he sketched a path.

"The chances are that Caillat will have found men to watch the gates now and report on comings and goings. These three gates, eastern, northern and north-western, they are not much use to us. No, it must be the southern gate. Ride here, along the road to Condé, cross the marsh and follow this road." Ferrand sketched the route onto the paper as he spoke.

"I will meet you at the southern gate tonight. From Raismes it is a three-hour ride and you will need to change at some point. You leave here as a Countess and dressed like a soldier. Make sure that you arrive tonight dressed as the niece of a colonel with some story as to how you were so late in arriving. I might drop the matter into casual conversation with Caillat at some point during the day that your arrival is expected."

Juliette nodded and tried to commit as much of the route as she could, in the knowledge that the last part of the journey would be completed after sunset.

"Until we meet again then and you have become Mademoiselle Courtois." Ferrand bowed and kissed the Countess's hand.

Dunkirk: 5th April 1793

Lazare Carnot had paused for no more than an hour at Mont-Cassel, inspecting the views from various positions around the windmill which turned at a leisurely rate in the gentle breeze. He scratched a series of observations with a freshly-sharpened pencil into a small, black, weathered notebook. The town was of strategic importance, it sat on bedrock towering a thousand feet above the flat, fertile farmland around it. To the south lay a military camp. Troops could muster there and strike out against the allies and unless the hilltop town had fallen, the strength and direction of such a stroke would be unknown until it was too late for the allies to react. He closed the black note-book and drew a smaller red one from a right-hand pocket, scribbling further instruction and handed it to a young stable-lad, who been had ordered by Carnot to act as his runner, the moment 'the Worker' had descended from the carriage. Gilles Tabary, Mayor of Mont-Cassel was summoned to meet Carnot at the Church of St-Éloi in Dunkirk, the following day.

Tabary arrived punctually to find the church doors guarded by soldiers in the blue of republican uniforms who, on recognising the mayor's sash of office, ushered him in. He blinked to adjust his eyes from the brightness of a Dunkirk spring day to the dimness of the church. Narrow shafts of sunlight pierced the gloom catching spirals of dust which drifted in the still air. St-Éloi, had been ransacked in the wave of uprisings in the summer, two years earlier, a pitiful cavern littered with the wreckage of medieval pews. Against one of the giant stone columns that ran the length of the church, two figures propped themselves. In the half-light, these were silhouettes he knew at once, friends from his days aboard the *Perseus*. Arnold Mahieu, now the captain of that ship and Jean-Francois Grison, the mayor of Dunkirk. The three shook hands and exchanged whispered greetings.

"I thought you were dead!" Tabary clapped a large paw of a hand on Mahieu's shoulder.

"Not too disappointed, I hope?" Mahieu grinned.

"How's my ship, still in one piece?" Tabary smiled.

"Which ship is that? Not many ships docked in Mont-Cassel, Gilles. But the *Perseus* is fine, thank you. And I might have a little something for you."

"That's what you normally tell the port whores." Tabary laughed.

Mahieu unwound a small leather pouch from around his neck.

"Look!"

He held the pouch over his hand and a dozen small diamonds fell out.

"Sweet Jesus Arnaud, where did you get those?"

"Payment for services, I swiped a couple more, of course."

Mahieu smiled proudly at the sleight of hand that had allowed him to steal an additional four small diamonds from under the nose of Genet.

"Not now, not here. Show some caution, man." Grison hissed.

Even though he was a head's height shorter than the other two men, Grison was as tough as any that Tabary had known.

"This is not right. Why have we three been summoned? This Carnot, a big name in Paris, what does he want with us here? I hate this building. I had ordered it closed ever since…"

Tabary could see that Grison's head was beaded in sweat. He knew what unnerved his friend; a man who had killed his share of men, fought bloody battles in the surf with the survivors of ship-wrecks and casually evaded British ships with nerveless seamanship. Grison had become the town's mayor not from a sense of duty but on the shoulders of sailors and dockworkers that had carried him to the post. The night in late June of the previous year when the madness of rioting came to Dunkirk, flames had spread through every building connected with King Louis. Then the mob had turned on the other symbols of monarchy, the ships of war, marooned in the dock. Had they been set alight; the hot winds sweeping through the city would have carried the threat of fire to hundreds of smaller craft. The *Perseus* and others like her would have been lost.

It had been Grison who had led the crew of the *Perseus* against the mob attacking the ships of the line, other dock workers and seamen followed him. The pitched battle offered no quarter, but eventually the melee broke into a series of running fights as the men from the port chased the rioting citizens back towards the centre of the town and towards St-Éloi. Only when the Church had been reached was the grisly discovery made. Timber from the seats had been lashed together to make two crucifixes, bodies had been stripped and appallingly mutilated. The town's former Mayor and his wife, both devout Catholics, had been crucified by

351

the townswomen of Dunkirk. The pair had been left as a warning to Catholics and Monarchists alike.

With the mob dispersed, Grison and Tabary had organised the citizens into crews to fight the fire that now raged out of control and threatened to consume the town. In the aftermath, Grison had been propelled into power and when Tabary had returned to his home in Mont-Cassel, where the Mayor had fled, rather than face the prospect of the hatred that had broken out in Dunkirk, Tabary too had been approached by the towns-people to be their new mayor, the news of his bravery in saving Dunkirk having spread to the hill-top town.

Grison had ordered St-Éloi to be closed ever since. The authority held by Carnot had reopened the Church for the engineer's inspection, without the need for any consultation with Dunkirk's mayor. Somewhere above them came the echo of footsteps, growing ever nearer. A minute later, from the doorway which led to the main church tower, a tall, slim figure emerged into view. As his distance to the group shortened, dark fringed curls of hair flopped in energetic motion, a right hand clenched a weather-beaten black hardbound note, with a smaller red one bound to it.

"Apologies gentlemen, I rather lost track of time. Thank you for coming so promptly. I am Carnot." Introductions and handshakes followed and the three men waited for Carnot to catch his breath after the rapid descent.

"I'm afraid I must ask you to climb these steps in a minute." Carnot smiled weakly.

"You might be wondering why I have asked you to meet me, perhaps you have already guessed. The British are coming here."

The three men exchanged worried glances.

"Not now." Carnot smiled, holding up a hand in apology, "soon, perhaps a month, perhaps three. It depends on a great deal, but they aim to capture Dunkirk. Of course, Paris has sent me to make sure that doesn't happen, but I am also responsible for a great many other matters along the northern border. I need help. I need your help to be precise."

Tabary spoke rapidly, "Are you sure? Of course, whatever you need." Then with more circumspection, "What do you need, exactly?"

Mahieu and Grison waited for Carnot to answer.

"I have already prepared lists," Carnot said, holding up the note books. "I am also supposed to tell you that files are held by the Minster of War about your conduct before the revolution and of matters recent too." He glanced at Mahieu as he spoke.

"I have little time for threats. In fact, I'm quite useless at them. Help me and I will help you. Paris is disorganised at the best of times. Files can disappear for a very long time. Am I sure that The British are coming?

Yes. The revolution has friends, even in London. The British will come here and we must beat them. Anyhow, let's not waste any more time. Shall we go?"

Carnot motioned towards the entrance to the tower that he had emerged from a few moments earlier and the three, exchanging looks which suggested that their curiosity had been piqued, meekly followed.

St. Amand: 5th April 1793

"I have no idea if this will do you good or ill, Julien, but, here," Dumouriez signed the document with a flourish and pushed it towards Beauvais.

"Are you sure you will not join me?"

Beauvais pocketed the letter safely. "Thank you for this, sir," the tone told Dumouriez all there was to know.

The dragoon captain stood to attention in barren command tent, the General's personal items already having been secretly transported to the Austrian camp. Outside, horses could be heard stirring. Dumouriez bore the serene countenance of one whose die has been cast.

There were no more deals to be brokered.

The commander of the fortress at Valenciennes had refused the army entry. Juliette had returned and then disappeared. Beauvais had pleaded ignorance of the matter; Dumouriez didn't have the will to press the subject further. The next morning, news came from Lille that the commander there had arrested the officer sent by Dumouriez, threatening to fire on the troops camped outside his city. Duty to the Republic had won out over the personal magnetism of Dumouriez.

"I admire them you know, Beurnonville and Camus, very brave, all things considered, don't you think?"

"Yes sir." Beauvais answered, wishing to be dismissed at the earliest moment.

Beurnonville, Camus and the two Girondin delegates had arrived late in the afternoon, four nights before, each with the message 'Republic or Death' chalked into tall, felt hats. In the courtyard of a small farmhouse that Dumouriez had taken for a headquarters, on the edge of the Raismes Forest, the delegates from the National Assembly had come to demand the arrest of the General. The interview between the group and Dumouriez had oscillated between legal debate and high farce. It had ended bloodlessly, thanks in some small matter to Beauvais disarming one of the Girondins who had moved to draw a small dagger from inside his jacket. Dumouriez had been surrounded by the men of the 1st Hussars, the old Berciny regiment; Germans drawn from Alsace, some of their regiment already defected to Austria in the previous year. Had the Hussars reached the assembly delegate first, there would have been bloodshed, of that there was little doubt.

"We came very close my friend. I owe you my life. That letter seems a poor repayment. I plan to return and when I do…"

"I don't doubt that for a moment, sir."

"Do you think the Republic will survive, Julian?"

"I don't know sir. I am just a captain of dragoons. But France will survive somehow."

"Yes, she will. She must. I am serving her as I know best, Julian. Thank you for your service to me."

The General offered his hand. Beauvais shook it, then stepped back one pace, bowed deeply and stepped from the tent.

Dusk was falling. Men loyal to Dumouriez would leave with him, tonight. It was an open secret in the ranks of the army. None of that mattered to Beauvais though. His mind raced again, as it had all day. Genet had been dismissed from Dumouriez' service earlier that day and was headed for Valenciennes. Juliette had made it safely to the southern gate on the same night that the delegates had been arrested; Demont had escorted her and reported back to Beauvais. But if Genet saw Juliette, he was bound to use the information for his own ends; the dragoon did not much like the thought of what that could be.

CHAPTER TWENTY-ONE

Esel Soldaten.

Enschede: 6th April 1793

The sign of the Green Cow hung limply on one rusted chain, the other chain waved gently on the morning breeze. In the narrow alleyway, a portly man in his late fifties ran his hands though thinning blond hair, his other hand shakily held a cup of steaming, black coffee. He spoke in a mixture of Dutch and German towards a Hanoverian provost. Two more stood guard at the passage way entrance, moving synchronously to shoulder their muskets at the sight of a party of officers who had arrived to inspect the damage. They wore the same redcoats as those who had torn his premises apart, the night before.

2nd Battalion shuffled into order in the watery sunlight of a Dutch morning; distant bells sounded out seven chimes which echoed across the encampment. Krombach joined the three ranks of men jostling into their positions and looked up and down the line. Reifener and Pinsk were unscathed as was he; others in the Company bore heavy bruises or bleeding knuckles. Krombach sensed Gauner's *Katzenjammer*, the angry headache that followed the drunken excesses of the hours before. They waited for the colonel and for judgement.

The previous night had been the culmination of three painstaking days and the twenty-five miles of toil from Bentheim. 2nd battalion had borne the brunt of the worst tasks. Krombach had felt his own grim humour sorely tested by the constant need for the battalion to halt, men to be detailed out of the column to help resolve problems with the Brigade's baggage train or traipse further back along the road, to the heavy guns which brought up the rear of the army.

The army had maintained the same order of march every day; 3rd brigade waded through the dust and detritus of the other brigades, three of infantry and one cavalry. Between each brigade, wagons laden with all the baggage needed for the campaign. Not only did 3rd Brigade have the dubious honour of being the last infantry brigade into camp, but the order of march dictated that the 1st and 2nd battalions of 5th Division marched in advance of the 10th who similarly followed, 1st battalion marching before the 2nd. With every broken axle, stranded wagon or accident which called for additional manpower, the foot-sloggers of 2nd

Battalion had found themselves formed into one work detail after another while the rest of the army marched away.

The camp around Enschede was to the south of the town, the army having passed through it. As 3rd Brigade finally exited the outskirts of the town, there were steady streams of redcoats heading back into Enschede, hoping to make the most of the remaining Saturday evening light and find a meal at one of the town's taverns, before the place was overrun with soldiers. A company of unshaven Dutch soldiers in grubby white uniforms followed the progress of the army with very little enthusiasm. If the war didn't spread to their corner of the province, all would be well. Many were more interested in a swift return to their barracks and the prospect to venture into the night to ensure that the redcoats did not take the opportunity to ravage the fair maidens of Enschede, at least not before the Dutch soldiers had taken their turn. There was little pity at the arrival of 2nd battalion from their off-duty comrades, a chorus of brays and gestures mimicking donkey-ears followed the column. Soldiers were keen to choose demeaning nick-names for other battalions; the army had christened the battalion 'Esel Soldaten', the 'Donkey Soldiers'.

Even the baggage and artillery trains had found a way of beating the battalion to the taverns or bakeries along the route, often feigning problems with horse teams to purchase food and beer. The battalion marched behind a series of mobile banquets, at which the men could only watch with ill-concealed rancour. The 'Donkey Soldiers' had drawn all of the short straws on the march and the mood of the men who finally slunk into Enschede was as black as the encroaching night sky.

Corporal Gauner, flanked by Hartmann and Corporal Krogh had led a crowd of Brandt's Company back into the town, determined to find their own share of beer and hot food. Most of the taverns spilled over with soldiers but eventually, with Hartmann leading, the men had turned onto a side-street followed by a snaking line of around fifty men of the company. The pair of giants pushed their way into a stable-gated doorway below a freshly painted sign of a green cow. Gauner, travelling in their wake forcibly suggested to a group of the grenadier corporals sat at one of the tables that their time in the premises was drawing to an end. Krombach and Henry Pinsk watched a tumbling stream of merry soldiers, clutching bottles and half-filled pots of beer trail out of the tavern, led by the gaggle of smirking two-stripers who began a raucous marching song as well as a few jokes aimed at the Esel Soldaten. The pair shared a concerned look as to whether a fight might break out in the confined space, but the most likely suspects to react to such insults had already pushed in to the Green Cow; the remaining line was more interested in food than fighting.

"I wonder if Tomas is here," Krombach shouted above the din.

"Perhaps, but he is the 1st Grenadier; they come from the Guards and our battalions. The facings are wrong. These are the 3rd Grenadiers, I think," Pinsk looked at the facings of soldier's uniforms and motioned to a couple of soldiers, trying to get them to confirm their unit above the din. Eventually one man held up three fingers. Krombach saw disappointment etched across Henry's face. The 3rd Grenadiers were from the 1st Infantry Brigade; no-one that either man had spoken to in the last three days had seen the 1st Grenadiers on the march so far.

Only when the men of the 10th had forced their way into the tavern, did it become obvious that there was very little food and no beer to be had. Gauner had taken it on himself to interrogate the owner and the two serving girls and then three more local men who were sat at a corner table of the pub. Despite the language barrier, Gauner was making himself understood with malevolent clarity.

Before the army had entered Holland, the soldiers had heard that many of the population secretly supported the Patriotic Party, a closet Republican movement, which sought to remove the Stadtholder from the throne. Fuchs, who had been close behind

Krogh, had wormed his way to the rear of the small
tavern and had started kicking barrels. Hartmann had
caught sight of him and while Gauner was holding
sway, Hartman began pushing aside a stack of large
empty barrels, allowing Fuchs to squeeze in to a second
row of stacked barrels. When he found two barrels
which gave a dull thud, he smiled broadly at
Hartmann. The giant of a man threw an empty barrel at
the wall which shattered into pieces and the room
stopped to look in his direction. Hartmann howled in
triumph as he pulled out a bung from the top of the
barrel and a warm amber jet of beer shot over his
fingers. In the chaos men scrambling towards the
barrels, Gauner head butted the owner and screamed at
the cowering maids to bring drink for his men. The
owner tried to rise but Gauner threw a punch which
caught him squarely on the left ear, which began to
bleed almost instantly.

"Republican scum, lucky we don't lynch you on the
spot." Gauner spat vehemently.

With the new source of beer discovered, Hartmann
had hoisted both fresh barrels into a position where
frothy tankards of free beer were passed around; the
men of the Esel Truppen enjoyed a welcome drink.
Some of the grenadiers who had not yet filed out of the
tavern tried to force their way back towards the liquid
treasure, but a series of punches and kicks were
exchanged and a running battle erupted in the narrow

passage way. Krombach and Pinsk suddenly found themselves grappling with men who had previously been merrily singing and had little interest in fighting. Eventually the 'Donkey Soldiers' held possession of the Green Cow; the hinged stable-door was bolted shut. The serving staff, the owner and the locals had fled and only when every barrel had been smashed open did the Esel Soldaten head back to camp.

Reifener missed the early morning parade, having risen an hour earlier to fulfil his sentry duty at just after sunrise. Sergeant Winckler had marched the two soldiers to replace the guard outside of the headquarters tent of 2nd battalion. The rich aroma of bacon and sausages had reached Reifener's nostrils, subconsciously he found himself listing the ingredients he would have added to bring out a richer flavour to both. So much was he lost in his world of culinary delight, he missed the order to halt and clumsily bundled into the redcoats who had just held their watch. The clamour drew the attention of one of two of the seated officers, forcing Winckler to berate the boy instead of ignoring the sloppy drill. Reifener snapped to attention and concentrated with all his might. It was as well for him that he did. Moments later, an officer arrived on horseback, hastily dismounted and entered the tent. Almost instantly Neuberg emerged to follow the young aide-de-camp of Field Marshal Freytag and Reifener clicked his heels to attention with proud precision, while the ordered world about his battalion began to unravel.

The colonel had left the breakfast table with his own meal only partly consumed; Major Volgraf, now the most senior officer present, piled a pastry and two more sausages from a freshly arrived tray. The four company captains and Surgeon Harris sat in uncomfortable silence. Volgraf dismissed the corporals who waited table in their white fatigue jackets, before adding a boiled egg onto his plate.

"I wonder what fate awaits our esteemed leader. The Field Marshal does not suffer indiscipline," he sliced the top off the egg with satisfaction, "or so I have heard."

Soft yoke splattered down the side of the shell as he dipped a bread crust into to soak up the residue.

"Adequate, quite adequate?"

"The food or the Colonel, sir?" Ernst smirked, looking around the table. Bachmeier smiled awkwardly back, the others ignored the comment and carried on with their own breakfast arrangements.

"Now, now Ernst, we must not speak ill of the recently departed. I'm sure all will be fine, eventually."

Harris looked up. "We don't even know it was our men. A few of the soldiers had been fighting but that doesn't mean it was ours who wrecked that tavern, the 'Green…'"

Harris, a man of receding hair and a plump ruddy complexion spoke German with the hint of a thick Derbyshire accent.

"Cow, Surgeon Harris. Yes, it was our men, sad to say. I had a whisper of this trouble at first light. I took the trouble to inspect 1st Battalion and none of their soldiers looked as if they had been in a brawl. Only our men or should I say only yours, Brandt," Volgraf spoke with a casual cheerfulness and then proceeded to relieve the egg of the rest of its contents.

Brandt shifted uneasily in his chair. "And you didn't have time to share this whisper with anyone; Colonel Neuberg or me?"

"Sadly not. It wouldn't have changed a jot though; besides, you seem a hard man to pin down, Brandt. One never really knows where to find you or where you might stand on various matters."

The hawkish stare issued a cold challenge to Brandt, who rose knowing that he needed to leave the tent, as much to establish the truth from his men as to avoid an exchange of words with the Major which might easily spiral out of control. Even as the news of the previous night had spilled out, the captain had the uneasy feeling that the trouble in Enschede would somehow involve his men.

"Excuse me, gentlemen, I had better go and inspect my men. Whatever punishment is due, the company will take, but I'm not sure I can completely blame them. We are the last battalion on the march. The men are sick of every menial task being given to them. Why the hell is our Brigade the last to march every time? I'm pretty tired of this myself."

Brandt wished he had said less but once he had started, he found curbing his anger difficult, besides it was a rhetorical question born of the frustration of the moment. He looked up to see Captain Thalberg nodding in silent agreement and then looking at Major Volgraf in the hope of answer.

"You may indeed ask, Brandt, a very reasonable question. And one to which I am surprised that you don't already know the answer. Why has the order of march been set like this? And why will it remain so for the next month? That is what I have heard anyway, another whisper which I share with my fellow officers... as a courtesy."

Volgraf helped himself to slices of cold beef, remnants from the previous night's meal.

"Of course, I have a theory, but I'm not sure that it's my place. After all, it doesn't seem fair, what with the colonel not being here to be able to refute it."

"For God's sake, spit out what you know man," Harris grunted, motioning Brandt to return to his seat.

"Fair enough, but your word as brother officers that this conversation goes no further."

Brandt squirmed awkwardly, wishing now that he had taken the opportunity to leave. Breakfast had become conspiratorial.

"Have you ever wondered why a man with the colonel's vast wealth of experience has not commanded before?" the Major asked acidly.

"Yes, uncle, you know I have. You should be…" Ernst began, but Volgraf shook his head.

"Another conversation for another day, Ernst," Volgraf placed a conciliatory hand on his nephew's arm.

"Unfortunately, our Colonel has had dealings with Field Marshal Freytag which did not end well. In fact, I'm not sure that the disagreement has ended at all; some nonsense about light infantry tactics, if you please. The matter escalated to the point that Neuberg was sent to Prussia, of all places, to learn proper infantry tactics. Freytag and others had had enough of his fanciful notions. Major Neuberg skulked back to the infantry school in Nienburg after his deployment in Berlin, having learnt nothing. Field Marshal Freytag of course has let the matter rest but his staff are not so forgiving. For our dear colonel, I would suggest the wound has festered ever since."

"So why did he receive command of the battalion?" Harris was the first to ask the question the others were thinking.

"Von Diepenbroick and Freytag haven't seen eye to eye for years. He probably did it to spite him. Whatever the reason, don't be surprised if we receive every filthy duty going while Neuberg…" Volgraf's voice trailed away.

"Remains the colonel" Harris finished the sentence for him. "All a bit convenient for you, isn't it?" His eyes met the Major's but Volgraf matched the Derbyshire man's look before continuing.

"What I have heard might go some way to explaining the reason for our brigade being last, and we are always the last battalion, unless any man around this table knows of a better reason?"

Silence and awkward glances between officers followed for a few seconds which Volgraf broke by calling the orderlies to clear all but Neuberg's dish. A few minutes later, Reifener thrust open the flap and did his best attempt at shouldering arms as Neuberg ducked under and returned to his seat. Neuberg ate a mouthful of congealed breakfast then swallowed a mouthful of cold coffee.

"Well you will be glad to know that with the events of last night, both battalions of the 10th and a battalion of the 3rd Grenadiers are to have money deducted from this month's pay to make repayments to the good folk of Enschede. It seems there was other trouble elsewhere in the town, which has somewhat diluted the behaviour of our men. For our part, we remain the 'Esel Truppen' as I believe the rest of the army is calling us, until we reach the British camp."

Neuberg sighed and returned to his meal unaware of the triumphant glint in the eye of Major Volgraf.

"Sir, I think it was my company…" Brandt felt the need to confess what would soon be obvious.

Neuberg stopped trying to eat. His appetite had deserted him and he was merely moving the food around on the plate.

"Yes, I bloody well know it was your men, Werner. While you have sat here breakfasting, I inspected the four companies."

There was a controlled anger in his voice.

"I have thought about what punishment should befall your company but we must face this together, as a battalion. I don't want any divisions. God help us we might have to fight the French after all and not just helpless civilians. I am rather hoping that we might be able to rely on one another when that moment comes."

He looked around the faces of the officers.

"One thing I have just heard from Freytag's aide is that a messenger from the Duke of York arrived within the last hour. An Austrian peace offer made by Prince Josias has been revoked by the Emperor Francis. We are to hurry toward Antwerp. We might just be needed after all."

Neuberg turned to Volgraf.

"Major, arrange for every senior non-commissioned officer to be here for three o'clock this afternoon."

The tent filled with around forty men sheltering from the afternoon sunlight. Senior corporals and the sergeants who made up the spine of the battalion filled the officer's dining tent. Neuberg's words were in part a plea and threat; uphold the honour and discipline of the battalion. Should any man be found wanting of his duty, he would be broken back to the ranks irrespective of his years of service. The trouble at the Green Cow had been led by a corporal. Neuberg chose to believe for now that it might have been a junior corporal drunk on power as much as alcohol. The file of non-commissioned men streamed away, as did Major Volgraf who caught the eye of Gauner and nodded for the corporal to follow him.

Antwerp: 7th April 1793

The buildings around the perimeter of the Grand Place, bathed in bright spring sunshine had shed their tricolours since the retreat of the 'Army of the North' and the subsequent defection of Dumouriez. Now only the palace, with overlooked the Grand Place bore any flags, those a curious mix of battle standards. A huge yellow Austrian standard bearing a double-headed eagle design casting a wary gaze over the Kings Colour of the 1st Guards on its right and an eagle on the Prussian infantry standard to its left. While these three flags flew with a degree of pomp, the fourth, a flag bearing the coat of arms of the house of Orange had become entangled on its pole and bore all the regal air of washing that had been hurriedly put out to dry on the spring breeze. To the citizens of Antwerp, the sight provided the only amusement at the time when the crushing collapse of the French army carried away their own hopes of liberty.

Only the merchants welcomed the return of allied troops to Antwerp. The first of the diamond traders who had sheltered some months in Amsterdam had returned that morning to re-establish their businesses, as soon as news of the arrival of Knobelsdorff's Prussian troops in Antwerp, had reached them. The city bore the air of a carnival or religious festival.

Major Trevethan looked down on thousands of townsfolk and traders from a palace window. A cacophony of sounds echoed in through the window and circulated around the hallway where walls rich with stucco friezes and burgundy and gilt paint, all of which looked tired, held a dozen officers and aides-de-camp from the four Allied powers. Inside the suite of rooms once the domain of General Dumouriez, a third day of planning and discussions were being held.

Trevethan checked his pocket watch; soon there would be a lunch break and he could deliver the latest dispatches to the Duke of York. He snapped the fob shut, remarking at how little stiffness remained in his left hand; the Dutch surgeon at the fort had carried out such delicate stitching that no dexterity had been lost. The bayonet scar, a reminder of the fight to save Willemstadt, would be a memento of his adventure with the Duke's army. The Cornishman studied the faces of the officers around him, all of them at least twenty years his junior. Henson-Jefferies was there, conducting some discussion in an excited voice with another Guards subaltern and an Austrian officer. The Guards officer had made a point of ignoring Trevethan and the Cornish engineer couldn't place why this irked him so much.

He returned to studying life on the Grand Place. A sea of colours met his eyes. Red uniforms mixed with the dark blue of Prussian and the crisp white of Austrian infantrymen. Cavalry-men paraded around like peacocks, Austrian hussars paraded in their finery, a riot of rich green jackets, deep red riding breeches matched by the tall cuirassiers with burnished black breast plates. Yet all were standing and watching the sad spectacle of the dishevelled blue and white uniforms of the French army of the North pass through the town.

Pushing his way through the square earlier, Trevethan had seen the state of the French soldiers at first hand. This was the remnants of the army left by Dumouriez to continue the siege of Willemstadt. There was a great deal of discussion and disbelief amongst the soldiers but the standing orders issued two days before had been quite clear. Prince Josias had made an accord with the French General. The enemy soldiers passing through Antwerp had chosen to join forces loyal to the House of Bourbon, under Dumouriez. Others, who had undertaken an oath to return and not bear arms against the allies, streamed south to the border. On the terms of such an arrangement, the fissures between the allies had begun to emerge.

The Duke of York was unhappy with the lack of consultation on the matter, even more unhappy about letting most of the French escape, but this paled against the cataclysmic rage which Knobelsdorff flew into. Trevethan had witnessed the Prussian General screaming insults at Prince Josias, across the large circular conference table, at least Trevethan assumed they were insults, the harsh tone did not offer much to suggest that the Prussian General was impressed with the choices made by his Austrian counterpart. From that moment on all further discussions had been held behind closed doors. Only the most senior officials had remained.

The doors opened and four of the representatives left the conference room. One of them, Sir James Murray, studied the hallway, saw Henson-Jefferies trying to catch his attention but shook his head. The eyes panned around until he found Trevethan, who waved a bundle of dispatches above his head. Murray beckoned the engineer to him and sorted through the envelopes.

"How is it in it there?" Trevethan asked.

"Not great. We have a plan of sorts but…" Murray's voice trailed off, perhaps cautious of being overheard. "Has the new brigade arrived?"

"Yes, God help us."

"As bad as that?"

Murray looked at Trevethan.

"There can't be many old men, boys and cripples left in England. They've shipped the job lot to us!"

"Wait here for a couple of minutes. I'm going to pass these to the Duke; you had better show me." Murray disappeared swiftly and returned a few minutes later with a heavy greatcoat folded under his arm. Henson-Jefferies again bobbed up to meet the gaze of the colonel.

"The Duke may need you later. Wait there!" Murray spoke, barely pausing, eager for fresh air.

The two men turned right from the Grand Place and made steady progress through the crowd and towards the mouth of Scheldt River and the port. Once away from the crowds, the fresh spring winds, straight off the North Sea whipped into their faces. Murray struggled into his greatcoat and only when they were out of earshot of anyone did his pace slacken.

"The last three days have felt unending. Hopefully those dispatches will bring some clarity, before this conference turns into a tragic farce!" Murray sounded resigned to the fact that any such progress would be slow.

"Who is holding up a decision?"

"Everyone; Prince Josias had backed himself into a corner with this deal with Dumouriez. Now the Emperor has overturned that agreement and rapped Josias across the knuckles. Baron Thugut has arrived to further muddy the waters. Every suggestion that the Baron makes is greeted with a sour face from Josias. As for Knobelsdorff, well Emperor Francis could just as well have sent Satan to be his advocate. Although Knobelsdorff might tell you that he already had, if he was speaking to anyone, which he currently isn't. And then there's the Prince of Orange."

"What does he want?"

"Half of Liege it seems, as reparations for the rest of Flanders and Brabant harbouring the French army."

"My head aches. I'm not sure I ever thanked you for inviting me on such an expedition. Suddenly that road from Falmouth to Plymouth seems a very attractive option."

Murray barked out a laugh. "You would have been bored within a week."

Trevethan shrugged and gave a wry smile "So what will the outcome be, do you think?"

"Well Josias' adviser, Colonel Mack, has a plan to besiege the key fortresses of Valenciennes and Lille. The Duke has sent the outline of the plan to London. It seems agreeable. Knobelsdorff has written to Berlin. Neither we nor the Prussians want to be a poor man's corps in the Austrian army. But if guarantees are in place then we can follow Mack's plan."

"And after the fortresses fall?"

"Ah, yes. Knobelsdorff wants to strike at once for Paris. Thugut will not countenance that without Austrian and British troops being present. Prince Josias is still of the opinion that at such a moment, the French will sue for peace."

"And us? What do we want?"

"Well apart from some of us who want to go home and build roads, we await orders."

The pair walked in silence for some way along the road that ran to the dockside at Antwerp. The Scheldt was busy with a variety of small single-mast craft, using the tide and breeze to make an easy passage south towards the French border. Further along the quay, merchantmen were docked. Trevethan had seen the sight earlier that morning but it was still impressive. For years harbour trade had dwindled as the Dutch had controlled the entrance to the Scheldt in an effort to drive trade to Amsterdam, now under British leverage the port had begun to flourish, like desert flowers after a long drought. An army needed supplies and new troops. Six hundred yards away, along the flat of the quayside, a column of redcoats headed towards the pair of men. Even from this range the column had no obvious cohesion, no sense of the rhythmic movement, of arms and legs in crisp drill. The newly brigaded British infantry were the stuff of nightmares for any sergeant-major.

Valenciennes: 6th April 1793

News of the arrest of the delegates from the National Assembly reached Carnot during his afternoon inspection of the defences of Dunkirk. He left immediately, the passage of his coach journey to Valenciennes interrupted by the further dispatches delivered by a messenger. One told of the defection of Dumouriez and a clique of senior officers, later another suggested that thousands of soldiers from the Army of the North had also gone over to the Austrian camp with the traitorous General. By late afternoon of the 6th, the coach had made Lille. Carnot paused to speak to the commander of the garrison before continuing his journey the remaining thirty miles to Valenciennes, leaping from the carriage almost before it had halted. The Governor's quarters were empty. In the room below Ferrand's he found Caillat with another man, thinly built with receding hair brushed forward to hide impending baldness and slender silver-framed glasses perched on the bridge of his nose.

"Caillat, what news? Where is Ferrand? Who the hell is this?" Carnot noticed that the black clerk's attire of the second man was punctuated by a tricolour sash of office.

Caillat stood in deference to Carnot as the engineer burst into the room.

"General Ferrand is at dinner with the niece of a friend. The latest dispatches are here. Ferrand has already read them. I was about to send them to Paris along with a list of..." Caillat paused, "Forgive me. This is Citizen Genet; he was helping me with the list. Genet was..."

"Dumouriez' man? His chief of staff?" Lazare Carnot looked incredulously at Caillat, who nodded dumbly.

"I have heard of you. Why did you not flee with your rat of a master?" Carnot was rarely drawn to anger but swept up with the rage and frustration of the journey, he grabbed Genet by the lapels of his clerk's jacket and pinned him against the roughly plastered walls. Genet's body gave an involuntary gasp at the force of Carnot's action.

"No, sir, it wasn't like that. Please, Citizen Carnot." Caillat spoke quickly.

"No?" Carnot stared hard into the eyes of Genet, whose glasses had skewed and dug into his deeply furrowed forehead. "Explain."

Genet drew breathe to speak.

"Not you." Carnot felt rage overwhelm logic and clarity and tried to focus on the words of Caillat.

"Citizen Genet has written regularly to Minister Beurnonville over the past weeks. He has kept us informed of the treachery." Caillat pleaded.

"Is this true?" Carnot asked coldly.

Genet nodded his head and Carnot slowly released his grip allowing the rather shaken Genet to straighten his jacket and re-adjust the wire frames of his spectacles before replacing them.

Carnot drew a deep breath. "Then tell me what is going on? The facts as you know them." He expelled a long stream of air from his lungs.

"The facts as you both know them. My apologies Monsieur, I am tired and this matter stands France in the gravest danger." Carnot offered a raised hand of apology toward Genet before continuing.

"I think I am going to need some wine: perhaps we all could do with some?"

An hour later, Ferrand joined them. By midnight, dispatches had been written to Paris, a list of conspirators in league with Dumouriez made and plans to rebuild and re-equip the Army of the North.

The following morning Carnot headed out to St. Amand to begin the matter of reviving the forces there. A commander needed to be found but the list of possible choices was to be reduced by a further list on which several senior officers were named. At the earliest convenient moment, arrests would be made. Ferrand was to bring men from the garrison of Valenciennes and Caillat was to affect the arrests in the name of the Minister of War. By the time the group of horsemen arrived from Valenciennes, the command tent that had once been the nerve centre of Dumouriez' operations once again held the future of the army under its canvas roof.

Carnot had furnished the tent with a dozen chairs; a line of the remaining senior officers, headed by General Miranda filed in and took what seating was available. Ferrand, Caillat and Genet joined on the end of the line and stood near the back of the tent. Carnot was deep in discussion with the governor of the Lille fortress. Ferrand made to close the flap but Carnot stopped him.

"Thank you General but the army has had enough of meeting in secret, please leave it open."

Behind Ferrand a semi-circle of men had formed, several ranks deep, peering into the tent and eager to hear the conversation. Carnot spoke plainly; he was to assume control of the army until a replacement had been selected. Those officers that were tainted by Dumouriez' treachery would need to return to Paris and answer for their own actions; Citizen Caillat from the Ministry of War was to deal with those matters. Carnot then made his way between chairs and out of the tent. He pulled at an empty ammunition box which he had placed near the flap of the tent and dragged it towards the crowd. Soldiers rushed to help him and within moments he was stood so that the press of men, a thousand strong and growing by the moment, could hear him. While this occurred, Ferrand's men positioned themselves around the perimeter of the tent.

"Soldiers, I am Carnot, hear me. I speak to you on behalf of the National Assembly."

He paused between each statement, allowing the noise of the soldiers to fall away to a hush and the gravity of his words to carry.

"Paris will decree that any oath offered under the direction of the traitor Dumouriez is contrary to the principles of the Revolution for which you fight. In one hour, the army will have a new commander. You will parade for inspection before him."

He paused again, allowing for the whispering of the message to reach the soldiers at the rear of the mass. In the distance, he could see more men streaming towards to crowd from every direction.

"Any man tainted by association to the traitor Dumouriez must answer to the National Assembly for his actions. The National Assembly will immediately instigate a series of arrests. Any soldier who interferes with this action will be subject to the harshest military justice. I have spoken with the governors of Lille and Valenciennes. Food, clothing and new weapons will arrive here shortly from their reserves. We must prepare for enemies to attack us at any moment. Return to your regiments and ready yourselves."

The press of men digested the words, somewhere in the crowd the words of the Marseilles broke out and only when it was sung to rapturous applause and wild cheering, did men start moving away. Carnot turned and walked back to the tent where a dozen faces looked anxiously at him, some already having guessed at the purpose of the meeting. He drew a list from his pocket and read each of their names in turn.

"In the name of the Republic, you are now under arrest for collusion with the traitor Dumouriez."

While Caillat dealt with disarming the officers, Ferrand slipped away to find the camp of the 3rd Dragoons. The cavalry had been billeted to the east of St. Amand; the battle tricolour of the regiment fluttered limply around one solitary tent. Hundreds of horses were held in roped enclosures which passed for stables. Ferrand had fallen in with a stream of cavalrymen who had been listening to the speech of Carnot and witnessed the scenes of the arrests and made straight for the command tent where he found Colonel Courtois deep in conversation with two other officers. When Courtois noticed Ferrand hanging back at the entrance to the tent, he dismissed the two men with a casual gesture and beckoned his friend in.

"Ah, Ferrand, you old dog, how is my niece?"

Ferrand smiled at the two officers who passed him before entering the tent.

"Fine, fine; she has already acquired a new wardrobe of clothes. The dress-makers of Valenciennes have a new favourite." Ferrand smiled, turned his head awkwardly to ensure that they could not be overheard, then whispered.

"A man, an investigator called Caillat, is coming to arrest Beauvais, his name and Juliette's are on a list of Dumouriez' associates."

Courtois sighed. "I expected as much. Sadly, Monsieur Caillat will be disappointed. Captain Beauvais is leading a scouting mission for at least the next ten days. They are keeping a tight watch on the Austrians at Mons. Until we have a new commander, I will not jeopardise the safety of the army. No other officer has considered the scouting needs of the army."

Ferrand expelled a deep breath. "That will only hold for so long Alain. Get in the way of Caillat and your name could be added to the list."

Then Ferrand reached inside his jacket.

"Here, from your niece for Beauvais. As you suggested, his name is not mentioned."

"Good, I have one in return for my, um, niece."

Ferrand took the offered envelope and pouched it in the same pocket he had just taken the letter from.

"Good luck, my friend." Ferrand offered his hand.

Outside the sound of horses' hooves clattering to a sudden halt could be heard. Ferrand exited the tent to come face to face with the investigator, who gave the governor of Valenciennes a most quizzical look.

CHAPTER TWENTY-TWO

Thalers.

Eindhoven: 16th April 1793

The morning of the sixteenth came as something of a relief to Krombach. The eight-day march from Enschede had ended at a camp south of Eindhoven. Reifener had returned to the tent and threw himself onto the damp grass of the tent floor with exaggerated exhaustion.

"My work is done" he sighed, feigning instant sleep followed by heavy snoring.

"Do try and remember you are meant to be an infantryman, Andreas" Krombach smiled. "I have cleaned your musket and whitened your belts but you still have your boots to do."

"Thanks 'Bastian," Reifener waved a thin, weary arm in the direction of Krombach. Each morning, Andreas had found his skills much admired by the 'Twenty', the selected soldier's wives who had been chosen by lot after over two hundred had wanted to follow their husbands on campaign. Four had been chosen from Brandt's company and although Krombach barely knew them, Andreas had arrived with news or gossip every morning. The Twenty managed the washing, feeding, and sewing chores for the battalion. When the time came, many would be called on to nurse the sick or wounded.

"Oh, and the pay will be arriving today, that's another reason why we have the day off." Reifener added.

"How do you know that?" Krombach asked, already knowing the answer.

"Anna told me."

Who is Anna?"

"Mrs. Weber, to you, of course; her husband is a corporal in Fourth Company. I have been showing her how to make sour dough" Reifener yawned.

"Is that what you call it? Just don't let Corporal Weber catch you" Krombach chuckled.

"What do you mean?" Andreas asked with genuine naivety.

The flaps of the tent were pulled back, and Corporal Pinsk craned his head in.

"Wake up you two, pay's arriving. Form a queue outside the battalion tent."

"We know," Krombach replied.

"How do you know? I've just been ordered to let the company know. You are the first tent I called in at. I haven't told anyone else yet." Henry looked slightly crestfallen.

"He can't tell you, it would betray a confidence," Reifener added, pulling his backpack towards him to use as a pillow, before returning to a completely prone position.

"Shut up, Reifener," Pinsk growled, shaking his head.

"Save my place in the line 'Bastian, I'm going to sprint around the tents, but there is bound to be a rush. We are allowed into town later, so we had better get a move on."

"Save mine too, but I have already got the three of us on a duty that will give us plenty of time in town," Reifener yawned again, before turning his back to the two men.

Krombach looked at Pinsk, shrugged his shoulders and hurriedly put on his boots; the tall corporal held the tent flap open as Krombach ducked out into the fresh morning air and left the sounds of heavy snoring behind him.

Bread and vegetables were in short supply and prices were increasing daily; in Enschede, Winckler had suggested to Major Volgraf that Reifener should be allowed to accompany the Commissary staff on the basis that his knowledge of grains might avoid the battalion being sold sub-standard produce. Both Pinsk and Krombach had been added to the detail of redcoats sent to collect rations. Both had felt the sealed note that

Winckler had given to Reifener to deliver to the grain merchant a coin wrapped inside the note; there had been a similar letter delivered by the baker's boy-turned-soldier in Enschede but he was at a loss to explain the letters.

The short journey was slow progress. The road was swollen by red coats, not as many as in Enschede though; each company was being released with a strict time of return to the camp. Even though the pay had arrived, there was no British bonus. It had been the main topic of camp fire conversation since the army had left Bentheim. The promise of British pay had given the hope of making the meagre Hanoverian wage stretch further. Many had run out of pay after Enschede so the continual marching had come as a strange comfort as everyone shared in the suffering and soldiers quickly learnt to pool resources to find a decent meal. Now Eindhoven promised nothing more than over-inflated prices and little chance of money lasting another fortnight, let alone another month. The only efficiency the army had shown were the deductions of wages from the men of the 10th for the damage caused in Enschede.

"Do you think there will be trouble?" Krombach asked, as the wagon jolted along.

"I don't know. While the men have got some money then maybe all will be alright. After that…," there was a hint of worry to Pinsk's words as he continued.

"You know there are Provosts in the town. There is talk of hanging men who are caught stealing or roughing up the locals. All it needs is the word of a Provost. We haven't even been gone a month. What a mess!"

"I'm sure it will be alright. The British pay will catch up with us soon. Or the war will end. Or Reifener's stews will kill us off," Krombach nudged his friend.

"I heard that," came a muffled voice underneath a firmly pulled down bicorne hat.

Private Reifener looked up readjusted his cap and returned for another cat-nap, allowing the gentle motion of the wagon to return him quickly to a happy daydream.

Back at the camp, soldiers from Brandt's Company, waited for the return of the men from Thalberg's so that they could head into Eindhoven and buy whatever might be left in the way of food and drink for the journey ahead. For those who had scrimped perhaps there was the prospect of wolfing down a quick meal or the warmth of a local whore. Most of the soldiers poked around two braziers waiting for various kettles and pots to boil. Dregs of tea leaves or coffee beans had been pooled to make the last of the hot drinks. Each of the company's redcoats made a contribution to the Twenty and their thrifty economy would provide these essentials but none of the women had been permitted to leave the camp yet.

"It's a fucking disgrace."

Hartmann rarely spoke more than one word; even Gauner was surprised. The giant of a man let a handful of Groschen and Pfennigs tumble through giant fingers and then gently deposited them into a tiny leather pouch.

"All of that horse shit about English pay and we get this. We will be marching hungry before ten days are done."

Krogh agreed, his own pouch as poorly stocked as Hartmann's. Gauner thrust some slivers of wood onto the fire and chuckled.

"Listen to you two old women. You're sounding worse than them," Gauner cast a disparaging look around at the rest of Brandt's Company who were milling around.

Krogh examined the sole of one of his boots muttering about the split that was starting to appear after only a few weeks of use; Hartmann stared angrily at Gauner.

"Now, now," said the corporal quickly, afraid that the red mist and fighting ire of the colossus from Hamburg might be rising.

"We'll be all right boys. Just stick with your old Uncle Conrad. Life has been pretty sweet so far and war will be just the same."

Gauner reached into his backpack and then motioned the two to draw close to him.

"I don't want prying eyes to see."

Hartmann turned his head toward the other men of the company, a look that challenged anyone glancing in their direction to avert his gaze. Gauner took out his own brown leather money bag. He pulled out four silver thalers, double the wealth of the other two combined, with more coins inside.

"There is more, much more, where that came from. Today we are going to lose this lot and find a nice little spot to hatch a plan or two," Gauner smiled and tucked the coin bag into a pocket inside his redcoat just as Fuchs arrived back with four mugs of hot, sweet tea.

He was met by three grinning faces "What did I miss?" Fuchs asked, but the three men merely took their cups in silence and returned to their stations around the fire.

Ghent: 16th April 1793

York's forces had made a rather ponderous journey by a combination of river and road towards Ghent. The arrival of a further infantry brigade had strained the limited capability of the army, even though the country was friendly and the weather had remained fair. Colonel Murray had predicted such events might unfold on the voyage to Hellevoetsluis. 'Teething troubles', Murray had called them. Every campaign suffered them until the cogs of the war machine began to synchronise. From the argument that Trevethan could currently hear, such synchronising was some way off yet.

The Duke of York had been offered a suite of rooms in an old chateau near the centre of Ghent; his own overlooked a large walled garden where a corridor of willow trees sheltered a path leading to a small pond and a series of benches. Yesterday evening, the officers of the British general staff had taken drinks near the pool to toast the bloodless success of the campaign to date. But the morning's dispatches had changed the mood. Henson-Jefferies entered the map-room, a small room adjoining the quarters of the Duke, partitioned by a series of concertina oak-framed doors. Trevethan, the only other officer in the room, watched as the Guards officer stood, poised to knock.

"I wouldn't if I were you. Not unless you want to spend the next year as a private soldier."

Trevethan spoke casually while reading a newspaper that had been delivered with the morning's messages and sipping tea from a delicate bone china cup. Henson-Jefferies' hand wavered, like the hammer of a bell about to strike mid-day whose mechanism had suddenly seized. He had taken a disliking to Trevethan since the night at Numansdorp but now he found himself forced to acknowledge the Cornish man's words.

"What shall I do with them, sir?" Henson-Jefferies asked, the last word a grudging recognition of Trevethan's rank.

"Leave them on the table, boy. And go and find something else to do until this blows over."

Trevethan had little time for the sons of the peerage who surrounded the Duke. Henson-Jefferies represented the worst of them in the engineer's eyes. The voices beyond the screen were raised again. Henson-Jefferies took that as a sign to drop the dispatches on the table.

"For the Duke, as a matter of urgency, from his Majesty."

Trevethan nodded and returned to the newspaper. A further ten minutes passed until the conversation had died away to something more muted. He folded the paper, took the dispatches and rapped firmly on the door. The central section of the door slid open, flooding the room with afternoon sunlight from the large window that looked out over the garden of willow trees. The Duke was sat at a desk, his back to the window, looking rather flushed. Murray, who had drawn back the doors, took the bundle of dispatches from Trevethan. The third occupant of the room,

Commissary General Brooks Jackson, stood and bowed his head in the direction of the Duke before turning and joining Trevethan. The Duke acknowledged the gesture with a pained smile, before Murray closed the doors again. Jackson slumped heavily into a wooden chair next to the one that Trevethan had occupied. Jackson blew out his cheeks heavily and gave Trevethan a look that suggested the afternoon had been somewhat strained.

"I think you need a shot of this."

Trevethan rummaged in the deep pockets of his waxed blue overcoat which hung at a peg on the door that led to the hallway and the world beyond the room. Jackson drew heavily from the silver hip flask proffered to him.

"Thanks. And my bloody foot is giving me grief; gout, no doubt!"

"Which one?"

"Ah the wit and wisdom of a Cornishman; I think I have a copy of that book at home. Very thin as I recall."

"Well, you can give me that bloody flask back, if you are going to be like that!" Trevethan grinned and waited for Jackson to draw another shot of rum before taking some himself.

"What was going on in there? Is it safe to ask?"

"A misunderstanding; a few misunderstandings actually; that and everything is moving too slowly for the Duke."

Jackson removed the boot from his left leg and placed the foot over the knee of the wooden-stumped right so he could massage his toes before he continued.

"The Duke has received word from opponents of Dundas that I am working for the Secretary of War and not for Prince Frederick. Whoever these people are, the Duke clearly trusts their word. They allege I have orders to hinder the progress of the army until Secretary Dundas can approve or challenge the Duke's decisions."

"And do you?"

"Of course I bloody don't!" Jackson snapped back, the repressed anger of the last hour surfacing in a flash and then dissipating almost as quickly.

"I'm sorry Stephen, of course I don't. Since we started to move from Holland the army has been dogged by one thing or another but not of my making. I'm here to do my job to the best of my ability and serve the army and the Duke."

Trevethan grinned as Jackson spoke.

"What's funny about that?" Jackson asked.

"I think the last person to call me Stephen was my sister."

"The thought of being related to you would be more than I could bear right now; today has been trying enough as it is." Brooks Jackson smiled and drained the last of the rum from the hip flask that Trevethan had placed on the table.

"So how does the land lie between you and the Duke now?" Trevethan asked, examining the empty flask that Jackson handed back to him, with a hint of dismay on his face.

"I told him of my conversations with Dundas, showed him the private correspondence that I had received from Henry. I like Dundas, I know he seems overbearing to most but he gave me this chance."

"But a man cannot serve two masters. You will find that in your book of Cornish wit and wisdom." Trevethan grinned.

"Remind me why I seek your company again?" Jackson's vivid blue eyes shone with warmth as he fired back the retort.

"Because I have booze; had booze, actually," Trevethan shook the flask as if to emphasise the point.

"Well there's not much point in being the Commissary General, if you can't lay your hands on a few bottles of grog."

Jackson stuffed his shoe back on, tightening the buckle to a degree that was bearable. "Come on, if you are free. I have an army to chivvy along and you can give me a hand to liberate a bottle or two for the Duke as a peace offering. Of course, we might need to sample it first."

Trevethan grabbed his jacket and followed Jackson, who moved with a sprightly gait for a one-legged man, into the warm sunshine of a Ghent afternoon.

Famars Camp: 24th April 1793

The French camp at Famars, situated in the open plateau to the south of Valenciennes, rang to the sounds of preparations for war as a once bedraggled army re-equipped for battle. Carnot had worked tirelessly, aided by Genet and Ferrand. The fortress too stood ready, the river Scheldt had been dammed to flood the valley south-east of Valenciennes and deny the allies the chance to outflank the town and the camp itself. The small village of Famars, a dozen small houses along a narrow street, had mushroomed into a small town, with tents, bivouacs and temporary shelters of every type of construction erected to house an army, growing in number by the day.

Since the defection of Dumouriez much in France had changed. Robespierre had seized power within the National Assembly and blood-letting had followed. Girondins were being hunted down and dragged to the scaffold. The guillotines of Paris were working ceaselessly. But not quickly enough for some it seemed. Serge Genet fretted inwardly. Beauvais had finally been arrested and sent to Paris but none of the generals or officers who had been associates of Dumouriez had yet been tried; Girondins were the current flavour for summary justice.

Working beside Genet, in the largest of the tents that had sprung up around the village of Famars, Caillat also fretted, as he read the latest dispatch from Paris. New powers had been conferred upon him and a new title; Maurice Caillat, 'Representative on Mission'. His authority was almost unchecked; Caillat now answered only to Robespierre and the newly formed 'Committee of Public Safety'. His word, the word of a former stable-hand and coach boy, was now all powerful. With this new power though came direct missives from the Committee, circumventing the National Assembly.

The primary order handed to Caillat was to watch the new commander of the Army of the North and report his every action to the Committee. The army was ordered to resume the offensive at the earliest opportunity and the Committee for Public Safety would brook no delay. Among a series of secondary instructions was the finding and arrest of Juliette, Countess de Marboré, one of a handful of conspirators to evade arrest and the only one still currently thought to be in France. Caillat had developed no new leads and considered discussing the matter with Genet again but the previous occasions had borne little new fruit in that regard.

The sentries outside snapped to attention and both men looked up and out to a sea of men, horses and wagons; Carnot and another man, shorter by a head's height, strode into the tent. Auguste Picot de

Dampierre, a marquis before the revolution, had not wanted promotion to army commander. Eyes that were once clear blue were now lifeless and framed with dark heavy bags which suggested that the Marquis de Dampierre had received little rest. Genet had earlier observed to Caillat that General Dampierre had greyed significantly in the last three weeks. Only a trimmed thick moustache and busy eyebrows held their recent jet black, but even here, streaks of grey had sprouted. He appeared crestfallen at even the most trivial of news, like a small boat in heavy seas.

At thirty-six, Dampierre looked twenty years older.

Carnot paced over to a table without pausing and studied a large map which showed not just the fortifications at Valenciennes but the works of Famars to the south and Anzin to the north. The pair had spent the morning inspecting the positions and Carnot began to transfer a series of scribbled notes from the worn black notebook into drawings on the map. Dampierre stood alone, peeled off his riding gloves and smiled weakly at the two seated men, as if waiting for further instructions. Caillat did not want to add to the man's obvious worries but a question needed answering.

"Pardon me, General. But Paris, the Committee, it wants to know when you intend to attack and where?" Caillat spoke in a gentle voice, almost afraid that anything more forceful might break the spirit of Dampierre.

"We can't attack until we know what we have to attack with. The men are still short of weapons and the battalions are at not yet at full strength. Paris will have to wait."

Carnot spoke without looking from the map.

"Is that what you wish me to report?" Caillat asked.

"Yes," Carnot answered, as if the matter needed no further discussion.

"No," said Dampierre at almost the same moment, before stuttering, "I mean, yes. We are not yet ready. We do not even know the current strength in the camp...how can we commit to?"

"I have the latest returns from every formation, sir. It was completed this morning in your absence. I took the liberty to make a copy for Citizen Caillat's records." Genet spoke with almost cringing sycophancy.

His role had been severely usurped with Caillat's rise to power; if only he remained at the Ministry, that job would surely have been given to him. While Beurnonville, the head of the ministry remained captive at the hands of the Austrians, The Spider would need to time his moment to pounce carefully; Genet coveted the power of Caillat's new rank.

The document was handed to Dampierre, who studied it for a few seconds before hurriedly handing it on. Carnot took it, ran a finger down through the columns, counting battalions, guns and cavalry as he went, passing over the name of the 14th National

Battalion; the Black Lions had made it to the safety of Famars and the return for officers and other ranks showed that the battalion was nearly at full strength again.

"Five days. Tell the Committee, we should be ready in five days. The Austrians may well be here then anyway so we have little choice." Carnot turned and flashed a smile toward Caillat.

"Don't include that last bit though."

He returned to reading the list and then looked up.

"I'm sorry General, that was not my decision to make. Do you think we should be ready in five days?"

"Me? What? Yes, I think. Yes, of course. Five days, good choice."

The Marquis de Dampierre returned to the task of dealing with truculent riding gloves which stubbornly resisted being turned out while fighting the urge to be sick.

CHAPTER TWENTY-THREE

Breaking point.

Etterbeek: 24th April 1793

Another week of marching had been completed under clear skies; Holland had been left behind, a passage across the Austrian controlled Brabant lay ahead before entry into Flanders. The army was destined for the town of Halle, north of Brussels, as it moved towards a union with the British. With the town a few miles distant, camp was pitched under increasingly leaden skies.

The tent flap had been flung open and the storm that had battered its way along the Flanders coast swept across the landscape, puffing out the cheeks of the tent and threatening to send both it and the bedraggled occupants into orbit. A cacophony of cries and curses met the entrant, who proceeded to thread his way through a score of arms, legs and prone bodies, all trying to sleep off a most wretched meal. A single lantern swayed as the frame on which the damp canvas clung rocked with another strong surge of wind. A dexterous man would have struggled. Reifener was not that and every step drew fresh curses and the occasional blow as he stepped on or over his compatriots to find a spot at the back of the tent, near Krombach. Someone near the front of the tent bolted outside, closely followed by a second body. More curses. The air was fetid and heavy. Even the storm forces of nature, penetrating the canvas walls at will, could not shift the stench.

"What the hell was in that stew tonight?" Krombach groaned.

"The best of what we could sort. Some of the meat had turned rancid and had to be left. A few bits of mouldy vegetables and rabbit, I think; at least I hope it was. The Twenty certainly weren't happy about it. They are thinking of complaining to the Colonel." Reifener said dejectedly. "Clara says she will see him tomorrow."

"Who is Clara?"

"Sergeant Richter's wife; don't you know anything?" Reifener knew all of the women who had been chosen to join the battalion camp on a firm first name basis and assumed that everyone else had such a luxury of knowledge.

"All I know at the moment is my guts are not happy."

Krombach could feel sweat forming on his brow and knew that it was only a matter of time until he would need to fight his way through the bodies to relieve himself. The tent flap opened again and another rush of air and driving rain cascaded through the tent. Pinsk entered, looked around and stooping more than most, picked his way through the mass towards Krombach.

He found a spot and crouched by his friend, "We've a got problem."

"I know, it's Reifener's stew," Krombach said wincing as his stomach rumbled.

"You look like death. And you don't smell great either." Pinsk was grim faced and lacked the cheerful tone that kept him on the right side of melancholy, "Thank God, I missed that, just finished duty; no, not that problem, Gauner and some of the others are doing the rounds from tent to tent. There's been a meeting."

"What sort of meeting?"

"One we might want to avoid unless we want to end up swinging from a tree. How much money have you got left?" Pinsk whispered.

"Not much, you? Why do you ask?" Krombach said through gritted teeth.

"Apparently men from 1st Battalion have signed a letter asking for their extra pay. Gauner, Krogh and Hartmann think we should do the same. What do you think?" Pinsk looked anxious in the pale-yellow lantern light.

"I think I need to go."

Krombach lurched forward and made the perilous trip up the congested aisle of the tent. As he reached to pull back the flap, the shape of Gauner blocked out the entrance.

"Where are you going? Get in and sit down, I need to talk to every man in here." Gauner grunted.

"I've got to go Corporal, that stew it's…it's not going to end well if I stay" Krombach ducked under Gauner's arm and kept going.

The barrage of wind and rain enveloped Krombach and Gauner decided that pursuing the boy was more effort than it was worth. Instead he ducked into the tent, cursed at the foul smell that met his nostrils and addressed the men of Brandt's Company on their current grievances.

Halle: 25th April 1793

The bedraggled army arrived in the centre of Halle late in the afternoon of the 25th April, a Thursday afternoon made longer by the fitful nature of progress through the streets of the town to a camp designated for the Hanoverians. The tedium of the march had been worsened by the battalion's continuing task of acting as the *Esel Soldaten*. The roads, a mixture of slick cobbled stones and muddy morasses after previous night's storm, provided continual work for the tired and hungry soldiers.

Captain Brandt shared the exhaustion of his men though for slightly different reasons. No post had arrived in the last week and the last message that Katerina had written mentioned that Aleksander's fever had returned. He knew his wife would have held the matter from him; the severity of the boy's condition had forced her to admit the facts to him. The message had tormented the captain and in a moment of desperation he had shared his concern with Doctor Wexler.

The encounter had been one of the rare highlights of the journey so far. Wexler had listened and counselled with compassion that Brandt had never seen him display. It seemed that time away from the temptations of rich Hanoverian society clients had begun to give August Wexler both sobriety and prudence. His skill at cards still appalling from the few games that Brandt had witnessed, but with Neuberg's embargo on officers from the battalion gambling, at least Wexler wasn't sliding back into debt.

The night after their conversation Wexler had returned with a prescription, carefully written with precise amounts, details of preparation and the quantities of the mixture that a child should receive. Brandt had dispatched the note with a message to his wife the next day. That had been four days ago, perhaps five, Brandt struggled to remember. But once the infantry column had arrived, Brandt dismissed his company to make its camp, leaving the task in the hands of Company Sergeant Roner and Lieutenant Schafer and made straight for the billeted accommodation of 3rd Brigade. Perhaps there had been a new message from Katerina that may have crossed with his. It was possible that the mail for the entire battalion was languishing there and been completely overlooked. Brandt considered that the young officer, now his senior lieutenant had, under the tutelage of Roner, become a more competent officer. He turned away but had only made it about fifty paces before Neuberg trotted past.

"You're in a hurry!" Neuberg reigned in to match the direction of Brandt's walk.

"Yes sir. Schafer can handle the men for a quarter of an hour, if that is permitted? I want to head to Brigade, see if there is news from Katerina," Brandt didn't break step but flicked a glance in the direction of the rider.

"Yes, Werner, I'm sure it will do Schafer some good. I have no idea about the post but if it's there, get a runner to deliver it instantly. The men really could do with some good news. By the way I received a letter last night. More of a demand, really," Neuberg said, somewhat guardedly.

Brandt stopped "A demand, from whom?"

"The men of the battalion, regarding food and pay; and I can't say I blame them." Neuberg pulled a leather riding glove off with his teeth, peeled his waxed blue riding cape to one side and searched around inside his uniform jacket.

"Here, as you are going that way, give these reports to Brigade and this to von Diepenbroick. Oh, and I am calling a meeting of all officers tonight at 7.00pm. I will tell the rest of the officers about the letter then."

Neuberg wheeled his horse away and Brandt felt the spectre of something far worse looming than the scenes at Enschede. He found 3rd Brigades headquarters after a quarter of an hour of searching. Columns of troops were moving into positions around a farm house which the army had hastily requisitioned hours earlier. The farmer and his family had moved into a large barn, converting part of it into a living area until the army moved on.

Oberst von Klinkowström, the Brigade commander was a soldier of frugal baggage; the large rectangular yard that connected the barn to the main farmhouse contained two wagons, enough for the brigade to function efficiently and at least a dozen horses, currently being cleaned before being stabled in the increasing crowded barn. Next to the house, on a small patch of grassland, a tent had been erected, a pair of clerks busily unpacking their baggage and storing it alongside a mahogany folding table, which already had a small collection of messages accumulated on it.

Brandt enquired as to the arrival of any post but found that nothing had arrived with the army for at least a week. One of the clerks, struggling to open a backless folding chair suggested bleakly that a popular whisper was that the mail was currently sat in Brussels, due to a mix-up, but that such matters were not divulged to the mere orderly.

"Excuse me, but where can I find Oberst von Klinkowström, please?" Brandt heard a voice that he instantly recognised and wheeled around to see mud-splattered Erich von Bomm, on a horse which was sweating heavily after a hard ride.

"Erich, you old devil, what on earth are you doing here?" Brandt was filled with a joy that he had been missing for a few weeks.

Von Bomm dismounted with ease and wiped a gloved hand over his mud sprayed features, before embracing Brandt with a bear hug and huge smile.

"I'm playing officer of the day, well more like officer of the fortnight to the Duke."

"The Duke?"

"Why York, don't you know; only the top of the society for me." Von Bomm grinned, white teeth and eyes shining against a mud-stained face.

"I'm still acting Captain, but about ten days along the road, a new officer arrived. And you will never guess who."

Brandt looked blankly at his good friend and shrugged.

"Your very good friend, Leopold Baumann. Seems he bought the Captaincy through the good Major Volgraf and now I'm at the head of the junior officers list. Not sure they really know what to do with me. Anyhow we got here a week ago and I was sent to act as an aide to the Duke. I'm getting saddle sores in all the wrong places. I know now why I never joined the Cavalry."

"Baumann? What the hell does he want with securing a commission in the 10th and our battalion too? Has he said anything about the duel? I remember Neuberg asking Volgraf for help in finding officers but God above. And why not make him a lieutenant. He might actually learn something from you."

Von Bomm's laughed at his friend's outburst.

"I actually meant about soldiering Erich, rather than philandering."

"Thank you, sir," von Bomm winked. "He's not said a word about the duel. Not that he actually speaks to me or acknowledges my presence. For the first week I was left in charge of the company, then my services were surplus to requirements. He even brought his own lieutenant, some spotty relative."

"Does Colonel Franke know of the matter?"

"Not from my lips. But I was given this job in quick time, so you can draw your own conclusions."

"So what are you doing here?"

"Delivering messages to the brigade commanders and then I will ride into Halle to deliver a message to Freytag. The Duke is on his way here and wants to meet Freytag before we meet up with the Austrians. Wants to make sure there is a united front I think. Apparently, we are all on the same side, but you'd hardly guess at that," von Bomm said.

"Seems like no one is home here, I came to find the mail, oh, and to deliver this..." Brandt hooked out the report for von Klinkowström. He turned to face the orderlies.

"Where shall I leave it?"

The orderly, having conquered the folding chair, took the message and added to the pile on the mahogany desk, "The General has already left for Halle, sir. I think all of the brigade officers are dining there with the Field Marshal." The man returned to his task of preparing a functioning headquarters.

The friends weaved their way across the busy yard to find a quiet spot to talk

"So where are 1st Grenadiers now?" Brandt asked.

"They were just outside of Halle, on the northwest road but that was a few days ago. There was some confusion about the route or where we would meet the British. Not my doing, I just carry around pieces of paper. Anyhow the battalion's moved further south."

Von Bomm looked around a grabbed a small sliver of wood and scratched out a 'V' shape in the mud.

"The British are using the Scheldt and coming down here," he pointed to the left-hand side of his marking.

"We are due to meet here, at Tournai," pointing to the base of the shape where the two lines met. "I'm heading back to Enghien at first light tomorrow. The Grenadiers are heading towards Tournai already.

"How is the mood amongst the men?"

"Don't know. I'm out of touch with that, just dealing with the Duke and his staff is challenging enough. Before I left, matters were a trifle tense, the men had expected more pay. They have been sat on their backsides slowly drinking, whoring or gambling what they had away, no doubt… God I miss that life," von Bomm joked. "Why do you ask?"

"I think trouble is brewing in our battalion. Neuberg has received a letter from the men. Just came to deliver the report as well as search for the post."

"Oh," von Bomm sounded as close to grave as Brandt had heard, "That is not going to make the powers that be happy. Is it bad?"

"The sergeants are solid men. Roner thinks that there are a few corporals who hold some sway over the new men but these same names crop up as the most effective men to train the troops. I have been dodging the matter, I think. I need to talk my NCOs tonight, after I have heard what Neuberg has to say."

"And once that is done, will you have to chance to have supper with an old friend?" von Bomm asked.

"Of course," Brandt smiled, "Which old friend is arriving?"

Brandt failed to catch the cursed reply; von Bomm had swiftly remounted, touched his bicorne in salute to the Captain before spurring his mount out for the farm and along the track toward the road to Halle. In his wake a spray of churned grass and mud flew in all directions as the horse accelerated to a gallop.

At the officer's meeting later that evening, each of the officers listened intently as Neuberg read the letter listing the battalion's grievances, asking any man, whatever his rank to express their opinion on the matter and share any observations they had of the current mood of the ranks. The meeting had ended with an agreement that Neuberg would address the battalion's sergeants tomorrow, before addressing the whole battalion. If there was an injustice, Neuberg would see it corrected.

Brandt had decided not to hold his own meeting with Roner, Winckler and the rest of the sergeants until Neuberg had acted. Von Bomm had attended the meeting at Brandt's suggestion and had stated that a similar undercurrent of unrest had swept through the Grenadiers. When he had last seen officers from that battalion, no one there seemed to know how best to deal with the matter.

Other men however who have some inkling of how to best deal with the matter met in Halle. A private

room of a small tavern just off the great square saw a
meeting between representatives of men from the 3rd
Brigade, soldiers of the 5th and 10th Regiments. All the
men wore hoods roughly fashioned by the various
camp-followers. An agreement was made that the army
and the Electors had broken their bond to the men.
Insufficient pay had been forthcoming; redcoats would
not be able to survive if the matter was not resolved.
The food that had been supplied was often rotten and
when soldiers tried to supplement their diet, the Dutch
and Brabanters, who they had come to protect, had
sought to overcharge them at every turn. A thick set
corporal from the 2nd Battalion of the 10th suggested
that the only way to make a man like Freytag listen,
was direct action. He outlined his ideas to the others in
the room. The hooded corporal left the inn and
disappeared into the night to rendezvous with his
accomplices.

Corporal Gauner had another agenda to fulfil, one he
failed to share with the hooded men in the tavern.

CHAPTER TWENTY-FOUR

Act of Riot.

Halle: 26th April 1793

A sickening feeling quelled the desire for food in the hours before but now that Krombach had arrived back from sentry duty desperation for some breakfast overcame him. There were fewer redcoats milling around the cooking pots of the Twenty than he had expected. Amongst the clusters of soldiers there was no sign of either Reifener or Pinsk. His head pounded with the enormity of the morning so far, he had the most shocking news to tell them. Neuberg had been in a fit of rage, the like of which Krombach had never seen before, having accused the young soldier of being complicit in a most heinous treachery.

Krombach had drawn sentry duty with Fuchs, who seemed less concerned with Colonel Neuberg's wrath. Krombach was sure he had seen the faintest hint of a grin from Gauner's lackey when the colonel and some of the senior officers were involved in a heated discussion. A large tear, probably caused by a bayonet, had been found in the back of the tent. The night before had been unseasonably cold and the culprits had left a series of footprints across the frost-encrusted grass. The lack of footprints from the position of either sentry supported the denials of both men. The enraged eyes of Colonel Neuberg dared Krombach to utter anything but the truth.

All the shocked boy soldier could picture was that his name would forever be associated with the shame of this moment. The Battalion's colours had been stolen.

The damp shirt under his redcoat was soaked with a heavy sweat. He wanted to change into the shirt stuffed into his backpack as if changing the garment might undo the events of the morning. Mind and body were already wracked with a nervous exhaustion, clear thought was impossible. He spotted Reifener deep in discussion with some of the wives, faces etched with tension, faces suggesting that the theft of the colours was already common knowledge. The gangling figure of Corporal Henry Pinsk stopped any further deliberations that Krombach had.

"'Bastion, thank God, you are still here. We are forming up now, get in line." Pinsk, the side of his face swollen and eyes reddened had charged up to Krombach, who stared at his friend's appearance; a rider thundered past the two redcoats, Krombach caught a glimpse of a grim-faced von Bomm.

"Wait. Henry, what the hell is going on?"

But Pinsk too had already bolted past not even stopping; around him redcoats scrambled for packs and muskets and Krombach followed blindly.

The Grote Markt, the market square at Halle, was filled with around two hundred redcoats. From the narrow townhouses that surrounded the square, curious inhabitants watched barricades of tables, chairs and even an upturned wagon being used to seal the narrow entrances at either end of the market place. A huge cheer erupted as a hooded soldier brandishing a battalion standard clambered over the northern barricade bringing another twenty men with him. Musket fire echoed across the square to celebrate the arrival of a battalion colour, 'The Reward for Bravery' clearly emblazoned on its rich green silk.

Brandt's head pounded; a night of drinking with von Bomm had left him with a headache on waking, coupled with the arrival of the most dreaded word, 'Mutiny'. Neuberg had summoned all of the senior officers to him as soon as the theft of the colours had been discovered. Throughout the morning the dispatches arrived with alarming regularity; little of the news was good. Redcoats had stormed the market place in Halle. An attempt to steal 1st Battalion's colours had been foiled but the perpetrators had escaped. A response was to be swift; by just after 8.30am, 10th Regiment, along with two six pounder guns and a squadron of light dragoons, marched on the town with orders from a furious von Klinkowström to bring the disgraceful scenes to an end.

Brandt knew that around thirty men were missing from his company, including Gauner and a couple of the other corporals. The redcoat column was full of sullen faced soldiers; ordering them to fire on their comrades could lead to open revolt. He fumbled for a hip flask with his right hand and drew a few deep swigs of water to try and revive his mind. For the first time since leaving Hanover, the army's *Esel Soldaten* found themselves at the head of a marching column. With soldiers from every battalion watching on, they had led out the brigade and within an hour they found themselves deployed around the entrance of Melkstraat, a short walk from the northern barricade.

The battalion waited for the next command

Brandt watched von Diepenbroick and Neuberg, both dismounted, deep in conversation. Major Volgraf had pushed his horse slightly ahead of the column and around a dog-leg in the cobbled street only to spark a volley of jeers from the men on the barricade, as soon as he had come into their view. On Basiliekstraat, parallel to the position of 2nd Battalion, the men of 1st Battalion would be anxiously watching for the return of their colonel. The other two battalions of the brigade were making their way around the outskirts of the town, approaching the Grote Markt from the north-east and south-west respectively. A messenger pushed his horse through the tightly packed Melkstraat and brought further news to the colonels.

Army Commander Wilhelm von Freytag, Field Marshal of the Hanoverian army was coming to observe the swift resolution of the matter at hand.

Krombach slumped against a shop doorway. The battalion had posted a dozen men at the dog-leg of the street, around fifty yards from the barricade, to act as sentries. Sunlight had filtered into the airless avenue, filled with soldiers, faces taut with tension. The cold of the night had long since gone. The press of bodies and lack of shelter would soon bring a radiating heat that would be magnified by the brickwork. The passageway promised to be an uncomfortable place to spend the day. All this suggested that the officers would not wait for negotiation; redcoat would soon fight redcoat.

He tried to picture which men were missing. Gauner, Hartmann and Krogh were the most obvious. The sergeants were still present; Winckler, Roner, Richter and Möller, were deep in conversation. Whatever was agreed, the four senior men turned and moved down through the ranks of sprawled soldiers, engaging in small talk with a few and giving looks of encouragement to others. Pinsk arrived and sat next to Krombach before setting out his flint and striking a pipe.

"I lost the colours. I was on watch with Fuchs when they were stolen. Neuberg thinks I am involved," Krombach said.

"I doubt it, he is angry at the moment, ashamed too."

Pinsk expelled a long jet of smoke at a fly that threatened to irritate the two men.

"It will pass and the truth will come out, no doubt. Not much of a mystery as to where they are or who has got them at least. One of the lads up there said that there is a colour flying from the barricade," Pinsk motioned in the general direction of the men standing sentinel further along the avenue.

"And if the truth doesn't come out?"

"Well if it doesn't Fuchs will be shot at dawn, along with you no doubt. But I will place flowers on your pauper's grave once a month until I forget you."

"Cock!" Krombach jabbed an elbow into Pinsk's ribs.

"Cock, Corporal, is, I believe, the correct term of reply."

Another jet of smoke expelled, Pinsk offered the pipe to Krombach.

"What happened to your face?" Krombach asked, noticing for the first time a dark swelling forming under Henry's left eye.

"I was punched by a masked man who came to the tent this morning. He wanted 'brave men who were prepared to stand up for their rights'." Pinsk smiled weakly and retrieved the pipe from Krombach.

"I stood up and challenged him. Fortunately, as I ducked to avoid the top of the tent, I missed the worse of the punch. I think it was Krogh but I can't be sure. His jacket was turned inside out so I couldn't see any stripes," a steady stream of smoke escaped from his nose, "only stars when I came around."

The rueful smile faded, "Half of the men in our tent had gone, the rest looked terrified."

Brandt and the other captains had been called to Neuberg, who had set up a temporary headquarters in a small coffee shop.

"Just so you are all aware, the Field Marshal is arriving. I hope we can resolve this soon and without bloodshed or repercussions. If any of you are worried about your military careers then don't be. I am the commanding officer. The blame is mine and not yours. I'm going to walk to the barricade and try and resolve the matter."

Neuberg looked at each of his senior officers. Volgraf, completely unperturbed by events, was the first to speak.

"Do you think that is wise, sir?"

"Wise? I don't know. Someone must try and do something. Those men will die if we don't. Or perhaps the battalion won't follow orders to attack. I'm not sure which is worse."

"Quite," Volgraf agreed, "but to offer oneself to these scoundrels? If they refuse your words of conciliation, you might look… weak."

The major offered a rather charmless smile to Neuberg. Every word was weighted with thinly veiled malice. As much as Brandt wanted to wring Volgraf's neck in that very moment, he also knew there was a degree of truth to the words.

"I have to say, I agree with Major Volgraf, sir…" Brandt interjected.

The ire in Neuberg's eyes at Volgraf's comments, worsened by the agreement of the one captain that the Colonel considered he could rely on. Volgraf's eyes sparkled with pleasure as Brandt spoke.

"…so, let me go. Some of those soldiers are my men and whatever you think, we have all been complicit in this, at least in the eyes of those in the square and probably many of the silent majority out there, too."

Volgraf rose without waiting for an answer, his nephew doing likewise, "If we are not needed, perhaps we should step outside and be seen. We don't want the men to think we have deserted them."

Brandt's interference in the matter was clearly unwelcome. Neuberg still considering the matter, nodded belatedly. The other captains followed Major Volgraf into the heat of the avenue, the gentle sound of a small brass bell signifying that the shop door had gently settled back into its frame.

Only Brandt remained with his colonel.

Within a minute the bell had wrung again, Neuberg turned and was about to berate who ever had disturbed the conversation only to find a party of three bicorned officers had entered followed by the familiar physique of a fourth, blonde hair thick with sweat and wearing a blue waxed riding cape.

Von Diepenbroick had returned accompanied by Oberst von Klinkowström, the brigade commander and Field Marshal Freytag.

"Gentleman, good-day," Freytag a rather portly septuagenarian, brushed an imagined speck of dust from an immaculate uniform, bedecked with gold braid. "Excellent idea to hold your meeting in a coffee shop, von Diepenbroick, some refreshments perhaps, as breakfast was curtailed?"

There was a sneering venom in the words. Chairs were found and the three men seated themselves.

"Do continue" said Freytag. "I would like to know how we might resolve this little drama before…"

Freytag waved his hand in the direction of the fourth person who was untying his cape and brushing back thick blonde hair. Von Bomm turned to see the room was looking at him. He brought himself to attention and announced:

"Gentlemen, the Duke of York sends his greetings. He is to inspect the men of 3rd Brigade at midday today in the Grote Markt. The grievances of the men will be addressed in a meeting after the parade and the matter will be settled," von Bomm bowed his head in the direction of the Field Marshal and then Neuberg.

"There" Freytag said. "Our Supreme prince will arrive, in…" he casually flicked open a pocket watch "…an hour. I suggest the colonels find a way to resolve the matter while we take a short break before the main act."

The owner of the store, who had arrived in the early morning to find the streets almost deserted, had hidden in the rear of the premises while the redcoats had rampaged towards the Grote Markt at the beginning of the day. Now he reappeared with two rather large pots of coffee that he had brewed earlier when there were six officers. The new arrivals looked much wealthier and so a second trip was needed to bring his best cutlery and plates of assorted pastries. The trading day might not be a complete loss after all. As drinks and refreshments were poured, the doorbell gave another gentle chime. In the street outside the men of 2nd battalion had risen to their feet and began cheering heartily.

Major Volgraf stepped into the gloom of the shop followed by a party of three men.

To Brandt they represented a grotesque version of the Russian nesting dolls that Eliza, his daughter, occasionally played with; Each a burlier version of the one before. The first, a thick set corporal carried, one of the missing battalion colours; behind him another corporal, taller and lithe in his movements with a physique that spoke of his bare-knuckle boxing days; the third was a colossus of a redcoat, who turned obliquely and dipped his head, to ease his entrance through the doorway. The men bloodied and bruised around their faces came to a halt in front of Freytag.

"Well, what's this? What splendid theatre, von Diepenbroick," Freytag's voice dripped with irony.

Neuberg felt a surge of relief tempered by the crimson embarrassment of Freytag's remarks to von Diepenbroick. The Field Marshal had given scant acknowledgement to the presence of Neuberg even though the men were less than four feet apart.

"Ah Johann, how are you my boy? Oh, of course, this is your battalion isn't it? Sorry to see you mixed up in such an episode. Now, what have we here, heroes or scoundrels?" Freytag rubbed his hands together with childish delight.

"Good morning sir," Volgraf was the embodiment of courtesy toward the Field Marshal, "I do indeed serve in the battalion under Colonel Neuberg," Volgraf watched as the two men finally exchanged cursory nods of acknowledgement.

"I believe these men to be the very best of Hanoverian heroes, sir, for they have rescued a colour at tremendous risk to themselves," Volgraf said.

"Only when I passed under a room where the men had been hiding, did they realise it was safe to bring the colour out and return it to the battalion."

"Splendid, splendid, let the heroes speak; tell us of your adventure, gentle soldiers" Freytag sipped at a black coffee and examined the rather splendid array of pastries that had arrived.

Corporal Conrad Gauner did the talking, as the three had agreed. The room learned of how the three had become aware of a discontent within the battalion and throughout the army: the shortage of pay; rotten food procured for meals; profiteering and unchecked Republicanism across the Austrian Netherlands had brought the men to breaking point. However, the three did not agree with the action taken and had followed the culprits who stole the colours. After mingling with the group, they had managed to regain one of the treasured flags, fighting a running battle through a maze of streets until they found somewhere to hide. Only when they saw Major Volgraf, a principled officer who they trusted, did they know it was safe to emerge.

Neuberg listened to the words with horror. Volgraf, Freytag's man 'a principled officer'. The death knell of his command was ringing before it had even had a chance to begin.

"Bravo, bravo," Freytag put down his pastry and gently applauded the story.

"Drinks and pastries for those heroes, I dare say our 'Lord Prince' will want to offer you a suitable reward. But I should do something. Let me think. A promotion for each of you of course and thirty thaler for each man," Freytag smiled.

"You will see to that Colonel Neuberg is that understood?" Freytag looked directly at Neuberg as he spoke, dead eyes resonating utter contempt.

"Yes, sir" Neuberg held the look for a moment before turning towards the three redcoats; Volgraf could barely conceal this moment of triumph.

III

Brandt, accompanied by von Bomm, felt relieved to be free of the pernicious atmosphere of the coffee shop. Preferring instead to take their chances at reasoning with the protesters, they slipped away. As they made their way through the sprawl of the battalion's men in the Melkstraat, Brandt whispered comments to the blonde-haired grenadier officer. They stepped past Krombach and Pinsk, now joined by Reifener. The three watched them disappear around the dog-leg. A few nervous glances were shared around between the men of the battalion. Winckler came and stood by the three crouched soldiers.

"What do you reckon, Sergeant?" Reifener asked.

But Winckler seemed lost in his own thoughts, his gaze fixed on the spot where the two officers had vanished from sight.

Ten minutes later, the two men returned, the blonde haired von Bomm in animated dialogue next to the brooding Brandt who moved through the stream of men towards Roner.

"Company Sergeant-Major Roner, will you take Volgraf's company and my men. Clear up the barricades. We have a parade and the visit of a Prince to prepare for in about three-quarters of an hour.

"Yes sir," Roner's voice filled with relief and a degree of questioning, "are you not coming, sir?"

"No. I think the men can do without officers for a bit. Make a good job of it, William; I can trust you to sort it out, can't I?"

Company Sergeant-Major Roner stood stock still "Yes sir, at once sir."

The bells of the Basilica of St Martin had just peeled midday when the men of 3rd Brigade caught site of the party of mounted dignitaries. There were scant signs of damage and the citizens of Halle had now taken to the streets to witness the events of the most unusual of days at first hand. The four battalions of the brigade were paraded in a contiguous line, each three ranks deep, in open order so that the mounted officers could take the salute of the colours. At the head of the party, slightly ahead of the now austere Freytag rode the Duke of York. His Hanoverian cream horse showing no signs of the eleven-mile ride that had brought the Prince and his party to Halle.

At the rear of the ranks of infantry, the cavalry and artillery which had been dispatched to Halle, also paraded. The Duke set his horse to a slow walk and examined the ranks. Krombach felt the weight of the Duke's stare, feeling the guilt of the early morning return along with pangs of hunger; York, having finished his review, headed to the centre of the parade ground.

"Soldiers of the 3rd Brigade and my father's most loyal subjects, how I have looked forward to the moment when I would meet you," he paused, his high

429

nasal voice carrying to the corners of the Grote Markt, "but not like this. The disgrace of today can only be washed away in the blood of the enemy when we meet them in the field. If rights that have been promised to you have been breached, I personally will ensure that they will be honoured. To this end, I and the other officers will hold council; any man here may come and state the nature of his grievance, free of the fear of retribution."

The Duke paused, looking up and down the ranks of soldiers.

"I have authorised the Commissary General to issue an extra ration of six pounds of beef per man for the remainder of our march through Flanders to France."

Smiles and words of triumph echoed throughout the ranks.

"The matter of your pay will also be resolved, you have my word."

The Duke removed his black bicorne and thrust it into the air

"God save the King."

3rd Brigade answered as one.

"God save the King."

In scenes of jubilation the parade was dismissed and the Duke and his staff were escorted into the town hall which looked onto the market place. From there, in a hastily arranged reception, drinks were served and the Duke was introduced by Freytag to the assembled

430

senior officers from the brigade along with the Mayor of Halle, who had materialised as soon as the danger of the hour had passed. News of the royal visit had spread from the moment that Roner had led the two companies into the market place. Now five chairs had been arranged behind a long table, the Duke taking his place in the middle, Freytag and von Klinkowström taking the seats to his right, Commissary General Jackson and von Diepenbroick the seats to his right.

"Thank you for brightening my afternoon, sir. Whitehall won't be happy with the extra expense but I will try my best to bury this in the returns, somehow." Jackson said, as soon as they were seated.

"That's alright. I know you won't let me down; should the Minister of War complain, bring the matter to me," the Duke smiled as he sipped a small glass of red wine.

"It's not just that sir, where we might get the meat from? It's a bit unexpected and will cost more for that, no doubt."

"You are going to tell me it's impossible. I'm going to tell you that I need these men alive, in good health and wanting to fight the enemy not one another. In the end, you will solve the problem and Dundas will bankroll it. And we can all be spared the tedium." York understood the roles that would be played but his patience had worn thin.

"I will speak to the mayor. I reckon we will need around two hundred extra cattle; rest assured, I will sort it."

Jackson drained his glass and looked to an orderly for a refill.

"Half measures in this place, I think; will have to have a word with our Hanoverian hosts." Jackson spoke before realising from von Diepenbroick's pained expression that he had an excellent grasp of English.

"No offence meant," Jackson smiled, apologetically.

Redcoats were crowded around the ebullient Gauner telling his story of how he, Hartmann and Krogh had rescued one of the battalion's Colours after deciding that the mutineers had gone too far.

Their reward for bravery had been promotions.

Krogh and Gauner were now sergeants and Hartmann, a corporal. Krombach and Pinsk milled around at the rear of the Kings Germans, the quadrant of the market street reverberated to the sounds of exuberance. Pinsk towered above the press of his comrades, intermittently relaying parts of Gauner's story. Krombach listened distractedly, his attention elsewhere

"Can you believe this? It's complete cock and balls!" Pinsk hissed, but Krombach was watching Sergeant Winckler who had ascended the short flight of steps and slipped quietly into the Town Hall.

Volgraf flicked open his pocket watch, "Half an hour, gentlemen, then we can get back for a bite to eat. All this excitement has left me famished."

The circle of senior officers, drawn from the 5th and 10th Regiments, along with the officer who commanded the light dragoons laughed politely and made stilted small talk. No officer had seriously expected any of the rankers to appear; those who did might drown the Duke in petty squabbles. The quickly established opinion was that this meeting was a waste of time apart from the fact that it gave the officers a chance to view the Duke at close quarters; further consensus was that York had nothing to gain from this meeting and by implication much to lose.

Neuberg stood apart, making polite conversation with the mayor, feeling very much alone in the room. Then his eyes were drawn to the movement of a shadow in the doorway and the sound of footsteps on the stone floor. A moment later and there was a knock on the open door and the figure of Sergeant Winckler snapped to attention. Every head in the room turned towards the soldier framed in the doorway.

"Sergeant, what is it?" Neuberg asked.

"Sir, a battalion matter, sorry to disturb you."

Neuberg felt the room turning its gaze on him. To dismiss the sergeant in the face of the morning's events would seem careless. Neuberg looked at the Duke.

"With your permission?"

"Yes of course Colonel," The Duke offered a congenial smile and returned to conversation with the men seated at the table with him.

Neuberg followed Winckler down the stone steps to the entrance, expecting the sergeant to step out of the building and onto the steps that lead from the main square. Instead Winckler opened a door opposite the main doorway, checked the room was empty and stepped inside; Neuberg followed and closed the door behind him.

"Well, Sergeant?" Neuberg's voice was clipped with impatience.

"Sir, it's about the missing Colour."

"Yes"

"Well, I can't prove it sir, but, don't you think the whole event was…" Winckler was uncertain as to how to frame the words.

"Well put it this way, sir, everyone's been struggling for pay; even a sergeant's pay didn't stretch to much more than that of the lads. But certain men have had plenty to spend since we left Hanover."

Winckler's fingers dug into his bicorne held by his right hip, there could be no more fencing around the subject.

"Corporal, now Sergeant Gauner to be precise."

"And?"

"Well sir, back in camp at home, most of the men needed more than army pay to keep them fed. Gauner did some building as I recall but was as short as every other man by pay-day. So, it makes no sense that he has a large pouch full of thalers. Where did he get it from?"

Winckler paused.

"Go on." Neuberg said, one hand still resting on the door handle and Winckler was unsure whether it was to prevent the two men being disturbed or to sweep the door open and terminate the meeting.

"Well sir, on more than one occasion, I spotted Gauner in conversation with one of our officers; Major Volgraf to be precise. sir. It may be that they were discussing battalion matters but what would the major want with a corporal from Captain Brandt's company? And then, before Halle, Gauner was a big voice in the airing of the men's problems. Yet when the matter comes to a head, he is the person who saves the Colour and just happens to find the major. And then you are embarrassed by the matter in front of the Field Marshal..."

"That's enough, Sergeant," Neuberg spoke quickly. "Are you expecting me to go upstairs and accuse Major Volgraf of paying one of my men to breed insurrection, then being complicit in the stealing of the Colours?"

Winckler stood stock still at attention.

"No, sir."

"Good, because it all sounds completely preposterous."

Neuberg fixed his sergeant with a withering stare; except that to Neuberg it didn't sound preposterous at all. However, if such an accusation were made or even spread, the consequences would be disastrous.

"Is that all?" Neuberg's hand gripped the door handle firmly.

"No, sir, there is another matter."

Neuberg half shook his head, "Do I want to hear this?"

"Perhaps sir, perhaps not; but the Duke and his Commissary will."

Sergeant Winckler was presented to the Duke and the dignitaries at the main table. As Winckler spoke Neuberg kept a cold eye fixed on Volgraf, who for his part returned an indifferent look before turning away dismissively.

"Sergeant Winckler, please speak. How can we help you?" The Duke smiled in an effort to relax Winckler, little knowing that after the meeting with Neuberg, this moment, this was a conversation that far easier for the Hanoverian soldier.

"Actually sir, I think I might be able to help you." Winckler smiled and the room broke out the sounds of stifled laughter.

"Good, good," York replied, "we could always do with extra help."

A chorus of laughter erupted from the standing circle of officers, Volgraf's laugh loudest amongst them.

"How can you help us?"

"Sir, I have been a soldier for twenty-three years. Sadly, one thing or two things I have learnt in that time, begging your pardon, is that the army doesn't always make the best choices for food. The ministers are a tight-fisted bunch at best of times. As for the promise of English pay, the men desperately needed it to arrive on time. Then there was Enschede..." Winckler's voice hesitated.

"Enschede?"

"The lads got carried away, broke some tavern up. But we were all short of money; the Dutch had been thieving us on the price of bread. Our wagons were empty and when we bought grain from them to try and make our own, it was mouldy. The only efficient thing the ministers managed to do was to dock our pay for what we did to the town and forget the extra money we were promised."

Winckler paused, hoping the Duke was following but York was nodding and had even scribbled a note on some parchment in front of him.

"Go on," York said.

"Well, sir, it seemed to me, being a soldier for twenty-three years that something like this was inevitable. Everywhere we go, bread is ten times more expensive than at home. If only we had a mobile bakery, sir. You see them at fairs every high day and holy day. I've heard some of them can bake five thousand loaves in a day, maybe more. We wouldn't need to be fleeced."

"Yes, very good idea, thank you Sergeant …" the Duke looked at his paper. "Sergeant Winckler, I will tell the Commissary General to begin searching for one."

The Duke looked at Jackson, who was smiling broadly at Winckler whilst von Diepenbroick translated.

"Yes, capital idea, Sergeant. Already started making enquiries across the northern German towns, but it could be weeks, months perhaps. Contrary to popular belief, I'm not a miracle worker," Jackson shot a look at York and grinned.

Again, laughter echoed from the officers, glad of this unexpected theatre before lunch. The Duke started to translate Jackson's reply, but Winckler held up a hand.

"There is no need sir, I understand some English, enough to follow the gentleman," he nodded in the direction of Jackson.

"Sir, there is no need to wait or search. It just so happens that I know of a mobile bakery a few miles from here," Winckler spoke, calmly now, knowing this was his moment.

"Most marvellous news," the Duke looked at the group of officers and grinned as laughter peeled around the room. "Where can we find our Brabant bread makers, so that I can coerce them to join us?"

"They aren't local, sir, they are Hanoverian. In fact, they have followed the army since we marched."

The Duke stopped his note making and looked directly at the sergeant.

Winckler spoke with a deliberately calm voice, knowing that the room now held his full attention.

"I took the liberty of arranging the matter six weeks ago. As I said, it seemed inevitable that the ministers would fail us. The men don't need much sir; bread, beef and beer will keep us going forward. So I made the arrangements and…"

"Oh, this is brilliant," Jackson having just caught up with the conversation thumped the table and bellowed laughter.

Winckler spoke again, slowly so that Diepenbroick could translate.

"There is a mobile bakery, Hanoverians by the name of Reifener. Waiting for your word to join the army and provide us with bread at a very reasonable rate. As I have said, I have been a soldier for a long time. I understand the army. When the politicians don't need us, we survive on half pay and so most men have a second job. Mine is…well let's say I know how to arrange a deal here, a deal there…So I was wondering, if I might be of more use to you serving the Commissary…" Winckler looked at Jackson enquiringly.

But Brooks Jackson had already stood up as the words were being translated and looked at Colonel Neuberg.

"Colonel, I'm requisitioning your Sergeant, if that is alright with you?" the room turned to look at Neuberg, who as transfixed as all the rest of the occupants, merely shrugged his shoulders.

"Good!" Jackson said "Sergeant…no…Sergeant-Major sounds better, if that is acceptable to your Royal Highness?" casting a glance in the direction of the Duke but not even waiting for the reply.

"Glad that is all settled. You have got to be paid better when you work for me, you know," Jackson walked around the table and slapped Winckler firmly on the back, "now, Sergeant-Major, we need to find two hundred cattle by this afternoon."

CHAPTER TWENTY-FIVE

Brother Redcoats.

Tournai: 30th April 1793

At Halle, The Duke of York had issued a challenge to the Hanoverians; make good forty-two miles distance in four and a half days and join their comrades-in-arms at Tournai.

Among Hanoverian ranks there was a feeling of bittersweet victory but Krombach could not share that joy. The colours were discovered to be stolen on his watch. The promised beef ration had arrived, mail had caught up with the battalion and soon the English pay would arrive. Brandt's Company now had one more sergeant than its quota but little was made of that for the battalion's lot had improved and every man took this as a proof that Sergeant-Major Winckler was already making his presence felt on the Duke's staff.

Worse still, for the young redcoat, Gauner, Krogh and Hartman had come out of the episode with credit. Around the evening campfires, toasts to Winckler's good health and Gauner's success were galling. Krombach felt betrayed by one and utterly outmanoeuvred by the other.

The hypnotic action of marching to the beat of a single drum soothed the musketeer; the bite of the pack across his shoulders and weight of the musket freed Krombach's mind. He knew he needed to lift his spirits and began constructing thoughts for a letter to his parents, another to Maren. Before Halle, the energy to write back had escaped him, now with post arriving these were overdue tasks. The young redcoat had taken the time to read letters for a couple of comrades, even drafting a reply for another over a hasty morning breakfast. Each task felt like a small act of contrition for what he perceived to be a personal failing.

Around the battalions that marched south, a gentle Walloon landscape revealed itself. Shades of fertile brown tinged light green with the early shoots of crops, compacted cobbled roads and warm spring sunshine made the journey pleasurable. However, as Tournai approached, the weather deteriorated into a succession of showers and cobblestones gave way to a morass of mud. From the grey cloak of mist that smothered the Hanoverians, emerged an incredible sight. Thousands of Prussian, Austrian and British soldiers assembled now that the commanders had agreed the strategy for the defeat of the Republican French.

Reds and dark blues greeted their arrival as British and Prussian soldiers formed an honour guard; 3rd Brigade brought up the rear of the four formations but the camp had been reached with two hours to spare.

Only when the redcoats began to unpack wagons and assemble their tents did the rain abate and a fine spring evening unfolded. With this change came the magnificent sight of the arrival of hundreds of horsemen. Two more brigades of Hanoverian cavalry, which had travelled on a different route made the camp just before sunset. Even the Austrians felt compelled to send a dozen white jacketed Cuirassiers to acknowledge the arrival of such spectacle. Krombach and Pinsk cheered as eight squadrons of red jacketed cavalry trotted past. Reifener tore himself from cooking duties and the three jostled amongst the other men of the 10th to identify the units that had arrived. The Life Guards, the 2nd, 5th and 7th regiments paraded through the camp and on to cantonments that had been allocated further to the east. A solitary figure remained, his horse trotted towards the Duke of York. Both men dismounted and then embraced. Around them, British soldiers who had also been watching the parade broke out into cries of 'God Save the King'.

Prince Ernest Augustus, The Duke of Cumberland, and York's younger brother, had arrived.

Krombach and Pinsk eventually joined the lines of men, milling around the cooking pots of the Twenty in the fading light. Darkness had settled by the time both crouched in the damp grass to eat a bowl of stew; neither spoke, intent on savouring the meal, a situation that might have lasted had it not been for the figure of a light dragoon trooper who walked past. Pinsk had seen the facings of the uniform before.

"Hey you, cavalry, which unit are you from?"

"The 9th," The trooper kept walking.

Pinsk shoved his near empty tin to Krombach and loped after the man.

"Wait up. You were with the advance brigade, weren't you? There were grenadiers with you, weren't there, the 1st?"

The trooper slowed and turned. In the flickering camp fires that were scattered around he saw the gangling man with corporal's stripes heading towards him and stopped.

"Yes Corporal, we were. Why do you ask?"

"Please, my brother is with them. I thought they might be here but no one has seen them."

"No, Corporal, they aren't here. We left them at Rumes two days ago, about six miles south; they are part of the cordon there. Anything else, only I'm on an errand for my captain?"

Pinsk shook the trooper's hand and settled down to finish off the last of his stew, then looked suspiciously at Krombach as there seemed less of it than before. Krombach had stuffed a chunk of fresh bread into his mouth and was grinning as he attempted to chew. When most of the bread had disappeared, he could finally draw breath to speak.

"I don't think the army can afford for you to grow any more. Come on, let's see if we can scrounge some more from Reifener."

A lack of extra food was the first of many disappointments that night; rain returned, harder than ever, driving squalls which buffeted the tent. Krombach had eventually found sleep, only for his dream to be disturbed by loud voices and the sound of drums. Tent flaps tore apart and the silhouette of Moustache Georg appeared.

"On your feet Brandt's Company. Stand to, now!"

The battalion stood and waited; rain continued; out in the darkness of the night, drums could be heard again. Sergeant Gauner prowled in the darkness too, at one moment thumping Reifener for attempting to sleep whilst stood up. Then Krombach felt the right side of his face alive with pain, his ear ringing. Gauner had taken the opportunity to cuff him for no apparent reason at all. The sergeant proceeded to walk on down the line without turning back; rank had its privileges.

Brandt waited for orders. Major Volgraf wearing his regulation waxed cape and additional protective cover over his expensive bicorne, paced past him.

"What's this Brandt, no cape? You will catch your death with this weather."

Brandt wore his redcoat only, his cape somewhere in his tent, forgotten in the alarm.

"It's in the tent. Anyway, the rankers have nothing but their jackets."

"Good God, man! Send someone to fetch it! The last thing I need is a martyr for a captain. They are used to being wet and miserable; hardens them up and it's good for the soul; but that is not the lot of a gentleman."

Brandt bit to control a rebuke; out of the heavy drizzle Neuberg appeared.

"Stand the battalion down. Get them under cover. We march in four hours. Senior officers, to the battalion tent immediately."

Six hundred tired and miserable men, their eternal souls much strengthened by the two-hour watch, scrambled for the luxury of the tent and vain effort to dry sodden redcoats.

A cluster of candles that adorned the table in the battalion tent shed dim light. Volgraf and the three other company commanders shed waxed jackets and found chairs. Brandt shed his redcoat, his shirt underneath drenched; he sneezed and Volgraf cast him a look, one eyebrow raised.

"Forget your cape, Captain?" Neuberg was busy sketching a pencilled map onto an envelope, which he had slit and opened out.

"Apparently, as the men do not have greatcoats, Brandt has taken a stance of sufferance." Volgraf sneered.

"I forgot my cape sir, nothing more than that," Brandt could feel another sneeze forming but was in no mood to suffer the sniping of Major Volgraf.

Neuberg continued his drawing. "The men do not have greatcoats. It is an act of folly on behalf of those who should know better. Best not compound that folly with our own acts of carelessness." He glanced up at Brandt then turned to the others.

"I will make this quick, as no doubt you could use rest and a change of clothes. Apologies for the sketch but no-one at headquarters has a map as far as I can see. This is the land ahead as best we know."

The drawing showed the camp of Tournai and roads leading south-east and south. Running parallel to the south-east road, a wavy pencil line marked the Scheldt River. Both the road and river met at a place called Condé and then carried south-east to the edge of the envelope.

"The Duke has received word that the French have launched a series of attacks along the Scheldt and here, around Condé, where the main Austrian camp is. The Prussians are marching on the south-east road now to be in position to launch a counter attack later today, should the opportunity arise. We will follow them at daybreak, unless the situation has changed."

"What about this road, sir. What do we know from here?" Volgraf asked, looking at the map with professional interest.

"Ah, apologies, Major," Neuberg replied, hastily jotted the name of Rumes onto the map.

"We have men there in three outposts. 1st Grenadiers to be exact. Nothing new from them yet but their last report which arrived at sunset mentioned no sign of activity from the French."

"Who are they posted with, sir?" Brandt spoke, having stifled another sneeze.

Neuberg sighed. "No-one: they are part of the cordon that the Austrians have constructed. It's a relic of the last war but now is not the time for that. Rest while you can, we march at first light. I really do hope you are not catching a cold, Brandt!"

The command tent of the British was unusually quiet. Apart from orderlies packing the last of the Duke's effects, the only senior officers present were Trevethan and Jackson. The Cornish engineer was in the process of sketching a copy of a map of Valenciennes which the Duke had managed to borrow from one of the Austrian cavalry commanders and had been delivered by an officer of the Esterhàzy regiment. Even without the rich blue pelisse Trevethan had marvelled at the rich colour of the cavalryman's uniform, cherry red riding breeches set against a sky blue jacket and gold braided riding boots: the hussar accepted the compliments on his dress with a casual air, as if such comments were common place.

Major Brennan, English by birth, had given eighteen years' service to the Austrian Emperor; he sat and watched patiently at the delicate markings made by the pencil clutched between thick muscular fingers. The Esterhàzy had scouted the road from Tournai to Valenciennes and the map had become a central part of the allied intelligence for the days ahead. On the table opposite Trevethan, Jackson was reading through a series of returns, the occasional sharp intake of breath as calculations were made followed by an equally frequent chuckle.

"When all of this is over I might have a job for that sergeant, you know. He is going to save me a fortune! Not only with this bakery, but he has negotiated grain prices all the way along the route so we aren't stuck with suppliers here in every province charging us through the nose."

"All sounds very exciting," Trevethan spoke without looking up. "Any idea when this might be over? There are half a dozen fortifications on this map. Might take a while to winkle these Frenchies out, you know."

"One or two more defeats and the French will have had enough, gentlemen, mark my words! Already handing a couple of good doses of the cane to them myself; can't think that they will be eager for too much more."

Brennan offered the comments, glancing from one man's paperwork to the other, keen to absorb any other useful information knowing that Mack had chosen him for that very purpose.

Outside the men heard a sentry issue a challenge and then the tent flap was thrust open. A soldier from the 1st Grenadiers, thick with mud and sweat, barrelled into the tent; large saucer-white eyes scanned the room and the soldier spoke in rapid German.

Brennan answered, asked a series of questions and then relayed the information.

"Your outpost at Rumes is under attack, has been for the last…," he checked an elaborate fob-watch, "…three hours; at least four battalions of French infantry. There are just two companies of 1st Grenadiers there."

Trevethan looked at the map. The Duke was already on the road towards the Prussian encampment at Anzin.

"Poor bastards, what do you think?" Trevethan and the cavalryman studied the map, calculating the time it would take the message to reach the Duke and then how long it would take soldiers to reach Rumes.

"I will take my men there now. At least if some cavalry arrive the French might think reserves are closer at hand."

Brennan was already up and rattling off a series of instructions to the messenger. He wrote a note detailing his own action onto the unopened envelope that the messenger carried, then spoke to the man in the calm voice of one used to commanding men in such situations.

"Take this to any brigade commander that you can find on the Anzin road; beg them to send a column to Rumes at once. Then find the Duke and inform him of the orders that I have given you."

The messenger nodded, turned and was gone.

"I will return for the map later, once I have attended to this matter; good-day to you both." Brennan bowed and without waiting for a reply, the hussar officer disappeared.

A squadron of the Esterhàzy, led by an Englishman, would ride to the rescue of the King's Germans. And without a single order to sanction the action from the general staff of either nation.

Tournai: 1st May 1793

Second battalion remained the *Esel Soldaten*. The curious badge of distinction that was taken broadly in good spirits even though the road had been thoroughly ploughed up by the passage of the Prussian troops earlier that day. Sergeant Gauner had been in a convivial mood during the march but Krombach knew he would need to tread as cautiously as the passage he and the battalion were taking through the glutinous Flanders mud. 'Moustache Georg', Möller and Company Sergeant Roner made up the compliment of senior non-commissioned officers. At least now that Henry Pinsk had been promoted to corporal he would have more regular contact with the sergeants and Möller was no friend of Gauner. A few new friendships within the company might not go amiss but as the column of infantry stopped in the midday sunshine and fell out along the grass verges of the arrow-straight Flanders road, it was Pinsk and Reifener that he sought to share food and discuss the events of the previous night.

As he did, a messenger thundered past lines of redcoats, sprawled along the banks of the road and on through ranks of cavalrymen, arranging fodder and water for their mounts, pausing at a distant wagon serving as a mobile buffet, a group of officers gathered around while an orderly served food and drink from a wicker hamper. Within seconds the messenger spurred his horse further down the road; the three redcoats saw von Diepenbroick and Neuberg in conversation.

"Someone's going to be for it, no doubt."

Pinsk spoke between heavy draws on a freshly-lit pipe, while Reifener sliced bread that he had baked the previous night, depositing chunks into the three bowls, then adding meat and cheese.

"As long as it's not us, I don't care." Krombach sat on his pack and wiped his boots in the grass to remove the worst of the mud and busily inspected them.

"These boots are leaking; there is a hole here I can fit two fingers through!"

"Everyone's boots are leaking, 'Bastion. Get a pair of cavalry boots if you want dry feet. Impossible to march long distances in, of course, but they never leak. The people who do the least amount of walking get the best footwear. That's the wisdom of the army for you."

Pinsk nodded his thanks to Reifener as he took his bowl of food.

"Have your boots been leaking?" Krombach eyed Reifener's footwear suspiciously.

"Yes." Reifener gurgled, "really uncomfortable to wear; like walking in a puddle the whole time."

"There, Reifener's boots are leaking, your boots are leaking, my boots are leaking. Every man in the company has wet feet right now."

Pinsk spoke with a corporal's authority, as if such logic determined the matter to be closed.

"My feet aren't wet. In fact, they are warm as toast." Reifener spoke as he poked large chunks of food into his mouth.

"I thought you said your boots leaked?" Krombach asked giving the redcoat a sideways look, as did the tall corporal.

"They did, but these aren't mine. I got one of the Twenty to swipe these for me. Much better fit than my last pair too." Reifener smiled disarmingly making Krombach want to punch him all that much harder.

Thirty minutes later, the messenger reappeared at a gallop and found von Diepenbroick, the horseman's arm jabbed to a direction north-west; moments later, the messenger was off, riding past redcoats being roused to their feet. The battalion reformed, facing back up the road from when it came. In a few paces the infantry column slewed off the road, taking to the flat, ploughed fields to avoid the train of baggage wagons; behind them a regiment of light cavalry and a battery of horse artillery were preparing to follow.

The *Esel Soldaten* were heading to war.

Valenciennes: 1st May 1793

Genet had watched Caillat struggle with an increasing workload with the secret delight of a man who felt unjustly usurped. It was a pleasure he took great pains to conceal but now every action he undertook served to add to Caillat's burden rather than reduce it. With Dumouriez, the working relationship had developed into one of synchronisation, even though Genet had been reporting to the National Assembly to protect himself. That choice had been fortunate but the freedom to control the day-to-day workings of the army had disappeared with the departure of Dumouriez. Now Carnot pulled the strings: Dampierre, the nominal commander, consented in relief that someone else was making the decisions; Genet, little more than a clerk, drafted the orders and Caillat approved each one. To Serge Genet, the new pecking order was an affront but the moment for a little manoeuvring and revolution of his own was close at hand. Paris, glorious Paris, with the new Committee of Public Safety would be Genet's salvation.

The first of the trials of those accused of conspiring with Dumouriez had commenced only to face immediate setback. The Committee had presumed the pronouncement of a guilty verdict within the same day of the trial opening. Instead, member after member of the National Assembly had arrived to speak in support of the popular Venezuelan officer, General Miranda. Following these were testimonies from senior officers of the Army of the Ardennes, each man risking his own liberty to tear to shreds the accusations made by the Committee.

A scapegoat for the palpable embarrassment of Robespierre and the Committee had been found in the Parisian lawyer who had prepared the case, but Caillat had received a severe rebuke of his own: his investigations, methods and evidence had all been called into question. More than his career was threatened with swift termination should more prosecutions fail.

The letter had remained on Caillat's desk for the last three days, weighed down with several other sheathes of paper under a polished grey pebble, pressed into service as a paperweight. Every so often the edges of the paper lifted, threatening to engulf the stone, on the warm breeze which streamed into the tent, carrying the heat of the day and the rich aroma of cooking pots as the few soldiers left in the camp breakfasted. The two men worked in silence, at either end of a large table. Only when an orderly had arrived to remove the discarded breakfast plates and bring fresh coffee did Genet determine that the moment to circle his prey was at hand.

"The first reports should be here soon, let's hope for good news."

Genet spoke as he carefully etched a new series of returns on equipment strengths of the army. The National Assembly had thrived on the minutia of war, the Committee for Public Safety even more so.

"Yes indeed. Good news would be most welcome."

"Paris thrives on news, so best to give her something positive."

"Yes, noted. Would you do me the favour of reading this before I send it?"

Genet looked up and smiled at Caillat, who was re-reading a report he had written in the late of last night and in the process of amending, in order that the message was indeed, more positive.

"Of course, Maurice."

Caillat for his part had taken advice that Genet had already proffered to heart, still considering Genet his mentor despite the reversal of their positions; when the pair were left to their own devices, a working relationship borne of a shared burden had blossomed. The latest dispatches spoke of the offensive being undertaken by the North. The army, also under severe pressure from Paris, had launched a series of attacks against the Allied cordon, designed to delay the concentration of forces east of Valenciennes.

"Here," Caillat rose and offered the corrected sheet to Genet, "please, let me know your thoughts."

The Spider knew how to spin out the slenderest of favourable facts and while burying the most damning. Caillat's effort showed promise but Genet offered his own thoughts with the end-game in mind.

"This last line; do not offer an assurance of success. We do not know how the matter today will turn out. Distance yourself, in case the matter ends in failure. Should this day be ours, emphasise your involvement in the next report. After all, you and I are not out there doing the fighting and therefore we cannot be blamed for the lack of valour in others, should attacks fail."

"Do you think they will fail?"

"And never ask or answer that question, Maurice," Genet chuckled.

Caillat looked blankly back at Genet, wondering what mistake had been made.

"If you ask my opinion on failure, then you risk a dialogue where your own opinions or sympathies could be gleaned. That would leave you vulnerable, especially with the power that your office holds now."

Caillat nodded, seeing the wisdom in older man's words, feeling more aware of a cloying self-doubt, rather than feeling the power of the Committee backing up his every decision in the field.

"But, if you are asking me as a friend, then yes, I'm afraid that we will fail. Valenciennes or Lille will soon be under siege and we must not be contaminated with that stench of failure."

Caillat retrieved the document and reached for fresh parchment, preparing to submit the final copy and hoping for the early arrival of news from any of the half a dozen attacks that were occurring along fifty miles of the front line.

"Thank you, Serge. I am not sure that I am the man for this task. I'm certainly no Carnot."

"No one is. But even the great Carnot has doubts. And he would not envy your assignment. His power is enjoyed with the freedom to move along the frontier. You are tied to the success of this army, my friend."

"Yes, I know. I am a man serving two masters. If I fail here, it is my own fault. But Paris…"

Caillat glanced in the direction of the grey pebble and the letter it restrained.

"Those investigations were sound, Serge. The evidence against Miranda was strong. The man should have been sent to the guillotine."

"I know, my friend, I know."

The Spider knew the moment had arrived.

"Maurice, I have given this matter some thought. Someone needs to go to Paris and oversee the next few prosecutions. Of course it should be you, but with your work here, that is impossible. But…" Genet paused then lowered his voice, "what if I were to go? I know the transgressions of every man on trial and the case against each."

Caillat stopped writing and looked at Genet.

"But, what if you fail? You would be tarnished, even dragged to the guillotine. I cannot ask it of you," Caillat hissed back.

The conversation had taken a conspiratorial tone. Even though no guard stood outside the tent and both men held unobstructed view out across the camp, their voices had dropped to the merest whisper.

"If I am in Paris, then you can be assured that every prosecution will be conducted thoroughly. Better to risk death for something we have control over, rather than be hostage to events out of our hands, don't you think?

You and I should both maintain a healthy distance from the decisions made in this place."

Genet continued in a whispered.

"Dampierre is no fool; he knows this command is a poisoned chalice. He is a man dying in front of our eyes. Your words may not condemn him but when matters on the battlefield sour, the Committee will recall recent events and heap the infamy of them onto his shoulders. Better to be the slaughter-man than the cattle, surely? Paris needs victories: military, political and judicial. You and I can, at least, deliver the latter."

Caillat put down the quill he had just loaded with ink and sat back; the material of the folding chair creaking subversively. Genet watched as the man twenty years his junior considered the matter. He said nothing: to Genet, the wait was an eternity, until Caillat reached for a new leaf of paper.

"Serge, these reports to Paris will be ready in an hour. I am authorising you to deliver them personally to the Committee. A month should suffice to gather and complete those investigations. You had better go and pack what you need."

Genet felt his soul lift. He was going to Paris: power would be in his grasp once more.

CHAPTER TWENTY-SIX

The Countermand.

Rumes: 1st May 1793

There had been little time to train the replacements to the Black Lions. Recruits in new blue uniforms tried to ingratiate themselves with an exchange of anxious smiles and the false bravado of small talk with men whom they considered veterans, whose own blue coats looked distinctly filthy and worn after just a few short weeks on campaign. In truth many of these were the levy of soldiers from the previous year who only had the good fortune to survive the campaigns of the later winter and early spring. The old white coats still formed the backbone of the battalion. Soldiers who had once served the king and now served the National Assembly. But their ranks were thinning. In February at Mont Cassel, perhaps three hundred had formed to parade and march away with the battalion. After the defeats at Herstal and Neerwinden, where the Black Lions had performed the role of rear-guard, Mahieu estimated there might only be a hundred left, including himself. Now they had been chosen as an advance guard, to deliver an attack against an enemy outpost.

The instructions that had been passed down were straightforward, 'overrun the enemy and withdraw before a reserve could be organised to counter-attack'.

Straightforward in theory, shambolic in practice.

"Still no sign, sir?" Mahieu spoke as the figure of Captain Davide stalked towards him.

"No, Sergeant. I'm afraid it feels depressingly familiar. We are stuck with our breeches around our ankles. Our General, the guns and cavalry are nowhere to be seen," Davide's voice was hushed, the conversation was not for the ears of the men around them.

To the watching soldiers the pair might have looked the perfect union of the new state. The blue coated officer of the Republic and white jacketed sergeant once of the Royalist army, come together to serve the will of the people of France. Their personal small talk however had little to do with singing the praises of the new model of the military system.

"Christ, this lot couldn't organise an orgy in a brothel. Now headquarters has these Parisian politicians sniffing around over every decision, we will be lucky to get bread and musket balls, let alone cavalry and some sort of plan."

The first attack of the day had gone badly. No one knew how many redcoats held the line of houses that populated the main road of Rumes. But the artillery support had failed to arrive and cavalry had been supposed to bypass the village and hinder the deployment of enemy reserves. The infantry had been left to their own devices and the attack had been badly executed and poorly co-ordinated.

"The men need a victory sir, especially if we are going to keep getting farm hands and pensioners to fill the ranks with," Mahieu was unusually sullen. He knew it was to do with Neerwinden, the battle that had nearly taken his life. The infantry had fought to cover the retreat of the guns and the cavalry had fled rather than support their foot-slogging comrades. How the Black Lions had survived had been a minor miracle, not that Mahieu could remember much of it. A cuirassier sabre blow had caught him on the temple and only fate and the bravery of the Grison brothers, who had retrieved his body, had kept the sergeant alive.

Into the clearing where 6th Company had gathered to reload and reorganise, a runner appeared. New blue and old white coats watched the man pass orders to their captain. Davide nodded and checked a pocket-watch then exchanged words with his sergeant who nodded in agreement and then turned to the faces which now stared intently at him.

"6th Company, on your feet and make yourselves ready. Prepare to form a skirmish screen. I want forty men, the rest of you will act as loaders."

Mahieu began to make his selection, a mixture of the veteran blue coats and the white coats. None of the new arrivals would be chosen. If they could manage to load the Charleville musket correctly and take it to one of the men in the firing line, that would be a blessing enough.

The French had called the truce and for twenty minutes of the hour-long peace, von Bomm had been dismissed to the bell-tower of the church, to note the French positions and observe the movement of their forces. Rumes was unremarkable, a series of small farms and houses stained dirty with clay-dust, clustered around a cross roads, where a postal road and earthen road met.

Those inhabitants who had remained took advantage of the pause in hostilities to flee. A variety of carts and wagons hastily piled with what could be salvaged moved south-west along the cobbled road across gently undulating farmland towards the French border. Very few had moved north-east in the directions of the allies, the majority had decided that their sentiments lay with the French.

The other road, more mud than shale, ran north to south. Two days before, one Grenadier company had followed it north two miles to Wannehain, the other had traipsed five miles south to Brunehat. Whatever help might come from either of these would be a long time in arriving, if any was coming at all.

Moving around to the other side of the parapet in the tower, von Bomm scouted the terrain to the north-east, using the telescope that Baumann had loaned to him. There were no signs of dust on the horizon, but that was only to be expected. The rain of the previous night had quickly turned all roads other than the postal roads into a morass. It would hamper the sending of reinforcements and mask the signs of their arrival, just as the boggy ground had hampered the French attacks of that morning.

Reserves were coming but not for the King's Germans.

The glint of bronze betrayed movement to the south-west. Light calibre horse artillery and cavalry. The flood of civilians would further slow the arrival of the enemy but once they were here, the fate of the two grenadier companies would be settled unless help arrived.

Messages had been sent from Rumes of the situation and south to Brunehat, where Colonel Franke had positioned himself. The 1st Grenadier Battalion represented the combined forces of grenadier companies from the Hanoverian Guards and 10th Regiment. Franke was a Guards officer, as was most of the 1st Grenadier's staff and for a while von Bomm had been the only member of his headquarters staff not

drawn from the Guards. The arrival of Leopold
Baumann had changed von Bomm's standing, not just
in the return to his lieutenant's rank but in the fact that
Baumann discussed matters regarding the company
with officers more junior and ignored von Bomm. If the
captain had to communicate to his most senior
lieutenant it was through one of the N.C.O.s. Baumann
had done so in his order to a corporal called Engel,
ordering him to 'ask Mister von Bomm to go to the
tower and conduct a search for the enemy and our
reinforcements'.

Outwardly von Bomm had taken the situation with
cheerful pragmatism; after all, he was still receiving a
captain's pay but whether Colonel Franke knew of
Baumann's hostility toward von Bomm or of the duel
three months earlier was uncertain. The colonel had left
the instruction that one of the corporals, who happened
to be an outstanding horseman, would act as a
messenger to the Duke should enemy forces be
observed. It had been Franke's grim prediction that
'every officer would be needed'.

Earlier that morning he had been proved prophetic.

The initial attack, uncoordinated as it was, had been
soundly repulsed. Three infantry columns tried to force
the passage of the postal road before the fourth had a
chance to deploy from its marching column and
support its comrades. One and a half companies of
grenadiers waited to meet the enemy, taking advantage

of every piece of cover that the houses and walls of the village could provide. Captain Baumann commanded soldiers posted around the northern road, in case the enemy made any effort to outflank the positions from there, but nothing came of that.

When the French attack did come, one battalion had advanced ahead of the others, perhaps to provoke the defenders into firing early and blunt the effectiveness of a first volley of the day. Whatever the enemy's plan it had not succeeded, the grenadiers holding their nerve until the enemy were no more than fifty yards. The front of the infantry column, densely packed with French soldiers, had visibly shuddered as the volley struck home. As the enemy struggled to re-form, a second volley crashed out from the fortified buildings. After that redcoats loaded and fired at their own pace but within a matter of a minute the attack was broken. Leading half of Baumann's Company, von Bomm had found himself, with the musket of a fallen grenadier in hand, taking speculative shots at an utterly disorganised enemy.

The second attack had been a more cautious affair. Clouds of blue-coated skirmishers had harassed the grenadier's positions. The enemy had perfected a method where troops who huddled at the rear, out of the danger of musket fire acted as servants on a hunt, loading weapons. Bolder soldiers took advantage of any cover and fired at leisure on the receipt of a freshly

467

primed musket. It was certainly effective in pinning the redcoats down and a form of stalemate had ensued.

The affair reminded von Bomm of swatting a hand towards a swarm of annoying midges, which after a few seconds circle again around the face and exasperate their host. That attack had led to the cease-fire but had also tested the defences to the north. While Hanoverian casualties had been light, the chance to buy time for the arrival of any reserves had been seized on by the Major Habmantel, the commanding officer of the Rumes outpost. Finishing the last details of the rough sketch, von Bomm smiled an acknowledgement to the soldier posted as the lookout, a young grenadier from one of the Guards companies, who watched the actions of the officer as much as keeping an eye out on the manoeuvring of the French.

"What do you think sir, will they attack again?"

A tall but gaunt youth in his late teens itched lank brown hair while using the brim of his Corsican hat to shade his eyes. It had become a standing joke that the politicians had felt generous enough to remove the battalion's treasured bearskins and replace them with a wide-brimmed infantry hat, which folded straight against the head on the left-hand side and seemed utterly impractical. The new apparel was meant to reflect the elite status of the 1st Grenadiers but no redcoat saw it that way. They christened the hats the

Korsisch and the word was spoken with as much venom as the rank of the present company allowed.

"Perhaps; but nobody tells me, lad. I'm just a humble lieutenant. Just keep your eyes peeled if you see anything of interest," he replied as he returned the telescope to view the position to the right of the Grenadiers' positions. Two French battalions had deployed either side of the northern dirt road which led away from Rumes, one of which was moving in dead ground and would be unseen to Baumann's men until the moment of attack. The enemy would need to fight their way through the chain of houses held by Baumann's Company who had barricaded themselves into a series of strong points. Von Bomm swept across the positions to see the captain was enjoying cordial conversation with a French officer as the blue coats removed wounded soldiers who had fallen in the later skirmish attack.

The telescope swung back to the south-west. The other two enemy battalions remained astride the postal road. One of these possessed the most splendid battle standard, A black, heraldic lion on a yellow background, a battalion colour that looked as though knights, pages and footmen should wear matching livery of the black lion. There was a strange beauty to the savagery of war.

The blonde-haired Grenadier officer made some additional notes on his sketch which showed four enemy battalions and estimated the arrival of the cavalry and artillery to be somewhere near the conclusion of the ceasefire. The two companies possessed a single small calibre three-pounder gun, currently covered the road south-west. The undulating ground gave it few targets. To the north the terrain was flatter, save for the depression of dead ground. It would be a point worth mentioning to the Major.

"Here, take this; a present from Captain Baumann. Make sure you give it back to him when we have won. Remember to keep waving until someone acknowledges your signal. Point out the direction of the movement. Keep your *Korsisch* on if you are signalling enemy movement and take it off if you spy the reinforcements. I think we will be mightily glad of good news in the next hour or so."

He smiled at the Grenadier who looked surprised and delighted in equal measure to receive the telescope.

"Just don't drop it or the cost of a replacement will come from your pay and mine."

With that he began the descent by a series of wooden ladders which led to three flights of stones steps and made his way to report to the major.

A precious ten minutes of the cease-fire remained when von Bomm took command of the eighty Grenadiers posted in three buildings to the right of a small earthen track that ran north across farmland, green with the early shoots of barley and wheat. The ground ran flat for five hundred yards and in the fields of earth and rich greens, enemy soldiers grabbed their last opportunity to eat, while others stood watch. Von Bomm scoured the horizon for any sign of the battalion that had been evident from the church tower but the terrain sloped away before rising again another few hundred yards distant; the enemy was hidden in a small valley that ran between cultivated fields. Elsewhere along the line and nearer to his position, within three hundred yards, clusters of Frenchmen crouched in loose skirmish chains.

Behind von Bomm, homes were being gutted of any furniture which could block the open spaces between the houses, where vegetable patches had been cleared and cultivated. A hastily gathered jumble of tables, chairs and bed-frames formed a flimsy barrier. Only the hardiest residents remained, barring the houses to the soldiers who scavenged for materials; hoping against hope that the battle would pass them by. Either side of the sodden brown dirt-road, the houses had been fortified too. Captain Baumann, stationed to the left of the road, had made the red-bricked farmhouse into a defensive strong point. On the inside of the six-foot wall that enclosed the large farmhouse, an assortment of barrels and boxes had been placed to make a fire-step. A quarter of company's one hundred and sixty men deployed here. Some had taken to the slate roof in order to find a firing position. The remaining portion of

Baumann's men was posted between two houses to the rear of the farmhouse to help protect the left-hand flank of the farm. The right flank rested on the road, mutually supporting von Bomm's left hand position.

Von Bomm ran his hands over his uniform and felt inside a jacket pocket to find a pencil and an unopened letter from Hanover. The writing was his father's heavy script but he had yet to open it. Turning it over, he sketched the outline of three houses and the barricades that his troops had erected. There was little to distinguish between the three houses, but his grenadiers, in gallows humour, had already christened them Apple, Broken Tail and Hell's Corner. Apple House, where he viewed the French from was nearest the road and supported by Baumann's men. Hell's Corner was the most exposed. Thirty Grenadiers were deployed there but they would only delay the inevitable. The French would attack from the right, he was sure of it. Whether Broken Tail house held would decide the fate of the defenders, in the lieutenant's mind.

A Grenadier appeared from the shadows of the room with a plate that had been 'liberated' from the house, on it were a small chunk of Flanders cheese, hard bread, a hard-boiled duck's egg and few thin strands of beef. Von Bomm nodded his appreciation and ate while observing the deployment of the French.

He grunted his thanks while gnawing at the bread, "Pinsk, isn't it?"

"Yes sir, transferred from Captain Brandt's Company seven weeks ago, after the Celle camp."

"I'd say that Captain Brandt is a good man to send me his best soldiers, Pinsk? Seven weeks ago. Feels longer than that, doesn't it?" von Bomm caught himself smiling at the chance remembrance of his friend.

"Yes sir, I suppose it does. One day has become much like another; march, camp, march," Pinsk replied, his voice sounded uncertain as to whether the question actually required an answer of him.

"Better than sitting around in the barracks though, eh? Anyway, today is different. No marching but a chance to shoot a few of the French and watch them run. The rest of the 2nd will wish they were here with us. Still, more glory for us come the end of the day."

There were faces around him, listening to his every word and von Bomm knew that the men wanted to hear good news.

"So, let's hope we can get the job done before troops from the column turn up and claim that we needed their help."

His voice and smile exuded confidence but nothing he had seen from the church tower could back up such a claim.

"You look like you have legs up to my armpits, Pinsk. Stay close, I will need you as a runner, I think."

The soldiers in earshot grinned, exchanging nervous smiles and von Bomm stepped away from the window at the front of the house moving to the stairwell then hurriedly making his way into an upper floor, partitioned into two bedrooms. The ceilings sloped towards the walls such that a man could only stand at full height in to the centre of the room; at least that had been the case before the soldiers had occupied it. The bed frames had gone, thrown out of huge holes gouged into the roof and added to the makeshift wall erected to block up the space between the first and second house. The wooden partitions had suffered the same fate and now sunlight poured into the open-topped room, its floor covered with broken terracotta roof tiles. Each of the half dozen grenadiers who manned the position could now load and fire whilst standing but still presented a very small target to the enemy.

"Good work, lads. Let's hope it doesn't rain though." More smiles and grizzled laughter met the easy remark.

"Any sign of our guns arriving, Corporal?"

Engel, a burly soldier, silvery-white hair tied in a tight pony tail elegantly tied in a long queue, held his *Korsisch* to shield his eyes as he peered from his corner perch, craning his neck down the street to look.

"No sir, no sign yet but look, a signal from the tower, sir," Corporal Engel spotted the movement as he had turned his head away from the view along the empty track that led to the centre of the village. The grenadiers around him turned to look and von Bomm waved his hand to acknowledge the signal. The lookout's movements were clear, his hand pointed to the right of the Grenadier's position.

Korsisch on: enemy movement.

Von Bomm waved his appreciation, seeing that the soldier in the tower had the telescope trained on him and made his way back down a wooden staircase worn smooth by years of use.

"Pinsk. Present yourself to Captain Baumann. Tell him we are ready on this side of the road and that the enemy is moving to our right. I have requested the battalion gun from Major Habmantel. Ask him if he wishes you to check on the progress of our artillery. I will examine the other two houses again. Oh, and you might care to mention that I left his telescope in the possession of the lookout," von Bomm pursued his lips in a tight smile, knowing that it wold irk Baumann to think of a common soldier using one of his possessions. Von Bomm only wished that he could see the captain's reaction when Pinsk delivered the message.

"Yes sir." Pinsk clambered out through a window in the back of the house, the door which led to the side door having been barred with furniture wedged tight against it.

The French would not be as clumsy as they were before the ceasefire. They would pin the Grenadiers along their line and then attack in overwhelming numbers on the flank of von Bomm's position. There, a cluster of houses that the Grenadiers did not have the manpower to defend would conceal their advance. Then they would prize the Grenadiers from each house in succession.

The doors having been barred, von Bomm shimmied out of the window that Pinsk had made his way through and moved on to inspect the rest of the defensive line, fighting the desire to turn and look up at the church tower again. The reserves would surely come soon. They had half an hour at most, or else it would be too late.

Three hundred horsemen of the 9th Dragoons, dressed in immaculate blue tunics, were a splendid sight. The *Esel Soldaten* cheered to a man. Four horse-drawn guns followed: a passage that necessitated the mass of infantry to leave the sticky mud of the road for the rutted and cloying earth of the fields. Rumes was two miles distant but the percussion of hundreds of muskets could be heard. Whispered conversations had died away, replaced by the rhythmic pounding of six hundred pairs of boots and hard breathing of men who strained under the weight of pack and musket. The battalion veered back onto the road and marched towards the sound of gunfire accompanied by the drone of flies brought to life by the warmth of the day even though the full heat of the day had yet to arrive. Krombach's world was the pack of the man in front of him: sweat streamed from his brow; mud and stones had worked their way through the splits in his boots, causing each footstep to jar. Minutes more of marching was abruptly broken only by fresh orders from Neuberg, to a barrage of muttered curses, as the battalion again swerved off the road and returned to the rutted fields. Krombach heard the thunder of horses.

Hundreds of cavalrymen thundered past; the same dragoons that had passed the redcoats minutes earlier were retracing their steps. For some reason best known to the Generals, the light dragoons and their guns were recalled. Between the bodies of the horsemen who streamed past, Krombach could just make out the sight of Colonel Neuberg deep in conversation with two other officers. One was clearly the colonel of the cavalry regiment, the other, who seemed to be on the sharp end of some finger pointing, bore the look of a brow beaten messenger who had ridden hard across country to carry the order. To grumbling redcoats, it made no sense; the infantry might cover the ground to Rumes in the next twenty minutes, but the cavalry should have been there already. Worse still the redcoats had no artillery save for two small battalion guns.

A regiment of infantry, two squadrons of cavalry and four horse guns had set out from the Hanoverian column to relieve Rumes. Now just the two infantry battalions steadily trudged towards the sounds of battle.

CHAPTER TWENTY-SEVEN
The Battle for Broken Tail House.

Rumes: 1st May 1793

In grim humour, von Bomm's soldiers had christened the houses in which they would make their stand. The house nearest the road became 'Apple House' with its beautiful shades of garden blooms. 'Hell's Corner' was the most exposed of the three houses and a delaying action at best when the enemy made to outflank the redcoats. 'Broken Tail', the middle of the three, was the position which von Bomm hoped he could somehow stall the enemy advance. The redcoats had christened the house because of the frightened young puppy that the grenadiers had found hiding in one of the rooms there. Soldiers took respite from the tension by playing with the small dog who had nipped at a few fingers before settling on a thin strip of beef that a grenadier had spared from his rations.

After twenty minutes of the battle restarting, Hell's Corner had fallen and a brief lull had descended while the enemy organised for the next attack. A dozen wounded men had been rescued and ferried to a patch of garden in the rear of Apple House, now a make-shift medical post. The oblong of garden, a dozen yards by ten, was flanked on either side by a wall of thick blackthorn bushes, a sea of delicate white spring blooms and stiff, spiny branches. To its rear ran a long, low wall of old brickwork, against which a large pile of compost rotted. A pair of apple trees bloomed within its boundary and under the pink blossom of one of these, Fourth Company's doctor fished with a bullet probe, long-necked scissors with flattened tweezers at their tip, for a spent musket ball which lodged rather doggedly in the right shoulder of a grenadier.

A table had been rescued from the barricade and as metal scraped against bone, then found the object of the search, silent tears rolled down the face of the grenadier who bore down on the table with grim determination. Scissors were withdrawn and a blackened musket round, covered in a claret sheen, was discarded unto lush green grass. Dark blood oozed over the Doctor's nimble fingers; he wrenched free the soldier's grip from the table edge and ordered his patient to place his left hand over the wound, where a torn patch of bedding had been placed.

By the foot of one of the apple trees, a stricken soldier laid deathly pale, his left leg now nothing more than a stump below the knee. The doctor cast an anxious look in the direction of the newly crippled boy then returned to the task of threading a needle with catgut. This done he moved the redcoat's hand and the swab of bloodied material which had been held in place, pinched together the skin around the wound and began to suture it closed. From the other side of the hedge came the percussive boom of the Grenadier battalion's canon. Win or lose, the doctor knew his day would be busy.

A sergeant and five grenadiers had wheeled the battalion gun into position. One man had died before the weapon had even been fired. A few minutes later the three-pounder had fired off its allocation of canister and was left with solid shot cannon-balls which held little fear for the thin blue skirmish line that had begun to advance cautiously towards Apple House and the walled farm, which stood on either side of the track. Without the canister rounds which had kept the enemy at a respectable distance, the gun served little purpose. The gunners had been forced to take shelter wedged between the wooden trail body of the small cannon and the wall of blackthorn bushes. Through the gaps in the greenery, the doctor could be seen working away with a small queue of soldiers sitting or slumped, waiting for his attention. In the fields ahead of the silent cannon, blue-coats swarmed, sensing the chance to rush the gun, kill its stranded crewmen and isolate the redcoats who resisted at Apple and Broken Tail.

The sergeant weighed the odds of survival. To stay with the cannon was to die. Across the track, no more than ten yards away, was the red-bricked wall which had become Captain Baumann's headquarters. The opposing wall was at least eight feet and by the time the gunners had left the safety of their shelter, and found a way to scramble, the odds were very slim. The only route was to retreat, keep as low to the hedge as possible and hook left into the garden where the doctor worked. Every man who could hold a musket would be needed if the French were to be held there.

For the second time that day von Bomm found himself clutching a musket. He counted himself as being a reasonable shot with a hunting rifle but the mule kick of the Brown Bess into his shoulder jarred unpleasantly and instinctively his face turned from the pall of smoke it discharged. He had positioned himself in the remnants of the roof space of Apple House and as von Bomm crouched to reload, fumbling for more ammunition in the pouch of a grenadier who lay dead at his feet, his eyes caught the movement of five redcoats who had edged their way from the battalion gun, crossed the wall and through the compost heap to traipse into the garden past the doctor and growing number of wounded grenadiers.

The iron rain of musket balls rattled the shingles and remaining roof slates; air thick with red dust and smoke mixed with bitter taste of cordite in von Bomm's mouth. The heat of the day slowly baked the redcoats on the upper floor; the Lieutenant's head pounded with the effort of concentration and decision making. Musket fire crashed around him. Grenadiers had fallen into a steady rhythm, working in pairs; von Bomm had taken the place of the soldier who lay dying.

As he groped for the twisted paper cartridge of ball and powder he craned for a view of Broken Tail house. Fire to the front of the house had thickened and from every vantage point in Hell's Corner, French soldiers could be seen. Enemy skirmishers prowled its garden adding to the weight of fire. The Grenadiers stood firm, a dozen puffs of musket smoke from the windows and the roof rattled in quick succession.

From the end of the room, he heard Corporal Engel curse and looked to see the silver-haired redcoat, now caked in red dust and black grime, kneeling and carefully pouring a stream of water from his canteen into the musket barrel; steam rose from the hot barrel and a thin dribble of black ooze ran over the lock and frizzen. Searching inside his ammunition pouch, the corporal brought out a strip of linen, bound it tightly around the head of the ramrod, and forced the metal ramrod down the musket barrel; a thin tube of sludge oozed out of the touch-hole. Only when the process was repeated did the corporal reload the weapon, movement catching his eye as he raced through the drill movements.

"Signal, sir!"

Turning to look in the direction of the church-tower, von Bomm could see the lookout waving for all he was worth, his black *Korsisch* hat removed: reinforcements, at last. The soldier pointed to the north. Whatever was coming was moving in a direction that would support Baumann's Company.

"Thank God!"

Erich von Bomm was certain now as to his course of action.

"Thank you, Corporal. Keep the French honest. I am going next door. We must hold these two buildings until our troops arrive, understood?"

Engels nodded, loosed off a shot at a target marked by another grenadier, then returned to reloading his musket with mechanical regularity. Von Bomm clattered down the heavy wooden steps into the thick smog of the room below. Musket balls thumped into the plasterwork around him. Two more grenadiers lay dead, sprawled against the back wall. A table which had been against the open window that led to the garden to allow the wounded to exit the building was slick with smears of blood. A lanky body climbed awkwardly in through the window.

"Pinsk, you still alive?"

A tall grenadier, face blacked and looking more like an overgrown chimney-sweep's apprentice, looked up and smiled thinly, white teeth set against the powder black stains.

"Yes, sir, compliments of Captain Baumann sir; you are to retire across the road and find cover on the buildings behind his position."

"I'm not sure that is going to be possible. Can you get back across the road again with a message?"

Yes, sir. I will need to work my way up the street but I can do it."

"Good lad. The French hold Hell's Corner and they are moving troops to attack us from the gardens. If we try and move the wounded, we will be overwhelmed in the open. Give Captain Baumann my compliments but tell him we need to hold Apple House and Broken Tail or his position will be lost. Understand?"

The tall, spectacled grenadier nodded.

"Good." Von Bomm smiled. "Glad you are here, Pinsk. Thought I would have to do something dangerous myself for a minute. Reinforcements are on their way too; inform Captain Baumann of that too, in case he did not see the signal." He shouted the last few words louder for the room to hear.

"Take care and use that cover. Watch out in case the French are already in the houses behind us."

Von Bomm pointed past the doctor and over the wall which the Grenadier gunners had just used to scramble into the garden. Pinsk nodded, grabbed his musket and slid over the table top and out through the window, closely followed by von Bomm. He had chosen to disobey a direct order but now there was no doubt in his mind. The only course of action that would buy the Company enough time was to stand.

The newly arrived grenadiers were busily loading muskets removed from the walking wounded. Nodding his appreciation to the doctor, von Bomm turned to the sergeant, who snapped to attention with parade ground formality.

"Sergeant?"

"Hahn, sir."

"Thank you, for joining our little party."

Von Bomm felt a sense of clarity; there was no changing the course he was about to take. From the rich dark blue facings, von Bomm could tell that Hahn, a trim, muscular man of medium build with a thick red moustache, was from one of the two Grenadier companies of the Hanoverian Guard Regiment.

"Reinforcements are coming to steal the glory I'm afraid but until then I want your men and any of the walking wounded from here to hold this garden. This is

Apple House, that's Broken Tail." Von Bomm pointed in the direction of the house screened by the hedge.

"Loophole this bush line as best you can and kill any Frenchmen who try and cross into Broken Tail's garden, understood? Take command of Apple House, it must hold at all costs. I am going next door to hold things there until our forces arrive."

Von Bomm stared down as a musket ball, its force spent by the passage through the dense hawthorn, dropped between the feet of the two men. Hahn remained stock still.

"If the garden can't be held, move the doctor and the wounded back into the house."

"Yes, sir" Hahn replied with a stoic voice, as if the orders had been nothing more than a series of drill instructions for the parade ground.

With that von Bomm turned and made his way along the white-bloomed wall of hawthorn to a gap between the hedge and Apple House. Ahead, French skirmishers had now reached the barricade which sealed off the dead ground between the two houses. He steadied himself to peer around the corner when the wall to the left of his face exploded, showering him with debris and shards of plaster. While the soldiers attacking the front and sides of the second house could not see him, the French skirmishers who now occupied the garden of Hell's Corner could. From the thick hedgerow of blackthorns, half a dozen musket barrels could be seen.

Two more fired and von Bomm threw himself forward, tumbling away from the house and back to the safety of the hedge. Regaining his composure and a little dignity, realising that Hahn had witnessed the whole sorry scene, von Bomm waved a hand as much in a rather feeble apology.

With frantic arm waving the officer attracted the attention of one of the men manning the roof space of Broken Tail house. Von Bomm dropped the musket by the side of the hawthorn bush, unbuckled his sword and left the scabbard with the stranded Brown Bess: he was to rush the gap between the two buildings, the less that could impede him, the better.

The doorways of both houses faced one another and each had been barred from the inside on von Bomm's orders. From either side of the doorway of Broken Tail were small rectangular windows, wooden shutters partially opened; every few seconds a Brown Bess discharged another round towards the enemy who had made it to the barricade to dissuade them from scrambling over the low wall of furniture. Beyond this, through the continual blooms of musket smoke, von Bomm could see shapes inside the doorway working to move whatever obstructions had been placed there. The barricade now firmly in the possession of the French, was just five yards to the left of the doorway. Blue jacketed troops were now huddled, firing up at the men on the roof or attempting to hit the slivered gaps between the shuttered windows. There were a half a dozen yards between the two buildings. If von Bomm misjudged the moment he would be pinned in the narrow earthen strip between the two buildings: death would be a certainty.

Musket balls plucked at the blackthorn bush around him. Through the tangle of the barricade von Bomm could make out the silhouette of a French skirmisher prone to the ground frantically reloading his musket and gesturing to his colleagues of von Bomm's position. The door had to open soon or the grenadier officer would be caught in a deadly crossfire.

A heavy scraping echoed out of the passageway. Time seemed to slow. The barricade buckled the efforts of the skirmishers; the house door creaked open fractionally; a pair of muskets jutted from the windows; two more from the doorway. The alleyway was filled with the crash of musketry and explosions of smoke as both sides exchanged short range volleys. One moment, he was crouching, curved infantry sabre nestled firmly right hand, ready to spin forward; the next he was running, hard and low, towards the doorway. The void of the passageway was filled with the jumble of upturned furniture. Through the wreathed musket smoke, appeared the silhouettes of four French skirmishers charging at von Bomm and the open doorway.

Von Bomm skidded in the soft earth and adjusted his balance. The first blue coat was on him almost instantly, bayonet thrust directly toward von Bomm's chest. As the Frenchmen lunged, the redcoat twisted his torso sharply left and then drove his shoulder hard into his opponent as soon as the bayonet had passed harmlessly by. The Frenchmen and von Bomm stumbled and crash together into the wall of Broken Tail house.

A second skirmisher was upon him, reversing his musket to drive the butt into von Bomm's face. In desperation the grenadier officer threw himself forward against the second man's legs, trying to get inside the downward arc of musket, absorb the blow that would impact on his back or shoulder and deal a killing blow of his own. Struggling to keep balance, he grabbed hold of the blue tunic and drove upward with his blade with all the force he could muster. The weapon pierced just above the groin: there was momentary resistance then the soft sucking sound of punctured flesh and an eruption of blood as the officer's sword severed an artery.

More musketry fire spouted from the doorway; the passageway was filled with redcoats driving back the French. Feeling himself being unceremoniously dragged by the scruff of his jacket, von Bomm passed from daylight into smoke filled darkness, leaving the passageway filled with the screams of dying men.

Once inside, there was a sharp rap of orders and the scraping of wood against stone as a table was once again wedged across the doorway to bar entry. Von Bomm's eyes adjusted to the gloom. Of the thirty or so grenadiers who held the building, three men were dead or dying, many more with wounds which had been bandaged by comrades.

"You all right, sir?"

The young voice that had issued the orders was by his side. Ensign Rausch was not yet eighteen, a tall clean-shaven youth with a mop of dark brown hair swept rakishly from a parting on his extreme right. Even in the heat of battle, he looked unblemished, white ceremonial gloves shone in the gloom of a room thick with powder and dust. He cast an anxious look at von Bomm, so often accustomed to seeing a man he admired as the gallant dandy and raconteur, caked in dirt, dust and blood.

"Yes, thank you, Rausch. We didn't lose anyone in that little escapade, I hope?"

"No sir. All present."

"Good," von Bomm drew deep breaths regaining his composure. "Thank you. And thank you, lads."

Soldiers in the act of firing or reloading grinned in appreciation.

Von Bomm continued, "Not long to hold on now. Reinforcements have been sighted. We must hold out here. Do that and victory will be ours."

Men too exhausted to cheer, nodded in understanding, kept on loading and firing, as automatons.

"How long until they do, sir?"

"Not sure but soon, Rausch."

"I think you might want to look from upstairs, sir. Keep low, the French are in the roof space of Hell's Corner and pinning us down. Still you need to see this."

Von Bomm nodded and followed the ensign up a worn staircase which led to an upper floor where the stonework ran to just above chest height. Wooden joists were all that remained of the ceiling; every tile had been torn down and thrown at the enemy to supplement the shower of musket rounds. Redcoats crouched, firing from whatever loopholes had been made in the stonework. The two men crawled forward to the end of the room, where a loophole overlooked the garden of Hell's Corner and beyond. Rausch had tapped a grenadier on the shoulder and the man had edged back to let the officers take his position.

"Look, there, sir."

The situation was worse than von Bomm feared. A dozen skirmishers were firing from positions in the garden but beyond that a full company was formed in the gardens beyond and another was moving through the alleyways that led to the low wall of Apple House. A skirmish duel had broken out with the men that

Sergeant Hahn had placed to guard the wall but it was a mismatched affair.

"How long have those companies been there?"

"A few minutes at most, sir; what do you want us to do?"

"Bring the wounded upstairs now. It's too late to get them out. Strip the ammunition and weapons from the dead men. We hold this floor, no matter what."

Rausch nodded and both men scrambled downstairs. Von Bomm moved quickly towards the small window next to the door by which he had entered. He could see the stream of wounded soldiers being helped into the temporary safety of Apple House; Sergeant Hahn came into view momentarily, barking instructions then taking cover behind the apple tree nearest the house. Grenadiers fell back to positions around him, preparing to reload. Behind von Bomm the sound of a bugle blew. The French attack against Broken Tail house was about to begin.

The front of the building was still being peppered with musket fire. Somewhere in the distance a cheer broke and within moments, the windows were surrounded with the shapes of French soldiers. Musket balls thudded against the wall of the house that faced the garden, some found their way through gaps in the window shutters. In the darkness of the crowded room, two grenadiers were wounded.

Rushing to the soldiers who manned the north wall that faced out into the open fields, von Bomm rasped, "Upstairs now, cover the garden side of the house. Go! Go!"

It would only be a matter of seconds until the skirmishers realised that the windows on the wall which faced north were unguarded. A dozen men now held the doorway and south facing wall. Rausch collected the cartridge bags from the bodies of the dead grenadiers, passing them on to a redcoat who waited for his turn to ascend the crowded steps.

"Mr. Rausch, take the men from the doorway. We will be hard on your heels. Give what covering fire you can and find something to block up that stairway space."

The officer nodded; the four men around the door needed little invitation to follow their companions to the comparative safety of the upper level.

Eight soldiers now held the two main window spaces downstairs. French musket butts crashed against the closed shutters of the small windows around the doorway. The door was being forced back, the wedged table would not hold much longer. A shuttered window on the north wall burst open. Daylight and then musket smoke filled the room; a grenadier rocked back clutching his face and slumped blocking the base of the stairs. propelled by those on the outside, a Frenchmen attempted to clamber through the unguarded window.

"Upstairs now, everyone," von Bomm screamed covering the short distance across the room to sabre the intruding blue coat in the throat.

The door began to groan ominously and the next moment it shattered from its hinges and flipped up over the table. The wreckage of door and table slowed the press of bodies from the outside just long enough for the last of the grenadiers to make progress up the stair-well, stepping over the body of their dead comrade. Von Bomm turned and jumped over the dead man, caught the third step and drove himself up to the sanctuary of the upper floor. Musket balls struck the wall and woodwork. Almost as soon as he cleared the stairwell, a rather battered ottoman chest, considered too heavy to be moved to form part of the barricade, was pushed across the stairwell. It left a narrow strip of perhaps three inches. The grenadiers who manned the doorway stood watch over the gap and within seconds the first of these fired his musket into the swell of French soldiers who had begun to occupy the room below.

"Good work, 1st Grenadiers. Now we hold this until help arrives." Von Bomm shouted against the clamour of musket balls which rattled against tile and masonry. A redcoat clutched a knee as a jagged ricochet found flesh in the confined space. Von Bomm turned to Rausch and spoke quickly.

"Make sure that stairwell holds. I want four men loading and two more firing at all times."

The ensign nodded and von Bomm pushed his way through the room.

"Every man not covering the stairwell find a loophole, or act as loader."

The grenadier officer scanned the room for a quick head count. His command was now twenty-six men, five of which were seriously wounded. He found a space on the west facing wall and poked out a tile three rows up in the half a dozen that remained. Musket balls thudded into the joists around him, the fire coming from three sides now. The view offered little comfort. Apple House held. Musketry came from both floors but no doubt the French would attempt to overwhelm it soon. Around him, tired soldiers worked to fire and reload. Some poured the last traces of canteen water into heavily fouled barrels, swiftly cleaning the weapons before reloading again. Von Bomm tapped the grenadier next to him on the shoulder.

"How many rounds do you have left?"

The redcoat shrugged, held open his black leather cartridge pouch. No more than a dozen tightly wound cartridges remained. The soldier grabbed one, smiled at von Bomm and crouching in the awkward space of the upper floor, bit into the cartridge and began to pour fresh powder into the recently cleaned weapon.

At the stairwell, a dozen rounds had been fired and then the French were gone. Rausch peered through the narrow slit; darkness was pierced by shafts of light which streamed in through shutter less windows and the open door. Bodies clustered around the base of the stairwell, blue and red coated dead. Rausch wiped away his face with gloves no longer a parade-ground white. Smoke stung his eyes, but not from the discharge of muskets; thick and black, it drew up through the gap from somewhere in the room below. Erich von Bomm had noticed it too. Stinging smoke began seeping through floorboards and dispersing in the freshening breeze around him. Enemy infantrymen piled out of the building, back into the cover of Hell's Corner's garden.

The officer who von Bomm had seen from the Church tower chatting politely to Captain Franke, had decided to burn down Broken Tail house, rather than lose any more men, in trying to capture it.

CHAPTER TWENTY-EIGHT

Brandt's Company.

Rumes: 1st May 1793

It had taken Major Brennan much longer than he had hoped to bring his men to Rumes. After leaving Trevethan and Jackson, he had run into a particularly fastidious staff officer, who insisted that the hussars would not be permitted to move without written orders. The deadlock of heated discussion ended by the chance arrival of the Esterhàzy colonel, who immediately sanctioned Brennan's action on hearing the details.

Stranger still had been the matter of the Hanoverian dragoons. On the junction of the road between Rumes and St. Amand, Brennan had met the colonel of the 9th Dragoons, furious that his orders had been countermanded by Field Marshal Freytag. Neither men could make sense of that decision; Brennan's Esterhàzy troopers resumed their approach overhauling two infantry battalions which were breaking out of column to form for battle.

A brief conversation with the assembled infantry colonels and an officer sent from the Grenadier Colonel holding the town brought forth a plan for joint action. The cavalry would sweep either side of the village and attack the exposed flanks of the enemy. 2nd battalion would move through the tangle of buildings and support the Grenadier's flank where the enemy pressed hardest. To the north of Rumes, a thick pall of black smoke rose ominously.

Brennan spurred his mount back to the cavalry which had now formed into two troops, each thirty men abreast and two ranks deep. The Esterhàzy moved efficiently, using the same folds of ground that had masked the approach of the French to von Bomm. Only when the horsemen crested the plateau did the French battalion, strung out in a long skirmish lines with three of its companies involved in fierce house to house fighting, realise that it was in mortal danger: That realisation was too late.

For the second time in a matter of weeks, Austrian cavalry crashed into the thin screen of French infantry and the blue coats ran. Brennan decided that there was little point in holding back his reserve troop. He signalled to his bugler and then spurred his mount on, poised for the nirvana which all light cavalrymen dream of; a routing enemy, with no cover to hide in and no enemy cavalry to rescue them.

The sergeant knew a fiasco when he saw one. This attack had long since turned into one. From what Captain Davide could deduce from a hastily snatched conversation with an adjutant who had passed 6th Company's position, the brigade commander sent to oversee the attack had been sent to Brunehat along with the artillery and cavalry. They had spent most of the morning staring at the enemy redcoats posted there, wondering when their own infantry support was due to arrive. It had taken until nearly lunchtime for a message to arrive back from Dampierre's command tent at Valenciennes to correct the error in the orders and send the cavalry, guns and a now apoplectic commander to Rumes, where the infantry had begun the third attack of the day. Five hours wasted because someone at headquarters had put the wrong name on an order. Had the Black Lions come from the south, Valenciennes, with their commander, as was the usual practice, Brunehat would have been attacked and overwhelmed in a matter of an hour at most. But the infantry had marched from the north, the guns, cavalry and commander from the south; the operation had been shambolic from that moment on.

Horse-guns crashed an opening salvo. Behind them, a squadron of rather skittish looking hussars deployed. Davide stood next to his sergeant and both men watched a skirmish screen of one of the Black Lion's companies carry out a steady fusillade, some four hundred yards ahead of the main body of the regiment and within fifty yards of the long chain of buildings that marked the western flank of the village. Theirs was just a holding action. A left hook was being performed that would either break the enemy or weaken the centre sufficiently for the two battalions that had remained posted to the west, to sweep over the redcoat's positions.

"I wouldn't like to be relying on that lot if it gets tricky," Mahieu grunted, nodding towards the cavalry.

More guns fired, completing a fragmented first salvo.

"Still, I don't imagine the foot sloggers on the receiving end of those boys will stand for too much more," Mahieu continued. But his captain was clearly occupied with his own thoughts and the sergeant watched the artillerymen attach ropes to the guns and begin moving them forward. Each round of fire would bring closer the time when the battery changed from iron cannon balls to deadly cannister rounds to scour the buildings, hedges and hiding places. Then the enemy would be forced to withdraw or die where they stood.

Still Davide didn't reply, his head was turned sharply left, in hawk-like observance of the undulated farmland to the north where the main attack was in full flow. The captain turned about swiftly, "Drummers, to me now!"

Half a dozen drummers, a mixture of youths and young boys, shuffled in front of their officer. The senior most, a corporal, stood to attention in front of his captain.

"Beat the retreat! Skirmishers to return to close order."

The corporal looked blankly at the officer. The company was already in close order, no more than three yards behind them, its best skirmishing troops watching the action from the safety of the ranks.

"For them!" Davide pointed to the pair of skirmish screens drawn from other companies, that were engaging the village. Elsewhere, drums and bugles sounded out a similar warning. Others had seen what Davide had spotted. Mahieu craned his neck and thought he could see movement.

Then the horsemen crested the rolling ground six hundred yards to his left. Austrian hussars, the same sky blue jackets and red breeches of the regiment that had cut down the Black Lions piquets at Herstal. Around the cavalry-men, the best part of two infantry battalions were routing in blind panic.

Mahieu watched the disaster unfolding far to his left and then sound and movement to his right caught his attention. The horse guns that had been in the process of being hauled forward were being made ready to leave as limber teams were being whipped forward from their station behind the deployed field pieces at the gallop.

Almost at the same moment, a body of enemy horsemen, more hussars had swung around from the southern edge of the village. An officer from the French cavalry ordered his men to counter the threat. There were three times the number of French light cavalry to the enemy but shamefully the French hussars were already pulling their mounts around preparing to desert the battlefield.

Somewhere along the line of Black Lions columns that awaited the order to advance, more drums played and the order to 'Form Square' was carried on the wind. Davide repeated the call and the sergeant moved to his post to ensure that the newer recruits didn't decide that now was an opportune moment to leave the service of the Republic. While nervous recruits shuffled to find their place, Mahieu glanced at the enemy cavalry. Around twenty had given chase to the French light cavalry, others made for the horse teams which were frantically attempting to pull guns and frightened gunners through the heavy soil. The balance had turned with deliberate intent on the stream of Back Lions skirmishers who had seen the deadly threat too late. The 'square' was a defence against cavalry. Normally it would have been formed by six companies. The Black Lions would make a defensive formation with just five. Unless there was a miracle, the infantrymen caught out in front of the village of Rumes were already as good as dead.

All the drill preparations, hours of changing formation from column of march to orderly firing lines counted for little. The men of Brandt's Company found themselves running through the narrow paths between houses to reach the northern end of the town. Drawing deep breaths, Krombach felt his heart pound with the effort, his heavy pack thudding against his back as he moved from jogging to running. Ahead he could hear the voice of the captain, then the first shots rang out. Something tore passed his head and he and another half a dozen redcoats ducked involuntarily. The *Esel Soldaten* were coming under enemy musket fire.

More orders were barked. Company Sergeant-Major Roner was shouting at men to stand up and then issuing orders to the other sergeants.

More musket rounds fizzed overhead and a dozen Brown Bess muskets hammered out a reply. Krombach felt a hand grab at the back of his neck and then heard Gauner's voice bark. "Stand there, boy," I want four ranks now. Ten men in each rank. Fall in on Krombach. Move your fat arses."

Order was forming from the red mob that had crowded into the narrow street. More musket fire and Krombach was aware of redcoats rushing passed him. Some smiled, others grim-faced. All had been in the front line and had discharged their weapons. Each sergeant now controlled four ranks of redcoats. There was no drill book for street fighting, this was clearly Captain Brandt's solution and Krombach listened as Gauner bellowed out the orders to load and make ready. Then the line advanced, another round of musket fire, less ragged than before.

"Advance! … Halt! … Make ready! …Present! …Fire!" Captain Brandt's voice was clear now. More redcoats pushed past Krombach, heading to the rear of what had become a dense company column. Through the smoke and press of bodies he could see blue-coated figures in the haze. Ahead to his left was a high red-bricked wall, to the right an abandoned cannon. In the middle of the road, a press of bodies, dead, dying and wounded. The French were attempting to form their own line to the new threat that Brandt's Company posed but were caught in a deadly crossfire from the buildings on either side.

"Advance! …Halt!" and suddenly Krombach was in the front rank. The moment felt surreal. He had stepped calmly over the body of a prone redcoat. Beside him another soldier fell, clutching at his belly. More flashes of white as the enemy muskets retaliated. But their response felt weak against the weight of shots that were being driven into the mass of blue shrouds in the chaos of the street. He was no more than thirty yards from the enemy.

"Make ready! ...Present! ..."

Krombach felt the butt of the musket nestle reassuringly into his shoulder and tensed himself for the mule kick that would follow. Before the words had left Brandt's lips, the French soldiers had begun to turn and flee, some had thrown away weapons in the hope of mitigating what was to follow.

"Fire!" the volley crashed out.

Krombach was blinded by stinging white smoke and when his eyes cleared the narrow road contained only the dead and the dying.

The enemy had fled.

"Brandt's Company...follow me!"

Sebastian Krombach held his musket, still trying to understand the scene of carnage ahead of him. A fist thumped hard into his left arm.

"Don't just stand there day-dreaming boy, follow the Captain!" Gauner's voice barked angry instructions.

The ranks broke into a run again, following the road and then taking a sharp right, passed a first house and on towards a second where the shouts for help could be clearly heard.

The fire in Broken Tail house had taken hold, flames greedily licked up the northern wall which faced onto the garden. As Krombach clambered over the barricade of broken furniture close to the burning building, French soldiers appeared from the shelter of blackthorn bushes, hands raised high in surrender. The young redcoat watched as Gauner drove the butt of his musket into the stomach of an enemy soldier who had been slow to drop his weapon. Through thick smoke, red coated grenadiers dangled down from the side of the building.

Like a man stumbling through a drunken dream, Krombach was aware of Captain Brandt shouting instructions to dismantle the barricade. Within a matter of precious seconds, a precarious ladder of tables and chairs had been erected against the eastern face of the building where, despite thick smoke, the flames had yet to take hold. Each man could spend no more than a few seconds working on makeshift ladder before reeling away with lungs full of blackened air. Yet the desperate work brought results. Through the choking smoke, grenadiers were helped down to safety.

Aping the actions of men around him, Krombach tied a neckerchief over his nose and mouth but it had little effect as he took his turn to clamber up the flimsy wooden structure. The smoke was unbearable; he felt his body searing inside his uniform as he thrust a hand quickly through the wall of smoke. He was about to retract his hand when Krombach felt someone clutch his arm so he hauled with the last reserves of strength that he had. The figure could barely balance and for a moment Krombach was afraid he and the grenadier would topple backwards but somehow the young redcoat helped the man down to Hartmann who gathered the grenadier over his shoulders as if he were a doll.

Retching with smoke Krombach slid a few feet and then fell the rest; the soft earth of the passageway between the buildings cushioned the fall. He pulled at the neckerchief for air. For the second time in a few minutes a hand grabbed him roughly by the back of the neck. This time he was dragged into the clear air of the garden and the words were far more soothing.

"Well done, lad." Sergeant Richter, Moustache Georg, was no more than a blur in Krombach's dazed vision, "Now, deep breaths. You will be alright."

Richter turned to the prone body that Hartmann had gently placed on the grass of the garden. Brandt stood over the man.

"Anyone else, sir?"

Brandt learnt over the blackened figure, whose chest was heaving, hungrily drawing in the clear air, listening to whispered words. Brandt turned to Richter and shook his head.

The sergeant nodded and turned to issue instructions, "Alright lads, secure those prisoners and help move the wounded."

Erich von Bomm sat upright with a degree of effort, coughed heavily and spat out blacked globules of phlegm then drank heavily from a water-bottle which Brandt held to his lips.

"God, Erich, you look more dead than alive."

Von Bomm flashed the hint of a smile, white eyes and teeth against a smoke charred face.

"Perhaps, but what a story to tell the fine ladies of Hanover and Paris, eh? How are my men, Werner?"

The French did not attack again. Two hundred men had surrendered to the Hanoverians, rather than continue the fight or face the wrath of the Austrian cavalry which had swept the field of the enemy and captured a horse gun as a trophy. Colonel Neuberg ordered his battalion to begin repairing the defensive positions while working parties of redcoats and French prisoners scoured the field for the wounded who might yet live.

Brandt watched Doctor Wexler and Surgeon Harris hurry to aid the grenadier doctor, the trail of wounded now led towards the grounds of the Church. Then he noticed Henry Pinsk's lanky frame run to embrace a tall grenadier with thick pebble glasses, his rich red uniform stained brown with dirt. An hour later two rows of bodies littered the cemetery grounds. The butcher's bill for Baumann's Grenadier company stood at fifty. More than thirty of those from von Bomm's command, in death one of those cradled the small furry form of a puppy: Broken Tail was dead.

Whatever Brandt had expected victory to feel like, it wasn't this. The trials of the long march where the battalion had come close to tearing itself apart in the utter dishonour of Halle and the threat to Neuberg from his own officers. Victory had washed some of that bitter taste away. The laurels of victory belonged chiefly to the two companies of 1st Grenadiers but 2nd Battalion could claim a share at least.

Yet one voice was determined that not all the redcoats would share in the honour of victory at Rumes. It was only when Colonel Franke reached Rumes that Captain Baumann demanded a private audience with his colonel, levelling accusations of insubordination and cowardice against von Bomm and demanding that the matter be referred to Oberst von Klinkowström, commander of the brigade.

Brandt heard of the matter after Colonel Franke had shared the details with Colonel Neuberg.

"That ungrateful bastard. I should run him through where he stands. Franke must be a fool to believe any of that. If Erich hadn't held this position, we would have arrived to bury these men, not rescue them. This isn't about today, it's about that damned duel. I have to go..." Brandt turned swiftly, hand reaching for his sword hilt.

"Werner, stop!" Neuberg's voice was calm but authoritative, "I know you want to help Erich; so do I. Stop and think! This will end both of your careers. I don't think for a moment that the colonel does believe him but such an accusation must be handled delicately. We need to speak to any of the officers and NCOs that were present and you had better tell me about this duel. Whatever happens, I promise that I will make a representation to von Klinkowström on von Bomm's behalf."

A dozen yards away, under the pink umbrella blossom of an apple tree, von Bomm had drifted into a deep sleep, the exhaustion of the last few hours had overwhelmed him. Doctor Wexler knelt over him, his palm gently pressed over von Bomm's blackened forehead. Brandt watched the doctor listen to his friend's breathing and then nod in satisfaction towards the captain and colonel. Werner Brandt felt relief at the prognosis of his friend's health but neither the doctor or his patient knew of the storm that would break around Erich von Bomm when he regained consciousness.

CHAPTER TWENTY-NINE

Oubliettes.

Paris: 7th May 1793

The Parisian air was thick and oppressive, the city busier than Genet remembered, frenetic with traders, soldiers, citizens and beggars. Once he had been the Spider; his web of information had helped in some part to propel Dumouriez from the War Ministry to the commander of the Army of the North. He had hoped that papers bearing the signatures of Caillat and Carnot, who had returned in time to affirm Genet's departure, would gain access to those in high office. Such hopes were soon dashed; his web had become gossamer strands drifting on the wind.

With the capture of Beurnonville by the Austrians a new War Minister, an ex-cavalryman called Bouchotte, spent his days shuttling between the Convention at the Tuileries and meetings at the Conciergerie, too busy to be disturbed. Genet's return to his former seat of power at the War Ministry found men who had once bent to the will of the Spider afraid to talk. As for a meeting with Robespierre, it was said that most waited months for such an appointment.

Three fruitless days of journeying back and forth across the city ended in unlikely success.

At a crowded coffee house on the banks of the Seine, which looked across at the Île de la Cité, Genet found himself in the company of men he did not know; new faces who had emerged in the last few months, pawns to those fighting daily political battles on the floor of the National Convention. The talk was of the desire for the 'maximum', the capping of the bread price, and little else. Politics were too deadly to be discussed, there had been polite interest in the war but for most Parisians, war was a distant problem. Life surrounding them was difficult enough, why look elsewhere for more troubles.

Genet, absorbed in his own problems, listened with indifference; his absence felt more like ten years, rather than ten months. Then a whispered name caught his attention. Three tables away, a solitary figure poured over the latest news from the one of the printed broadsheets; Jean-Baptiste Bouchotte, Minister of War looked a care-worn man. Serge Genet sensed it was time to rebuild his web.

III

Blank rectangles of clean Persian-green paint spoke of a dozen paintings that had once hung in the room. Only the overhead tableau of a hunting scene from the Normandy countryside that lay framed within ornate gilded architraves hinted at the former splendour. The hastily arranged interview of the previous afternoon was not proceeding to the satisfaction of either man. Two separate lines of conversations were taking place in the apartment of the Tuileries that Bouchotte used for an office. The Minister of War was vaguely interested in matters concerning the Army of the North, pursuing a line of questioning to add detail to what he considered the flimsy reports signed by General Dampierre. Genet had offered what information he could but took every opportunity to steer conversation towards the fate of the traitors who had supported Dumouriez and the potential flaws of the 'Representatives on mission' role, an argument he had honed on the trip from Valenciennes. Newly spun gossamer threads of intrigue were brushed aside by Bouchotte, too blind to their potential to France and the Spider.

Salvation came with a brief rap at the door; Maximilian Robespierre did not wait for permission to enter but swept into the room. The very man that Genet had spent four days seeking out had sniffed political blood in the water. In the briefest exchange of terse words, it was clear that there was little warmth between the pair. Quickly it was established that matters concerning the prosecution of the confederates of Dumouriez or matters concerning the Representatives on Mission presided with the Committee of Public Safety not the Minister of War. Genet was Robespierre's property.

A second meeting convened in a room larger than the first, lavish with works of art; half a dozen of the surrounding suites had been raided and their contents crammed into the one room. Genet outlined his ideas and arguments to a far more discerning and sympathetic ear.

The Conciergerie was a pragmatic Revolutionary solution to the problems of the vast number of prisoners who waited for trial and either execution or release, a curious middle ground in the system of justice. The grand building on the Île de la Cité, a mixture of architecture from across the centuries, afforded cells with the privilege of privacy and the prospect of daily exercise within its grounds for those who could pay and the oubliettes, the forgotten places, for those who could not. Swift death from the guillotine might well have been a better choice than the certainty of disease, starvation and the base animal struggle to survive the oubliettes.

Much to the chagrin of the gaoler fresh orders had been received; a huge set of shackles from one of the lower levels to the single cell that Beauvais occupied. The dragoon sat on the edge of his bed and checked the lateral and vertical movement of the restraints with quizzical interest like a child intrigued by a new toy. He looked well for his time in captivity; too well, to the mind of man now appointed to lead the prosecution of the supporters of Dumouriez. Clearly Beauvais, or a supporter, had made his time at the Conciergerie as comfortable as could be bought. Genet had considered that possibility and how to use it to his own advantage. Even with the giant dragoon incarcerated he feared Beauvais more than ever, transfixed upon the actions of the man as he tested the limits of movement in the shackles. Having watched the dragoon, Genet summoned the courage to step from the shadow of the corridor and into the cell.

"What are you doing Beauvais? Those links cannot be broken by a dozen men."

"I'm not interested in breaking them; just wondering if there is enough movement in them to wrap this chain around your neck."

Beauvais replied in the casual manner of a man who might have been asked for his preference of drink with an evening meal.

Genet, who had remained standing, took an involuntary step back nearer the open door.

"Very humorous, Julian, I'm sure."

"It's no joke. I mean to kill you soon enough. My only regret is that I didn't do it before," the dragoon shrugged his shoulders, his face expressionless, the one living eye as cold as the dead one that followed the retreat of Genet.

"Try it and death will be certain, for you murder a prosecutor and official of the Republic." Genet drew on his reserve of inner bluster to conquer Beauvais will the inescapable logic of the law, "Help me and you will live. Be free from this place. Return to the army for all I care."

"I'm a dead man already, we both know it; don't pretend otherwise."

"Only if you face trial; help me and you are pardoned. Not only you, but Juliette too."

A flicker of interest registered across Beauvais' face.

Serge Genet continued, "I am to bring prosecutions against the remaining traitors. You will stand in front of the court and affirm their guilt; a simple matter for which you and Juliette will receive a complete exoneration. I'm offering you your life back, Beauvais. Don't be pig-headed!"

"You have Juliette?"

Genet knew that the question would arise. Lying to the dragoon would have been the easier option but there was something to gain from telling the truth.

"No, not yet, but there are only so many places she can hide. If she is found and brought to Paris the matter may be out of my hands. Right now, there is still time. She may have taken in with the Austrians but I'm sure we would have heard. We have watched your regiment of course. My suspicion is she will be found in either Lille or Valenciennes."

Genet had paused between the two options. There it was; the faintest twitch at the mention of Valenciennes. Beauvais struggled up from the bed and leaned forward under the restrictive shackles.

"Tell you what Genet. Why don't you come over here and I will whisper my answer in your ear."

Beauvais shuffled slowly forward and Genet stepped briskly back, collided into the door frame. The arm of his tunic caught in the metal lock catch and as Genet turned on his heels and tumbled into the corridor, a sharp ripping sound was followed by the howls of derisive laughter from the dragoon's cell.

Gaoler LeGrand, a bulbous man, neck and waist hooped with thick rolls of fat, could barely suppress a grin himself at the sight of the bespectacled clerk plucking at the tear that had appeared in the right arm of his black jacket. The gaoler wiped a grubby rag of a handkerchief over his face and mopped large beads of sweat that formed on his brow in the sultry afternoon air and tried his best to compose himself. There was always a backlash when such indignities occurred. He had witnessed or pretended not to witness such scenes many times before. The high and mighty arrived only to be rebuffed by those who, without hope, had lost all fear. Genet slowed his pace and approached the gaoler.

"Monsieur, you see this document?" LeGrand strained to read it but literacy had never been his strongest suit. "I am authorised on behalf of the Committee of Public Safety to take whatever action is needed to secure the prosecutions of the traitors who followed Dumouriez."

The ink had barely dried on the document drafted and signed by Robespierre before Genet was waving it around.

"This man is to be moved today. I know how things work here. I don't care what has been paid to you or what money is offered. He is to live in the darkest, shit-infested cell you can find until I say otherwise. Do you understand?"

LeGrand had noticed only one fact of the neatly folded document, the signature. He nodded solemnly.

"I will send a man here every day to check that this has been carried out. If I find that my instructions have not been met to the letter, the man who has crossed me will take this traitor's place at the scaffold!" Genet jabbed a thin finger toward LeGrand who nodded in speechless assent.

St Amand: 7th May 1793

Battalions had regrouped in the shelter of the forest. The action at Rumes had been one of a series of diversions to mask the main French assault against the Austrian camp at Raismes. Sergeant Mahieu had listened to the report of that action with a sickening feeling that he already knew the reason for its failure.

After a hard fight, the white coated Austrians had routed from their trenches and the infantry pressed forward in the moment of triumph. All the while, French Chasseurs, light cavalry who had idly stood and watched the infantry shoulder the burden of battle, fled at the first sight of the appearance of wild looking Austrian uhlan. A single enemy squadron of lancers chased the panicked Chasseurs from the field while the balance wheeled onto the exposed flank of the French infantry lines and began a merciless slaughter.

Several hundred lives had been lost and only the shelter of the forest saved countless more. Even in the woods, the lance-armed horseman had shown no mercy and hunted the fleeing soldiers until they grew tired of the sport.

Now the Black Lions had been deployed into the last strip of land wedged between the Austrian and Prussian camps. Somehow their own losses at Rumes had been remarkably light. The skirmish company that had been caught in the open had managed to flee to the safety of the square while the enemy cavalry had concentrated on the much easier target of the horse battery. One gun had been taken as a prize while the other limbers had made straight for the gap between the two infantry squares that had hastily formed. The Black Lions had spared the blushes and lives of the artillerymen and there had been plenty of ironic cheers towards the gun crews who had spent no more than ten minutes on the field. Eventually the Austrian hussars lost interest and returned to Rumes. The Black Lions had marched away, not waiting for the remnants of the other two infantry battalions to join them.

Now they laboured in the cool darkness of the forest. Tomorrow the enemy would attack and when they did, no cavalry would be able to intervene.

Tomorrow, the Black Lions of Flanders would have their revenge. This would not be a forgotten place, it would bring a victory that would live long in the memory.

East of St Amand: 7th May 1793

Krombach had been an unwilling hero in rescuing Lieutenant von Bomm from the roof of Broken Tail house, although he felt anything but heroic. A week had passed and he could still taste the smoke in his throat and the stench of it on his tunic. Clara Richter, Moustache Georg's wife, had even washed it twice to try and clean it; the sergeants had allowed Krombach and some of the other men to parade and march in their fatigues while the wagons of the Twenty resembled a mobile laundry.

The previous evening Reifener had somehow found the ingredients for a celebratory cake to mark the passing of Brandt's Company's first action. To the delight of the redcoats, each of the soldiers who had made the perilous trip up the makeshift furniture ladder received the most blackened and charred wedges of cake, liberally washed down with wine liberated from the houses around Rumes.

Tomorrow, there would be another battle but this time the whole army would be in action. The French would be pushed from this new position and then the siege of Valenciennes could begin. It had become the new mantra around the camp fire. Valenciennes and Lille, the keys to the northern frontier. Then Paris, no more fortifications or rivers, just a straight march. One of the officers had told Gauner as much; the sergeant repeated the words as though they were scripture.

Valenciennes, Lille, Paris and then home.

Enschede, Halle and the hardships in between would be forgotten on the road home.

All Krombach had to do was survive.

The King's Germans Book 2

The King of Dunkirk

Prologue
Rosendael: 9th September 1793

The young soldier lay motionless, vacant eyes struggling to focus on clouds of blackened cinders that drift away on the eddy of a morning breeze. His woollen infantry jacket, drenched in cold sweat and dew, had once been a proud, bright scarlet. Now it reeked of the burnt flesh that lay around him. The movement of bloodshot green eyes and a mouth that gulped for air were the only signs of life other than the congregation of sand flies who busied themselves in the light of the new day.

Memory and understanding returned.

Another man had given his life so the soldier might live. Fingers edged up to a welt of congealed blood and sand. Pain throbbed across his forehead in response. Smoke had scorched his nose and throat. The blow to the head was the result of a body collapsing on top of his: a small price to pay for survival. Dragging the sleeve of his jacket across his face, the redcoat began to focus and organise his mind.

A wooden canteen lay a dozen feet away, strapped to the side of his horse's carcass. The violence of the explosion that had ripped through the battery of heavy siege guns had left nothing else alive. The soldier crawled over to retrieve canteen and musket, slumping back to the patch of ground next to the body that had shielded him. Sensation returned: every breath felt like a punch to badly bruised ribs. How long had he lost consciousness for? Two hours, perhaps three?

The redcoat gulped back warm water. A first mouthful was vomited up almost as soon as it was swallowed; the second, slower and measured, felt sublime.

He tried to picture the orientation of the land. In the last month he had travelled the roads and crossed its waterways in his service to the British engineer in charge of the siege artillery.

North were the dunes and sea; the army had waited four weeks in vain for the arrival of the fleet. Today the bombardment of Dunkirk was scheduled to begin; even if the Royal Navy arrived, how could he hope to attract their attention?

South were the network of canals and marshes; land firmly in the hands of the French by now. To the west was Dunkirk, still held by the enemy.

Follow the coast east and head to Furnes. It was the only direction of flight that made sense.

The redcoat was a King's German and knew his duty. Survive, find the army and find his battalion.

Furnes was twelve miles away; the French would be patrolling the road to Ghyvelde, the halfway point. Escape on foot would be near impossible. His body was still too exhausted from the events of the last thirty-six hours.

He needed a miracle; he needed a horse.

Remy Pasquier pushed blood-stained hands through a mop of lank brown hair. Thankfully his watch would soon be over. A bath, a hot meal, the warm body of a grateful woman and sleep were what he needed. The Sixth had patrolled throughout the night but had not followed up the retreating British. Instead, they had contented themselves with easy plunder. Every dragoon knew that standing orders forbade such practice. The reality was that only the careless or the greedy got caught.

The appearance of the British ships curtailed the morning's pilfering.

A trooper had been dispatched a quarter of an hour earlier to alert Dunkirk to the presence of the enemy vessels. Pasquier worked with skilled efficiency knowing that time was against him. Liberty and fraternity were the watchwords of the age but equality was a virtue that rankled the looter. The man who risked his neck took the greatest share of the profit.

With practised skill, corpses were quickly assessed. Back pack and pockets were searched for coins and practical necessities that might sell easily. He had several customers for an officer's sword but when he reached the body of a young ensign, the scabbard was already empty.

"Bloody thieves!" the dragoon muttered, slicing away with a small fishing knife at a finger that was reluctant to yield its prize of a thick gold band. Half a dozen teeth were deftly removed with small pliers, fillings glinting with promise.

Flat against the peak of a sweeping dune tufted with marram grass, his sergeant trained a battered telescope onto jolly boats that wrestled in the swell, next to the hulls of two warships. The pilferer's head twitched at movement in the corner of his eye as the telescope pointed back towards the town. A gruff voice edged with concern ordered him to remount. A column of riders, more dragoons from the Sixth, were approaching fast. The morning's work had been poor pickings: nothing worth risking the noose for.

As Pasquier's wiry frame rose, the early morning light reflected off something in the sand near a group of bodies he had yet to search. Silver coins were scattered near a slumped body. Another officer, nearly a costly and careless error. There was still time, perhaps three minutes until the cavalrymen arrived. He walked the horse quickly over to the spot, looked left and right, suspicious of such an easy find. Three bodies were nearby; two sprawled near the corner of a trench and a third face down, near the body with the coins. Kicking each of these carcasses in turn, the dragoon stood poised to silence any signs of unwelcome life with his bloodied knife.

Returning to the corpse, Pasquier removed his gloves to prize the coins more easily from the cloying sand and frisk the man's thick blue jacket. With the instinct of a seasoned looter, he knew there were more. In vain, he tried to roll the body and for a briefest moment considered calling the sergeant but rejected the notion: this find might just be too good to share. He knelt quickly, removed his cumbersome brass helmet and reached under the body with his right hand, his face near the ground. Finger tips touched the edge of a leather pouch, he could feel the coins inside but dead weight pinned the prize. Pasquier grunted and fought for leverage, trying to move the lifeless torso just a few inches and wrap his hand around the pouch.

His horse stamped at the ground impatiently. Pasquier sensed movement from behind him. He twisted his arm free, rolled away and reached for the blade but all too late. A young redcoat, now more alive than dead, loomed over him and drove the brass butt of a musket square into the side of his face, shattering eye socket and cheekbone and driving bone fragments into his brain.

Remy Pasquier, 6th Dragoon trooper and master pillager, collapsed into the sand, a lifeless, bloodied eye fixed on the pillar of smoke and ash drifting into the morning sky.

Dunkirk Beach

The First Lieutenant scanned the horizon again. By now the beach should have been alive with redcoats. King George's soldiers were always glad to see the arrival of the Royal Navy.

Whether the turn of the morning's events had gone dreadfully wrong was impossible to determine in the half-light of dawn. Sand that would soon become golden white under the rising sun held its secrets in long dark shadows from bluffs and dunes that separated the beach from the inland. The view that motioned through the telescope changed from dark browns back to the deep blue of water. In the chop of the heavy sea, the jolly boat of HMS *Thunder* was making painfully slow progress toward the beach.

The evening before, the commanding officer of *Thunder*, First Lieutenant Geoffrey Dowdes, had agreed

a plan to send a party ashore with the commander of
HMS *Racehorse*, who would no doubt be keeping a
similar vigil. Since then, around three o'clock that
morning, the skyline had illuminated with a massive
explosion beyond the dunes, near the proposed landing
site. Communications had been exchanged between the
ships. The plan stood; his vessel, a Royal Navy mortar
ketch, busied herself for action.

Dowdes slammed the telescope shut and observed
the broader canvas. Fires that had illuminated the
coastline the previous evening had been replaced by
columns of grey smoke. To his right, smog from a
myriad of chimneys and open hearths formed an early
morning haze over the town of Dunkirk. He pondered
the unknowns: too many for his liking. Small trails of
steam drifted lazily from his mug of tea, each fresh curl
swayed by the swell in which the *Thunder* was anchored
as the officer battled the nagging doubt of having made
an error of judgement.

The small flotilla of three ships were anchored in
order that *Racehorse*, a swift sloop which bobbed
gracefully some three hundred yards off her bow, could
protect *Thunder* and the HMS *Argosy*. This smaller
vessel, the handmaiden to *Thunder*, was filled with the
powder to service the two heavy mortars and waited in
the gloom, a further three hundred yards to the
starboard.

Minutes dragged. Again, the telescope swept the water, gauging the remaining time and distance that the small craft, crewed with a dozen oarsmen and some half-dozen marines, had to travel. Ahead, half a mile to the east of Dunkirk, was the position held by the Duke of York's army where a dark tower of dense smoke rose to veer east, pushed away on the westerly that had brought the flotilla in good time from Greenwich. The beach swept back into view; the improving light revealed the nature of the dark shapes on the beach. He fought the urge to recall the jolly boat, not that it would do much good, the craft was nearly landed and his men could gauge the situation more clearly than he could from twelve hundred yards distant.

Lieutenant Byron Summersdale felt the jolly boat buck in the heavy surf and fought the urge to be sick. Being a Royal Marine was little or no assurance of being a good sailor. He craned his neck to see if he could spot the small boat from the *Racehorse* which was also charting a path to the beach but sprays of salt which drenched his tunic were the only reward for his efforts. Instead his gaze returned to the beach, aware that his men were looking at the same sight as him, no doubt wondering what fate awaited them.

The boat dug into the sand; oarsmen nimbly bailed out left and right of the small craft to secure it. Careful not to fall over his own sword, Summersdale leapt into the surf, relieved to find the water no more than knee deep. His red-coated marines followed close behind and once out of the surf, worked to load their sea service muskets, the Royal Navy's version of the redcoats 'Brown Bess'. Practicality had changed wooden ramrods from iron, which corroded with exposure to sea-spray. Further economy removed the brass cap onto which a bayonet was fixed, at the fore of the musket. Their Lordships at the Admiralty would rest easier at the money saved, no doubt. Besides there was little call for fixing bayonets on board a ship. Silently, Summersdale cursed such economy, wishing he could issue such an order, as much for his own morale, as for any other reason.

The beach was ghostly quiet, even the sea had calmed. The crew of the *Thunder's* jolly-boat, feeling the vulnerability of sailors perched on an unfriendly shore, worked silently to make sure that the small craft did not beach itself in the receding tide. The Marines scrambled from wet sand that became dry and deep, sapping their energy in just a few paces. Along with their muskets, Summersdale's men carried little else except for ammunition pouches and canteens. Still the sand clawed at their heels as they threaded a route through the first of the bodies. Summersdale slowed and knelt by the corpse of an officer.

"Heathen bastards," he cursed, his mind racing.

A neat, round hole in the side of the skull was thick with congealed blood. Death had been recent, perhaps at the time of the explosion. His eyes dropped involuntarily to the what was left of the mouth where sand flies crawled in the air morning air. Most of the lower jaw was missing. Deep and deliberate blade marks had prized out teeth. On the right hand, a finger had been hacked off, a wedding ring no doubt. He fought to control nausea brought on by the journey in the jolly boat. Feeling horribly exposed on the open expanse of beach only worsened matters.

"A month's pay for the first of you to pouch one of these scum, lads."

The shore party lurched forward again. Moving in a column of twos with Summersdale at the head, they picked a careful path through the dead redcoats until they saw the lone horseman, three hundred yards away and closing at the gallop.

"Halt," the ensign growled. "Marines on the left, kneel and make ready."

Redcoats to the left of the column dropped to one knee, cocking their muskets without further instruction. Lieutenant Summersdale gripped his long straight sabre. The redcoats on the right of the column had also trained their muskets at the approaching figure but had remained standing.

Two hundred yards.

One hundred and fifty; the figure was waving and shouting, his uniform was impossible to distinguish but the helmet with a horse-hair plumed peak was that of a French Dragoon. The rider, approaching fast with the sun behind him, showed no signs of slowing.

One hundred yards; Summersdale chose a marker, a line of dried seaweed on the beach. That far and no further. If horse and rider hit the soldiers at speed the redcoats would be cast about like nine pins.

Fifty yards; still he could make not make out what the man was shouting.

At thirty-five yards, the horse galloped over a green smear of dried seaweed. Summersdale gave the command to fire.

CHAPTER THIRTY-ONE

Cast list

Who's Who in The Black Lions of Flanders...

The King's Germans.
Brandt, Captain Werner.

Ordered to assume command of leaderless 2nd Company, Brandt is a loyal supporter of the new colonel, Jacob Neuberg. He is firm friends with Erich von Bomm and married to Katerina Brandt.

Krombach, Private Sebastian.

Enlisting in the army in search of adventure and a life beyond working in his father's fishing fleet, Krombach finds Second Company a dangerous and divided world, being forced to choose between Sergeant Winckler and the sadistic Corporal Gauner.

von Bomm, Lieutenant Erich.

A rake and eligible bachelor but his potential to make a good leader is untested until von Bomm is offered command of the battalion's Grenadier company.

Officers of 2nd Battalion.
Bachmeier, Captain Gerhard.
The officer commanding 3rd Company.

Harris, Regimental Surgeon.
A plain-speaking Englishman, from Derbyshire, who is a loyal supporter of the changes implemented by Colonel Neuberg.

Neuberg, Lieutenant-Colonel Jacob.
His appointment causes resentment from within the battalion and from enemies in the hierarchy of Hanoverian society. Neuberg must hope to unify his battalion before the realities of war threaten to tear it further apart.

Schafer, Lieutenant Christian.
A rather hapless officer who finds himself in temporary charge of 2nd Company until the appointment of Captain Brandt.

Thalberg, Captain Hugo.
The officer commanding 4th Company.

Volgraf, Captain Ernst.
The commander of 1st Company and a loyal supporter and mouthpiece for his uncle, Johann Volgraf.

Volgraf, Major Johann.

Usurped of what he considers his rightful claim to command the battalion, Major Volgraf enlists forces from inside the battalion and powerful friends without, to ensure that the tenure of Neuberg is as brief as possible.

Wexler, Doctor August.

Second Company's doctor, a poor card player and partial to more than his share of medicinal brandy.

Other ranks of 2nd Company.
Gauner, Corporal Conrad.

A disciplinarian, Gauner wants to control and shape Second Company in his own image and finds an unexpected and powerful ally to attempt his goal.

Fuchs, Frederick.

The lackey for Gauner, Fuchs feeds off the gossip of the Company.

Hartmann, Thilo (The Ox)

Nicknamed 'The Ox', Hartmann rarely speaks, brute force does the talking. An enforcer for Gauner.

Krogh, Peter.

A tough Dane, the only man ever to fight 'The Ox' to a standstill, Krogh has forged an easy alliance with Gauner.

Möller, Corporal.

A quietly spoken N.C.O. who feels alarmed by the growing power of Gauner within Brandt's Company.

Pinsk, Henry.

Younger twin of Tomas, Henry's fiery temper is matched by a laconic wit. A firm friend to Sebastian Krombach.

Pinsk, Tomas.

Elder twin of Henry, Tomas is transferred to the newly formed Grenadier battalion as the plans for war progress. He is placed under the command of acting Captain Erich von Bomm.

Reifener, Andreas.

A baker's boy who was enlisted by his uncle to avoid payment for pregnancy out of wedlock, Reifener is full of surprises. His culinary skills bring life to dreary meals and his scrounging makes him a useful accomplice for Sergeant Winckler. He is a friend to Krombach and the Pinsk Brothers.

Richter, Sergeant Georg.

In the divisive world of Second Cowman, 'Moustache Georg' is a firm favourite of the redcoats, offering patrician care while overseeing the training of the new recruits.

Roner, Company Sergeant-Major William.

Transferred from the Grenadier Company with the arrival of Brandt, Roner is responsible for raising the standards of drill and discipline. He must also check the growing power of Conrad Gauner within Second Company.

Winckler, Sergeant Tobias.

Giving the nickname of 'Old Boots', Winckler is an opportunist who knows how to turn a situation to make a profit. He is opposed to the brutal methods of Gauner but has his own agenda to keep himself from life in the front-line.

The ladies of the regiment.
Brandt, Katerina.

The daughter of a Polish emigre family and the wife of Captain Werner Brandt.

Neuberg, Frau.
The redoubtable wife of Colonel Neuberg who is keenly aware of the ambition of Major Volgraf and appeals to Werner Brandt for his loyalty to her husband.

The Twenty.
A selected number of wives of the men Second Battalion chosen to campaign with the men including Anna Weber and Clara Richter.

Westerberg, Renee.
Barmaid and daughter of the owner of the Blue Angel public house, she encounters Sebastian Krombach, when he is sent to Celle on behalf of Captain Brandt.

Soldiers from 1st Grenadier Regiment
(to which von Bomm and Tomas Pinsk are transferred)
Baumann, Captain Leopold.
After his brother is bested by von Bomm in a duel, Baumann arrives to assume seniority of von Bomm's command.

Franke, Lieutenant-Colonel Manfred.
Colonel of the Battalion.

Hahn, Sergeant Fritz.
Sergeant from 1st Guards in command of one of the battalion's artillery pieces.

Keithen, Sergeant.
Sergeant from 1st Guards who becomes the senior Sergeant in the skirmish company commanded by von Bomm.

Rausch, Ensign Johannes.
A young officer from 2nd Battalion's Grenadier Company.

Other Hanoverian Characters.
Diepenbroick, Colonel von.
The senior commander of the Tenth Regiment and the man responsible for offering the role of Colonel to Neuberg, ignoring the seniority of Major Volgraf.

Freytag, Field Marshal Wilhelm von.
Commander of the Hanoverian Corps, with an uneasy relationship with both Wallmoden and the Duke of York.

Klinkowström Oberst von.
Commander of Third Brigade in which Second Battalion are located.

British characters.
Craufurd, Captain Charles
An Aide de Camp to the Duke of York who is sent as
the Duke's representative to the Austrian camp of
Prince Josias.

Dundas, Henry.
The Home Secretary and Minister for War,
responsible for the appointment of Brooks Jackson, to
control the conduct of the war from Whitehall.

Henson-Jefferies, Lieutenant Simon.
An Aide De Camp to the Duke of York from 3rd
Guards Battalion.

Jackson, Brooks.
Appointed Commissary General to the Duke by the
Minister of War, Henry Dundas, Jackson must grapple
with the suspicion of the Duke towards his motives and
lack of co-operation from Dutch allies. He finds a
friendship with Stephen Trevethan.

Murray, Colonel Sir James.
The Chief of Staff to the Duke of York.

Prince Frederick, the Duke of York.

The second son of George III, the commander of the British and German forces sent to Holland.

Trevethan, Major Stephen.

By accident rather than design, Trevethan finds himself appointed as the engineer advising the Duke of York. The Cornishman, more used to building roads, must quickly adapt to a world where events are always outside of his control.

Austrian characters.
Baron Thugut.

The chief adviser to Emperor Francis II and a bitter opponent of Colonel Mack.

Clerfayt, Count François Sébastien Charles Joseph de Croix.

An Austrian General under the command of Prince Josias.

Ferraris, Count Joseph Jean François.

An Austrian General under the command of Prince Josias.

Francis II Holy Roman Emperor.

The man recognised by many as ruling the most powerful military land empire in the world.

Josias, Prince of Saxe-Coburg.
Commander of the Austrian army in Flanders and keen to see an end to war with France at the earliest opportunity.

Mack von Leiberich, Colonel Karl.
The Chief of Staff to Prince Josias, the man responsible for co-ordinating operations of all the forces along the northern border of France.

Hessian Characters.
Louis X.
Landgrave of Hesse-Darmstadt and the cause of a potential rift between Prussia and Great Britain.

William XI.
Landgrave of Hesse-Kassel.

Dutch Characters.
Bentinck, General.
The Military adviser to the Prince of Orange.

Boetslaar, General.
The General commanding the strategically important fort Willemstadt.

de Bylandt, Count.
The commander in charge at Breda fort.

de Haan, Pieter.
The Mayor of Hollands Diep.

Kinsbergen, Admiral.
Naval adviser to the Prince of Orange.

William V.
Prince of Orange and Stadtholder of the United Provinces; a difficult ally for the Duke of York to deal with.

Prussian Characters.
von Knobelsdorff, General.
Commander of the Prussian forces on the northern French Border.

French Characters
Beauvais, Captain Julien.
Officer of the 3rd Dragoons, wounded in battle at Jemappes, in saving the life of General Dumouriez.

Caillat, Maurice.
A stable boy turned investigator, thanks to the vagaries of the revolution.

Carnot, Lazare.
One of the most influential people in the effort to save the fledgling state. Carnot is nicknamed the 'Worker' in his tireless efforts to resolve several crises.

Courtois, Colonel Alain.
Commander of the 3rd Dragoons and friend of Julian Beauvais.

Dampierre, Marquis de.
Commander of the Army of the North in early May 1793.

Davide, Captain Valerie.
Officer in the 'Black Lions', captain of 6th Company.

de Beurnonville, Pierre de Ruel, Marquis.
Minister of War sent by Paris to confront Dumouriez.

De-la-Faye, Colonel.
Commander of the 14th Nationals, the 'Black Lions'.

Demont, Captain Claude.
Officer of the 3rd Dragoons, friend of Julian Beauvais, commanding the patrol that finds Beauvais and Arnaud Mahieu.

Dumouriez, General Charles François.

A man treading the world of Revolutionary and Royalist camps with care. The Commander of the Army of the North, with an ambition as great as his ego.

Ferrand, Jean Henri Becays.

Governor of Valenciennes and friend of Colonel Courtois of the 3rd Dragoons.

Genet, Serge (the Spider).

A one-time lawyer in provincial Dunkirk, France has made use of the legal and organisational skills of Serge Genet. The Chief of Staff to General Dumouriez, with contacts in every department of Paris, earning his nickname of the Spider.

Grison, Fabien.

Soldier in the 14th Nationals, the 'Black Lions'; son of Jean-Francois Grison and older brother to Guilbert.

Grison, Guilbert.

Soldier in the 14th Nationals, the 'Black Lions'; son of Jean-Francois Grison and younger brother of Fabien.

Grison, Jean-Francois.

The Mayor of Dunkirk, a close friend to both Gilles Tabary and Arnaud Mahieu.

Juliette, Countess de Marboré
The beautiful emissary of Dumouriez, aware of the dangers of the world into which she has been pitched.

Lavigne, Major.
Officer of the 3rd Dragoons with who holds a personal grudge against Julian Beauvais.

Louis Philippe
The Duc de Chartres, an ally of General Dumouriez.

Mahieu, Arnaud.
Captain of the Perseus and older brother to Jean-Baptiste. Close friends with both Jean-Francois Grison and Gilles Tabary.

Mahieu, Jean-Baptiste
Soldier in the 14th Nationals, the 'Black Lions', younger brother to Arnaud.

Miranda, General.
Commander of the Army of the Ardennes.

Robespierre, Maximilien.
Leader of the Committee for Public Safety.

Tabary, Gilles.
The Mayor of Mont-Cassel and close friends with both Jean-Francois Grison and Arnaud Mahieu.

Valence, General.
present at the battle of Neerwinden

CHAPTER THIRTY-TWO

Authors notes.

Author's Notes

Dryden to Lawrence:

When we told lies, you told half-lies. And a man who tells lies, like me, merely hides the truth. But a man who tells half-lies has forgotten where he put it. Big things have small beginnings.

Lawrence of Arabia (1962)

Thank you for reading this book, if it gave you half as much pleasure as I got from writing it, then you might want to read the others that will follow. The Black Lions of Flanders is the curious mixture of historical fact and fiction which seems to be called 'faction', so I thought I might shed a little light on the stories behind this narrative. For those who might like to dig a little deeper I have included a reading list at the end of this book with some key texts.

The Hanoverian regiments, the 10th and 1st Grenadiers were real regiments. During this story and the subsequent three books, I will try and place their movements as faithfully as possible. Senior commanders such as Freytag, Wallmoden, von Klinkowström and von Diepenbroick were real people; all of characters within 2nd Battalion and 1st Grenadiers are my own creation. From the Hanoverian perspective, Ompteda of the King's German Legion, tells of the lack of time for war preparations. There is evidence of problems along the march with soldiers attacking Dutch citizens who they felt were 'revolutionaries', made worse by the failure of 'English Pay' to materialise and the soldiers experiencing profiteering along the line of march. The result was the riot at Halle. The Duke of York did intervene, the Riot Act was read to the Hanoverian soldiers. There was also an action soon after at Rumes, an outpost towards Lille. The scale of the attack was somewhat less than I have portrayed but Field Marshal Freytag saw fit to countermand a direct order from the Duke of York. This was an inauspicious start to the campaign!

As for the British, before researching this book, I had little clear idea of why the army was on the continent at all. Fortescue's book 'British Campaigns in Flanders', suggests that British involvement was part of a greater Austrian plot concerning much broader aims in Europe. It's an idea I quite like but these machinations have still to play out so I will come back to this point in later notes.

The British army certainly wasn't in a fit state to do much when it arrived in Holland other than stiffen the resolve of the Stadtholder. The three Guards battalions suffered from similar poor preparations to the Hanoverians, the incident during the embarkation was taken from Fortescue, as well as the observation that no medical supplies had been packed in ships ready to sail. Politicians do not escape Fortescue's ire either, he has few kind words for Henry Dundas, whose political meddling will be a running theme in these books, in the way that political interfering and military shortages have been inexorably linked since the dawn of warfare. Parts of Fawcett's letter (Chapter 13) are quoted here, I would have enjoyed reading the original in full. The second brigade being sent to Holland was unfit for service in the field, and I hope I have given some indication of the drain on manpower that the Fencibles units would add to the already dire shortages.

Brooks Jackson, the link between Dundas and the army is based upon a person called Brooks Watson. His is a story worth researching and packed with far more adventure than I could dream of inventing.

The lack of manpower and the need to call upon loyal Hanoverians and Hessian 'mercenaries' are outlined by Fortescue. How King Louis X of Hesse-Darmstadt managed to spend all the cash that he had pocketed from selling his troops to Prussia in two months, I will leave to your imagination. He did, and the British government found itself paying Prussia off to release the Hessian soldiers and then paying Louis X for their services. Dundas was keen that the army should not move to unite with Austria, feeling that the force was so small it would become a poor man's corps in the huge imperial force. Within a year, it was a viewpoint that had turned around completely but that's for another book.

The situation with poor morale of the Dutch troops was mentioned in the contemporary accounts from Officer of the Guard and Ompteda. Breda fell despite being well garrisoned and no attempt was made to destroy the magazine. Dutch guns were used in the attempted siege of Willemstadt, but I can find no account of a serious assault against it. By that time, manpower was being bled away from the Army of the North to the Army of the Ardennes. Had Willemstadt have fallen, Overfrakkee was likely to have been taken too. The ability of the port of Helleveotsluis to service the needs of the British army would have become questionable. Helleveotsluis has a particularly long and narrow entrance to the harbour and a well-positioned howitzer battery would have played havoc with transport ships being manoeuvred into port. Both Willemstadt and Helleveotsluis are worth visiting, if you find yourself in the area.

On the French side, Charles François Dumouriez (sometimes written as Dumourier), is possibly one of the most interesting characters in the 'Revolutionary War' who you may never had heard of. While I had a keen interest in the Napoleonic period, Dumouriez was a find for me. A courtier, politician and latterly commander of the Army of the North, Dumouriez was one of the last people to speak to Louis XVI. He did attempt to negotiate an alliance with Prince Josias, which was being discussed around the time of Neerwinden. The arrest of the four National Assembly members who arrived from Paris, to demand Dumouriez' own arrest also happened. Dumouriez later wrote his own account and justification of these actions and was certainly vilified in political and emigre circles in London as an opportunist. Whether he was tilting for power for himself is more difficult to judge but it's not beyond the realms of possibility. France does have a history of being rescued by a 'soldier on a white horse', as one of my old history professors used to love to quote.

The rest of the characters around Dumouriez are fictitious but Maurice Caillat, is drawn from the kind of interference that Dumouriez loathed, the 'Representative en Mission'. These men acted with the full power of the National Assembly. The result of the failure of Dumouriez to bring his army over to the

Austrians was that French political interference into military decisions worsened. However, the fate of the unsuccessful (and sometimes the successful) commanders of the Army of the North was far less forgiving than those of their counterparts in the allied ranks.

Lastly, I want to thank Bernard Cornwell. I don't know him, and I doubt that he will ever read these words but like the countless millions who had read his books I felt as though they spoke directly to me. I loved Sharpe and Harper and would read every word, cover to cover and in the last line breathe a sigh of relief with the words that 'Sharpe and Harper will march again'.

It's time for Krombach, Brandt and von Bomm to have their own voices and write their own adventures.

I hope they do.

'Big things have small beginnings.'

And, more importantly…

The King still has need of his Germans.

CHAPTER THIRTY-THREE

Reading List

Reading List:

Bayonets of the Republic - Lynn, J.A

British Campaigns in Flanders 1690-1794 - Fortescue J.W

French Revolution - Hibbert, C.

Noble Duke of York - Byrne, F.A

Memoirs of Dumouriez - Dumouriez, C.F.

Officer of the Guards Volumes 1 and 2, an accurate and impartial account of the war - Officer of the Guards

Ompteda of the King's German Legion - von Ompteda